Other Books & Stories
by Lynn Bohart

Inn Keeping With Murder
Grave Doubts
Your Worst Nightmare
Something Wicked
Also published in the anthology of short stories:
"Dead On Demand"

Mass Murder
(A Giorgio Salvatori Mystery)

By
Lynn Bohart

Cover Photo: John Bohart
Cover Design: Jaynee Bohart

Published by Little Dog Press

ACKNOWLEDGEMENTS

My sincere thanks go to Compulsion Reads for endorsing my book. It feels great to be acknowledged as an "indie" author. Thanks also go to my friends, family, co-workers, and fellow writers who continue to support this obsession I have with writing. It can't be easy. Special thanks to my good friend Chris Lavender for giving me Grosvenor's name. So perfect! Thanks to those who vetted fact: Kevin and Pam Miles (retired Catholic priest and nun) and retired police officer, Don Persson. Thanks to my friend Valerie O'Halloran and Liz Stewart for editing and revision advice. I couldn't have written Detective Giorgio Salvatori so authentically if it weren't for my long-time friend, fellow thespian, and now retired police detective Mike Magnotti, on whom some, but not all, of the character is based. He actually did say that becoming a police officer cured his insatiable desire to be on stage. That statement was one of the things that inspired me to write the book.

I would be remiss if I didn't acknowledge my home town of Sierra Madre, a lovely community of about 20,000 that really is nestled in the foothills of the San Gabriel Mountains. While I lived very near the resident Catholic monastery there, I chose to create a completely fictitious monastery for this story. And for those familiar with the area, I also changed a few street names.

This is dedicated to my dad, who loved a good mystery.

† Chapter One †

Premonitions were taken seriously in the Norville family. When Syd Norville was six years old his mother abruptly aborted a trip to Florida to celebrate the birth of her niece because of a dream she'd had the night before in which the plane crashed. The plane she'd been scheduled to board the next day did, in fact, crash on take-off due to a faulty suspension rig, killing all two hundred and forty passengers. When Syd was twelve, his older sister abandoned her millionaire husband-to-be at the altar because of a bad feeling about the honeymoon. The groom went on to Aruba alone and was killed two days later when his rented car flew off a cliff. When Syd was home on leave from the Navy, he'd been about to cross a downtown street when an inexplicable feeling made him suddenly retreat to the curb. A moment later, an old van barreled through the intersection followed by a police car, both passing within inches of where Syd would have been walking.

Yes, premonitions were taken seriously in the Norville family.

Syd's old Chevy truck pulled into the west parking lot of the massive Catholic monastery where he worked five nights a week as a janitor. He climbed down from the cab and let his right hand linger on the tattered steering wheel cover. A glance at the hazy moon peeking through a clump of trees at the south end of the property made him shudder. Something was wrong. He could feel it. And his impulse was to run.

He turned his head to listen, remembering the night several months before when a child's voice had sent him scurrying through the mammoth building looking for the source.

Since then, cold spots had stopped him in the middle of heated hallways and once, when a pair of invisible fingers slid across his forearm, he'd thought seriously about finding another job. The acid pouring into his stomach now made him wish he had.

A penetrating breeze rising up from the southern tip of the property sent shivers across his shoulders like a thousand sand crabs running for cover. It was five minutes to nine. He had to make a decision.

Syd grabbed his lunchbox from behind the seat and closed the battered truck door. He needed to ignore the voices in his head and get to work. His fingers flexed around the Rosary in his pocket for comfort. With a shake of his shoulders, he hurried toward the west door before he could change his mind.

Lights blazed in the banquet room, and the sound of laughter replaced thoughts of impending disaster. The white catering van was still parked in the lot. The young Miss Fields would depart soon, leaving behind a small clean-up crew. These parties often lasted until well past midnight, so no telling when he'd have access to the banquet room, where his job was only to pick up the trash, vacuum, and spot clean the carpet.

The ignition of a car engine made him turn around as he reached for the door. A pair of headlights flicked on in the parking lot. A moment later, a familiar Toyota Camry pulled out.

Syd slipped inside the back door and turned down a short hallway towards the cleaning closet. He would start tonight at the other end of the building in order to avoid the party guests. He liked to mix up his routine, sometimes going through the building clockwise, sometimes counter-clockwise, sometimes all out of order. It helped to relieve the boredom. Thirty years as a shop manager made this work meaningless, but the job helped to pay his wife's medical bills. After surgery to remove a kidney, her prognosis was good. The image of his plump little wife sitting comfortably at home warmed his insides, helping to further reduce his jitters.

With the feeling of dread beginning to fade, he stepped into the closet and flicked on the single 40-watt bulb that served as an overhead light. It only illuminated the area right next to the door, but Syd could have found his way around blind, he was that familiar with how things were organized. His lungs inhaled the comforting sweetness of the powdered soap that sat in boxes on a shelf to his left, but an almost imperceptible tingling at the back of his neck made him think there was something more. It was an odor he didn't recognize, something dank among the aroma of pine and borax. With trembling fingers, he tucked his lunchbox under one arm and reached for the small flask he now carried in his pants pocket. He removed the cap with practiced ease and took a swig. The searing flow of whisky inflamed his throat. Within moments, his muscles relaxed, and the tremors in his hands began to disappear.

Now he had to get to work. He returned the flask to its hiding place and placed his lunchbox on an empty shelf, surprised to find one of the monk's wool blankets there. He reached for a handful of cleaning rags and then grabbed a spray bottle filled with his favorite cleaning solvent. A wire brush, rubber gloves, and a couple of old sponges completed his list of supplies. He stowed this all carefully onto a large metal cart, loaded on the vacuum cleaner, and then stepped around a supporting column to grab the rolling mop bucket.

A small dark object sitting on the floor half in shadow caught his attention. Something had fallen off one of the shelves. Syd leaned down to pick it up and took a sharp breath. It was a woman's patent leather pump, looking completely incongruous in such functional surroundings. The shoe probably belonged to a party guest who had rendezvoused here with a male counterpart earlier in the evening. The thought disgusted him, but the woman would be back. He'd have to take the shoe to the kitchen. How was she walking around with only one shoe anyway?

He reached down again to pick it up when the back of his hand bumped something just above it, causing whatever it was to swing back and forth ever so slightly in the dark. Surprised, Syd glanced up, peering into the shadows just in front of his face. His eyes adjusted, and a small cry escaped his lips.

He backed away with a jerk, knocking over a box of paper towels in the process, stopping at the door, his lungs incapable of drawing breath.

He remained frozen, staring at the back wall, the meaning of his premonition finally revealed.

Just above the shoe dangled a slender foot encased in a black silk stocking, attached to the body of a dead woman.

† Chapter Two †

Tension gathered in the courtroom like electricity forced through a high voltage cable. Every eye was focused on the dark-haired young man in the center of the room and the buxom blonde in his arms. The young man had been acquitted of murder, making him careless, careless enough to turn his back on the only real threat in the room — his wife.

With the delicacy of a whisper, she slipped up behind him and slammed the evidence knife between his shoulder blades. One juror screamed. The judge jumped to his feet. Everyone else watched in horror as the man crumpled to the floor. The buxom blonde shrank back, while the wife remained poised above her husband's body, her lips drawn back with the hint of a satisfied smile.

Giorgio Salvatori stepped forward on cue, his robes rustling against the hushed stillness. The wife's steadfast confidence, which had helped secure her husband's acquittal only moments before, was gone. She'd been betrayed by the man she loved; life as she knew it was over. She relinquished the blade as the court constable moved in to take her elbow.

"Guilty my lord," she muttered to the judge.

The constable led her toward the exit while the audience remained in stunned silence. A moment later, the heavy velvet curtains drew closed, awakening the first sounds of a rousing applause.

†

It was closing night, and Giorgio Salvatori faced a bank of glaring light bulbs using a handful of tissues to remove the heavy makeup that had helped create the illusion he was an aging British prosecutor. The cramped room bustled with chatter as actors changed into street clothes. Members of the production crew kept poking their heads in to shout closing night orders, while cast members entered and exited in various states of undress.

Giorgio reflected on the closing of Agatha Christie's *Witness for the Prosecution*. It had been one of his favorite movies as a boy, and he'd waited his entire life to do the stage play. Even so, he'd nearly lost the lead role ten weeks earlier when the director cast John Wilson as Sir Wilfrid — the crusty prosecuting attorney — arguing that a practicing lawyer would bring a sense of realism to the role. Giorgio had pouted for weeks. Wilson was a tax attorney and had probably never seen the inside of a courtroom other than to argue his own parking tickets. On the other hand, Giorgio was a veteran police detective and understood murder investigations and court proceedings.

But Giorgio had swallowed his disappointment and offered to serve as stage manager. Fortunately, three weeks into rehearsals, Wilson fell and broke his leg repairing the gutters on his roof. Giorgio didn't cheer exactly, but as stage manager he was the logical replacement. Besides, he was the better actor. He'd once told Angie that becoming a cop had replaced his irresistible desire to be on stage. But he'd never lost his love of the theater, and it was only moving to a small town with a rotating work schedule that provided this new opportunity.

He glanced over at the costume table with a pang of regret. The discarded black robe and powdered wig were now only fond memories. Everything would be returned to the costume department to be saved for another production.

"Jo Jo, you were great!"

Giorgio looked up to find his brother's six-foot, two-inch frame filling the doorway. Giorgio's younger brother, Rocky, stepped forward and threw one long leg over the bench, grinning like a Cheshire cat.

"I can't believe it," Rocky continued, "a cop playing an attorney. You're gunna get ribbed about this one." He gave Giorgio a rough slap on the shoulder, his dark eyes gleaming.

"Glad you liked it," Giorgio mumbled. "I'll be ready in a minute."

Giorgio reached for another tissue watching Rocky out of the corner of his eye. At thirty-six, Giorgio was the older sibling by only two years, and yet he wondered why anyone would ever mistake the two as brothers. Rocky towered over Giorgio by at least four inches, and his broad shoulders and thick, dark hair made him look like he was still in his twenties. His brother's casual good looks had always intimidated Giorgio. While Rocky took after their father — tall, slender and athletic — Giorgio had inherited all the flaws from his mother's side — high forehead and a tendency to put on weight. Giorgio sucked in his stomach, believing that whatever he lacked in looks and grace, he made up in bulk and muscle.

"Man, those wigs were cool," Rocky chattered on, rapping his fingers on the makeup table. "But I never thought I'd see you wearing a dress."

"It was a robe, not a dress." Giorgio curled a lip as he slicked back the brown hair that was just beginning to show strands of gray.

"Yeah, well, it looked like a dress," Rocky laughed. "But you get better every time I see you, you know? What's the next play, a musical or something?"

Rocky grabbed a powder puff and clasped it between his fingers, sending up enough fine dust to obscure his image in the mirror. Giorgio watched him, thinking his brother was like a teakettle--always simmering and ready to whistle. He contemplated whether his mother had ever considered putting him on medication.

"How'd they do that knife bit at the end, anyway?" Rocky continued. "It looked so real I thought I was gunna have to come up on stage and arrest somebody."

He faked a punch at Giorgio's belly and laughed as Giorgio used a Kleenex to wipe off the mirror.

"I'm glad you liked it. Where's Angie?"

"She's waiting for you in the lobby with the kids. Hey, Tony loved the stabbing." Rocky set down the powder puff and grabbed a makeup sponge. "He wants you to show him how they did it."

With a patience that belied his mood, Giorgio rescued the sponge and replaced it in a makeup box that belonged to another actor.

"What did Angie say?"

"Oh, you know Angie." Rocky fingered the powder puff again, his dark eyes glinting as if the powder puff was a chocolate truffle. "She never says much, but she loved it. She loves everything you do."

Giorgio carefully closed the box that housed the powder puff and caught the faint smell of alcohol against the dense aroma of face paint and hair spray. He threw a suspicious glance at his brother, but said nothing. Rocky pulled his leg out from under the bench and stood up.

"C'mon, let's go. We promised to take the kids for ice cream."

"Ice cream," Giorgio perked up. "I'm right behind you."

†

The two brothers approached the theater lobby where Angie stood talking with an enormous woman dressed in a bulky red caftan and green cap. As though her size weren't statement enough, Giorgio thought she looked like a giant tomato. He turned to Rocky with a snide remark poised on his lips when the woman's husband glanced his way. Giorgio recovered quickly, faked a cough, and turned to find his children.

Tony and his sister, Marie, were peering into a glass case that displayed props from the previous fall's production of *Dracula*. Eight year-old Tony knelt with his face pressed against the glass, staring at the bat. Marie, a year older, stood with her hands behind her back rocking back and forth so that her blue taffeta skirt flipped like waves on the ocean. Something caught in Giorgio's throat at the image. Marie was so like her mother, slender and pretty, with honey-colored skin, and large doe brown eyes. The only thing that marred what Giorgio thought of as perfection was the slightly crooked teeth that flashed whenever she smiled. Braces would fix that, he thought. Just a little more overtime.

Marie's eyes lit up when she saw her father, and she ran to him. He scooped her up in one easy movement.

"Daddy, you were wonderful."

Her lips touched his cheek, flooding his nostrils with the smell of the chocolate pudding she'd had at dinner. He sucked it up like hummingbirds suck nectar and then set her down and ruffled her hair.

"Thanks, honey. What'd your mom think?"

8

"I think she liked it. We're going for ice cream." She grabbed his hand. "Mom promised."

"Okay. Let's get your brother."

Giorgio yelled for Tony, but the appeal of the rubber bat suspended from the top of the case had glued him to the spot. Tony was slender like Marie but a head shorter. The uncomfortable looking suit and tie required by his mother for the show tonight made him look like a miniature used car salesman.

"Hey, Tony!" Giorgio bellowed. "Apparently your hearing is impaired! Let's go!"

Everyone in the lobby turned with a jerk except Tony, who rose obediently and followed his father without a word. Angie said goodbye to the giant tomato, and the family walked outside and down the steps towards the street.

"You're not on stage anymore, Joe," Angie reprimanded him as they followed the cement walkway into the park. "You don't have to yell."

"I know," he snarled.

They rounded the corner of the old granite courthouse converted years earlier into a community theater. The bulky, two-story building anchored the southeast corner of the town square and was flanked by a small parking lot, graceful eucalyptus trees, box hedges, and a stone marker commemorating 1930 as the year the old courthouse was built. It was late October, and leaves covered the sidewalk. Marie kicked at them playfully while she walked in between her parents. The news station had predicted a storm, and the air was dense with moisture. Rocky chased Tony around the swing set making Giorgio think how glad he was they had all moved here two years earlier. Life was good.

Marie reached up and took the keys from her father's hand and ran ahead to unlock the car leaving the couple to themselves.

"So," Giorgio began, "what'd you think?"

Angie moved over to put her slender arm through his. "About what?"

Her voice chimed the way a mellow church bell draws the hour, and Giorgio inhaled the sweet scent of her floral perfume.

"Now, don't do that to me, Angie. You know what I mean."

"I thought it was good," she said simply.

"That's all? Just good?"

"No. Very good. It was very good."

"Hmm," he mumbled.

"You were very good, Joe. You always are." She lifted his hand and kissed the back of it. "I liked it."

He threw his arm around her slim waist drawing her close. "Thanks. I always wanted to do that part, you know."

"I know," she said quietly.

"Perhaps I should send Wilson a card thanking him. After all, I couldn't have done it without him." He chuckled, winning a look of eternal patience from his wife. "Okay, maybe not a thank you, but I should at least see how he's doing. Tell him how the play went."

"That would be nice, Joe," she said, squeezing his arm. "There's something I've been waiting to talk to you about."

They were nearing the parking lot when a loud rattle interrupted them. Fifty feet ahead, a man was digging through a trashcan. Only his legs were visible. He looked as if he'd been swallowed up by Jonah's whale. He emerged holding an empty bottle, his straggly hair falling to his shoulders. Angie stopped short.

"It's okay. That's just Oliver." Giorgio called out to the old man. "Hey, Oliver! Get some good ones?"

Oliver leaned forward, squinting in the low light. He was short and slightly built, wearing dark baggy pants and a heavy quilted coat. He smiled at Giorgio showing the darkened hole where his front teeth should have been.

"Hey, Detective. You bet. I got me enough for a th-teak dinner." He gave a hoarse laugh.

Just then, Tony and Rocky ran up behind them tagging each other and laughing. At the same moment a Sierra Madre squad car pulled into the lot. Two patrolmen got out. Giorgio turned back to find Oliver, but the old man had evaporated into the night.

"Joe, we got a call."

It was Officer Samson. Samson was in his late twenties and wore a patrolman's uniform and leather jacket. He sauntered forward with one thumb stuck in his belt as if being a cop was as good as it got in this small town. His partner trailed behind.

"Swan's on duty tonight," Giorgio said, opening the car door for Angie.

"I know, but the Captain is out of town and wants you in on this one."

Samson tipped his hat to Angie just as Tony snuck in to stand just below the officer's elbow. Angie stepped forward and twirled him around and marched both children to the opposite side of the car. The officers took the cue and walked a few feet away. Samson greeted Rocky with a quick nod before introducing him to his partner.

"This is Officer Maxwell. Rocky's with San Marino."

"What's going on?" Giorgio asked.

He wanted to go for ice cream and bask in the glow of his family's admiration. Then he wanted to stop by the closing night party. Whatever this was, he could take care of it in the morning.

"There's been a murder."

Maxwell spoke this time. He was a short, stocky man in his mid-twenties who stood with his arms across the ample girth Giorgio thought would probably send him to an early grave.

Murders were rare in a town this size. Disturbance calls and assists to other agencies were more common. The low incidence of homicides had been one of the reasons Giorgio had moved his family here.

"Where?" he inquired with only a hint of enthusiasm.

The two officers exchanged looks before Samson replied.

"At the monastery."

A sudden breeze swirled a handful of leaves around their feet just as one of the tall parking lights flickered and dimmed. Giorgio glanced up thinking the city needed to replace a loose bulb.

"When?"

"She was found around nine o'clock tonight. It's a woman – strangled and hung by her bra in a supply closet."

Rocky shoved his hands into his coat pockets. "Jesus, Jo Jo. Not many murders at a Catholic monastery. Can I tag along? Maybe I could help."

Giorgio sighed knowing he couldn't avoid this one. "Yeah. Let me tell Angie. We'll take your truck."

"There's one more thing," Maxwell said, glancing a second time at Samson. "The tip of her little finger was cut off. We can't find it."

This information was met with a long moment of silence. Giorgio felt a deep chill settle into his bones.

"We'll meet you up there," Giorgio said briskly.

Samson nodded, and the two officers returned to the squad car, while Giorgio went to relay the disappointing news to his wife.

He'd known Angie since before junior high school, and she'd endured a lifetime of sleepless nights while he labored over hopeless and sometimes grisly murder investigations in New York City. The last case had nearly killed him with a bullet wound to the chest. He'd promised things would change. The move to California was part of that promise. But he didn't have a good feeling about this one, making him wish he could blow it off and go for ice cream instead.

Angie got out of the car as he approached and switched to the driver's side, a look of solemn resignation on her face. He reached in and quickly unlocked the glove compartment to remove his gun and badge and then caught up to Angie as she climbed inside.

"I hope it won't be too late."

"I won't wait up. I teach Sunday school tomorrow." She offered her cheek for a quick kiss and then slid behind the wheel. "Just be careful."

Her brown eyes impaled him with reproach. With a flick of her wrist, the car's engine roared to life, and she backed out of the parking space. Giorgio watched his family drive away in the direction of the only restaurant in town open this late, knowing the bloom of his performance would be dulled by morning.

He started for Rocky's truck just as a heady gust of wind forced its way through the trees like a runaway locomotive. A metallic clinking sound caught Giorgio's attention, making him turn to squint into the wind. A small object rattled its way down the walkway. When it reached the curb, it flipped off the sidewalk and landed at his feet. Curious, Giorgio bent over and picked it up. It was an antique brass button encrusted with age. Its rounded edges were battered and bent. One side was polished smooth with four hollow eyes for thread holes. The image on the other side caused gooseflesh to crawl up his arms.

It was an elaborate Latin cross. The kind usually displayed at Catholic churches.

† Chapter Three †

The deed was done, and from recognition, to planning, to implementation, it had all taken less than ninety minutes to eliminate a threat, secure his identity, and craft a coded message that would reach the other side of the country. Not bad. Not bad at all.

He'd slipped in and out of the closet with the dead girl flung across his shoulders. No one had even noticed. Then he'd made it back to his room, stashed the disguise, and returned to his previous activities without a question from anyone. Fucking amazing. Now, he waited patiently to be interviewed by the police and continue the charade. Life was good.

Occasional voices echoed at the far end of the hallway, then faded to silence. What the hell was taking so long? The time spent cooling his heels had all but dulled his senses, and frankly, it was pissing him off.

He stood up and rolled his neck in frustration. His blood began to flow again, bringing his muscles back to life. It was a far cry from the buzz he'd felt after killing the girl. After that, he'd been forced to dance around the room to use up excess energy. He couldn't afford to appear manic when the body was found. Manic might have put even these idiots on alert. So he'd exhaled slowly and counted backwards. Minutes later, he'd rejoined the group downstairs as if nothing had happened.

He'd almost regretted the deceleration, because for him the risk of getting caught had become a drug. The act was all about the art of getting away with the deception. The feints. The parries. The near misses. In grade school, he'd taken great pleasure in setting up his classmates by stealing from someone's locker, spreading rumors, or placing blame on someone else for practical jokes. Most of the time, no one knew who the culprit was, not even his victims.

By the time he was in college, he'd used that cleverness to make a name for himself in the theater, feeding off the tension just before stepping onstage. Would he drop a line? Would the audience see past his disguise? Or could he make them believe the lies, defrauding them once again?

Eventually he'd entered law school and found he excelled at mock trials. One of his professors had even nicknamed him "The Closer" because of the ease with which he could craft a closing argument from either point of view. It was a gift he now took for granted.

When the girl's body was finally discovered tonight, he was already back downstairs giving a perfectly choreographed response, indistinguishable from the rest of the Greek tragic masks in the room. When the police arrived, they'd quickly sent everyone to their rooms. That was over an hour ago. Now he wanted back in the game.

He moved to the window as a way to ignore the urge to open the door. His gaze fell on the darkened shadow of the statue of Christ rising from the center of the garden below. A bent figure sat in the shadows. It was a monk, no doubt praying for the soul of the dead girl. Or perhaps he was praying for the soul of the monastery itself, now that a murder would mar its reputation.

The solemn picture of the monk stirred fleeting images of his father on the steps of St. Anthony's Cathedral when he was just seven years old. It was a scene that played often in his mind. His father had been talking to the priest when a car had appeared out of nowhere, screeching around the corner and careening past the broken steps of the church. A flurry of bullets had erupted from a darkened window, ripping through his father's chest and slamming his body against the large cathedral doors. Father Allejandro stood untouched by the carnage, but his mother's scream as she dropped to her knees still reverberated in his ears. For one brief moment, his father's eyes had fluttered open to search the nearby faces, finally landing on that of his only son.

"Il vostro percorso è scelto, Cato" he'd whispered. *Your path is chosen, Cato.*

His father had used a family nickname to emphasize the words that would provide a roadmap for the next fifteen years of his life.

He pushed off the wall and paced the floor. He was on edge. In the closet was the small padded envelope with the blood-soaked baggie and severed finger.

He remembered holding that delicate finger many years before, remembered it stroking parts of his body. He flexed the muscles on the back of his right hand at the thought, putting into motion the tattoo of an eagle. Pity he hadn't had time tonight to revisit the pleasures of his youth. Pity there was no time now to satisfy the urge he felt at thinking of her. But the voices next door signaled the police were close. So as quickly as the thought arose, he deflected it. Discipline. That's what his uncle would reward.

When his uncle came to mind, he thought again about the padded envelope. It would be mailed to the Sierra Madre Police Department in the morning to create chaos. His lips curled into a smile. The police were no threat. They were small town cops who were more used to handling domestic disputes than solving a homicide. The envelope would serve as a diversionary tactic. And it would send a message. In the end, the case would go unsolved, and he would be able to resurface using this new identity.

The sound of footsteps brought him to attention. He checked his watch. It was eleven-fifteen. He snuck a peek in the mirror to make sure he'd combed out the gray at his temple. The fake moustache and goatee were hidden along with the padded envelope. With seemingly little effort, he had taken care of business and eliminated the only evidence that he ever existed at all. When the sharp knock resounded on his door, he took a deep breath and turned to answer it.

Show time!

† Chapter Four †

Rocky's small pickup rattled its way north, past middle-class neighborhoods with perfectly manicured lawns and well-worn basketball hoops hanging off garage doors. There were few cars on the road and most windows were dark. The town was going to sleep.

Giorgio glanced at the illuminated dial on his watch. It was eleven-thirty. Cold air forced its way through a broken seal in the cab window, bringing with it the smell of stale cigarette smoke and the faint aroma of perfume. Giorgio knew Rocky had gone out the night before and briefly wondered which leggy blonde had occupied the seat before him. Something clinked as it rolled across the floor, and he peered into the darkness at his feet. It probably wasn't an empty Coke bottle. He contemplated saying something, but changed his mind, turning instead to watch the darkened homes flash past the window.

A golden moon stood alone in the night sky to challenge a bank of clouds gathering to the east. Nestled at the foothills of the San Gabriel Mountains, Sierra Madre was a small bedroom community to Los Angeles, one where people knew their neighbors, mothers still volunteered for the PTA, and kids looked forward to decorating the annual Rose Parade float. The only points of interest were an old Victorian bed & breakfast reputed to be the most haunted house in Southern California and a bronze replica of a violin spider in the central park. When Giorgio received the call for lead detective two years earlier, he hadn't hesitated. It was exactly what Angie wanted –a normal life away from the dirt and crime of New York City. A few months later, Rocky followed, taking a position with the police department in San Marino, a posh community only a few miles to the south.

The little pickup passed through a set of sturdy iron gates with a cast-iron plaque that read "St Augustine's." Beyond the gates were two hundred acres of undeveloped church property, bordered on the west by a row of homes and on the east by a large drainage ditch. The sprawling Spanish monastery held a commanding place at the top of the hill, while the distinctive bell tower loomed into the night sky like the centerpiece from a stage play. The dark outline of the mountains presented an overpowering backdrop framing the whole picture in relief.

Giorgio knew more than the average person about the monastery because he'd helped Marie research a paper the year before. St. Augustine's had been a landmark in the area since the early 1920s, when it was built as a rural church on top of the ruins of an eighteenth-century Spanish rancho. Patterned after the Franciscan missions constructed along California's coastal trail, the complex had been expanded over the years to include a monastery, commercial bakery, extensive library, and elaborate gardens. An important part of the tradition of the Benedictine monks who owned the property was education, and for that reason, the building had been divided in the late 1930s to accommodate a boy's school. Unfortunately, a major scandal closed the school only a few years later. The monastery disappeared from public view for several decades until the monks opened the west wing in the early 1990s as a conference and retreat center.

The road veered right at the top of the hill passing a small parking lot where the medical examiner's van sat with the back doors open. A single news van was parked along the downside curb. Outside a young female reporter and her cameraman assembled their equipment. Giorgio recognized the local station. Fortunately, Sierra Madre was out of the direct line of media fire, and the main media wouldn't pick up the story until the next day. But he was under no illusions. A murder at a Catholic monastery was almost as good as a political scandal. By the next afternoon, Sierra Madre and its monastery murder would be front page headlines.

Rocky circled around a three-tiered fountain and stopped where two police cars were parked head to toe.

A uniformed officer stood next to the walkway interviewing a man clad in a white dinner jacket, bow tie, and pencil moustache looking very much like the late Don Ameche.

A woman stood off to one side dressed in a Flapper-style white tailored suit, complete with a narrow slit-skirt and shoulder pads the size of saddle bags. While Don Ameche absently stripped the moustache from his upper lip, the woman used a small mirror to lazily apply fresh lipstick as if she were waiting to be called to the set.

As the brothers approached the main entrance, Giorgio couldn't help a curious glance back at Don Ameche.

"Must be a costume party," he mused out loud.

"Either that," Rocky retorted, "or we never left the theater."

Giorgio chuckled as they moved up a set of wide brick steps that curved towards the front door and past cactus gardens dotted with weathered benches, bird baths, and earthen pots filled with flowers. The path ended at a massive wooden door that could have come straight out of Grimm's Fairy Tales, complete with iron metal work. The doorframe was topped by a Moorish arch. Some ten feet above that, a small rose window was cut into the stucco. In between the arch and the window hung an ornate metal cross, reminding Giorgio of the brass button in his pocket.

Before entering, Giorgio glanced to his right where a metal door led into the base of the bell tower. The door was marked with yellow tape announcing it was under construction.

"I wonder if it's locked."

"I'll check." Rocky jogged over and tried the knob. "Locked," he called back.

"This place is huge," Giorgio said, his eyes following a colonnade of arches along the front of the building. "We'll be here all night."

Rocky rejoined him as he pulled open the main door and stepped into a wide entry where they were met with the smell of leather and incense. A large harvest-colored tapestry depicting Jesus being baptized by John covered the wall to their left. A darkened door to the administrative office sat quietly to the right with a plain cross mounted just below the window. Next to the door, two stenciled lines of verse stood out against the aging stained stucco.

"Let them prefer nothing whatever to Christ.
And may He bring us all together to everlasting life!"
Rule of Benedict

A few steps further in and they passed the darkened door to the gift shop. A hallway ran the entire length of the building to their right, connecting to the chapel at the east end. Just in front of them opened an expansive lobby.

Giorgio's gaze swept across the terra cotta floor tiles and up a wooden staircase that descended from the second floor like a tongue lolling from an open mouth. Above their heads hung three authentic oiled wagon wheels, their electrified candle bulbs casting golden halos of light across the surrounding walls. A large oil painting of the Resurrection hung to the left of an imposing river rock fireplace where small votive candles lined a rough-hewn wood mantle.

The lobby was filled with dark mission-style leather furniture. Heavy amber glass lamps anchored each corner of the room, while brass wall sconces dotted the walls like small glow bugs. If it weren't for the three women sitting in front of the fire dressed in gowns circa 1940, Giorgio could have pictured Father Junipero Serra taking up residence here. Either way, he felt he was in the wrong time period.

Blending in with the foot of the staircase stood a monk clad in a traditional, cowl-necked brown robe. One hand rested on the elaborately carved banister, while the other fiddled with the crucifix that hung from the tassels of his rope belt. His small stature made him inconsequential in such expansive surroundings and Giorgio would have missed him if the priest hadn't noticed them first. The presence of the two strangers seemed to give him purpose, and he stepped forward.

"May I help you? I'm Brother Rosario."

Giorgio produced his badge. "I'm Officer Salvatori. So is he."

The monk's pale eyebrows arched in question, so Rocky produced his own identification.

"We're brothers."

The little man squinted through a pair of wire-framed glasses.

"You'll want to go through there," he said, smiling briefly. He used the crucifix to point through an arched opening behind the staircase, thought better of it, and retracted his arm as he cleared his throat. "Sorry. I believe you'll find what you want down that hallway to your left and through the kitchen."

"Thank you. Who are all these people?" Giorgio nodded toward the women huddled by the fireplace.

"We're hosting a writer's conference. They've been asked to remain available for questioning. I really don't know much more than that."

"Why are they dressed like that?"

The little man shrugged, and his hooded robe nearly encased his head. Watching him, Giorgio couldn't decide if he was the real thing or another character at the costumed ball.

"I couldn't tell you," he said, eyeing the women with a pinched expression, "but I can tell you that we've never had a murder here. It's all quite troubling."

Without comment, Giorgio turned and led the way around the base of the stairs, past a portable bar, and down the hallway. They passed several closed doors before the hallway opened into a large square kitchen. A dichotomy in time, the kitchen sported shiny, commercial size appliances, in contrast to a worn tiled floor, dirty stucco walls, and two small antiquated windows set near the ceiling. A chunky wooden table marred by years of knife cuts and mallet whacks now served as crime scene central; Patrol Sergeant Abe Terrero had set up shop there. Tall and lanky, Sergeant Terrero was a man of few words. With an almost inaudible grunt, he shoved a clipboard at the brothers as they entered. Rocky and Giorgio logged in and then donned rubber gloves and booties before picking up radios. Terrero shrugged in the direction of a short hallway, mumbling, "Down there."

The brothers passed through the kitchen to a short hallway that ended with a door to the outside. To their right was a tiny tiled bathroom with only a toilet and a sink. Another hallway cut off to the left where they met Francis Mulhaney, who often acted as the police photographer.

"Joe! Glad to see you. We didn't take you away from a standing ovation did we?"

Mulhaney grinned as he swung his camera over one shoulder. Giorgio returned a brief smile.

"After three curtain calls, I told the stage manager I had to go. What do we have?"

Mulhaney turned and gestured to the other end of the hallway where a small Asian man in a white jumpsuit and rubber gloves dusted a door for fingerprints.

Sierra Madre was too small to employ a full-time forensic specialist and so partnered with neighboring communities when the need arose. Giorgio recognized Jon Fong from the Pasadena Police Department and felt a flood of relief. Fong was one of the best they had. The door he was dusting stood open, revealing a set of shelves with cleaning supplies stowed neatly beyond.

"A woman," Mulhaney replied, allowing Giorgio to duck under the crime scene tape. "Looks like she's been strangled. Whoever did it hung her in the closet. Literally," he emphasized, following behind. "The closet tucks back in there a bit. She's been hung on a utility hook by the back strap of her bra. The M. E. has done a preliminary on her, but they were waiting for you."

"Was she raped?" Rocky asked, bringing up the rear.

Mulhaney turned as if only now realizing Rocky was there. He acknowledged Rocky with a nod before answering.

"Don't know. But she's fully clothed. And she's missing the tip of her little finger."

"We heard. Who found her?" Giorgio asked, moving toward the open doorway.

"The night janitor," Mulhaney replied, following him. "He comes on about nine o'clock and went into the storeroom for the mop bucket. As you can see, the light ain't too good in there and he bumped into her. The old man's pretty spooked, to say the least."

Giorgio approached the door, glancing up at the ceiling as he passed through the hallway.

"No security cameras, I take it?"

Mulhaney shook his head. "No such luck. I doubt they had any reason before tonight."

The forensics man acknowledged Giorgio and then stepped aside, allowing him to poke his head inside. The overhead light did little to illuminate the room.

The closet was large, as closets go – big enough for a full set of shelves on one wall, an industrial vacuum, floor buffer, and various cleaning supplies. On the back wall, cast in deep shadow, was a row of hooks that held mops, brooms, utility jackets, and now the dark outline of a dead woman.

"You done inside?" he asked Fong.

"Just be careful."

Giorgio stepped inside, taking shallow breaths to minimize the stench left behind by death, made all the more unpleasant by the sharp odor of cleaning solvents. He glanced around. One door, no windows. The floor was clean – cleaner than his kitchen at home. All the supplies were lined up in rows and clearly labeled except for the strewn rolls of paper towels the janitor had probably knocked over when he found the body. No trash thrown into corners and no dirty cleaning rags. Just a few of crime scene markers and a dead body.

She was hung next to a pair of painter's overalls, her feet dangling in mid-air. One foot was bare except for her black stockings. Giorgio guessed she wasn't more than five-feet tall, if that. Her head was flopped forward with several long curls of red hair hanging free. Her petite frame was encased in a long-sleeved black velvet cocktail dress, her arms hanging limply at her sides. Except for the dress and the bags used to protect possible evidence underneath the fingernails, she looked very much like the rag doll he'd given Marie on her fourth birthday.

A gold chain encircled her slender neck, and a large amethyst pendant was cradled just above her full bosom. Giorgio looked past the necklace to the translucent flesh beneath. Even in the poor light he could see the wide, uneven ligature line that extended underneath her chin making him suspect the weapon was a scarf or piece of cloth.

The dead woman's face was puffy and looked bruised as the blood settled into her cheeks. He lifted the corner of an eyelid and a bloodshot blue eye peeked out, staring straight ahead. A thought made Giorgio lift her hair at the nape of the neck, using his penlight to identify the bruising he knew he would find. He touched her cheek with two fingers just behind the ear. The skin was cool to the touch, not clammy, indicating she'd been dead less than six hours.

Rocky stood at the doorway. "So?"

"She's been strangled, sometime earlier this evening. Doesn't look like she struggled much, but the autopsy will have to tell us that."

He lifted her right hand, noting the blood stain on the corner of the bag covering her hand. It was a natural reaction to turn and look around the small room as if the missing appendage might reveal itself only to him.

Just below where her hand dangled lay a pool of blood marked with an evidence marker. Lying close by was the woman's black pump, outlined in chalk, and also marked. Everything else seemed in place.

"I doubt she was killed in here," he concluded out loud to Rocky. "But this is where her finger was removed."

Giorgio stepped into the hallway allowing Fong to resume his work. Mulhaney was gone, so the brothers went to find someone who could provide more information. They pushed through a swinging door off the kitchen and entered a modest-sized banquet room filled with round tables. Cigarette smoke hung in the air along with the smell of cheap wine. Tables had been cleared except for the wine glasses and opened bottles of Crystal Moon Chardonnay.

Six or seven people sat huddled at the far side of the room. Two of the men were dressed in black pants, white shirts, and black vests. Probably the bartenders. One officer questioned a slender woman dressed in a long silver lame dress with shoulder-length hair draped alluringly over one eye. Another detective, Chuck Swan, talked to a tall monk with gray hair. When Swan saw Giorgio, he broke away.

"Joe, glad you're here. How was closing night?"

"Good." Giorgio answered, his eyes searching the room.

"Sorry you had to leave the party, but the Captain's gone and thought you should take the lead on this. I didn't think you'd want to get the information secondhand tomorrow, so I sent Samson to pick you up after the performance."

"No problem. What do we know so far?"

"Not much. A writer's conference booked the monastery. During their dinner tonight the janitor found the body. We have a list of every guest in attendance and every priest on the premises, but we've sent most people back to their rooms until we can interview them. The people you see down here have all been questioned. We're also working on a list of employees who were here tonight."

Giorgio looked at Swan. "First of all, they're monks."

Swan shrugged. "What's the difference?"

Giorgio continued to survey the room. "Priests are ordained to public ministry. These guys like to stay all to themselves. Is the janitor still around?"

"He's waiting outside." Swan indicated the back door.

"Who's the woman hanging in the closet?"

"Her name is Mallery Olsen. She was attending the conference."

"When was the last time anyone saw her alive?"

"So far no one's really sure. She was dressed for the dinner, but we haven't found anyone who saw her come into the banquet room. The coroner will have to tell us what time she was killed and whether she even ate dinner."

"How many people attended the dinner tonight?"

Giorgio studied the people at the back of the room, taking in the details of their clothing, their demeanor, and blank expressions. He felt himself entering a familiar groove, gathering information quickly and making determinations later. Swan consulted his notes.

"There were about forty people in the banquet room. Four employees in the kitchen. Two bartenders out in the lobby."

"What about the monks?"

"About twenty live on the premises."

Giorgio sighed and ran his fingers through his hair, setting a few strands free to fall across his forehead. This would be a long night.

"We interviewed the caterers and sent them home, but we've warned everyone else not to leave." Swan closed his notebook. "But there's a problem. The conference ended tonight. Everyone is scheduled to leave tomorrow."

"Then we've got to finish the interviews tonight -- at least preliminary statements."

"We've called for extra help."

Swan glanced at Rocky.

"I'll stick around," Rocky offered. "Who's got a pen and paper?"

"Ask Father Damian over there. He's the abbot." Rocky left and Swan turned back to Giorgio. "The woman was a literary agent from Marina del Ray. According to the conference chairperson, she showed up at the last minute, pinch-hitting for someone who couldn't make it. No one really knew her, although a few of the would-be writers interviewed with her."

"Who was she replacing?"

Swan consulted his notes again. "A woman named Beth Tomlinson, also from Marina del Rey."

"Okay. We'll need to talk with Ms. Tomlinson. See if you can get someone over there tonight."

"Will do. Anything else?"

"Yeah, I need a cup of coffee."

"No problem."

Swan paused, his hazel eyes peeking coyly out from under a set of straight brows. "You know, Joe, you don't look too bad in eye makeup. Makes those soft brown eyes really pop. Know what I mean?"

Swan gave him a seductive wink and walked away smiling to himself. Giorgio rubbed his eyes, knowing that some of the eye makeup lingered. This would be a long night.

† Chapter Five †

Father Damian rested a limp hand across the shoulder of a woman dabbing at her eyes with a burgundy cloth napkin, his face an expressionless mask of boredom. Yet the moment Rocky approached, the monk's visage became suddenly animated, and he stepped away from the weeping woman to give the detective his full attention. Giorgio watched them. After a brief exchange, the abbot pointed to a set of double doors and Rocky departed. The monk gazed after him as if Rocky had taken the only light from a darkened room. Giorgio decided the abbot required some attention of his own and headed in that direction.

"May I ask you some questions, Father?" he called out, weaving between tables to cross the room. The abbot made a full turn as Giorgio approached, his generous mouth stretching into an expectant smile.

"Are you with the police?"

His thick white hair matched a set of unruly brows that crowded narrow eye sockets, making Giorgio hunt for the small brown eyes hidden within.

"I'm a detective. Is there somewhere we can talk privately?"

The monk snuck a glance at the tearful woman behind him, perhaps feeling guilty for leaving her to her own devices. "We can go to my office," he offered.

He led Giorgio out the door and across the now empty lobby, the room's silence emphasizing the soft rustle of his robes. The abbot paused at the foot of the staircase where a wall niche held a delicate, painted statue of Christ on the cross. Father Damian quickly touched his forehead and each shoulder just as a door opened, and Rocky met them coming out with pen and paper in hand.

"I'll find Swan, get a list of names and touch base with you later," Rocky told his brother. He pulled his radio from his belt. "What channel are we on?"

"Three," Giorgio responded.

Rocky adjusted his radio and returned to the banquet room, leaving Giorgio to follow the priest into a warmly lit office. Floor to ceiling bookcases filled with gold-leafed religious texts covered one full wall, while an impressive carved writing table sat in front of a wall closet. The table's clawed feet grasped for a burgundy fringed carpet, its ribbon carving filled with enough shadow to make it appear as if a brown snake had coiled itself around its edge. A large brass lamp weighted one side of the desk; a computer monitor balanced the other.

To Giorgio's right was a large, gold-framed painting of Christ's descent from the cross. It hung above a highly polished oak library table that sat against the wall. The table was graced with a red silk runner, hand painted porcelain bowl, twin brass candlestick holders, and a large gold-leafed Bible heavy enough to anchor a small ship. On the opposite wall was a red velvet settee and small marble coffee table. As a lifelong Catholic, Giorgio felt right at home here and could almost hear the rich voice of Father Michael O'Hara patiently explaining the difference between obligatory prayer and true spiritual prayer.

"Praying is a discipline, Mr. Salvatori," Father Michael would say with a stiff lip. *"However, God wants your heart, not merely your mind. When you pray, you talk directly to God. Let go of everything you think you already know. Be humble and speak from your heart."*

Father Michael would tap Giorgio on the head after that as if to say, "Get that, Salvatori?" Then he would retreat with his hands clasped behind his back.

To this day, Giorgio prayed because he'd been taught to do so, not because he held out any hope his prayers would be answered. His view of God was surprisingly cynical for someone who had at one time considered going into the ministry. When he caught himself staring at the limp figure of Jesus, Giorgio allowed the ghosts of his youth to fade and lowered himself into a richly upholstered Queen Anne chair facing Father Damian.

"How can I help you, Officer…uh…?"

"Salvatori. I'm a detective with the Sierra Madre police."

"I'm afraid we're at a bit of a loss, Detective. Nothing like this has ever happened here."

Father Damian pressed his fingers together as if kneading bread dough.

"I understand, Father, but we have a problem. All your guests leave tomorrow. We have a lot of information to gather before then. I need some background. For instance, how are these conferences booked?"

"People find us through travel agents and travel guides. Our own Chamber of Commerce mentions us in their material. We even have a website."

"Who provides the food?"

"We have a standing contract with a local catering company."

"May I have their name?" Giorgio pulled a small pad from his pocket.

"Food for Thought." The monk smiled when Giorgio appeared confused. "The name is meant to be clever. They specialize in conferences both here and at several other locations in the area. Their owner is Mary Fields. I'm sure she'll be happy to talk with you."

"Were any of the catering staff still here when the body was found?"

He looked thoughtful for a moment. "Yes, I saw Mary when the police arrived. I don't know who else might have been here."

"What time did the dinner start?"

"We don't have much to do with the conference schedules. Our coordinator arranges everything. I can give you her name and phone number. She isn't scheduled to be back here until Monday. Her name is Anya Peters." He pulled out a Post-it Note from a drawer and wrote down a number. "I'm afraid she was only just notified about this. She leaves once the event is running smoothly."

Giorgio took the phone number, noticing the monk had known it by heart. Possibly an innocent fact, but one he would remember.

"Would she have been the person who booked the conference?"

"Yes. We try to keep the monastery separate from the retreat center."

Giorgio made a note and then remembered that some priests move around. Father Michael had been relocated to a parish in Brooklyn when Giorgio was only a year short of graduation.

"Have any new monks arrived recently?"

"Many young priests come as postulants for one or two-year programs. They live here on a temporary commitment. Some remain, while others conclude this isn't the life for them."

"Did anyone come recently?"

Father Damian paused, his hands crossed at his abdomen like the bodice of a period dress. "Three came to us within the last few months," he said, exhaling.

"May I have their names?"

He sat forward, bristling. "They are referred to us by their seminaries and come with the highest recommendations."

"I'm sure you're right, but this is a murder investigation and we have to consider all possibilities.

The monk blinked once or twice and then licked his lips, leaving a layer of moisture behind. To Giorgio, his lips looked like two large glazed doughnuts, and he dropped his gaze to his notepad. He was hungry.

"Brother Francis arrived from San Francisco in August," Father Damian explained, "and Brother Julio in early September. He came from Chicago."

Giorgio recorded the names and paused, waiting for the third. When he looked up, Father Damian was staring at him, the bushy eyebrows twitching like restless caterpillars. Finally, he relented.

"Brother Daniel arrived some six weeks ago from New York."

Giorgio stood to leave. "Thank you, Father. We'll also need to know where each monk was at the approximate time of the murder."

Father Damian's long fingers grasped the edge of the table. "I can tell you where we all were. We had a nine o'clock prayer."

"I'm sorry, Father, but the body was merely found at nine o'clock. We don't know when the murder took place. Our job is to interview the guests tonight and as many of the monks as possible. It would help to have all of them stay in their rooms, and I'd prefer they didn't speak to each other."

Father Damian seemed to hold his breath in an effort to control his temper. When he exhaled, he relaxed only slightly.

"I'm sure you believe these precautions are necessary. We'll help in any way we can. However, I must tell you that this investigation must be wrapped up within a few days."

"Why is that?" Giorgio couldn't believe what he'd just heard.

"The Bishop is scheduled to arrive next weekend. Preparations are on a fast track, including repairing the cracks in the tower caused by last month's earthquake. I daresay a murder investigation would not be to the Bishop's liking."

Giorgio was speechless. Under other circumstances, he would have assumed Father Damian was joking, but the man's face lacked any hint of humor.

"Father, we don't conduct murder investigations on a timetable."

"I don't think you understand, Detective. The Bishop is coming for a regional forum. He will be joined by about twenty abbots from all over Southern California. Once the forum has begun, it cannot be interrupted. So I would encourage you to complete your investigation as quickly as possible."

"I make no promises, Father," Giorgio stated flatly.

He left Father Damian and met Swan at the foot of the stairs.

"Joe, we've found something interesting. One of the guests says she saw the victim arguing with someone earlier this afternoon. She didn't know the man, but we have a description and will stay on it. And several people have already left the conference. I guess the dinner was optional."

"Do we have a list of everyone who has left already?"

"Yes. And the times they left."

"Well, leaving the facility could just be a diversion. Who's the conference chairperson?"

"A man named John Marsh. He's still in the banquet room. You can't miss him. Tall, with a mustache and a beard."

"Okay. Keep at it." Giorgio stopped him with a hand on his shoulder. "And where can I get that coffee?"

Swan's normally placid face broke into a grin. "I'll find someone. I recognize a star personality when I see one."

Giorgio went back into the banquet room and spotted John Marsh sitting with a glass of wine. A short bald man was bent next to him talking earnestly into one ear. Marsh had thinning gray hair and a sparse gray moustache and beard clipped close to a protruding chin. His head was much too small for his body, looking like the period at the end of a sentence. When Giorgio approached, the bald man moved a few feet away, but leaned in their direction, listening intently.

"Mr. Marsh, I need to ask you some questions."

"I've already talked with one of the uniformed policemen," he replied, rubbing life back into his dull brown eyes.

"I'm a detective and need to hear the information for myself." Giorgio glanced at the bald man who couldn't have been more obvious if he'd held a small glass up to his ear. "Perhaps we could step into the lobby?"

Marsh rose reluctantly, and they went into the lobby leaving the bald man to retreat to a corner alone with a look of abject disappointment on his face. A long, ebony wooden bench offered them a seat against the wall.

"You're in charge of the conference?"

"I have a committee working with me, but I'm the chairman...*was* the chairman," he corrected himself.

Marsh slouched forward with his elbows across his knees. His dated tuxedo was too small and when he stretched his hands forward, the sleeves pulled up to expose black and white cufflinks fashioned in the form of dice. Giorgio had the feeling he was still on stage and had merely changed plays.

"We've been planning the conference for over a year," he said. "We announced the date and location at the closing dinner last year. It's sort of a tradition."

"Tradition?"

"To build up excitement for the coming year. We usually include some gimmick. That's why we're all in costume. We scheduled a mystery game this year to promote next year's conference in Burbank."

Giorgio just stared at Marsh.

"At the movie studios," he prompted. "We're called the San Gabriel Writers' Association, so we look for locations in the area conducive to an intensive two-day writing conference."

"Are all of your guests writers?"

"Most of them. But out of the sixty or so who registered, we had six agents this year. We also have some fans who attend."

"Fans?"

"Sometimes we have well-known authors who come and speak."

"Ms. Olsen was an agent, not a writer or a fan?"

"That's right," he replied, stiffening at the mention of the dead woman's name. "She came in the place of someone else."

"Is it the usual practice that an agent would be replaced without telling you first?"

"No. We're usually notified in advance. Sometimes that person will find a replacement, but often we're faced with the task."

"Did anyone know Ms. Olsen would be attending?"

"We were only told when she arrived. Of course, we were grateful Ms. Tomlinson asked her to step in. Otherwise, a cancellation at this late date would have caused a problem. You see, we recruit agents who represent all sorts of works. Fiction, non-fiction, children's books, mysteries, things like that. People sign up in advance to meet with the agents. Seven people had signed up to meet with Ms. Tomlinson."

"Then Mallery Olsen and Beth Tomlinson handled the same kind of books?"

Marsh seemed to hesitate before answering. "Ms. Tomlinson handled a broad list. I assume Ms. Olsen did as well."

"Do you have the names of all the people who interviewed with her?"

"I'm sure we can provide that. I'll ask the Program Chair, Ms. Levinsky."

"Is there anything else you can tell me that might be of help?"

"I didn't know her myself," Marsh said.

His dark eyes darted away, and he rubbed his large hands together as if he were wiping something sticky off his fingers. Giorgio thought he was lying.

"You never met her?" Giorgio asked.

"I introduced myself at the opening reception. She seemed pleasant enough. As chair of the event, I don't have time to pay attention to anything but the details of running the conference. I'm afraid I can't tell you very much." He said this rapidly, his face devoid of all emotion.

"Do you know of anyone who came late to the dinner tonight?"

He raised one hand to his chin, bringing attention to his nicotine-stained fingers and long fingernails.

"I'm not quite sure, but I can find out. I'll ask the woman who was in charge of the table arrangements."

"Did you see anyone leave any time before nine o'clock?"

Marsh gave a throaty laugh. "Detective, many people left the room all through the evening. The bathrooms are down that hallway." He pointed behind the main staircase. "And the bar was set up out here."

Giorgio rose, and Marsh took the cue he was free to go and stood up as well. "I'll probably want to talk with you again."

"I don't check out until tomorrow afternoon. I'll be sure you have my contact information."

Although Marsh was a good five inches taller than Giorgio, he seemed ill at ease. Giorgio thought it was either the costume, or there was something Marsh wasn't telling.

"Thanks for your help. I know this is very hard."

"You have no idea. I just fear it will damage our reputation. We want this wrapped up as quickly as possible, Detective."

As Marsh walked away, Giorgio was left thinking about the work that lay ahead. He would have to concentrate on searching through pages of useless information from hundreds of potential witnesses in order to find one needle in a haystack. It was a familiar process. As a boy, he'd excelled at putting together complicated puzzles. No surprise, he'd grow up to do it again.

Inside his coat pocket, his fingers found the strange button from the parking lot. He took it out and studied the outline of the ornate Latin cross stamped into the tarnished brass. Giorgio didn't believe in coincidences. This button had come out of nowhere, and it meant something. He just didn't know what.

He glanced up to where a round plaque hung on the wall above the head of the stairs. Etched into the wood was an exact duplicate of the cross imprinted on the button in his hand.

† Chapter Six †

He lay on the small, uncomfortable bed with his arms folded behind his head. The interview had gone well. A young cop with red hair had asked simple, even cursory, questions meant to establish the basics. He'd applied just the right inflection of sadness in his answers. After all, a young woman had just died. He would be expected to feel badly about that.

In return, he'd gleaned important information of his own. The police had no suspects and couldn't figure out how someone had gotten the victim into the closet without being seen. The girl's name was Mallery Olsen, and she'd been strangled. So far, no one had reported seeing anything suspicious. But something else, something more sinister had happened that the young cop wouldn't reveal. Of course, that sinister "thing" was sitting safely tucked away in an envelope inside the closet. The officer had also divulged there was only one detective on the force trained in homicide investigations, but he wouldn't be available to take the case tonight. That was a fucking stroke of luck.

He rolled onto his side thinking about the girl, Mallery. He'd dated her for a short time in college when her name had been Mallery Young. They'd met in the theater; she'd played Guinevere to his Lancelot. Like most stage romances, it had lasted only until closing night. She'd briefly dated his best friend as well, saying the only way she could tell them apart was by the color of their hair and how well they performed in bed. He just assumed he was the better lover.

Perhaps he should have indulged himself tonight. They hadn't seen each other in over five years and yet, clearly, she'd been interested. She'd appeared out of nowhere to join him on the bench in the garden as he sat enjoying the fading sun. She'd been chatty and curious about his appearance.

Although he'd tried to engage himself in their conversation, his mind had raced ahead in an effort to resolve the situation. She could blow his cover, now, or when the conference was over. Fortunately, she'd suggested the rendezvous in her room before the banquet. All he'd had to do was suggest keeping it private. She'd gone back to the conference while he'd returned to his own room to figure out what to do.

His initial panic quickly morphed into a concentrated planning mode. The "what" (what to do) was answered immediately. He had to get rid of her. The "how" was a little more difficult. Fortunately, the location of his room came to his rescue. In the end, it had all been incredibly easy, and he remembered the odd sense of detachment when he wrapped the green silk scarf around her neck. She'd struggled and squirmed, but when the small bone in her neck snapped, her legs had gone limp, and he'd dropped her to the floor.

He'd stood over her for a moment, wondering at the perverse sense of power he felt at having killed another human being. When he'd shot Mangano, the man who had killed his father, the power had been contained in the gun, dissipating quickly once the gun was eliminated. With the girl, the power had been in his bare hands. But that feeling hadn't lasted long. A mist had formed above her body, breaking the spell and making him step back. The memory gave him a chill even now. He thought perhaps it was her soul leaving her body. That hadn't happened with Mangano, but then, maybe Mangano didn't have a soul.

Getting Mallery down to the closet had been the biggest challenge. She hadn't weighed much. Even rolled in a blanket, she'd been easy to balance on one shoulder. The real risk had been running into someone. But even the caterers had been too busy to notice him as he'd entered the rear hallway. Once he was in the closet, he'd been relatively safe. Hanging her on the utility rack and then removing her little finger was meant to achieve maximum attention. That was important. He wanted news of this to reach across the country.

After he placed her on the hook, he'd had time to indulge himself with a feel beneath the fabric of her dress for old time's sake. Her perfume lingered yet on his fingertips, and he dragged the back of his hand across his upper lip, inhaling the full aroma of her scent.

Shit! The perfume!

He sat up, flinging his feet to the floor in one fluid movement. Had the young cop smelled it?

He jumped up and ran to the bathroom with a curdled feeling filling his stomach. Grabbing the hand soap, he lathered up.

Stupid mistake. Stupid, stupid mistake! He had to get rid of the smell and hope the officer hadn't noticed it. Thank God he'd been fortunate enough to draw the biggest novice in the bunch. A mistake like this could have given him away. He scrubbed until his fingers were almost raw, even lathering up the back of his hand and putting the wings of the eagle tattoo into motion. He kept this up until only the crisp smell of the soap filled the small bathroom. Then he dried his hands and leaned on the sink, staring at himself in the mirror.

He'd killed a girl he'd once had feelings for, and yet he didn't really care. It was just something that had to be done. Survival. There had been no hesitation, no moment of question, and no guilt. Was that how his uncle felt when he took care of business? When he'd ordered his only nephew to disappear because he'd made a mistake?

He turned off the water and watched the soap disappear down the drain. This was no time for sentimentality. His uncle would expect more. Hadn't he always said, *"Never underestimate your adversary?"* Even dim-witted police could identify mistakes, so there couldn't be any mistakes. Not if he wanted back in the family.

The girl was dead, and the disguise had been hidden away. He was invisible again. He was safe. Tomorrow, he would use the disguise to mail the envelope, sending this small-town police department into a tail spin. After all, deception wasn't so hard. All you had to do was help them focus on all the wrong places. Like any good magician, it was only a matter of misdirection. And that was something he was very, very good at.

† Chapter Seven †

Giorgio dropped the button back into his pocket. Marsh wasn't telling all he knew. That was clear. But what did the deception mean? As Marsh disappeared around the top of the stairs, a red-haired officer appeared from the opposite direction.

"McCready!" Giorgio called up to the young man. "Where's Swan?"

The officer lifted his eyes from the tablet in his hands. At twenty-four, McCready was the youngest member of the Sierra Madre department and the tech whiz.

"Joe, I didn't think you'd be here tonight. Swan's interviewing two women up here," McCready said, jerking his head back and to the right. "Do you want me to get him?"

"No. Thanks." Giorgio grabbed the carved finial at the foot of the stairs and took them two at a time, stopping to look over McCready's shoulder. "Are you sure you're not playing solitaire on that thing?"

McCready was never far from a keyboard and looked at Giorgio, his blue eyes lost in a curious expression.

"I'm putting in my notes, sir."

Giorgio smiled and continued around the head of the stairs. He found himself in a dreary, narrow hallway. Voices drew him into the first room to his right where Swan was finishing up with two older women. The room was sparsely furnished with twin beds covered by eyelet bedspreads and green chenille blankets. Giorgio gave Swan a nod, encouraging him to continue with his interview. He decided to look around while he waited.

The hallway extended forwards for about seventy-five feet with rooms on both sides. Giorgio's footsteps were muffled by a series of threadbare, Middle Eastern carpet runners laid end-to-end. Two amber wall sconces splashed soft arcs of light across the faded floral wallpaper.

The hallway ended at a window that looked out onto a small roof. Giorgio glanced out the window and then tried the window. It was securely locked. Retracing his steps, he passed the brunette from the driveway, the one wearing the slim, white suit with the split skirt. She glanced his way, her eyes lost in shadow as she disappeared into her room.

Giorgio made it back to where the landing at the head of the stairs had been made into a sitting area. Two windows covered by heavy brocade curtains looked out over the north side of the property.

Giorgio pushed one set of curtains aside and found a tall leaded window. Dust lifted off the curtains making him pinch his nose to avoid sneezing. When the urge subsided, he reached out to test the crank window. It was also securely locked. He checked the second window and found it locked as well. The view from either window revealed little. It was virtually dark outside except for a string of lights strategically positioned along the walkway below. Yet even these were obscured by a canopy of mature trees now restlessly moving back and forth in a healthy breeze.

Since there was nothing to learn here, Giorgio turned away and started to leave, when a sharp "click" stopped him. He paused. Perhaps someone had opened one of the nearby doors. But all doors in close proximity remained closed. A soft whapping noise directly behind him made him turn back to the window.

The heavy curtain billowed away from the wall now as if a floor heater had been ignited. Slowly, he reached out to draw the curtain aside again, forcing the hairs on the back of his neck to stand on end. The old-fashioned crank window stood open now, allowing a crisp breeze to fill the narrow hallway.

Giorgio cautiously craned his neck forward to see below, half expecting someone to suddenly appear on the windowsill. But there was no one outside, just a damp pocket of mist hanging in the air just beyond the ledge.

He reached down and jiggled the antique hardware, curious as to how the window had popped opened. The crank moved generously from side to side. Convinced it was just old hardware, Giorgio shut the window tight and cast a final skeptical glance into the misty night before returning to Swan.

"Where's Olsen's room?" Giorgio snapped when Swan emerged into the hallway.

"Over here. Number 18. You okay?" Swan asked with a defensive posture.

"Fine. Just tired," he said, on edge.

They crossed the landing into a matching hallway and passed two rooms before stopping at the yellow tape marking off Mallery Olsen's bedroom. The hallway ended with a supply closet. Olsen's bedroom was the last room on the right, directly across from a large guest laundry and an alcove with a single vending machine that offered juices and candy bars. Giorgio noticed the apparent isolation of Olsen's room and made a note to find out who occupied the only room adjacent to hers.

"Make sure Fong gets up here as soon as he's done downstairs to dust for prints."

Swan nodded before slipping paper booties over his shoes and handing a pair to Giorgio. Olsen's room was similar to the one Swan had just left. It was spartan and without personality. A cheap nightstand and small chest of drawers filled one wall, while a worm-eaten writing desk and straight-backed chair sat under the window. A small bible sat in the corner of the writing desk, along with an inexpensive wooden crucifix. There was one, bell-shaped lamp on the writing desk that did nothing more than light the area right around it. A single upholstery fabric suitcase sat at the foot of the single bed with the same green chenille blanket laid across the end.

"Not much to look at, is it?" Giorgio said with some sadness.

"No," Swan agreed. "The rooms are all basically the same, although a few are a bit larger. It is a monastery, after all, and I assume the cost of the conference reflects it."

Giorgio wandered into the bathroom with its dated black and white mosaic tiled floor and frosted double-hung window. Olsen's bag of toiletries sat on the top of the commode's water tank. Her toothbrush and toothpaste lay on the chrome shelf above the sink, a small dab of water pooled under the bristles.

The bathroom still held the faint aroma of the White Diamonds spray perfume that sat off to one side. A plastic cup wrapped in cellophane was placed upside down at the end of the shelf.

As Giorgio looked around, he asked Swan, "Anyone report seeing her at any time before the dinner?"

"One of the other agents said she saw Olsen going back upstairs just before six o'clock."

Giorgio turned to Swan. "Going *back* upstairs? Did the woman say why?"

"Olsen said she was having a drink with a friend and would join the banquet later," Swan said.

Giorgio's eyes narrowed. "A friend? I wonder if it was someone from the conference."

Swan shrugged. "Maybe one of the caterers. Who knows? Could've been anyone."

"A caterer couldn't have left his post. They were working."

Giorgio wandered back into the bedroom. The room reminded him of his dormitory room at the police academy, except this room was peaceful. Here, he could picture a monk sitting at the desk late into the evening with only a candle to light his studies. It was that kind of solitary life that had prevented Giorgio from entering the seminary – that and the vow of celibacy.

"So, she was dressed for the dinner, but didn't go."

"Looks that way," Swan confirmed.

"Someone changed her mind," Giorgio said.

Giorgio moved to the writing desk where a bottle of corked red wine sat next to another plastic cup. This one had been used, and he bent over to take a sniff.

"It looks as if this is where she had her drink." He twisted around. "But where's the other cup? The one in the bathroom hasn't been used."

"Maybe they didn't meet in here."

"Where else would she go? We're three miles from the nearest restaurant, and she left the cocktail party downstairs and didn't leave the premises. No," he said pulling a handkerchief from his pocket, "I think she came back here to meet her mysterious friend and never left."

Giorgio used the handkerchief to begin opening drawers. Swan pulled out a pair of rubber gloves and joined him in a careful search of the room. Giorgio found nothing but Olsen's neatly folded clothes and personal belongings in the small chest. Swan looked into her briefcase and purse and then searched the suitcase. The room was neat and clean, offering no evidence to identify a guest, or a murderer.

Giorgio put the handkerchief back in his pocket. "Get Fong up here fast. I want forensics to check the remaining contents of that glass." Swan started to leave as Giorgio glanced at the bed. "Chuck," he said. "This woman was incredibly neat, wouldn't you say?"

"I guess so, yeah," his colleague shrugged.

Giorgio gestured around him. "Look around the room. The bed is neatly made. All her clothes are folded and put away in the drawers. Even the bathroom is neat as a pin, although she'd just gotten ready for a fancy dinner. Nothing is out of place."

"So?"

Giorgio pointed to the bed. "Why is there a pair of pantyhose lying crumpled up in the middle of the bed?"

Swan followed Giorgio's gaze and shrugged again. "I don't know. Women always leave those things lying around. I know my wife does."

"Doesn't it seem out-of-character to leave something so personal out in the open when a guest is expected?" Giorgio pulled a pencil from his pocket and lifted the toe of the nylon foot off the bedspread. "I have a feeling we may have just found the murder weapon."

"But you don't know she was killed up here," Swan said skeptically. "If she was killed in this room, the murderer would have had to carry her all the way down the stairs, down a hallway, and through the kitchen in order to get her to the supply closet."

"Maybe there's a back staircase," Giorgio said. "She didn't look very heavy. Under the cover of darkness, it could have been done pretty easily, especially for a man."

"Then you're eliminating any female suspects?"

"Not necessarily. I saw a few women downstairs built well enough to accomplish the task." Giorgio gave a wicked smile.

"But how did he get to the back stairs? The hallway ends right here," Swan said.

Giorgio arched his back, feeling his fatigue. "I don't know, but I bet there's a way."

"She could have been killed somewhere else," Swan argued. "The parking lot, for instance."

"The parking lot is lit. Plus, the caterers probably parked there. Too risky."

"What about out in the garden, then? She could've been killed out there."

"Her shoes will tell us that," Giorgio said. "But something tells me she was strangled right here, with this pair of nylons."

"Why?"

"The dead woman in the closet is wearing a black cocktail dress and black pantyhose."

Giorgio drew Swan's attention to the pale colored nylons lying on the bed.

Swan lifted his eyebrows. "Oh."

† Chapter Eight †

Swan went to help the other officers, allowing Giorgio to step outside for a short break. He stretched his arms above his head, groaning a bit as his muscles pulled. A bank of clouds had begun their march across the night sky, snuffing out stars one by one, while a brisk wind stirred up the rich aroma of sage from the bushes near the entrance. Giorgio sucked in the tantalizing smell and then ambled along the gravel path that led him into the center of a large cactus garden.

A tall, unadorned wooden cross rose out of a round, cement slab. It was the same kind of religious symbol Giorgio had come to associate with the church − rigid, unyielding, and solid as a rock. He stood for a moment lost in thought, until a tap on the shoulder startled him. Giorgio turned to find Swan holding out a steaming cup of coffee.

"This ought to strip the lining from your stomach."

"Finally," Giorgio smiled, rescuing the Styrofoam cup from Swan's stubby fingers.

Swan was an imposing figure, even in a suit and tie. Giorgio remembered that Swan had been a wrestler in college. At a good fifty pounds lighter, Giorgio contemplated with some anxiety what it must have been like to face Swan across a wrestling mat.

"Where's the janitor?" he asked, taking a swig of coffee.

"He's in the kitchen. I told him you'd be in soon."

"Okay, I'll go talk with him."

The sound of men's voices raised in chant made both officers stop and turn towards the arched windows on the other side of the bell tower.

A line of monks holding candles was visible through the window, descending a staircase and crossing into the chapel. Their faces were hidden by hoods, and the hypnotic chant filled the night like a doomsday warning.

"What the…?" Swan uttered.

Giorgio swallowed another swig of coffee and stared at the eerie scene, feeling the hairs on the back of his neck stand up for the second time that night.

"Mass. Probably for the girl," Giorgio speculated.

"Gives me the creeps," Swan shuddered, as the monks continued to file like lemmings into the chapel, their voices undulating in a Latin verse.

"Yeah, well so much for keeping them separate so they can't share information. I'll have to have another talk with Father Damian."

Giorgio turned and made it back to the front door just as the local female reporter came running up from the driveway. Her microphone was extended for a statement; the cameraman loomed behind her.

"Detective, can I have a minute?"

Giorgio turned to Swan. "Handle it," he snapped and then disappeared inside.

He returned to the kitchen where he found a man in his sixties sitting hunched over the small table, staring at his hands as if he were mapping them for later reference. Giorgio took a seat across from him. The man didn't look up. He just sat staring at his hands as if Giorgio didn't exist.

This kind of shell shock reminded Giorgio of a case in New York, in which a father had been rendered helpless by the hedonistic murder of his only son. The man had arms the size of canoe paddles, and yet he sat lifeless as a doll on a toy store shelf while Giorgio tried without success to interview him. Giorgio could only hope this time it would go better.

"I'm Detective Salvatori."

The man turned vacant gray eyes in his direction and said nothing for a full five seconds. Finally, he dropped his head and whispered.

"I've never seen a corpse up close."

"I understand," Giorgio nodded. "What's your name?"

"Syd Norville." His chest heaved. "I've never been through anything like this. That young girl was dead, you know?" His lip twitched.

"I know. You're the janitor?"

"That's right. I come on duty at nine o'clock."

Norville was a handsome man, with wide set eyes and skin as supple as soft leather. Coarse gray hair was cropped close to his head, and he wore a blue work shirt and crisp blue jeans.

"What's the first thing you did when you arrived tonight?"

"I went to the supply closet, like I always do. That's where I found her."

"Had you ever seen the woman before?"

Giorgio knew what the answer would be, but the question had to be asked.

"I only come in at night. I don't know any of the people who attend these things."

"Where do you park?"

A gnarly finger gestured towards the back door. "That's my truck out there."

Giorgio nodded, took a sip of coffee and wrote a note in his book. "Did you come straight in from the parking lot and go directly to the closet?"

Norville finally looked up at Giorgio. "Didn't have nowhere else to go."

"I understand, but it's important. You didn't come in here first for coffee or go see Father Damian?"

"Father Damian would have been at the night prayer. I went straight to work. I take a break at eleven-thirty. That's when I have my coffee. I bring it in a thermos, in my lunchbox."

"And where is the thermos now?"

"Oh!" The gray eyes expanded into near circles. "It's in the closet."

"We'll make sure it's returned to you. Did you see anyone else when you came in?"

"No. I went straight to the closet." His hands relaxed a bit and he looked back down at the table again.

"You didn't see the catering staff?"

"I heard them, but figured I'd start at the other end of the building."

"Did you see anyone at all? Inside or out?"

"Just Ms. Peters." The wide shoulders shrugged as if this fact was unimportant.

"Ms. Peters?" Giorgio asked her.

"She organizes the events. Just as I was coming in, she pulled out of the parking lot."

Giorgio made a note. "Is she usually here this late?"

"Sometimes."

"Did she see you?"

"I don't know. Why?"

"Tell me what happened when you found the body."

"Like I told the other officer, I went in there to get the mop and found a shoe on the floor. I was leaning over to pick it up when I bumped against something hanging on the wall. It was her foot."

His shoulders jerked at the memory. Giorgio let him relate the story at his own pace.

"What did you do then?"

Norville gazed at Giorgio as if he were looking right through him. "I went to find the abbot."

"You didn't call the police first?"

"No. Should I have?"

"What you did was fine," Giorgio assured him. "Did you see anyone when you went to find Father Damian?"

"I went through the kitchen, and the bartenders were still in the lobby. They were getting ready to leave. I started toward the chapel thinking Father Damian would be leading the night prayer, but I saw him just outside his office door. I told him what happened, and he called the police."

Giorgio put his notebook away. "Thank you, Mr. Norville. I hope you'll remain available if we need to talk again."

"Father Damian knows where to find me. Can I go now? I don't feel too much like cleaning up tonight. I haven't even told Mabel, yet."

"Mabel?"

"My wife."

"You can leave, but don't clean anything up until I let you know."

Norville pushed away from the table and stood. "Most likely I'll be finding a new job, anyway. This place gives me the creeps."

Giorgio stood with him. "By the way, Mr. Norville, did you find anything besides the shoe on the floor?"

Norville paused, giving Giorgio a curious look.

"I don't understand."

This was one of the parts Giorgio hated most about his job, destroying the image people like Syd Norville had of the world. As big as he was, he was clearly someone who had not been exposed much to violence. But if he hadn't seen the severed finger, there was no reason to tell him.

"I was just wondering if there was anything else you could think of."

"No. I don't think so."

"Well, thank you. Are all the doors to the outside locked at night?"

"I lock up as I move through the building. I don't finish until after one o'clock in the morning."

"Do you ever see any of the monks?"

"Not usually. They go to bed early. They have a pretty strict routine. I've been told they're up at four o'clock most days. I've seen the odd man about, taking a short walk or grabbing a snack from the kitchen, but not often."

"Does Father Damian go to bed at the same time?"

"Sometimes he works late. I've seen the light on in his office past midnight at times, but he sleeps out in the bungalow, so I really couldn't say what time he goes to bed."

"I see. Can I get a copy of the building plans?"

"You'd have to ask Father Damian for that."

"Thank you. We'll be in touch if we need anything else."

The older man grabbed his jean jacket from the chair before leaving through the back door. Giorgio followed him outside, stepping into the glow of the small light mounted above the kitchen door. Giorgio peered over a four-foot wall to his left topped by large clay pots. A truck engine flared and a moment later, the headlights of an old Ford pickup came on as the janitor pulled out of the parking lot.

Giorgio watched the taillights disappear and then glanced around, mentally calculating distances and angles. From where he stood, the row of planters blocked any view from the banquet room windows only a few feet away. To his right, bushes crowded the exterior wall, spilling onto the walkway as a path curved around the building.

A second path led up the slope to where an ivy-covered trellis opened onto a flower garden.

Giorgio was familiar with the garden because he'd attended a wedding there earlier in the summer. It was protected by a low trimmed hedge, with a circular patch of lawn and a shrine set off to one side.

He turned and scanned the building behind him. The kitchen doorway stuck out about ten feet from the main building. A metal ladder bolted to the wall extended up to the flat roof. Another ladder, perhaps a fire escape, extended from the roof above the door to the window at the end of the upstairs hallway. Although this could provide a means of escape, it was doubtful anyone could climb out the window and down the ladders carrying a dead body.

He decided to follow the walkway around the northwest corner of the building and entered a winding tunnel of low-hanging trees, old-growth bushes, and a series of buttresses that braced the exterior wall. The outdoor lights were practically useless, making him realize that anyone using the walkway would be invisible above the knees. A hundred yards farther on, he encountered a statue of the Virgin Mary flanked by two plain cement benches. Here, a second path disappeared up the hill into the dark.

The sound of a door opening from somewhere behind him prompted him to duck behind the statue. A draped silhouette glided silently up the hillside into a clump of bushes. There was a scratching sound, followed by a glow that pierced the darkness. One of the priests was having a cigarette. Giorgio smiled, thinking even a man of the cloth has his vices. This interested him less than the fact a rear door was missing a security light, something he would check the next day.

Giorgio returned to the main lobby where he ran into Swan.

"I sent the janitor home," he informed Swan. "He left a thermos behind. Let's make sure we secure it for him."

Swan nodded just as the front door swung open. A woman in her early thirties, with shoulder-length bleached blonde hair and tight green slacks blew in with the wind. A cashmere sweater and leather waistcoat accentuated her trim figure. She approached Giorgio, her eyes focused on him as if he were the biggest lobster at a seafood restaurant.

"I'm Anya Peters. I need to know what happened here. Where's Mr. Marsh? Where are Father Damian and Ms. Levinsky?" She only caught her breath at the end of her list of questions.

Giorgio noticed the heavy makeup used to cover pockmarked skin. He produced his badge.

"I'm Detective Salvatori. This is Detective Swan. You're the Event Coordinator?"

"Yes." She seemed surprised he knew who she was. "Tell me what happened."

"Perhaps we could go into Father Damian's office."

Giorgio started for the office, but the woman remained where she was, her jaw locked in stubborn determination. Caught in between the two of them, Swan shifted his weight uncomfortably.

"I don't think you understand. I need to know what happened, and then I need to speak with Mr. Marsh"

Swan drifted in Giorgio's direction. Inwardly, Giorgio smiled, thinking how easily an angry woman can intimidate a man, even one the size of Swan.

"I understand, Ms. Peters. But we're conducting an investigation here, and you may have information that could be helpful. Now, if you don't mind..." He allowed his sentence to trail off as he gestured to the office door.

She looked at him and then at Swan, finally making a decision. As she strode past Giorgio, he noticed the pearl earring that pulled at her ear lobe. She stepped into the middle of Damian's office, while Giorgio crossed behind her toward the red upholstered settee that sat against the wall.

"Why don't we sit over here? You'll be more comfortable."

"No!" she blurted, stopping Giorgio halfway to a sitting position.

He faltered, feeling more than a little confused. "Okay. Why don't we take these chairs?"

He pulled a couple of straight-backed chairs away from a round table. She plopped down and crossed her legs, exposing one shapely ankle accented with a gold ankle bracelet. Despite the blotchy skin, she was an attractive woman and seemed to know it as she slipped off the leather coat, exposing the firm fit of her sweater. With a short flutter of lashes, she looked at him as if she suddenly had all the time in the world.

"You were saying, Detective?"

He opened his notepad by way of distraction. When he looked up, he caught her glancing in the direction of the settee.

"I understand you handle all booking arrangements and that you were here this evening?"

"I'm always here for the events, just to make sure things are running smoothly. Some of these events are complicated. I want my customers to be satisfied."

She stretched her foot out, again bringing attention to her ankles.

"What time was the banquet scheduled to begin?"

"Cocktails began at six. We opened the doors for dinner at six forty-five."

"And the bar was set up in the lobby?"

"Yes." Her answers were short, forcing Giorgio to ponder her defensive attitude.

"What time was the dinner scheduled to end?"

"Around eight-thirty. It was only three courses."

"And there was to be a program after that?"

"It was some kind of game. They asked for a microphone and podium at the head table. I give them whatever they want."

She smiled in the same way she might swallow good wine and then shifted in the chair so that her back arched, pressing her breasts against the confines of the sweater. Giorgio wondered at the charade.

"Once the dinner began, your job was over for the evening?"

She stared at him before answering, her green eyes impassive. "Yes. I only stay to make sure there are no problems. I think I said that."

"So you left around seven o'clock?" Giorgio watched her reaction, noticing that she hesitated before answering.

"Around seven-thirty, I think. I said goodnight to Mr. Marsh. You can ask him." She stuck her chin out as if making a challenge.

"You're not under any kind of suspicion at this point, Ms. Peters. I'm only trying to get the facts. After saying goodnight to Mr. Marsh, you left and went straight home, I presume."

Again, she hesitated, pulling her purse into her lap. "Yes."

"And you remained there until Father Damian called you a little while ago."

"Yes."

"What time did he call you?"

"About eleven o'clock. He was quite upset."

"Did anyone else contact you during the evening? Anyone from the monastery?"

"No. Why do you ask?"

As the green eyes searched his face, he could've sworn the turned-up nose twitched, as if casting a spell.

"Just wondering," he replied. "Do you use the same catering company for every function?"

"Yes. Food for Thought. They're very good."

"And you're familiar with the staff?"

"Many of them, yes."

"Did you see anyone with them tonight that you didn't recognize?"

She pondered the question, seeming to grasp the diversion with relish. "I'm not sure. Let me see. I hadn't seen one of the bartenders before."

"What did he look like?"

"Medium height. Muscular. He had dark eyes and an earring."

"Earring?"

"Yes. I think in his left ear."

She raised her hand to her own ear by way of clarification, but a brief expression of panic crossed her face as she noticed one of her own earrings was missing. Her eyes darted in the direction of the settee again. Giorgio pretended not to notice.

"Had you met the deceased?"

"Actually, no one has told me yet who was killed."

Her lower lip extended in a petulant expression as if she'd been left off the invitation list for a sorority party.

"It was a woman named Mallery Olsen. She was a literary agent." He watched her closely and was more than a little curious to see her sigh, as if relieved.

"I really only know Mr. Marsh and Ms. Levinsky."

"You didn't happen to see anyone come to the dinner late?"

"I was back in my office getting ready to leave."

"And where is your office, Ms. Peters?"

"Just around the corner from here." She gestured and then drew her fingers across the soft fibers of the sweater just above her bosom.

"Where do you park your car?"

The question caught her off guard and the fingers froze somewhere around her cleavage.

"In the west lot."

"Did you see anyone outside when you left?"

She hesitated again.

"Just what are you implying?"

The game was over, and Ms. Peters didn't like losing.

"I just need to know if anyone can verify what time you left," he said.

She got up, the alluring green eyes now ablaze.

"I'm not sure what you're up to, Detective, but I don't like it."

He also rose. "I hope you're not going out of town soon," he said. "We may need to talk with you again."

She brushed past him and left the room, leaving a vapor trail of animosity behind. The moment the door closed, Giorgio turned to the settee and ran his hand around the seat cushion. When his fingers hit something sharp, he withdrew a large, pearl stud earring.

† Chapter Nine †

By two-thirty that morning, Giorgio had to blink several times to read the hands on his watch. It was normal to be tired on the last night of a production. After all, six long weeks of rehearsals and three weeks of performances were exhausting. Add to that the long workdays, a wife and two kids, and now a murder investigation, and he was running on empty.

Swan was in the lobby talking with McCready, who was putting information into his tablet. McCready would begin a background check on everyone first thing in the morning. Swan acknowledged Giorgio as he approached.

"I just got a call from Samson. He's over at Tomlinson's apartment. She's not there. The neighbors said her father died, and she flew home to Atlanta. Apparently that's why Mallery Olsen stood in for her. We're working on finding her phone number in Atlanta."

Giorgio rubbed his eyes, making them tear up. "Where's Rocky?"

"He's interviewing one of the monks. We're trying to get as many done tonight as possible. By the way, there's a helluva storm brewing."

"Okay," Giorgio replied, wiping away the moisture, "we'll get out of here soon." He checked his notes. "See if you can find Fathers Francis, Julio, and Daniel. They're the newest recruits. I want to talk with them tonight, but not together."

"I think I just met Father Daniel. He was in the chapel, praying. I'll send him out and then find the others."

Giorgio stopped Swan as he turned to leave. "Where do I get more coffee?"

"I'll get it," McCready offered. He locked the tablet's screen and turned towards the kitchen.

Swan retreated down the corridor towards the chapel. Giorgio decided he needed more air and stepped outside. A burly wind now whipped the graceful neck of a Bird of Paradise along the walkway, making it look like a hen pecking for crumbs. He wandered down the brick path, past a clump of billowing Pampas grass, to the drive. The valley lights, which had burned so brightly only hours before, had been replaced by pregnant clouds threatening to deliver their load at any moment. Even the palm trees that lined the drive had become a row of dancing men swaying in rhythm to the wind.

Giorgio stuffed his hands into his pockets and took a deep breath, hoping the cool air would revive him. He stopped on the far side of the marble fountain. All three fluted tiers of the basin's edges were lit by underwater spotlights. A single water jet erupted from the top tier like a flower opening to the sun. The floor of the lower basin was inlaid with colorful tile depicting richly plumed birds perched in the midst of a garden of bold flowers.

The clear water splashed and gurgled above them, reminding Giorgio of a time when he was twelve and his father had taken his sons to the zoo. While his dad stood in line for hotdogs, the boys ran to a nearby fountain with the intention of getting each other wet. Floating in the leaf-strewn water was a dead blue jay, its eyes glazed milky white. Rocky tried to grab it, but Giorgio just stood there, trapped in the gaze of its dead eyes. It wasn't until his father appeared with the food that he reluctantly turned away.

Giorgio's eyes were fixated now on the small beaked face of a ceramic bird at the bottom of the fountain. It wasn't until a clanging noise engaged his brain that he withdrew his attention and turned back toward the building. Fatigue worked on his body like a drug forcing him to gaze at the massive structure through half blurry eyes. The wind rattled a large, knotted oak tree that stood against the front of the building, manipulating its strong branches into a kind of mechanical stage apparatus. Along the pale stucco exterior of the front façade, bushy shadow puppets danced a mambo energized by the wind, while three statues bobbed in and out of a row of palmettos along the colonnade as if playing hide and seek at a carnival sideshow.

Giorgio turned his head to look up at the bell tower. Perhaps the clanging was coming from one of the bells.

Three arched windows stretched across the front of the tower, staring silently at the valley below. Only the shadow of a dangling rope was visible to one side, swinging from a second floor window to the left of the tower. It appeared to be weighted by a large sack. Scaffolding was erected against the west side of the tower, and Giorgio remembered reading that the bell tower was under repair after being damaged in a recent earthquake.

He stepped around to the other side of the fountain, hoping to see how things looked earlier that evening, but the clanging noise was giving him a headache. With a groan, he glanced over to the large metal statue of a monk standing just under the corner of the bell tower. A crucifix hanging from a chain around the priest's waist was being slapped against the cast iron robe by the wind. The monk was a formidable figure in the dark, with a raised sword pointed to the heavens. The priestly robes had been cast as if blowing in an unearthly wind, while the real wind seemed about to bring the commanding figure to life. Giorgio shuddered, partially from the cold and partially from the feeling the priest was about to step off the huge platform into reality.

He turned his attention back to the rope, wondering why it was there and what had been tied to it. But the rope was gone. There was no rope and no sack to weight it, making him doubt he'd ever seen it. After all, the entire building seemed to be wrestling with the approaching storm. When a fountain spray drenched the back of his head, he cursed and decided it was time to go inside.

Leaving the ghostly statue, the rope, and the belfry behind, he returned inside, shutting the fairytale door behind him with a dull thud. The inside warmth was a welcoming change. Outside, the wind dragged bushes across the exterior of the building with the same spine-tingling sensation fingers create crossing a blackboard. Behind the wind, the echo of the crucifix continued to punish the iron priest. When he turned away from the door and saw the boy at the top of the stairs, he stopped so short his feet could have been planted in cement.

The boy was nine or ten years old, with round eyes rimmed in shadow. He was dressed in a long-sleeved white shirt and dark knickers, with thick suspenders pulling at his narrow shoulders. A pale, vaporous mist illuminated him in a halo of light and he stared at Giorgio from the landing like a barn owl in the dark.

No one had mentioned anything about children on the premises, and Giorgio stared back, dumbfounded. It was several moments before he noticed the boy was clutching something in his left hand. Before Giorgio could make out what it was, the heavy wooden door behind him blew open again, bringing with it a cold draft of air. He turned and shoved the door closed, making sure it latched this time. When he swung back around, the boy was gone.

Giorgio leapt into action. He took the stairs two at a time, skidding to a stop at the landing. The hallway on both sides was empty. There was no sign of the boy anywhere. He dared not start knocking on doors for fear of disturbing guests, but when a cold pair of fingers brushed against his cheek, he flinched backwards down the stairs, his eyes focused on where he'd seen the boy. When he reached the foyer he paused, almost willing the boy to return. But nothing moved at the top of the stairs.

He waited until a soft noise made him spin around, his hand automatically reaching for his weapon. The chandeliers had been extinguished, leaving only the wall sconces to provide light in the large, vacuous room. When something by the far window moved, he pulled the gun halfway from its holster. The shadow shifted again, and he realized it was a woman sitting on a window seat staring out the window. He moved in cautiously to stand above her, his hand still resting on his weapon. She leaned on her inside hand, while she stared into the brewing storm outside, either ignoring him or oblivious to his presence.

"Excuse me." Giorgio spoke softly thinking she might be asleep. "Are you all right?"

She looked up, her eyes cast in deep shadow. She seemed to study him for a moment before turning back to the window. The branches of the oak tree raked the window, while leaves fluttered grotesquely in the shallow light outside.

"You're with the police." She made it a statement rather than a question.

"I'm Detective Salvatori. Has someone taken your statement yet?"

"No."

"Have you been here all night?"

"Yes. I've just been sitting here." Her reply was lazy, as if she'd been drugged or perhaps dazed by the tragedy.

"Can I get you something? Coffee? Water?"

"I don't want anything." A long pause stretched between them until she sighed. "We were supposed to have a mystery tonight. Did you know that?"

"No." He relaxed a bit and sat on the arm of a nearby chair. "Why don't you tell me about it?"

"I wrote it," she said distantly. "A game, called *Dead to Rights*." She chuckled, but it caught in her throat. "It was a play on words, you see."

When he didn't respond, she turned and looked directly at him. Although her eyes were still obscured by darkness, he realized this was the woman Father Damian had been consoling in the banquet room earlier in the evening.

"Writers sell their rights." She emphasized the words as if Giorgio were an idiot. "But we never played it. We never had a chance."

"Because the body was found?"

"Yes." Her throat seemed to close around the word in disgust. "That stupid woman was found. Now everyone's running around trying to solve a real mystery."

Giorgio was shocked by her lack of compassion, but chose to ignore it. "And your mystery was never used?"

"I can't believe it. I worked so damned hard on it, and for what?"

"Miss...uh...."

"Levinsky."

The name registered and he acknowledged it. "You're the Program Chair?"

"Yes."

"Did you know Mallery Olsen?"

"Who?"

"The woman that was killed."

"My job was to oversee the speakers, not the agents. I didn't even meet her."

"Would you have known her if you saw her?"

"Maybe. I saw all the agents at the opening reception. They all had ribbons on their nametags, but I didn't pay much attention."

"You're an aspiring writer like the rest?"

"I'm a playwright. I've written several one-acts and two full-length plays. Mostly mysteries. That's why I volunteered to do the mystery tonight. Arthur Wright was here from Samuel French."

Finally, Giorgio understood her enduring disappointment. Samuel French was the premier publisher of working plays. Most of the scripts Giorgio had ever used in the theater came from Samuel French. Ms. Levinsky missed her one big opportunity to impress someone important, and she couldn't stand it. Just then McCready returned with the coffee.

"I had to heat it up in the microwave," he apologized.

Giorgio accepted the cup. "Why don't you go home? You have a lot of work ahead of you tomorrow."

McCready said goodnight and left, while Ms. Levinsky continued to stare out the window as if her parents had just left her at boarding school. Giorgio decided he had little patience for the self-absorbed Ms. Levinsky.

"Ms. Levinsky, did you see anyone come into the dinner late tonight, or did anyone leave early?"

She turned as if she were being inconvenienced by the question. "I really couldn't say. I was concentrating on getting set up for the game."

"Was everyone at the conference aware of the game?"

"It was in all of our promotional materials, and we'd asked for special permission to use other parts of the monastery to stage it."

"So, you weren't sitting down and eating tonight with the others?"

"I told you. I had last minute details to take care of."

"And where were you taking care of these last minute details?"

He realized his voice was beginning to take on a strident quality, but he didn't care.

"Several places. I was laying out clues and I was back and forth to my room."

This piece of news interested him. "When did you go to your room?"

"I forgot my copy of the script."

"Yes, but when did you go to retrieve it?" he pressed her.

She took a deep breath and looked toward the ceiling. "Oh, I don't know."

Giorgio wanted to slap her.

"I think the cocktail party had just started," she continued. "Everyone was at the bar."

"Which room is yours?"

"It's at the end of the hallway to the right of the stairs."

Giorgio perked up, but attempted to hide his interest. "What number?"

She turned her dark eyes his way. Shadows billowed across the window behind her like a cheap light show. Although he couldn't see her features well, she looked to be about thirty-five. Long, stringy hair draped over one shoulder while two plump legs were stretched out on the window seat like logs in a fireplace. She resembled Deborah Carr in *An Affair to Remember* and Giorgio pondered whether this woman could even walk. Everything about her seemed incapable of movement of any kind.

"Ms. Levinsky, what is your room number?" he asked again.

"Seventeen. Why?"

His mind raced. This woman had the room next to Olsen's and may have been upstairs around the time of the murder.

"Did you see anyone in the hallways or on the stairs when you returned to your room?"

It seemed she understood his urgency and purposely stalled her answers. "No. I just popped into my room for a moment to get the script and left again."

"You didn't hear or see anything?"

"I heard voices," she said.

"Voices? Where?"

"I was reaching into my closet to get my briefcase, and I heard someone knock on the door next to mine."

"Which side?" he asked.

She looked at him with a blank expression, then her brain engaged and she replied, "To the right."

"To the right if you were looking out the door?"

"That's right. John Marsh had the room to the left of mine, closest to the stairs. At first, I thought it was him. Then, I realized the voices were coming from the room to the right."

"Did you see who came to the room next door?" Giorgio had to restrain himself from shaking the information out of this woman.

"I told you. I didn't see anyone."

"You're sure it was a man's voice?" Her eyes were drifting around the room, and Giorgio felt his muscles tense. "Ms. Levinsky, this is important. Are you sure it was a man's voice?"

"I told you, I thought it was Mr. Marsh."

"And you're positive it wasn't?"

She paused. "It sounded like him, but he was downstairs. I didn't really pay much attention. I had to find another prop since one of mine had disappeared. After all, it was critical to the mystery."

"What was it that disappeared?"

"A green silk scarf. I had it in my bag at rehearsal this afternoon, but it must have dropped out. I had to find something else at the last minute."

A fierce gust of wind rattled the old windowpanes, and a rush of cold air forced its way through with a low whistle. He leaned forward, anxious to ask a follow-up question, but Swan returned with Father Daniel. The men entered the room behind him, and Giorgio halted them with a wave of his hand.

"If you'll just wait over there, Father."

Swan returned down the hallway. The young monk stepped to one side, hands clasped in front of him. Giorgio turned back to the self-indulgent Ms. Levinsky, but now she was focused on the waiting monk.

"Ms. Levinsky." He tried to get her attention. "Where did you rehearse this afternoon?"

"The chapel. All the meeting rooms were filled with educational sessions."

"And what role did the scarf play in the mystery?"

He spoke as if to a deaf person, but there was a telltale ringing in his ears. It happened every time he was about to make a discovery. On the other hand, Ms. Levinsky seemed distracted by Father Daniel.

"He's awfully good looking for a priest, don't you think?"

Giorgio turned to locate the object of her attention. Father Daniel stood as still as one of the statues, his face only half lit by a wall sconce. He turned back to the woman.

"Ms. Levinsky, how was the scarf going to be used in your mystery?"

She shifted her eyes away from the monk and smiled. "To strangle the victim, of course."

A branch from the tree outside finally broke free, smacking the window with a heart-stopping crack. The wall sconces flickered and went out, leaving the room as dark and silent as the inside of a grave.

† Chapter Ten †

It was after three o'clock in the morning when Rocky's truck rattled up to the curb in front of Giorgio's house. The entire monastery had remained in the dark, eliminating any hope of finishing the interviews. The team would arrive early the next morning to develop an investigation strategy. Giorgio knew he was expected to fill out the daily call sheet, but it had to be accurate, and right now he felt there was a chance he might misspell his own name.

The storm had finally broken. A drenching rain obscured his two-story, stucco, Spanish-style house, sending rivers of run-off down the sidewalk. A brusque wind whipped nearby trees, sending loose branches and twigs across the sloping front lawn.

"I can come tomorrow, if you'd like," Rocky yawned next to him.

"Thanks. We could use your help. Make it early...if you can."

Rocky's eyes narrowed, and Giorgio wondered if he'd implied too much. But Rocky merely nodded. Giorgio pulled his jacket over his head and ran for the door. Inside, he dropped his jacket over the back of a chair and grabbed a kitchen towel to dry off. He stopped at the refrigerator for a long swig of milk and then headed for the hallway, stealing a glance out the grated window before locking the front door. The sound of the bottle rolling across the truck floor came to mind, and he silently prayed Rocky would go straight home.

Giorgio locked the front door and started for bed, stopping to salute a full suit-of-armor standing at the foot of the stairs.

"Good night, Prince Albert."

It was a ritual he hardly noticed any more.

He'd rescued Prince Albert from the theater's green room where the visor had been used as an ashtray. The insult had given Giorgio the idea to name it after his father's favorite tobacco.

Though Giorgio had long ago accepted Prince Albert as part of the family, his presence never ceased to spook Angie in the dark. She'd threatened more than once to melt the armor into scrap metal. When the armor disappeared one day, Giorgio thought she'd made good on her promise, but she'd only sent it out to be cleaned. Giorgio had to admit it returned looking and smelling much better.

While the prince stood guard, Giorgio climbed the stairs and checked on the children. He continued to the end of the hallway where the door to the master bedroom opened at the touch of his hand. The nightlight was on in the bathroom, as it always was. Giorgio slipped out of his clothes and climbed into bed, hoping not to wake Angie. When he settled back onto the pillow, though, she turned with a sigh and tucked an arm across his chest.

"I brought some ice cream home for you," she mumbled. "It's in the freezer."

He smiled and leaned over to kiss her cheek. "You're a good girl, Angie. Mama will like you. I think we should get married."

She popped open one eyelid. "Fat chance. You stay out all hours and come home with coffee on your breath and eyeliner on your eyes. My mama will never approve. I'll marry the baker." She tried to turn away.

He grabbed her and drew her close. "You've threatened to marry that baker for fifteen years. Who the hell is he, anyway?"

She leaned in to whisper in his ear, and he could smell toothpaste and a hint of the perfume she'd worn to the theater. Everything about this woman entranced him. It always had, and he wrapped his arms around her slender body, feeling the warmth of her skin beneath her nightgown.

"I'll never divulge the name of my lover. You might shoot him with your six-gun in a fit of jealous rage. Then, what would the children do for a father?"

"Ha!" he yelled as he slapped her bottom. He rolled her over so that he lay on top of her. "So, he's the father? Then why the hell hasn't he been putting clothes on their backs for the past nine years?"

He nuzzled her neck as she wiggled beneath him, giving rise to a potent desire. She giggled, pulling his face around to kiss him first on the eyelids, then the nose, then ever so gently on the lips.

"God, woman. I can't ever seem to get enough of you," he said, sinking into her embrace. His tongue played with her ear until her breath caught. "Tell me you're mine forever," he whispered, reaching a hand under her nightgown to stroke her breast. "Tell me."

She pulled back to look at him with her rich sable eyes, and he felt himself sink into their depths like a man sinks to the bottom of the ocean.

"I'm yours forever," she said breathlessly. "Forever and one day," she emphasized, before clamping her mouth over his.

His hands moved across her body knowing every curve, every soft spot, and within seconds, she was on fire, reaching for him, bringing him to her and laying his soul bare. It seemed there was room in this night for at least one more standing ovation, and this one would be the sweetest of all.

† Chapter Eleven †

Giorgio woke to the smell of coffee and bacon, and he turned a sleepy eye to the digital clock beside the bed. Angie was already downstairs fixing breakfast. He smiled. How lucky could a man be? When his brain registered the time, he jumped out of bed catching his toe on the foot of the bed.

"Shit!"

He'd never been an early riser and always had trouble making that first adjustment to the new day. Angie, on the other hand, popped out of bed like a piece of toast. The thought of toast made him forget his foot as he hobbled to the bathroom.

Fifteen minutes later, he entered the kitchen, patted his wife on the behind and nibbled his favorite ear lobe. He received a slap in return and was told to sit before she called the cops. It was a game he never tired of. It was Sunday, and the kids would sleep another half hour, allowing him to lean back on the chair legs to eye his wife. She was still in her nightgown, and the curve of her breast caught his attention.

"What happened last night?" she inquired, pouring him a cup of black coffee.

"I think you know what happened last night," he said, reaching for the object of his desire.

"At the monastery," she exhaled, pushing his hand away.

He retreated with an apologetic grin and took a sip of coffee.

"A young woman was found hanging by her bra strap in a supply closet. Dead, of course."

Angie turned to him, the fry pan in her hand. "Giorgio, you shouldn't be flippant. Someone died. That's not a joke."

"Sorry. It was just so weird. She was hung like a doll on a utility hook in the supply closet of a Catholic monastery." He twisted his mouth in a dry smile. "It was like one of those things. What do you call it? An oxymoron. Like naval intelligence." He chuckled and held up his hand when she turned with a stern look on her face. "I know. I shouldn't make fun of the dead. I'm sorry. It appears she was strangled."

Angie drained the bacon grease out of the pan and proceeded to make pancakes. "One of the cable stations already reported on it. I turned it off. I'd rather hear it from you. Who was she?"

"A literary agent," he said.

"You mean, like books?"

"Mysteries, as a matter of fact. Funny, hunh?" He smiled, but kept his mirth in check. "Anyway, she wasn't supposed to be there. They were having a writers' conference, and she was standing in for someone else who couldn't make it. So, no one really knew her." He purposely omitted the part about the missing finger. No need to remind Angie of the kind of crimes they'd hoped to leave behind.

"Someone so young," she ruminated. "It's so sad." Angie flipped a pancake. "Somewhere a mother suffers."

He watched her thinking it wasn't easy being a cop's wife. Although Angie never complained, he saw it in her eyes. The shooting in Queens had been a turning point he couldn't quite explain. Before then, she hadn't always waited up for him. Now, there were signs. A half empty coffee cup or a warm television set. Sometimes, like last night, it was the simple mist left behind in the bathroom after a late night shower. He got up and put his arms around her waist.

"You won't ever lose a child, Angie. God won't let you."

She patted his hand, and he kissed the top of her head before returning to the chair. She piled a stack of pancakes onto a plate, added the bacon, and placed it in front of him, bending over so that he could just see the crest of her breast.

"What time do you think you'll be back tonight?"

"I don't know," he replied, diverting his attention to his breakfast. He slathered butter onto the pancakes. "Late. Rocky's picking me up in a few minutes. He's still on medical leave and offered to help."

"Do you think it's a good idea – I mean, having him work on this case?"

"Yeah," he replied with a mouthful of pancakes. "I think he needs some focus. And frankly, we could use the help."

She rinsed off dishes in the sink while he devoured his breakfast. Finally, she turned to him.

"Joe, I wanted to talk to you about something."

"Aren't you going to church?"

"Yes, of course. I teach the little children today, and Marie sings in the choir."

"Oh," he looked up with a frown. "I forgot."

"It's all right," she said quietly. "She'll understand."

"I'll bring her a surprise tonight."

"You don't have to do that, Joe. She understands."

He bent to take another mouthful of food. "She sings like an angel," he slurred through pancakes and saliva. "I should be there."

He continued to eat as if food would blot out the disappointment he felt. Angie came and sat across the table from him, her hands folded in front of her.

"It's me who needs your attention right now, Joe. Not Marie."

"Can't it wait? We could talk tonight."

He wiped syrup off his chin and grabbed a slice of bacon. She watched him with a pained expression.

"It can't wait much longer."

Her eyes blinked several times, and he recognized the oncoming tears. He swallowed quickly.

"What is it Angie? What's wrong?"

"Nothing's wrong, at least not according to God's plan."

"What do you mean? What's according to God's plan?"

Her eyes glistened, and he felt the pancakes turn to cement in his stomach.

"What are you talking about, Angie?"

She paused before answering. "We're going to have a baby."

Whatever he thought his wife was going to say, it wasn't that. He sat for a moment, staring at her, all thought of pancakes and murder investigations gone.

"I thought we agreed not to have any more children. Two was what we said."

"I know, but I'm pregnant."

"But how? I mean, we took precautions. Didn't we? Didn't you?"

He grasped his fork like a fourteenth-century warlord, a wad of pancake dripping syrup all over the table.

"Precautions are never one hundred percent accurate, Joe. You can't control everything. God makes his own decisions. We're going to have another baby."

He knew what she expected from him – expressions of joy. But he didn't feel joy. He felt trapped. He dropped his fork and forced his chair back and stood up. He had to think, process. He moved to the kitchen window and looked out at the neighbor's garage, irritated the man never took in his trashcans.

"How long have you known?" When she didn't answer, he turned. "How long have you known, Angie?"

She barely whispered. "About four weeks."

"Dammit, Angie! What do you mean four weeks? Why didn't you tell me? How could you keep something like that from me for a whole month?" He circled the table once while she began to cry. "Christ. I can't believe it!"

She shrank into the chair, and he realized how miserable she was. He hesitated, confused. Finally, he went to her.

"Why didn't you tell me, Angie?" he said more softly. "I'm your husband. You should've told me. You should've been more careful."

She lifted her tear-streaked face. "I was careful, Joe, but I prayed for this child. I wanted another baby. I knew you didn't, but I did. When the doctor told me I was pregnant, I was happy. I was afraid if I told you, it would ruin your concentration. So I thought I'd wait until the play was over. I'm sorry, Joe."

He watched her, this woman he loved, filled with a mixture of anger and fear. He'd acted like an idiot, and he had to make it right. He reached out a hand to comfort her, but just then a horn blared out front.

"Shit! It's Rocky. I've got to go. We'll talk about this tonight. Okay?" He kissed the top of her head. "Okay?"

He moved towards the door as she lifted a napkin to wipe her eyes. She avoided looking at him and got up to take his plate to the sink. He knew better than to push it and so grabbed his leather coat and went out to meet his brother.

Rocky sat with his head resting on the seat cushion, his eyes closed. Giorgio slid into the seat and slammed the door, waking him with a start.

"Hey! Have some respect. I'm doing you a favor."

"I know. Let's go."

Rocky looked at his big brother. "Everything okay?"

"Yeah. Let's go."

Rocky yawned and stretched the muscles in his face before starting the engine. "So, what's the order of the day?"

"Have trouble getting to sleep last night?"

Rocky shot him a reproachful look. "We did work until three in the morning, in case you forgot."

He turned back to the road, so Giorgio decided to ignore it.

"I want to interview the woman who organized the dinner. We need to find out if anyone came in late. We also need to talk with each of the people who spent any time with the victim, and I want to know everything Mallery Olsen said while she was there."

Rocky turned to look at him. "That's a tall order. Who else is helping?"

"Swan and two others."

They drove the rest of the way in silence. Rocky finally spoke when they pulled through the monastery gates.

"Maybe she didn't like it as much as I thought."

"What?" Giorgio's thoughts were pulled back to the present.

"The play."

The truck climbed the hill and Giorgio sighed, rubbing a hand through his hair.

"That's not it. Angie's pregnant."

"Whoa. I thought you said you were going to stop at two."

"We did, but I guess…we didn't. Something went wrong. It happens."

"So, Angie's upset about it?"

"She is *now*. Instead of being the caring, understanding husband I am, I blew up."

Rocky parked in the west parking lot along with two news vans.

"Like I said, Angie's upset."

"I think that's putting it mildly." Giorgio sighed deeply. "God, three kids on a detective's salary. It's tight now. I want good things for Angie. For the kids. I don't want to have to scrape all my life."

"Angie could go back to teaching."

Giorgio gave his brother a cold look. "I don't want Angie to have to work!"

"Jesus, Jo Jo. You can't control everything. This is the twenty-first century. Women work. What's the big deal?"

"The big deal is I don't want her to have to work," he emphasized. "And I'm not trying to control everything!"

"She loved teaching," Rocky argued. "She wouldn't mind."

"Look, I'd support anything Angie really wanted to do, but she doesn't really want to work. She wants to stay home with the kids. It's all about kids with Angie. Besides, this isn't what we planned!"

Giorgio turned back in his seat, hoping to let his anger cool. When he saw the same young female reporter and cameraman approaching, he got out and strode right past her. She spun around after him, but he ignored her pleas for a statement. He would have knocked over a second reporter if the pudgy guy hadn't moved aside. The media frenzy had begun.

Giorgio entered the monastery ordering a patrolman to keep anyone but police personnel out. Inside, the monastery was cool and quiet, and he paused a moment to take a deep breath. A couple dressed in casual clothes chatted in the lobby, their luggage by their side. The power had been restored sometime during the night and Giorgio peeked through the gift shop window. A man in a tweed jacket and turtleneck browsed through a bookcase along one wall. Giorgio opened the door and stepped inside. A woman appeared from an alcove behind the counter, smiling at him.

"May I help you? We're not usually open on Sunday," she offered, "but I thought under the circumstances," she paused awkwardly, "Well, you know, I thought maybe there might be people looking for solace. Is there something I can help you with?"

Giorgio glanced at the man by the bookshelf, but he was absorbed with a book, stroking his goatee in thought.

"I'm with the police. I'd like to ask you a few questions."

Her eyes grew wide. She was in her mid-forties and wore a gray wool sweater.

"I wasn't here last night, but I'll tell you anything I know."

Just then, the man with the goatee approached and held out a book to purchase. The woman excused herself to take care of the sale. Giorgio stepped to the side, glancing at a glass case holding a selection of rosary beads and crosses. Next to the case was a beautiful antique oak wash stand with a locked box labeled "Mail." No mail today, Giorgio thought. It's Sunday.

"Oh, shit!" he muttered to himself. He hadn't thought to ask Father Damian if Sunday morning services would be canceled. The last thing he wanted was a hundred or so worshippers arriving.

"Excuse me," he called out to the sales lady. "I'll stop by later. I need to find Father Damian."

Back in the hallway, he almost bumped into Rocky.

His brother excused himself, backing away. "Sorry. I just saw Swan and he gave me a list of people who still need to be interviewed."

The man from the gift shop emerged with his purchase safely tucked under one arm. He turned and retreated up the staircase. Several other people milled about, probably waiting for taxies or friends. Giorgio looked about with a fleeting sense of panic. They needed to get this done before they were inundated with more people.

"I need to find Father Damian. I'll see you later."

The brothers parted, and Giorgio went to Father Damian's office. He wasn't there. Giorgio took a chance and went looking for Anya Peters. He found her in an office around the corner from the abbot's. She was talking with John Marsh, the conference chairman. The door was ajar, so he poked his head inside.

"Come in, Detective. You've met Mr. Marsh?"

She was wearing a pale green pantsuit that softened the green glaze of her eyes, but her demeanor was as cool as the floor tiles. She wasn't happy to see him. He acknowledged Marsh.

"How are you feeling this morning?" he asked the chairman.

Marsh looked like the star of a cheap horror flick. His eyes were ringed with shadow, and he'd only briefly run a comb through his hair. The dated tuxedo from the night before had been replaced with an ill-fitting, rumpled gray suit. A dark speck of blood on his chin broadcast that he'd nicked himself shaving.

"I'm afraid breakfast was rather somber," he mumbled. "We canceled the closing activities and just bid everyone a fond farewell until next year. If there is a next year."

"Are most people in the banquet room now?"

"Anyone who felt like eating," he said cynically. "I believe a few people called cabs, and some have checked out early this morning."

"I found two keys in the box outside my door when I arrived," Peters confirmed. She gazed impassively at Giorgio as if having a detective in her office was an ordinary occurrence.

Giorgio sighed. "Please make a note of who they were. Also, I was wondering if Father Damian had thought to cancel Sunday services."

"This church doesn't have a parish anymore. They only hold public services on Christmas and Easter. Is there anything else we can help you with today, Detective?"

Murder seemed to be a mere imposition to Ms. Peters. It didn't mean she was guilty of anything more than rude behavior, but he often found that rude behavior camouflaged something else. In high school, a boy named Jason Wright had beat up boys half his size on a regular basis. No one knew why until they realized he couldn't read and had successfully hidden it for years. A little tutoring had changed more than Jason's reading skills. The thought made Giorgio wonder what Anya Peters was hiding.

"I'd like to talk with the woman who organized the dinner," Giorgio said to Marsh.

"I'll get her for you."

Marsh rose and left the room. An awkward silence stretched behind him. Peters shuffled papers on her desk, attempting to ignore Giorgio. A feeling of irritation swept over him. Motivated by the bitter argument with Angie, he fished in the pocket of his leather jacket and placed the pearl earring on the desk in front of her.

"I believe this is yours," he said.

The air went still between them. She openly stared at the earring while her hand fluttered to her left ear lobe. When she realized she had on a different pair of earrings, she attempted to resume her composure.

"I don't think that's mine," she stated with little confidence.

"No? I noticed you were missing an earring last night that looked just like this. I found this one tucked into the sofa in Father Damian's office. It appears to match the one you were wearing."

She reached for the earring, but he closed his hand around it first. Her eyes betrayed a smoldering distaste while she contemplated her next move.

"I had a meeting last night with Father Damian," she responded almost too quickly. "I remember sitting on the sofa. Perhaps it came off then."

"Was that before you left at seven-thirty, or before you left around nine o'clock?"

Her eyes snapped wide open exposing green glacial pools. "I don't know what you mean. I told you when I left the premises."

"Yes, but someone has contradicted your story. I thought perhaps you'd like to set the record straight."

Just then Marsh reappeared at the doorway. "Ms. Chase is waiting for you in the foyer, Detective."

Giorgio rose, his hand still resting on the earring. "Please ask her to wait. I'll be there in a minute."

Marsh left, and Giorgio lifted the earring and dropped it back into his pocket.

"You were seen leaving the parking lot around nine o'clock, Ms. Peters. I must assume you were here when the murder took place."

"I had nothing to do with that." Her green eyes darkened as if a cloud had moved across a small pond of water.

"Then why did you lie about the time you left?"

"Because," she paused, "I was working on something personal, that's all. Father Damian doesn't like me to do personal business here, so I said I left at seven-thirty."

"Wouldn't he have seen you here after your usual time?"

"He would have been in the chapel." She stuck her chin out as if she just made a masterful move in a chess game.

"I see," Giorgio said, remembering what the janitor said about meeting Father Damian in the hallway instead of at the chapel. "Well," he paused at the doorway, "I'm sure I'll be able to confirm that."

He left Peters' office with a feeling of intense satisfaction he couldn't explain, but knowing he'd probably only uncovered an illicit affair. He would have to decide later if it had any significance.

Coming into the main lobby he found a short, rotund woman sitting like Humpty Dumpty on the bench, her feet barely touching the floor. Heavy jowls framed her billiard ball face. When she saw him, she attempted to rise. Instead, she flopped her immense bottom back onto the wooden seat. He waved away her attempts and joined her.

"I'm Detective Salvatori."

She offered a warm, mushy hand that reminded him of an overripe grapefruit.

"I'm Olivia Chase," she said with a throaty voice. "I made all the arrangements for the dinner. Mr. Marsh said you wanted to talk to me about the murder."

She seemed pleased to be discussing the murder and peered at him through small eyes lost in folds of flesh.

"Well, actually," he said, wiping his hand on his pants, "I was wondering if anyone came late to dinner or didn't show up at all."

She coughed suddenly, the way someone does when they're trying to loosen phlegm. Giorgio tried to look casual as he backed away a few inches.

"Sorry, I've got a cold," she gurgled. "Let me see. We were going to play a game, so everyone had assigned seats. As I recall, one man arrived late, and one didn't show at all."

"Do you know their names?"

Giorgio rested his hand on his chin as if in thought, but in fact he was trying desperately to cover his mouth and avoid taking a breath.

"Oh, yes," she said confidently. "Because it would have affected the game you see. I had to sit in for Cory Poindexter, and Mr. Marsh sat in for Jeff Dorman."

"Which one never showed?"

"Jeff Dorman. As it turned out, he had checked out earlier, and I wasn't told."

"Do you know where Cory Poindexter had been?"

"No. He came in eventually and took my place. It was rather awkward, because I'd already eaten the main course and had to move."

"What time did he come in?"

"Oh, I don't know," she said, wiping her brow as if the interview were taxing her strength. "It must have been about eight o'clock because I'd already finished the quail. When he arrived, I moved to the head table and finished my dessert up there. It was a lovely chocolate mousse."

Her eyes sparkled with appreciation, and he suspected she'd enjoyed a good many desserts. It was fascinating how people could always remember particulars about food in the midst of adversity. He'd once interviewed a woman whose husband dropped dead at a Mandarin restaurant, yet she could recount every detail about the elaborate meal down to the pattern on the dinnerware.

"Can you describe anything unusual about how Mr. Poindexter might have looked when he arrived?"

She flicked a finger at her nose, for what reason Giorgio couldn't be sure, but now he counted the seconds before this interview was over. The beady eyes looked at him as if a light bulb had just been turned on in her squat little head.

"I do remember something. He wasn't dressed for dinner."

"What do you mean?"

"Well, that was part of the game. We announced in the registration materials that we were going to stage a vintage murder mystery. Everyone was to dress accordingly. He was rather casually dressed. I remember because he apologized for not even wearing a tie."

"Did he seem to be in a hurry, or otherwise distracted?"

"Yes, he kept looking at the door as he took his seat, as if he were expecting someone."

"How long did he continue to do that?"

"I don't know. Once Mr. Marsh began to speak, I forgot all about him."

"Was he in the room when you were notified about the murder? I mean the real murder."

"Yes. We had only just started the game. Father Damian came in and took Mr. Marsh aside, but by then we could already hear the sirens approaching."

"What happened next?"

"Mr. Marsh told everyone to stay in the room. He and Father Damian went out to meet the police. When he returned, he told everyone that a woman had been found dead in the kitchen."

"Did anyone get up and leave?"

"Yes, but an officer appeared and told everyone to stay put. He said they would be interviewing everyone before the night was over. Another officer came and stood at the door."

"Who was it that tried to leave?"

"As a matter of fact, it was Cory Poindexter."

"Thank you, you've been very helpful. Please don't leave town for a few days without letting us know."

"I live right here in Pasadena. I can come in and talk with you any time."

Giorgio hoped to God it wouldn't be necessary, but merely smiled as she slipped off the bench and waddled away. Just then Swan and Maxwell arrived.

"Where do we start?" Swan inquired.

"I want to interview Mr. Poindexter. You and Rocky can finish with the priests and then check to see if anyone remembered anything after we left last night."

Swan nodded and left. Giorgio went into the banquet room where about twenty people sat in small groups having a light breakfast. He found Marsh near the kitchen door talking to a young woman.

"Do you know a Cory Poindexter?" he asked Marsh.

"Just a minute." He gestured to an attractive woman sitting nearby. She got up and came over.

"Miriam, do you know a Cory Poindexter?"

She pointed to the back of the room. "He's the young man with blonde hair looking our way." She indicated a man in his mid-twenties who quickly glanced away the moment he was noticed.

Giorgio circled back in his direction. "Mr. Poindexter?"

"Yes," he said, turning to Giorgio as if he was unaware of his presence.

A thick blonde mustache matched heavy eyebrows giving his face an imposing quality. He was wearing a long-sleeved polo shirt, khaki slacks, and expensive shoes. A gold watch glittered at his wrist, accenting an even tan. He looked like a man who was acutely aware of his appearance.

"May I have a few minutes?"

Poindexter quickly scanned Giorgio from head to foot, much the same way an electronic scanner would check for weapons at the airport. To a man like Poindexter, every other male was competition, and it was clear he was mentally calculating whether Giorgio was an equal adversary.

"I've already spoken with an officer," he said dimly. "I told him everything I know."

"I'm following up on a few things," Giorgio placated him. "Why don't we go outside?"

Poindexter preceded Giorgio into the lobby. They stepped outside, and Poindexter emerged into the morning light as a world-class athlete might enter a stadium full of fans. The sun was beginning to warm the day and Poindexter paused, lifting his chin until the sound of running feet interrupted his pose. The young female reporter was back, a brown lock of hair flying free. She was only about twenty-three, but showed the determination of a pit bull.

"Detective," she called, "I'd like to…"

Giorgio turned to the patrolman standing close by. "Officer, I want you to escort this reporter back to the parking lot and then escort all media back down to the main entrance. Only police personnel will be allowed up here from now on."

"Yes, sir," the officer chirped. He threw out an arm to block the young woman, who then hurled an angry look at Giorgio.

"Detective, the public has a right to know what's going on here."

"Let's go, miss," the officer ordered. He held out both arms, swiveling her around without actually touching her. She cast a frustrated sneer over her shoulder.

"I'd like a statement, Detective," she called. "That's the least you can do."

Giorgio watched the officer usher the protesting young woman back down the curved path.

"That won't stop her, you know." Poindexter gave him a half-smile.

"I know. Let's sit over here."

The ground was still damp, and debris clogged paths adding to the rustic nature of the gardens. They moved further down the colonnade to where a dark, heavy wooden bench sat propped against the building. Poindexter reached into his pants and pulled out a packet of cigarettes.

"Care for one?"

His manner was casual as he sat and crossed his legs at the knee. A gold bracelet dangled from his sleeve and across the edge of a tattoo on the back of his hand.

"No. Thank you," Giorgio said.

Giorgio had never smoked and prided himself on the one vice he had avoided all these years. He couldn't say the same for pastries and touched his midriff, silently comparing himself to Poindexter's lean physique.

"I need to ask a few questions about the dinner last night."

Poindexter lit the cigarette and took a long draw, while Giorgio joined him on the bench.

"What time did you arrive in the banquet room?"

Poindexter inhaled and looked out towards the valley as if carefully considering the question. Giorgio knew he was stalling for time.

"I'm not exactly sure," he said, exhaling a stream of smoke and watching it curl upwards into the cool morning air.

"Had the dinner begun?"

He now eyed Giorgio with suspicion. "I think you already know that, Detective, or you wouldn't be asking it. I came in late. And, yes, the dinner had already begun."

Cautious arrogance replaced his casualness, and Giorgio sensed a cat and mouse game about to begin.

Giorgio wondered why it was that young males so often looked upon this line of questioning as a tennis match. Even if they weren't guilty of anything, they revealed their fragile egos through their need to win.

"Can you tell me why you were late?"

"I went for a walk. It was a beautiful night."

His answer made Giorgio remember the storm the night before.

"Can anyone substantiate that?"

He turned to Giorgio with a smirk. "The weather or the walk?"

Giorgio was losing patience. "The walk."

He smiled and returned his gaze to the view. "Jeremy Slater went with me. You can ask him."

"What time did the two of you go for a walk?"

"I think we left around six-thirty," he replied slowly, letting the smoke emerge from his mouth as he spoke.

"And Jeremy was with you the whole time?"

The question caught Poindexter off-guard, and he paused, glancing sideways. Giorgio pressed for an answer.

"Did Mr. Slater also arrive to the dinner late?"

"We parted at the back door," Poindexter said. "I don't know if Slater went directly to the dinner."

Poindexter emphasized this point and seemed pleased he'd just thrown suspicion on someone else.

"And where did you go?"

He turned to Giorgio, a brief look of caution flashing in his eyes. "Just because I came into the dinner late doesn't mean I killed that girl."

"We're just trying to put facts together."

Poindexter shifted uncomfortably on the bench. "I continued around the building. Then I returned to my room. I had some things on my mind. I wasn't even sure I was going to go to the dinner, but I finally did."

"Did you see anyone when you came back downstairs?"

The young man paused, his mind working. Suddenly, his eyes flashed as if he'd remembered something, and the thought made him visibly relax.

"Actually, I did see someone. I thought I saw someone from the window when I was at the head of the stairs. Just a shadow really. I couldn't tell who it was. It was too dark. I happened to pause at the window and glance below. Someone was going in the direction of the kitchen."

"What time was this?"

"Around seven-thirty."

"And you couldn't tell who it was?"

"No. It was too dark."

"Could you see where they went?"

"I didn't pay any attention. I just continued down the stairs."

Giorgio's mind was buzzing. He was trying to determine if what Poindexter had just told him was the truth, or a lie to create an alibi.

"What is your room number?"

He paused as if he thought he'd just gotten caught in a trap. Finally, he replied, "Number eight."

"Thank you, Mr. Poindexter." Giorgio got up to go. "One more thing. Was there a reason you didn't dress for the mystery?"

Poindexter stopped smiling. "I just forgot," he said quickly. "I mean about the mystery."

Giorgio nodded and thanked him again, leaving Poindexter to gaze to the valley below as if he didn't have a care in the world.

† Chapter Twelve †

Giorgio decided it was time to examine the monastery by daylight. He followed the rear hallway east along the north side of the building past the bathrooms, two small classrooms, and a large meeting room set up with a projector screen and folding chairs. An intersecting hallway served as the boundary between the retreat center and monastery.

On the monastery side, Giorgio passed a small meditation room and a large laundry. Finally, the hallway opened into a stairwell where a metal door led to the backside of the property, probably the escape route for the cigarette-smoking monk.

When he opened the door, Giorgio stepped through a wooden awning covered by a thick tangle of vines. An ancient light fixture was tucked up under the overhang, but when he reached in and flicked the light switch, it didn't work. No wonder he hadn't noticed it.

A worn brick path led away from the building to a circular courtyard and pond. The pond languished in the cool morning air, its green water bubbling up like the headwaters of a mountain stream. Several small tadpoles kicked around the bottom looking for cover under the floating lily pads.

Giorgio glanced around thinking that by day the monastery and its elaborate grounds only added to the mystery. Almost every view was blocked by something – trees, bushes, cement statues, or vine covered arbors.

He reentered the building and rounded the rear staircase, stepping into a wide hallway that fronted the commercial kitchen and chapel. An open-air courtyard was visible through a set of double doors to his right, complete with another fountain, two flowerbeds, a second pond, and a large statue of Christ standing on a pedestal.

Giorgio looked up and realized the monks' bedroom windows looked out onto this courtyard, making it unlikely any of them had seen anything the night before. With a sigh, he retraced his steps and then climbed the stairs to the monks' quarters.

If the conference wing had felt worn and old, the monks' quarters were cold and empty. The hallway was all hard angles, bare wood paneling, and a hardwood floor. Three tall windows on the exterior wall were flanked by plain, dark green curtains. It all reminded Giorgio of the first time he'd attended classes at Sacred Heart Catholic School when he was six. His earliest memories were of being trapped in a frigid classroom with uncomfortable wooden desks and a harsh-looking woman encased in black, flowing robes and some sort of bonnet. The ruler she held became a weapon, and to this day the image filled him with a mixture of awe and dread. While there was nothing to fear here, the austerity of the monks' existence was intimidating.

Giorgio counted eight doorways before the hallway turned left. He passed four more rooms before the hallway turned again, returning along the south side of the building. There were no embellishments, not even room numbers. At the end of the south hallway, a second staircase led to the first floor and the chapel. He suspected it was down this staircase that he and Swan had witnessed the line of chanting monks.

Turning around, he walked the route in reverse, this time peering out the windows and stopping to explore a supply closet at the west end of the wing. The closet was stocked with toilet paper, blankets, and other basic necessities. If his calculations were correct, it backed up to the closet just outside of Mallery Olsen's room. Giorgio returned to the first floor.

It appeared the building was shaped like a hammerhead shark. When he stepped into the east hallway again, just outside the open air courtyard, he was standing where the shark's brain would be, if hammerhead sharks had brains. At the end of the hallway was the chapel; to his left the baking kitchen.

The smell of baking bread drew him to the arched kitchen doorway.

The room was large and equipped with two sets of big, black wall ovens, several work tables, a stand that held a large, copper kettle, and two walls of shelves and cupboards. Five monks were busy kneading dough, sorting ingredients, and working the ovens. Two additional monks worked in the rear, wrapping and packing loaves of freshly baked bread. Giorgio swallowed the saliva that flowed freely into his mouth. Father Rosario, the small monk who had greeted them the night before, saw him and approached.

"Detective, can I get you a sample?"

"Oh, no," Giorgio replied, his gaze drifting to where a short monk was just pulling a long metal paddle from the oven. On it sat six round loaves of steaming brown bread. Father Rosario followed his gaze.

"We don't eat butter, but let me get you some fresh bread."

He lifted a fresh loaf of bread from where it sat cooling on a nearby table and retrieved a long, serrated knife to cut off a large hunk. He placed it on a paper towel and gave it to Giorgio.

"Thank you," Giorgio murmured. "You're well known for your bread." He took a mouthful as Father Rosario smiled.

"We sell to all the local supermarkets and even many of the bakeries. It's a labor of love." He smiled. "That's the name of our business, of course, 'Labor of Love.' We thought the name was catchy. We've been approached to expand our market, but as you can see," he gestured to the other monks, "we have a limited labor pool." He smiled again, exposing a set of crooked teeth.

Giorgio sunk his own teeth into the soft bread. "Mmmm," he mumbled. "How do you resist? I'd eat this all day long."

"Actually, today is a fasting day. We fast two days a week to commemorate the death of our Lord Jesus."

"But it's Sunday. Don't you eat at all?"

"We are allowed one nourishing meal, which will be shared in the refectory after the morning service. No other food will be taken for the day."

His voice reflected his surrender to a life of poverty and lack of convenience. Giorgio had always wondered why the lack of anything was somehow more holy than actually having those things. It was a conversation he'd had often with Father Michael.

"*Life is not about things, Giorgio,*" the good priest had said. "*Life is about love; the love of God, love of life, love of family. Remember that,*" he added, "*and you'll do just fine in life.*"

The problem was that Giorgio liked his things. He didn't think he was materialistic. There was just a certain comfort in having things like his favorite chair and his big screen TV.

"I never understood fasting," Giorgio mumbled, swallowing another chunk of the heavy but tasty bread. "If God meant for us to eat, why would anyone choose not to eat?"

"Fasting has its roots in the very beginnings of Christianity," the small monk offered. "Many believe you cannot know God unless you fast, just as you cannot know God unless you pray. Fasting has many physical and mental benefits, as well as spiritual, not the least of which is to slow us down and force us to pay attention to the essence of life. When you fast, you let go, and by letting go, you see and hear more clearly." The little priest clasped his hands over his abdomen and smiled. "Perhaps it would even prove helpful in your line of work, Detective."

Giorgio knew when he'd been bested and decided to change the subject.

"So, this is the kitchen the monks use?"

"We have three kitchens on the premises. The one you saw last night was built when the boys' school was created. When we began baking commercially, we had to create this kitchen out of the old library. Because this is the commercial one, we keep it separate from a smaller kitchen that serves to make our meals."

He gestured for Giorgio to follow him through a doorway to a smaller kitchen that wasn't much bigger than his own. There was no outside window making him think it had been converted from something else.

"As you can see," Father Rosario began, "it's quite small in comparison, but adequate."

Through the opening in the far wall was a well-stocked pantry; to the left was a door leading into the dining room. This was a long room with a high ceiling and large arched windows, looking out to the east parking lot where a delivery truck sat. Two long wooden tables ran the length of the room, dotted on both sides by wooden chairs. The room was mostly unadorned, except for two fresco-style wall paintings at the far end.

"Is this how most of the monks spend their time during the day, Father, working in the business of bread baking?"

"This or gardening. Of course, there is always time for prayer and meditation, and we also hold classes for our novitiates and guests. In fact, twice a year we offer one week of fasting and meditation for guests who come from all over the world." The monk's eyes lit up. "You might want to consider joining us, Detective."

Giorgio made an immediate left turn.

"Do any of the guests mingle with the monks?"

"We'll often run into guests when we're working around the grounds. We are not a mute society, so we have no problem conversing with others."

"I appreciate your time, Father, and thank you for the bread. It was delicious."

"You're most welcome. You can return to the hallway through the door at the end of the room." He pointed to a set of double doors at the far end and retreated to the work area.

Giorgio returned to the main hallway and found Rocky sauntering toward him from the direction of the main lobby.

"Whassup?" he slurred.

"I'm trying to figure out how someone might have carried Olsen's body to the kitchen. What've you been doing?"

"Interviewing some of the monks. A Father O'Leary was taken ill last night and isn't up to talking yet, but I've met with two of the young ones." Rocky stuck his nose in the air and sniffed. "What's that smell?"

"Bread. Which ones?" Giorgio asked.

"Francis and Julio," Rocky replied. "What bread?"

"They bake bread here. What did they say?"

"Who?"

"The two monks," Giorgio sighed with exasperation.

"Francis was very forthcoming. Julio was more difficult. What do you mean they bake bread here?"

"To sell," Giorgio snapped. "What did you learn?"

"Nothing much. Can we get some?"

"Not so fast. I want an update first. Let's go into the chapel."

Giorgio opened the door and they stepped inside.

The room embraced them with its hushed silence and strong smell of incense. A row of stained glass windows glistened with the little bit of sunlight outside. Overhead, the spindly slivers of richly polished cherry wood arched across the cathedral ceiling like the skeleton of a large whale.

More ornate carvings filled each corner in graceful curves, giving the appearance that the entire room had been carved out of one large piece of wood. An octagonal stained glass window sat high above the altar where the ceiling came together in a point. A single monk silently polished tall, golden candlesticks near the altar.

Giorgio and Rocky quietly took seats in one of the back pews where Rocky stretched his long legs underneath the pew in front of him, clasping his hands tightly in his lap. As comfortable as Giorgio might feel in being here, his brother looked like he'd just been sent to the principal's office. Rocky sighed before speaking in a whisper.

"You know, I haven't been in a church since Rebecca died," Rocky murmured. "In fact, I haven't been in one since we picked out the church for our wedding. You remember? We were going to use St. Anthony's."

Rocky allowed an awkward moment to stretch into two. Finally, Giorgio leaned forward, resting his arms on the pew in front of him.

"You never talk much about that night," he said quietly.

"I try not to think about it," Rocky said.

"But you do." Giorgio glanced at his brother. "You do think about it."

Rocky raised his eyes to look at Giorgio. The handsome face had all the attributes Giorgio's lacked. His brother had a strong jaw, an irrepressible smile, and the only straight teeth in the family. But when Rocky was ill, it was a face that resembled a charcoal drawing someone had started to erase -- all definition seemed to disappear. He was looking into that face now.

"I think about it all the time," Rocky said in a whisper. "It's why I drink, Joe. It's why I can't stop drinking."

They sat quietly, each with their own thoughts. The monk busied himself at the altar.

"What does the department say?"

"I have another week to make a decision. Go into rehab, or get clean on my own."

"And?"

Rocky turned and the two brothers locked eyes. "I'm not sure I want to get clean."

The two brothers had never been competitive. Instead, they had shared an unusual bond from the time they were small.

When their father died, Rocky had turned to his big brother and Giorgio had risen easily to the task. The decision to move to the West Coast and to leave his brother behind had been difficult, but Rocky was happily engaged to Rebecca, a beautiful girl in the police academy. One week before the wedding, Rebecca had been raped and brutally murdered in her own apartment. The killer was never found.

It had all but shattered Rocky, and he moved to Southern California six months later hoping to put his life back together. It hadn't worked. Rocky had only been a social drinker in college, but now he sank longingly into alcohol's fatal embrace. When he'd been ordered to take medical leave, Giorgio had avoided the urge to lecture his little brother, knowing that what he needed was support. But Rocky hadn't asked for it. Giorgio thought perhaps this investigation might help get Rocky back on track. Now he wasn't sure.

"Rehab wouldn't be so bad," Giorgio said, looking away. "I'd probably give it a try."

"You didn't hear me, Joe," Rocky cut him off. "I'm not sure I want to recover. It's a part of me you've never quite understood. You have it all, Joe. You always did. You laid your life out long ago and everything fell into place. You don't know what it's like for me."

Giorgio felt the heat rise in his belly. "What do you mean everything fell into place? Because I worked hard to get where I am? Because I worked overtime every chance I got in order to provide for my family? What all do you think I have?"

"That's not what I meant."

"You mean because I have Angie?" Rocky flinched but Giorgio ignored it. "You forget little brother that I lost someone, too. I know damn well what it's like."

"You mean Dad," Rocky replied matter-of-factly.

"I was closer to him than you, and I was older. I understood what happened. I was at the morgue. I saw the hole blown in his chest." Giorgio stood up and moved away a few steps, unable to control the anger. "Shit, Rocky! I used to lie awake at night willing myself not to cry because you were in the bed next to me. Sometimes, I'd climb to the rooftop just to be alone – me and New York City!"

The monk at the altar turned in response to Giorgio's raised voice, prompting him to turn back to his brother and lower his voice a notch.

"I was the one who had to comfort Mom. Do you have any idea how hard that was? I was just a kid, but everyone said I was the man in the family now and had to be strong for the two of you. Crap, I was just as torn up." He stopped and took a breath and lowered his voice even more. "I do know how you're feeling. You want to scream and you want to cry. Sometimes, you just want to run in front of a bus and end it all. But most of all, you just want someone to take away the pain. You want someone to fix it. But they can't. Because death can't be fixed, Rocky. And that's why you feel so helpless." He paused and took a deep breath. "And that's why you drink."

Rocky's face had grown ashen, and he dropped his head.

"Drinking won't fix it either though, little brother. And that's the truth. Life isn't a promise. It just is what it is. Nothing more. We get what we get!"

There was a pause. Then Rocky whispered, "And don't throw a fit."

Giorgio recognized that Rocky had just finished a childhood rhyme and chuckled.

"Yeah, and don't throw a fit." He moved over and sat next to his brother. "I don't know what it's like to lose someone like Rebecca. I'm sure it's a pain you'll never get over, but there are people here who don't want to lose you, too."

"I know," Rocky whispered.

"Then don't quit on me," Giorgio said.

Giorgio recognized the moment was about to crumble into a sophomoric show of emotion and decided to end it. He took a deep breath. "Okay, so you interviewed Julio and Francis. They're two of the new recruits, right?"

Rocky nodded and took a deep breath. "Julio is from the Chicago area, apparently a 'boys in the hood' kind of background. Joined a gang and got arrested a few times. Father somebody-or-other got a hold of him and turned him. He decided to become a priest and attended seminary school in Forest Park. When he graduated, he was referred here. He's been here only about six months."

"Not much to go on."

"No. Of course, he says he didn't know anyone at the conference and was working in the library last evening with another monk. An older monk, a Father O'Leary, was with the two of them most of the time."

"Most of the time?"

"After dinner, O'Leary became ill and went to the infirmary. Not an airtight alibi, but he doesn't seem to have any reason to commit murder."

"What about Francis?"

Rocky took a deep breath and pulled his shoulders back. "Not much better. He's from San Francisco. His parents were both teachers. He lived there most of his life. Both parents dead. No siblings. Decided the monastic life might be for him and came here just five months ago. Likes it, but says it gets pretty quiet." Rocky smiled. "He strikes me as the kind of guy who won't make it."

"Why do you say that?"

"He seems a little too slick for a place like this. He seemed more interested in knowing if I'd ever been to San Francisco than talking about life here at the abbey."

"No literary writing in either one of their backgrounds?" Giorgio asked.

"None. In fact, in the case of Julio, I doubt there is writing of any kind. I've got a feeling he got a lot of help in school."

Giorgio sighed and got up. "Make sure McCready gets your notes. We still have to talk to Father Daniel."

"I think Swan has him cornered now."

"Good. Then, let's go."

† Chapter Thirteen †

He watched the two officers leave the monastery grounds just before noon − the tall, good-looking one and the shorter one he'd passed in the gift shop. Someone had told him they were brothers, although they didn't look alike. He'd spoken briefly to the tall one in the hallway. The man had introduced himself as Officer Salvatori. An Italian. A brother of sorts. The officer had asked him much more probing questions than the young red-haired cop had. He'd quickly realized he had to be careful not to contradict anything he'd said earlier.

It was the shorter officer that worried him more. This was a man with an unwavering sense of confidence, a man focused on the outcome. He was clearly in charge and someone who knew what he was doing. He had to be the detective with homicide experience, the one who wasn't supposed to be available to take the case. Something had changed to make him available.

A murder like this had probably never happened in this sleepy little town. It almost made him laugh. They should live in New York where murders were commonplace, where he'd been weaned on death, where he and his older cousins grew up knowing that to live on the streets you had to have ice in your veins and follow the code or you were dead.

He turned and retreated down the hall thinking about his uncle and his many cousins left behind. He'd been gone six months, unable to call or talk with anyone he knew, living as a ghost among people he generally detested, never being able to let down his guard. Until he was twenty-two, he'd had only one thing in mind – avenging his father's death. But he'd screwed up. Someone had seen him, and his uncle had stepped in as he always did. Even now the echo of his uncle's words rang in his head.

"You were always my favorite nephew, Danny. You're like a son to me, but your mistakes are now my mistakes. Mistakes I can't afford. So now you disappear – for good. If I ever see your face again, if I ever hear of you again, I'll kill you myself. That's a promise."

An accident had been staged that very night on a lonely road in upstate New York. A body, burned beyond recognition was found next to the twisted frame of his BMW. His identification was found next to the body, and there was an eyewitness who would swear he saw the car go off the road. His uncle had given him money and the name of a willing plastic surgeon. But he had no intention of staying hidden forever. He had a life back in New York and wasn't willing to give it up. He'd always had a plan to return, and this little situation would help him get there.

† Chapter Fourteen †

Rose Calhoun sat on a stool behind the cash register at Mom's Diner, her dyed blonde hair pulled up into a French roll, her skin showing every wrinkle of her seventy-plus years. Posters of Elvis Presley and Marilyn Monroe scattered the walls, along with chrome hubcaps, and a framed poodle skirt.

"You boys want some lunch?" she slurred through a set of heavy dentures. "You should try the chili today. Made it myself."

Giorgio smiled, thinking that would be the last thing he'd order. "We'll probably go for the pepperoni pizza today, Rose."

"Suit yerself," she said, dismissing him. She hopped down from the stool, grabbed a couple of menus and led them to a back booth. "I heard about that murder up at the monastery." She leaned a gnarled hand on the table as the brothers slid into their seats. "You ask me, that monastery should have been torn down back when the abbot was murdered."

"Whoa, there was another murder up there?" Rocky said in alarm.

"When they ran the boy's school," Giorgio informed him. "One of the students killed the head priest."

"Now, here we go again," Rose pursed her lips, accentuating the ruby red lipstick that crawled up the lines of her mouth. "It don't seem like such a holy place to me." She winked a heavily made up eye, turned on her heel and walked away. "I'll be back with your drinks. The usual, I presume."

"You didn't tell me about that other murder," Rocky scolded.

"It doesn't have anything to do with Olsen's murder, but it will give the media a lot to talk about."

"No kidding." Rocky drummed the table with his fingers.

"By the way, have you heard anything about any kids on the grounds?"

"No. Why would there be any kids there?"

"I saw one on the second floor landing last night."

"It probably belonged to one of the conference attendees. That or you're imagining things."

Giorgio grimaced, keeping his thoughts to himself.

"Got any theories, yet?" Rocky asked, tapping the table.

"I think whoever Mallery Olsen had a drink with strangled her in her room. What I can't figure out is how he got her down to the kitchen closet. The only way to the first floor from her room is by that main staircase. The two back staircases only lead to the monks' quarters, and there's a wall in between the two wings of the building on the second floor."

"Pretty risky to bring her down the main drag."

"Someone at that conference knew Mallery Olsen. The question is, did they come to the conference with the intention of killing her, or did something happen at the conference that precipitated her murder?"

"Are you going to her apartment this afternoon?"

Rose returned with their drinks. Rocky reached for his root beer. Giorgio waited until she was out of earshot.

"I want to talk with the caterers first. Why don't you finish with the monks? Someone had to see something." He took a sip of his drink. "When do you come off medical leave?"

Rocky stopped drumming his fingers.

"Three weeks, depending on rehab."

Giorgio shrugged his shoulders. "Great. I'll keep you busy."

"You don't have to keep me busy, Joe."

"I just thought you might find this more interesting than watching the World Wrestling Federation." He attempted a smile but came up short.

A young waitress saved the moment when she arrived with their food. Rocky grabbed a slice of pizza, successfully landing a large bite in his mouth. Giorgio just stared at the table.

"I think I'll buy her a dog," he announced.

Rocky looked up with grease dribbling down his chin. "Who? Angie? Is that the new Millennium way of saying you're sorry?"

"No. She wants a dog."

"You're not suggesting the dog will take the place of the baby, are you?"

"Don't be silly. Angie wants a dog. Ever since we had to put Butch to sleep."

Giorgio reached for his own slice of the pepperoni pie.

"Butch was *your* dog."

"She loved him just as much as I did."

"She hated that dog." Rocky swallowed a large bite and then wiped his chin. "He shit on the carpet and pissed on the stairs. Why would she want another dog?"

"Angie wants a dog, I'm telling you. She misses Butch. She said so. And he only made a couple of messes. It's not like he used the house as a kennel." His brother arched his eyebrows, but Giorgio ignored the implied reproach. "Maybe I'll go to the pound this afternoon and see what I can find."

"And you think that'll do it?"

"What?"

"Patch things up?" Rocky swallowed again.

Giorgio thought for a moment, toying with the pizza he hadn't tried yet. "I don't know. I still don't know how I feel about having another baby. I just know I want to make it right with Angie. I can't stand fighting with her. She's the best thing that ever happened to me."

"You got that right!" Rocky chided, taking a drink. "But a dog!"

"You'll see. It'll be great. After Butch died, the whole family wanted another dog. But I said no. Angie says that I only think about me. Well, this time, it's just for her. She'll see. Not all men are insensitive." With that, he finally leaned into his pizza and took a huge bite.

"You're an idiot, you know that?" Rocky said.

† Chapter Fifteen †

Food for Thought was located in the middle of a strip mall between a shoe repair shop and a UPS store. The name on the front window was embellished with an image of Rodin's "The Thinker." A bell jingled when Giorgio opened the door and a pleasant-looking young black woman looked up from behind the counter.

"I'm Mary," she said cheerfully. "What can I do for you?"

"I'm Detective Salvatori." He produced the badge. "I'm investigating the murder at the monastery last night."

The cheery face fell. "How can I help you?"

"We have to get statements from anyone who was there. I'm afraid I'll have to talk with each one of your employees who was with you last night."

"We talked with the police last night," she said, fidgeting.

"Yes, but I'd like to hear what you have to say for myself."

She sighed. "We have another party this afternoon and one tonight. We're very busy. Can't it wait?"

"I don't think so. Maybe I could start with you. It'll just take a few minutes."

She looked through an open door to the kitchen beyond. Two people busied themselves packing boxes. "Okay," she said, coming around the counter to sit at the small table. "But it'll have to be fast."

Giorgio sat across from her and took out his pad and pencil. "You're the owner?"

She nodded.

"And the caterer of choice at the monastery?" he asked.

"That's right. We do all of their gigs. Have for over two years."

"What time did you arrive there last night?"

The brown eyes seemed to turn inwards as she thought back to the day before.

"We do most of the cooking here and only use their ovens for warming, so I guess we got there around five-fifteen."

"Did you go straight into the kitchen?"

"Where else would we go?"

He ignored the rhetorical question. "The kitchen was open?"

"The monks use another kitchen at the other end of the building so that we don't run into each other."

"Was there anything unusual about the facility when you arrived?"

"No. We would have noticed." She paused. "I saw on the news that the body was found in the supply closet. Of course we don't use the supply closet."

"Why is that?"

"We don't store anything on the premises, and the janitor does the heavy kitchen clean-up after we're gone."

"So you've never been back there?"

"I've been in there a couple of times to grab paper towels."

"Have you ever seen anyone else go in or out of that supply closet?"

"No," she said, shaking her head. "We're very busy and can't even see the supply closet from where we're working. We go from boxes, to the counter tops, to the banquet room."

"Does anyone ever use the restroom down that hall?"

"Sometimes, but I can't say if anyone did last night."

"Could someone come in that back door without you knowing it?"

"I'm sure they could. We're just not paying attention."

"Did any of your staff leave for any reason last night that you're aware of?"

She rubbed the back of her hand over her forehead, setting loose a few curls. "I told you. We're busy during that time. I don't pay much attention."

"Wouldn't you know if someone wasn't there to do their part?"

"Catering is a little bit like a performance, Detective. If someone wasn't there, someone else would have to step in. So, yes, I'd know."

"Who did you have with you last night?"

"I brought two other employees." She leaned around to point into the back. "The same two here now. I also took Colin and Peter to serve, but they won't be in until one o'clock."

94

"So, there were actually five of you?"

She thought for a moment. "Yes. Plus two bartenders."

"Have they all been with you a long time?"

She rubbed her forehead again. "Nancy and Austin have been with me since I started. Peter just started working part-time. Colin came on about four months ago. I contract for the bartenders. I'm sorry, Detective. It was a pretty standard night for us."

He stood up, extending a card. "Thank you. Call me if you think of anything else."

"I'll send in Austin first," she said, standing. "Nancy has to finish the crepes."

She disappeared into the kitchen and leaned over to speak into a man's ear. The man named Austin glanced in Giorgio's direction, finally coming out to the front. He was about the same height as Giorgio, but he had a slight build with a long nose and tortoiseshell glasses.

Giorgio asked him many of the same questions, eliciting the same answers. It seemed the caterers were single-focused in their tasks and took little notice of anything else. Austin did add one important piece of information. John Marsh came through the kitchen saying he was going to use the bathroom. Austin couldn't remember the time or seeing him return.

Nancy appeared shortly after Austin. She was about thirty-five with a mole in the middle of her left cheek. She fluttered behind the desk, and Giorgio attempted to calm her by making her sit down. It only seemed to restrain her nervous energy until she disintegrated into giggles.

Nancy didn't remember seeing Marsh, nor did she remember seeing anyone else. She only remembered serving the quail so late that it was nearly cold.

"Peter and Colin do all the serving?"

"That's right. We prepare. They serve. Colin likes to have his cigarette, so he was hustling. They picked up around eight and we had the mousse up by eight-fifteen. We were ready to leave right around nine o'clock."

"You work fast."

"We all know what to do," she said, beginning to calm down. "Mary and Austin and I have been together a long time. We have things down to a routine. We're almost packed by the time the dessert is served. Austin and Colin stay behind to clean tables."

"You mentioned that Colin likes his cigarettes. Did he go out to have one last night?"

"Yes, I think so. I think I remember him saying he'd be right back." She looked up, realizing she may have implicated a co-worker. "But Colin couldn't have done anything. I mean, why would he?"

"I'm sure he didn't," Giorgio lied. "But he may have seen something that could be useful. I'll need both Peter and Colin's phone numbers and addresses."

She stood and backed up from the chair, nearly knocking it over. "I'll get Mary. Oh, I didn't mean to get Colin in trouble."

A moment later, Mary returned and gave him the required phone numbers. Giorgio left the shop thinking he hadn't learned much except that Marsh had indeed left the head table at some point, and Colin Jewett had gone out for a cigarette. Both men would now be added to the growing list of people who had opportunity to commit the murder. The question was, did either one have motive?

† Chapter Sixteen †

Giorgio left Mary Fields to her crepes and used his cell phone to call the station. Swan wouldn't be back from the monastery for about an hour, so he decided to take a little side trip.

Fifteen minutes later, he pulled into the dirt parking lot of the Pasadena Humane Society, focused now on assuaging his guilt instead of solving a murder. The manufactured image of Angie's look of surprise when he came home with a new dog gave him all the confidence he needed.

He parked in front of a one-story gray building surrounded by a bunch of scrub oaks. The words "prison camp" came to mind as he emerged from the car. He entered a small dreary office and stood at the counter until an affable young man wearing gray overalls appeared through a side door.

After explaining his mission, the young man led Giorgio through a metal door into the back of the building, where fluorescent bulbs cast a pallid wash across a line of tall metal cages. The odors of urine and feces rose distinctly above the bleach used in a vain attempt to neutralize the smell. It was enough to make Giorgio's nose twitch.

The young man left Giorgio to look around while he went to attend to the dogs in another room. Twenty cages lined each wall, and behind each gate was a friendly face.

Wet noses pushed against the gates and every tail wagged in anticipation of a ride home. Giorgio remembered getting Butch at a place much like this, a forlorn puppy with brown spiky hair and a long wiry tail.

Butch spent six happy years with the family, guarding their small apartment with a ferocious tenacity that intimidated everyone except his mother.

Giorgio thought about that.

His mother would snap the dog on the snout and say, "Not now, Butch!" It worked every time, making Giorgio wonder if that was how she'd managed his father's equally ferocious libido. It wasn't until he was in his twenties that Giorgio realized his mother's frequent headaches had miraculously stopped after his father's death.

Staring into the eyes of all these homeless dogs, he remembered how much he'd enjoyed taking Butch to the park. Butch loved to play fetch, and Giorgio would always tuck a tennis ball into his pocket. One day, the ball took an errant bounce into the street. Before Giorgio could stop him, Butch followed the ball to the bitter end, coming to rest under the front wheel of a delivery truck.

Although he'd maintained a stoic exterior for the kids, Giorgio was devastated. When Marie and Tony whined about getting another puppy, he'd cut them off. Even Angie said they should consider another dog, but Giorgio was adamant. Too much work. Too expensive. Too much trouble. Eventually, the requests stopped. The truth was, he didn't think he could handle the emotional strain of losing another canine friend. But now, he would get a dog for Angie.

He walked the kennel with his hands behind his back, glancing from side to side as if he were General Patton inspecting the troops. He didn't know exactly what he was looking for, but felt sure he would know it when he saw it. A small collie mix caught his attention, and he stopped for a closer look, squatting down and stretching out a finger for an enthusiastic lick. Her long brown and white fur felt like silk, and he imagined her sitting demurely in Angie's lap. This one had possibilities.

He finished the right side of the aisle, passing a bulky black dog with runny eyes and an overgrown cocker whose eyes were barely visible. The walkway ended at a cement wall. He turned around to start up the other side intending to visit the collie mix again when something in the last cage on his right stopped him. Sad, droopy eyes peered out from beneath a large tattered blanket. A long, heavy snout lay flat against the floor. Giorgio stared through the wire, curious about this dog. The young kennel worker appeared again, and Giorgio flagged him down.

"Is this dog ill?"

"No," he said, coming down the aisle. "He's lonely. We found him on Pascal Boulevard about three weeks ago."

"How long do you keep them, before you...you know?"

"Only about three weeks," the worker replied. "This little guy's time is about up I'm afraid."

"May I see him?"

"Sure." The worker pulled out a large ring filled with keys and opened the gate. "He's very gentle."

Giorgio stepped in and the dog rose. The blanket slipped off revealing a young Basset Hound. Giorgio squatted down, and the dog pushed a wet nose into his hand. It was then Giorgio realized what had kept the dog from being adopted. Across his back were a series of small, round burn marks, as if someone had repeatedly placed a lit cigarette against the fur until it singed the flesh beneath. The wounds reminded him of the murder case of a small boy who was tortured to death in a similar fashion by his mother's boyfriend. It was one of the last cases Giorgio had worked in New York and a big reason why he'd left. The haunting image of the fresh skin of a four-year old child disfigured in that way was still almost too much to bear. Now, here was a young dog, equally trusting as a child, and equally abused. It was cruel and unfair.

Although the dog's burns were scabbed over and would probably heal without much scarring, he looked as if he had small pox. Giorgio cupped the dog's chin and turned the head sideways. Behind his right ear was a fresh, jagged scar.

"Someone's abused this dog."

"Yes," the voice spoke softly behind him. "He was in pretty bad shape when we found him. The doctor stitched him up, and the burn marks will go away, but people think he can't be trusted. But, honestly, he hasn't shown any aggression since he's been here."

The dog allowed Giorgio to look him over as if he were a patient having his yearly exam. The liquid brown eyes watched him, and the long tongue found its way to give Giorgio one good lick. Giorgio wondered why dogs had ever allowed man to tame them. He'd read once that horses aren't really broken--they allow themselves to be ridden. Dogs are different; they welcome human companionship. And a dog's deep-rooted trust is with them for life.

Giorgio played with the long ears, carefully avoiding the recent injury. The dog began to relax allowing his long tail to whip back and forth across the floor. There was no anger in this dog. No hatred for what humans had done to him. Only a longing to be taken home and loved. A tag hooked to his collar was inscribed with the name "Grosvenor." Giorgio attempted to say it out loud.

"According to my supervisor, you don't pronounce the *s*," the young man corrected him. "I guess it's an English name. You pronounce it like a grove of trees. Grove-ner." He enunciated it as if he were instructing someone in a foreign language.

Giorgio looked down at the dog again, completely smitten with the droopy eyes and heavy, bowed legs. The Basset had beautiful black and brown markings and was clearly eager to please. He'd already tucked his head under one of Giorgio's legs, pushing against him for more attention. Before he could think of a reason not to, Giorgio said, "I'll take him!"

The young man gave a broad smile. "You won't be sorry. He's a nice dog. My aunt used to raise Bassets. They make wonderful pets. Do you have kids?"

"Yes, two," Giorgio answered, as they started for the office.

"Great," the man said. "Bassets are very good with kids."

When they reached the exit the dog let out a melodious woof, telling Giorgio to hurry back. The paper work took only a few minutes, and Grosvenor emerged from the wire kennel as if he knew he was embarking on a new life. Giorgio took the new leash and collar he'd just purchased and snapped it around the dog's thick neck. The dog wiggled in between his legs as a way of accepting Giorgio as his new owner. Dogs, Giorgio thought, were amazing animals. Forgive and forget.

"Bye, Grosvenor." The young man leaned over to pat the dog on the head. "I'm glad you're getting a new home. You be a good dog."

Grosvenor whined and slapped him with his tail, then pulled at the leash to be gone. Giorgio led the dog into the parking lot, shortening his stride to match his new friend. When they reached the car, Grosvenor needed a little push from behind to get into the police-issued sedan.

When Giorgio attempted to shut the door behind him though, the latch didn't catch and Grosvenor almost fell out again. Giorgio opened the door and slammed it a second time, but it just bounced open, making him curse under his breath. He'd reported the malfunction several times to the maintenance department, but gotten no response. Finally, holding the handle up, Giorgio pressed the door closed with his hip until it latched.

When Giorgio walked around to the driver's side, Grosvenor met him. Giorgio held him back and climbed in behind the wheel.

"Okay, buddy, we're off," he said.

The oversized head, squat body, and long ears made the young Basset both humorous and endearing. Giorgio couldn't help but chuckle. Unaware of his funny looks, Grosvenor sat down, happily waiting for what the rest of the day would bring. More than once in his life, Giorgio had felt things had happened for a purpose. He had that feeling now.

Giorgio returned to the station and left Grosvenor in the car while he went in through the back door to see if Swan had returned. Swan was still at the monastery, but McCready had information he wanted to share and offered to ride with Giorgio to Olsen's apartment. When McCready got to the car, he took one look at Grosvenor and cooed.

"Whoa, that's a good-looking dog. Where'd you get him?"

"He's a present for my wife," Giorgio responded, opening the back door. "Let's put him in the back."

He and the young cop hauled Grosvenor onto the back seat. It was a little like wrangling a sea lion, but eventually the two men got him safely situated and climbed into the front seat. McCready turned around and scratched the dog under his neck. Grosvenor whined in pure ecstasy.

"My family had a Basset when I was little," McCready chattered good-naturedly. "I used to ride him around the house pretending I was a cowboy. I'll never forget that dog. His name was Rags on account of his ears used to wipe the floor like two dishrags."

Giorgio snuck a glance at Grosvenor who was now happily looking out the back window, his short legs up on the arm rest. Giorgio couldn't help but think how sometimes the stars align for good luck. This was his lucky day.

He started to back out of his parking space just as the same young female reporter appeared. She saw Giorgio and made a beeline in his direction.

"Shit, she must have radar or something."

He made full use of the car's power steering, laying a small patch of rubber as he sped away. Grosvenor gazed balefully out the back window at the retreating reporter. Giorgio found his way to the 210 Freeway heading west, and McCready began to fill Giorgio in on what he knew about the dead girl.

"She was twenty-six and divorced," McCready read from his notes.

The young cop was sitting with a folder open in his lap.

"She left her husband about two years ago. He's an electrical contractor and beat her up pretty good a couple of times. She finally moved out. When he began following her around, she went to court for a restraining order," he finished saying.

Freeway overpasses whizzed past, and traffic squeezed around them. Driving in the Los Angeles basin was like serving a tour of duty in Iraq--you had to stay alert and drive offensively or die. Giorgio deftly switched lanes back and forth while McCready continued his report unabated.

"We checked her bank records and she declared bankruptcy around the same time she left her husband."

"How did she make a living back then?"

"Real estate. We finally got a hold of Beth Tomlinsen in Florida. She said Olsen only became a literary agent about eighteen months ago. She bought her home in Marina del Rey when she sold real estate. She was born in a small town outside of Chicago. Her parents were Elaine and Jack Young. Her father died six years ago, but her mother lives in San Diego."

"Any brothers or sisters?" Giorgio switched lanes to pass a slow moving delivery truck, checked his rearview mirror, and then pulled in front of the truck again.

"She had a sister named Lisa who lives in Tucson. The two women have been estranged for some time according to the mother. Apparently Lisa loaned Mallery money a few years ago and wasn't paid back. The mother said the loan was pretty substantial and the two sisters haven't spoken since."

"Hmmm," Giorgio murmured, thinking. He kept his eye on an elderly couple in an old Subaru station wagon next to him as McCready talked.

"Interesting," he murmured. "Family squabbles can complicate matters. Anything else?"

McCready referred the notes again in his hands. "The mother hasn't seen Mallery since last Christmas when she came up to visit. She said everything seemed fine then, although Mallery had just broken up with a boyfriend."

"Any names?"

"Pedro something. She never met him, but Mallery said he had a nasty temper and liked to hang out in bars too much for her taste."

Giorgio looked over at the red-haired young officer. "We need to find Pedro and the ex-husband."

"The mother is flying in this afternoon to arrange for the burial. I'll see if she knows more about Pedro." McCready made a note.

Thirty minutes later they pulled up to a small one-story Spanish-style home with a manicured lawn. McCready produced a key ring extracted from the dead woman's purse, and they entered a tiled foyer. The two officers wandered around to get a general picture of the place before beginning a complete search. The house was neat and tidy, just as her room had been at the monastery. Olsen's bedroom offered the only indication she had gone on a trip. An empty satchel sat on the floor, and an open make-up case sat on a nearby dresser. A computer was set up in an extra bedroom and Giorgio turned to McCready.

"Let's take it. It may have something we can use."

McCready nodded and pulled on a pair of rubber gloves and the two men spent the next hour and a half searching every room of the house. In the end, they filled three boxes with bank records, unopened mail, old high school and college year books, unpaid invoices, letters from old boyfriends, loan papers, and even medical records.

Giorgio found a series of framed pictures displayed in the hallway and contemplated throwing them into a box as well. They included the dead woman with what appeared to be family members and friends. There were several other pictures with various young men, dating back to when she was a teenager. In each picture, a happy Mallery Olsen smiled for the camera as if she might cheat death forever. But Giorgio knew better. He remembered her bruised neck and pallid skin. The beautiful young woman would live on now only in photographs, never growing old, but never smiling again either. As his eyes passed over the fresh and innocent faces of the boys from her youth, he couldn't help wondering if somewhere amongst them was the face of a killer.

✝

It was six o'clock when Giorgio pulled into his driveway. Leaves and twigs blanketed the yard, a sure sign he would have to drag out the rakes and trash bags sooner than he'd planned. Perhaps Tony was old enough to help this year.

He remembered his own father carefully raking the leaves into piles. When he would leave to gather up the bags, Giorgio and Rocky would take flying leaps into the piles, rolling around with shrieks of laughter. Giorgio could still hear his father's gruff voice.

"Here, here! You two stop that! Go inside and help your mother."

The first year after his father died, Giorgio talked his mother into paying someone else to rake the yard to avoid having to rake alone.

The rich smell of lasagna met them when they entered the house. Grosvenor pulled at the leash, heading for the kitchen as if he'd been in the house a hundred times before. A shrill cry surprised them both as Tony and Marie came bounding down the stairs.

"Is he ours?" Marie bubbled.

"What's his name?" Tony wanted to know.

Within seconds, the children and the dog were a jumble of arms, legs, ears, and snout. Grosvenor couldn't get enough of them. His tongue sought every inch of exposed flesh while they attempted to wrap arms around his wriggling body. Giorgio stood back watching approvingly.

"What's the matter with his back," Marie asked, her pretty face suddenly twisted into a sneer.

"I think he had some warts, and the vet burned them off. He'll be fine."

"Oh!" his daughter exclaimed, happy to engage herself with the dog again.

Slowly, Giorgio became aware of someone standing at his elbow and turned to find Angie, her dark gaze directed at the dog. She dangled a long, sharp knife by her side.

"I hope that knife's not for me," he joked.

With barely a glance of acknowledgement, she turned and disappeared into the kitchen, leaving an icy chill behind.

† Chapter Seventeen †

By seven-thirty, the family sat in the living room with the television blaring, but only Giorgio pretended to watch it. The children played on the floor with Grosvenor, while Angie sat at a desk in the corner paying bills. She hadn't said much during dinner and the subject of the baby hadn't come up. Right now her graceful brows were clenched just above her nose, something she did whenever she concentrated on a task. Giorgio flicked the remote control impatiently, all the time stealing glances at his wife. The newspaper lay unopened by his side.

"Look, Dad! Watch this."

Tony perched on his knees above Grosvenor who lay prone on the floor with his eyes closed. Giorgio glanced at the dog with little enthusiasm.

"What is it?"

"He plays dead."

"He did it on his own," Marie interjected. "Tony just said, 'bang!' and he dropped down like he was dead!"

She clapped her hands and Grosvenor came to life, wiggling his way into her lap.

"You guys should get ready for bed. Which one of you wants to take a bath first?"

"I'll go," Tony said. "C'mon, Grosvenor!"

The children raced out of the room with the dog hot on their heels. Giorgio watched the canine heft his way up the stairs in lumbering pursuit. He smiled in spite of his black mood until a quiet voice interrupted his thoughts.

"A small bottle of perfume or a little necklace would have been more appropriate."

Angie stood looking down on him, her eyes devoid of their normal luster. The light at the desk had been turned off and her bills put away.

"What d'you mean?" Her reprimands confused him. They always had.

"You missed Marie singing in the choir. The dog doesn't make up for that. And it doesn't make up for your boorish behavior this morning."

She turned to leave, but he stood and grabbed her hand.

"Angie, I'm sorry. I told you, I got the dog for you. I thought it would make you happy."

She pulled her hand away before turning back.

"You don't get it, do you Joe? I don't care about the dog. What I care about is that you don't want this baby."

With that, she left the room. He was about to go after her when the phone rang. It was Swan calling with the preliminary report from the coroner. Giorgio listened, torn between the information he needed to solve a murder and the retreating image of his wife.

"Mallery Olsen was strangled sometime between four and nine o'clock last night," Swan reported. "There was no evidence of a struggle, but chloral hydrate was found in her system, along with a small amount of alcohol."

Giorgio's interest was piqued. Chloral hydrate was a knock-out drug.

"What about the ligature mark?"

"According to the coroner, her assailant had to be several inches taller and strangled her from behind. A small bone in her neck was actually fractured."

"Nothing under her fingernails?"

"Like I said - no signs of a struggle."

"Okay, thanks. I'll see you in the morning."

Giorgio hung up and went to the refrigerator for a glass of milk. The fact that Mallery Olsen's assailant was much taller wasn't surprising. She probably didn't stand much over five feet tall. The narcotic found in her bloodstream proved more interesting.

The children's laughter floated down from the floor above, and he put the dirty glass in the dishwasher and climbed the stairs. When he opened the bathroom door, a suffocating burst of steam enveloped him.

Tony and Marie's wrangling bodies were barely visible, draped over a stoic Grosvenor standing in the middle of the bath tub. Although soapsuds covered his back and slid down one ear, the dog seemed sublimely happy. Water blanketed the tiled floor as Tony and Marie busily worked at rinsing him. Grosvenor turned towards Giorgio, his rear end moving from side to side with the rhythmic motion of his tail. His eyes said it all. He was home.

Giorgio knew he should scold the kids for making such a mess, but instead told them to skip their own baths and dry off the dog. He found Angie already in bed with the lights out, images of the intimate night before fading like so many high school memories. Since Angie never retired before ten o'clock, he recognized this for the message it was. He returned to the bathroom where Tony was working on Grosvenor with a plush towel while Marie wiped up the floor. Always neat and tidy, that Marie. Just like her mother.

"Good enough. You kids get in bed."

"But, Dad, it's too early," Tony groaned.

"Close enough. You have school tomorrow."

"Who gets Grosvenor?"

Always the equalizer that Tony. Everything had to be fair and Giorgio anticipated future struggles over the dog.

"I do. I have to go back to work. I'll take him with me."

Tony threw a disappointed look over his shoulder and finished rubbing down the dog. With a scowl, he gave Grosvenor a hug and disappeared down the hallway. Five minutes later, Giorgio was kissing the kids good night. Grosvenor accompanied him, licking each small hand.

"Is Mama mad?"

Marie was tucked beneath her pink butterfly comforter with only those brown eyes to tell him she suspected more than she should. The question made him pause as he reached for the light.

"I think she's just tired," he said.

"I don't think she likes the dog," his daughter replied.

She turned over and disappeared into balloons of colorful tufted cotton. He looked at the spray of honey brown hair across her pillow, thinking she wasn't much younger than Angie when they first met. Angie was eleven. He was twelve. They had met at a church social when they reached for the same meatball on the buffet table. The coincidence made them giggle helplessly until they were forced to hide themselves in a corner.

They spent the rest of the evening talking about baseball. Soon they began walking to school and doing their homework together. They were inseparable, at least until Giorgio was old enough to date. Then, whenever Giorgio called, Angie was busy. Giorgio spent most of his teens confused about Angie. Yet when his father was killed at a police standoff when he was sixteen, Angie sat with him all night after the funeral, looking through family picture albums and helping him to sort through a mixture of sadness and anger. She was the one person who had never made him feel inadequate or foolish.

Six months after his father's death, Giorgio's mother extracted a promise that he would enter the priesthood after college. Grudgingly he allowed her to believe in that dream until he was eighteen and getting ready to select a seminary school; instead he decided to become a policeman like his father.

He made a special trip to Angie's apartment to tell her and was shocked when she ran from the room crying. It would be ten years before she confessed she shared his mother's fear of losing him the way he'd lost his father. Thinking back to that moment, he realized that Angie's sensitivity balanced his lack of it. Now, when she needed him most, he'd failed her, and it was eating him up.

He turned off Marie's light and closed the door. Stealing only a quick glance at the master bedroom, he descended the stairs, checked to make sure Grosvenor was dry enough to venture outside, and decided to head back to the monastery. Perhaps by the time he returned, Angie would be in a deep sleep, and he could slip into bed unnoticed.

He parked down the hill from the retreat center and left Grosvenor in the car while he trudged up the drive in a growing mist. Several cars were parked at the front entrance, including a stretch limo decorated with white streamers. The police had released all but the back hallway and closet earlier in the day to allow a scheduled event to take place. Looking at the gathering fog, it seemed like an odd night to be getting married, especially on the heels of a murder.

Giorgio cut through the staff parking lot in the direction of the flower garden, thinking he'd map the grounds at night in an attempt to see things as the killer had. He climbed the short path and stopped near an ivy-covered trellis to look back at the building, noting again how little light there was around the grounds.

Only a low wattage bulb hung above the kitchen door, and the short walkway lamps that marked the path around the building were practically useless. None of the other paths were lit. The mass of trees, bushes, and statues that filled the gardens obscured everything, a fact probably not lost on the killer.

When Giorgio reached the top of the hill, the dim lights from the two cottages were barely visible on the east side of the property. He glanced down to the main building, wondering if the light over the back door had been purposely eliminated the night of the murder. He used an intersecting path to cross over the top of the hillside, moving towards the abbot's cottage. The path wound around a vegetable garden and a sagging shed that resembled Quasimodo in the dark. The foothills just beyond the vegetable garden had been blotted out, as if someone had drawn a black curtain across the vista.

Giorgio stuffed his hands into his pockets. Why was he here? Did he think he would actually learn something relevant to the case, or was he really just avoiding Angie? He stood gazing into the shadows trying to focus on the murder. If the body had been disguised somehow, the killer may have been able to bring it through the lobby and then down the back hallway to the back door without raising questions. That would mean Poindexter could have been telling the truth when he said he saw someone moving along the outside path towards the kitchen.

From the second story window, however, it would have been impossible to identify anything more than a human shadow. In this scenario, the killer would have had to slip past the bartenders twice – once on the way up to Olsen's room and once on the way down. Giorgio couldn't think of any way to disguise a dead body without calling attention to it, yet no one had seen anything suspicious.

The soft thud of a door closing interrupted his thoughts, and he squinted into the mist. A dark shadow flitted across his field of vision. Was this another monk catching a smoke?

A second noise made him snap his head to his right. Emerging from the kitchen, he caught the fleeting glimpse of a second figure heading into the garden. Had he caught two individuals sneaking out at the same time? What were the odds of that?

His peripheral vision picked up the first shadow moving up the hill in the direction of the flower garden.

If the two figures were planning to meet, he wanted to be there when they did. He cut down the hill at a right angle as quietly as possible hoping the music from inside the building would cover his descent.

The ground sloped so sharply that twice he almost met with disaster. He'd just tucked himself safely behind the shrine at the north end of the garden when the soft creak of a gate at the south end made him turn in that direction.

Someone had entered the garden. Before he could move, a shadowy figure appeared from behind a tree to his left, gliding through the bushes in his direction. Giorgio was situated to one side of the shrine, near a gate in the wall. He quickly backed behind a tree. The figure appeared out of the mist and silently disappeared through the gate, his face obscured by a monk's hood.

Giorgio moved to the gate with caution. He was right behind the shrine now and didn't dare go through the gate. There was a large, open lawn just in front of the shrine, which would leave him without cover. Instead, he planted his feet in a small ditch and leaned against the short cement wall while he listened. Harsh whispers reached him from the other side of the shrine, but the music eliminated any hope of decoding what was spoken.

He was just about to chance a closer inspection when the robed figure suddenly reappeared, forcing him to melt into the shadows. The figure stepped through the gate, leaving the path again and striking out through the undergrowth.

Giorgio made a quick decision and fell in behind the retreating figure of the monk, assuming the second individual was one of the caterers. Keeping a safe distance, he followed the monk down the hill. The monk paused at the back door, making Giorgio duck behind the statue of the Virgin Mary. Peeking through her elbow, he could just make out the shoulders of the dark figure. The monk turned in his direction as if listening. A moment later, the monk stepped into the building.

Giorgio followed the monk inside. Although the door had to be fifty years old, the knob turned without sound, a point he'd failed to notice that afternoon.

He slipped inside the empty stairwell shutting out the penetrating mist. Giorgio darted over to the staircase and glanced up the stairs leading to the monks' quarters. He stopped to listen, trying to discern which way the elusive figure might have gone.

There was only silence. He poked his head into the richly carpeted hallway that led to the chapel and then circled back into the stairwell to peer down the back hallway. Neither hallway offered up a retreating figure.

Returning to the back door, he paused, fearing he'd lost his edge. How could someone disappear so quickly? The bell tower began to chime the hour, filling the small enclosure with a jarring clang.

By the time Giorgio detected the soft rustle of cloth behind him, it was too late. Something smashed the back of his skull, sending a searing pain through to his eyeballs. His knees buckled and he collapsed onto the cold cement floor. As darkness invaded his mind, he was only barely aware of a door scraping closed somewhere behind him.

† Chapter Eighteen †

The unearthly shadows of four hooded men circled a splashing fountain like witches circling a simmering brew. A young boy stood off to the side, his face veiled in shadow. Giorgio crouched before the boy, his gun ready to fire, but there were no bullets housed in the chamber. As he shook the gun wondering where the bullets had gone, a guttural wail pierced the darkness, scattering the hooded men like beetles. The horrifying sound trailed off, and the boy's image evaporated.

Suddenly, something wet slid across the back of his hand making him recoil as if a rat had skittered across his skin. He tried to open his eyes, but they were glued shut. Then, a gruff voice said, "Let's get him off the ground." Rough hands pulled him to his feet and moved him forward. All he could do was shuffle helplessly along. Finally, a light appeared through the darkness.

"Put him on the sofa," the same voice said.

Red material swam into view, and his body sagged down. Someone lifted his feet, allowing his head to fall back onto a soft pillow. Something wet slid across his cheek, and he opened one eyelid, flinching when a furry, wet shadow appeared only inches from his face. There was a high-pitched whine and his arm was buffeted as if someone was trying to stuff something underneath it. Eventually someone placed a cool towel under his head, where he felt a painful knot on his scalp.

"How are you feeling?" Father Damian's voice finally cut through the haze of pain.

Giorgio lifted both eyelids this time, but it was a moment before he recognized the monk who peered down at him. A young, anxious monk stood behind him. Grosvenor's head rested under his forearm, leaving patches of drool on his leather jacket.

"Like hell!" Giorgio groused, squinting at the bright light.

The pained expression on the abbot's face made Giorgio rephrase his response.

"Like a building fell on me."

"You need to relax. I'm afraid you've been injured."

Giorgio managed a quizzical look. "I think you mean attacked."

Father Damian exchanged a glance with the other monk, his generous brows scrunched in confusion. "I'm not sure what you mean. Who would attack you?"

Giorgio was beginning to regain full consciousness and lifted himself up, dislodging Grosvenor's head.

"That's what I'd like to know," he choked out, holding his hand to the back of his head. His head was throbbing, making his skull vibrate. "I was hit from behind, by something very hard."

Father Damian's face betrayed his confusion. Giorgio was quick to explain.

"I came to the monastery unannounced tonight. I saw two people meet out in the garden. I followed one of them back to the stairwell and was hit from behind. Whoever it was must have been hiding under the stairs." He gave the monk a wry look. "Did you ever think of putting lights back there?"

Father Damian looked startled. "We...uh...implemented some cost-saving measures last year since none of the monks go out after dark. I use a small flashlight when I go to my quarters."

Giorgio smirked at the absurdity of his comments and swung his legs around to sit up. "Well, you may be accommodating a murderer. Not to mention a number of monks who seem to have private business of their own outside after dark."

"Now, just a minute, Detective...," the abbot erupted, but Giorgio waved him off with one hand, holding the cold compress with the other.

"Forget it. It doesn't matter now. But I must tell you that it was a monk I followed back to the building."

Father Damian's eyes grew wide. "Do you mean to tell me you think...?"

Giorgio cut him off again. "And, it was a monk who hit me on the back of the head."

"That's impossible," the younger monk cut in. "No one here would do that."

"This is Brother Daniel," Father Damian introduced the young man.

Giorgio looked up at the monk he'd only seen briefly the night before. "God moves in mysterious ways, Father."

Giorgio stood up leaning heavily on the arm of the settee. Father Damian reached out a hand to steady him.

"What do you intend to do?"

"Ask a lot of questions. Beginning with -- how did you know I was in the stairwell?"

"The dog," he said bluntly. "He was standing at the back door howling."

Giorgio looked down at Grosvenor's somber brown eyes and wondered for the first time how Grosvenor had escaped from the car. Then he remembered the broken door handle.

"I need to talk with the caterers," Giorgio said.

He walked with halting steps toward the door. Father Daniel hurried to open the door. Still unsteady on his feet, Giorgio headed out of Father Damian's office, leaving the two men to exchange confused looks. When he reached the kitchen, he saw Mary Fields at the far counter packing away food. Grosvenor went and politely sat at her feet, waiting for something to fall his way. Giorgio leaned against the doorjamb.

"You're here late tonight," Giorgio said weakly.

Fields turned. She saw the dog first and looked surprised. When she saw Giorgio's ashen face and the towel held to the back of his head, she came forward.

"Are you all right, Detective? You look awful."

"I've had an accident," he lied, bringing the towel forward. There was a small amount of blood nestled in the center of it. He quickly folded the towel in half. "Maybe you have some ice."

She went to a large stainless steel refrigerator and opened up the freezer compartment.

"I was wondering if either one of your servers are here tonight?" Giorgio asked.

"Yes, both Colin and Peter were here, but they just left," Fields said, returning with some ice. She wrapped it in the towel. "Peter had a date, and Colin had already asked if he could leave early. Why?"

Giorgio grunted. "Did either Peter or Colin go outside tonight?"

114

She looked at him with a perplexed expression. "Actually, I think they both did. Colin almost always goes out for a cigarette. And Peter went to the garden."

"He went to the garden?"

"Like I said, he had a date and wanted to take her some flowers. Is that a problem?"

"I think it was tonight; I just don't know for which one. Tell me, does Colin go out for his cigarette at the same time every night?"

"About the same time, I guess. I never thought about it before."

"It is the same time every night," Nancy interrupted. She had come over from the sink and held a dishtowel in her hand. "I've noticed it." The fluttering in her voice had disappeared. "He always goes out right after the main course has been served. So if it's not the same exact time, it's at the same point in our routine."

Giorgio turned his attention to Mary's partner. "How long is he gone?"

"Maybe five minutes," she replied.

"Does he come back with anything?"

They both stopped to think, then shook their heads.

"No," Mary said. "I don't think so, but he always wears his leather jacket. We've teased him about it because he comes in with his hand stuffed inside his pockets like he's cold, even in warm weather. I don't understand, Detective--are either one of them in some kind of trouble?"

"I'm not sure. No one else came through here in the last half hour?" Both women shook their heads. "What about the bartenders? Were they the same ones as last night?"

"No," Mary was quick to respond. "As I said, I contract for them through another agency. I often get guys I don't know." She peered at him closely, her dark brown eyes softening. "I can get you more ice, Detective."

"No, I'm headed home. Thank you."

Giorgio returned to the main lobby thinking that Anya Peters may have thrown him a red herring by mentioning the bartender with the dark eyes and earring. Grosvenor sauntered after him as he went to Father Damian's office. Father Damian was gone, so Giorgio turned the corner into the main hallway thinking he'd go to the outside bungalow, but stopped when he saw a light in Anya Peter's office. He knocked softly and heard a voice say, "Come in." Ms. Peters was at her desk reviewing some paperwork.

"Working late?" he inquired.

She looked up, her face illuminated by the harsh light of her desk lamp, her demeanor as repellent as always.

"I'm afraid that, with everything that's happened, I've fallen behind."

Grosvenor lumbered over for some attention.

"Is this your dog, Detective?" Her eyes blazed as she pushed her chair away from Grosvenor's long snout.

"Yes. He helped me out of a difficult situation tonight."

"Oh, yes," she said, her eyes riveted on the dog. "Father Damian stopped in."

She seemed to have little sympathy for Giorgio's predicament. Instead, she was preoccupied with Grosvenor, who was sniffing at her ankles. Clearly, she wasn't a dog person.

"He must like your perfume," Giorgio quipped, stepping around the desk. "Grosvenor!" he commanded.

The hound turned his head so quickly one long ear slapped his face. Giorgio took him by the collar and pushed him into the hallway and closed the door.

"You didn't see anything unusual tonight, I suppose?" he said, stepping back into the room.

Anya Peters had drawn her legs back under her desk and attempted to resume her work. She responded to his question without looking up.

"Of course not, Detective. I've been in here, working. Now if you'll excuse me."

It probably wasn't the truth, but Giorgio wasn't up to sparring. He needed to go home and lie down. He said a curt goodnight and made his way to the car where he found the passenger door open. With a sidelong glance at Grosvenor, he helped the dog into the car before getting in himself.

Before turning the key, his eyes drifted up to the big building. Something was obviously going on up there after dark. But how was it all connected? Giorgio believed Olsen had been killed in her own room. Yet, how was she transported to the kitchen closet without being seen? Giorgio had followed a monk into the stairwell tonight and then lost him. Yet he was sure it was the monk who had assaulted him. Why? And where had the monk been hidden? Details. Details.

He sighed and rubbed his eye sockets before starting the car.

"God is in the details," he said under his breath, patting Grosvenor on the head. "And you're a good dog."

Grosvenor merely wagged his tail and licked his hand.

† Chapter Nineteen †

The next morning, Giorgio rolled over and winced at the sharp pain in his head. A cursory examination told him he'd grown a lump the size of a golf ball overnight. When he threw an arm out to his wife, he found only a rumpled pile of cold sheets beside him. Raised voices downstairs reminded him it was Monday, and that Angie would be getting the kids ready for school. Groaning, he hauled himself out of bed and staggered to the shower.

By the time he entered the kitchen, he was thinking that God had a way of healing bad situations. His harrowing experience the night before was sure to evaporate Angie's foul mood. And the physical evidence, namely the lump on his head, would bring out her natural instinct to nurse him back to health. He could almost feel her fingers gently probing his scalp, which woke up other parts of his body. He slumped in the kitchen doorway just waiting for the right moment to tell his story.

The kitchen was alive with activity. Grosvenor sat behind Angie as she busied herself at the counter making lunches. Both children sat at the table having cereal and arguing over which one would sleep with the dog that night. Angie turned from the counter to give Tony his lunch, just as Grosvenor decided to snatch a discarded Cheerio from the floor. Her foot caught under his belly, throwing her forward and catapulting the lunchbox out of her hand. Grosvenor tracked its path as it opened mid-flight, throwing the sandwich and bag of chips against the wall and dropping the apple squarely into his mouth as if it were a well-rehearsed trick. The dog accepted his good luck with grace and removed himself to a corner to enjoy the unexpected snack. The children just sat with their mouths open.

"Oh, that animal!" Angie fumed, steadying herself with a hand on the back of a chair.

Tony looked down with a smile. "Hey, thanks, Grosvenor. Now I don't have to eat it!"

Angie crossed around the table to pick up the sandwich and chips and return them to the lunch box. Then she shoved it across the table to tony with a look even a moron would understand. Tony decided to act.

"I have to get my books, Mom." With a flurry of motion, he was out the door.

"Me, too." Marie disappeared after her brother.

Giorgio and Angie exchanged looks. But as he started to speak, she abruptly turned her back and returned to the counter.

"What do you want for breakfast?" she said over her shoulder.

And a cold shoulder it was. He paused, feeling he'd just dropped a line on center stage.

"Just toast and coffee. You okay?"

"I'm fine," she replied flatly.

She opened the bread bag and slipped a piece of wheat bread into the toaster. He went to pour his own coffee, watching her from the corner of his eye.

"Angie," he started, "what's the matter? I mean…really the matter?" When she didn't answer, he continued. "I guess it's the dog, isn't it? You said you'd like another one."

She slammed a cupboard door, making him reach for the sore spot on his head in a weird act of self-defense.

"I never said I wanted another dog! YOU wanted another dog."

He felt warmth rise to his cheeks and that certain part of his body went right back to sleep. There would be no sweet reconciliation this morning.

"You said you missed Butch."

She turned on him, her normally soft brown eyes ablaze. "I said I missed him, like I might miss an itch I couldn't scratch. That doesn't mean I wanted another dog. This is just another juvenile attempt by you to divert attention from the real issue."

"What do you mean? I got the damn dog for *you!*"

"Well, then, take it back! I don't want the smelly thing."

The toast popped up, and she turned and caught it as deftly as if it was merely another well-rehearsed trick in her side show. With a swift movement, she smeared butter across it and threw it onto a small plate, dumping the whole thing unceremoniously onto the table in front of him.

He realized he was walking on thin ice and decided to tone it down.

"Angie," he pleaded, "I can't take him back. The kids love him."

She tossed the butter knife into the sink and wiped her hands on a towel. "You knew what their reaction would be, but if you think that dog makes up for the fact you don't want this baby, you're more clueless than I thought." With that, she stormed from the kitchen.

Grosvenor watched her depart, drool spilling over his lower lip. He lumbered over to where Giorgio slumped against the counter and dropped his head back to look up at his new owner. Giorgio stared back knowing he couldn't return Grosvenor to the pound. His whole demeanor had changed overnight. He fit the family like a glove. Now, if Giorgio could only make Angie see that. For the umpteen-millionth time, he'd blown it, and didn't know why.

Rolling thunder alerted him the kids were coming back downstairs, so he grabbed the toast and coffee and went into the entryway. Angie was putting on her coat as the kids donned theirs.

"Aren't they going to take the bus?"

"It's supposed to rain again."

She opened the door to a gray sky, and the kids tumbled outside, backpacks in hand. Angie grabbed her purse from a small table and started after them.

"Angie," he stopped her, "what about Grosvenor?"

She turned and gave him a cold stare. "Take him with you."

"I have to work."

"They have police dogs in the department, don't they? I won't have him in the house while we're gone. I have no idea if he's trained to do anything but catch fruit."

She turned and went down the steps, leaving Giorgio and the dog staring after her like two little children left behind at the bus stop.

"Oh, brother," Giorgio said with a sigh. "I'm really in trouble this time."

He looked down at Grosvenor who stood with his front feet splayed in a clown stance, his long snout turned in Giorgio's direction, clearly confused by everyone's departure.

"Sorry, old boy, I'm afraid you're stuck with me today."

Giorgio returned to the kitchen to dispense with his meager breakfast and read the morning paper.

The murder had happened too late Saturday night for the Sunday edition, but today the story of Olson's murder was front page news. While the report was sketchy, there was enough information to paint a grim picture of a young woman strangled at the monastery during a writers' conference.

He finished his toast and went to turn on the television. One of the cable stations had just begun their report on the grisly murder of a young woman at a Catholic monastery in a small town in California. The reporter went on to speculate about whether this was a random killing by a deranged individual or something much closer to home. After all, the newsman said with a raised eyebrow, why would the killer take the victim's little finger?

Giorgio hated reporters. How had this idiot found out about Olsen's severed finger? Giorgio had been hoping they could keep that little bit of information from the media a while longer. When he'd been shot in New York, the media had distorted the entire situation, making it sound as if he'd stumbled onto Anthony Cordova's hiding place by mistake and taken a round to the chest as a result of his own carelessness.

In fact, he and his partner, Ben Attner, had gone to the warehouse on a tip, with backup on the way. But they'd arrived only moments after the weapons buy had taken place and Cordova and two of his henchmen were just coming out of the building. Bullets started flying, pinning Giorgio and Ben down on either side of their car. The bullet that hit Giorgio entered the left side of his chest, crushing a rib and puncturing his lung. Ben wasn't so lucky. While no one had ever accused Giorgio of getting his partner killed, the implication was present in the eyes of every reporter that covered the story.

He looked down at the newspaper in his hands. A small picture of Olsen accompanied the short article. There was no mention of a missing finger or Giorgio as the lead investigator. Giorgio decided that Max Dougherty, the department's public affairs officer, had done a credible job. Now he had to go do his.

It was eight o'clock when they arrived at the police station. Stares and chuckles followed them down the wide hallway that led to the office he shared with Swan. Swan took one look at the dog following close on Giorgio's heels and pushed his chair back to slap his leg. Grosvenor lumbered over, lowering his head submissively.

"Great dog, Joe. Where'd you get him?"

"Humane Society. I thought it would be a nice surprise for Angie." All the confidence he'd showed Rocky earlier about buying the dog had disappeared.

Swan looked over at his troubled friend. "I take it the dog wasn't such a nice surprise."

"That's an understatement. I think the only thing she hates right now more than that dog, is me." He pulled his face into a wry grin and sat down at his desk.

The small office they shared was painted a faded pea green and held two old, chunky wooden desks, a bank of dented metal file cabinets, and a water cooler that appeared to have been created around the dawn of time. An old framed map of the city was mounted on one wall. File folders and papers were stacked everywhere, and the only clean surface was a small Formica table set in between the windows. On it was a carved mahogany chess set in play. Swan was always in the middle of a challenge, sometimes with the Captain, sometimes with someone in another city.

"My wife and I used to raise Bassets," he said, holding the dog's noble head in his hands. "He's got good breeding." He pulled the ears forward and noticed the injuries. "What happened here?"

"He was abused. Somebody just dumped him. The Humane Society was ready to put him down."

"Tragic." Swan stroked the dog's back, careful to avoid the burn marks. "Do you know how old he is?"

"No. Although I think he's young."

Swan looked him over from the heavy head to the short, wrinkled back feet. Grosvenor allowed the evaluation with a polite wag of his tail.

"I'd say he's between two and three years old. Probably not much more than that." Swan stroked the velvet-soft ears and Grosvenor groaned in ecstasy, the heavy folds of his throat twitching with pleasure. "He's a beautiful dog, but somebody really did a number on him."

The officer ran his fingers across Grosvenor's back in an expert fashion. Most of the scabs had come off during the bath, leaving small pink marks in their place and a shiny, healthy multi-colored coat.

"These will heal all right. He'll be just fine."

Swan patted Grosvenor on the head and dropped his ears back in place. Grosvenor pushed up against his leg hoping for more attention.

"They're very clever dogs, you know. You ought to train him if he isn't already. They make great hunting dogs. In fact they were bred with those short legs so that hunters could follow them easily in the field."

"I just hope Angie lets me keep him."

"Sounds to me like you may be the one in the dog house," Swan chuckled.

Giorgio ignored the comment while he flipped through things on his desk. He picked up a copy of the coroner's report when Grosvenor came to lie at his feet.

"How's your head?" Swan inquired. "I heard about last night."

Giorgio looked up, reaching for his scalp. "I won't be playing soccer any day soon."

"Any clue who hit you?"

"I followed a monk into the garden where he rendezvoused with someone from the kitchen. When I followed the monk back inside, he caught me from behind."

"Were they both monks?"

"I don't think so. It was some sort of planned meeting, though. I just don't know what for. I think the person from the kitchen may have been one of the caterers."

"Could have been Colin Jewett."

"Why do you say that?"

"We ran backgrounds on the entire staff. Something Ms. Fields may want to do in the future," he added smugly. "Colin Jewett has a record for drug trafficking."

"Really?" For Giorgio, two and two had just added up to make four.

"According to McCready's notes, Fields said last night that she hired him because he's the relative of a friend. That's probably why she didn't run a check."

"We need to have a talk with Mr. Jewett, but we also need to talk with her other caterer, a guy named Peter. He was outside last night, too."

"I'll get somebody on it."

Giorgio scanned the coroner's report until the phone rang.

"Detective Salvatori?" a female voice said at the other end.

"Right. Who's this?"

"I'm Rebecca Browning from KBTV. I'd like to get a statement."

Giorgio winced. "Sorry. I don't have anything to say. You'll have to talk with our Public Affairs guy."

"I've already spoken to him, Detective. I need to speak with you."

"Look, I really don't have time. I have a murder to solve. Give Max a call." And with that, he hung up.

Swan rolled his eyes. "Well, that's the way to make friends with the media."

"I really don't have anything to say. I mean what am I gunna say? We don't know who the killer is, or if he'll kill again."

"Point made," Swan acquiesced with a shrug.

"Okay, tell me more about what the coroner said."

Swan leaned forward, resting his arms on the desk. "Olsen hadn't eaten since lunch, and there was a fair amount of alcohol in her system, along with the chloral hydrate."

Giorgio continued to read the report as he talked. "But it seems there was more alcohol in her system than what was missing from the wine bottle in her room." His eyes narrowed as if he were trying to make a calculation.

"Maybe she had a drink at the bar before she went upstairs," Swan offered.

"Perhaps. But maybe her visitor brought a bottle of something with him. She could have had a drink before he arrived. That was the glass we found in her room. Then the friend brought his own bubbly with the drug."

"But where's that bottle, or the glass?" Swan challenged him with a raised eyebrow.

Giorgio shrugged his shoulders. "I don't know. Maybe he took it with him."

"How? If your theory is correct, he killed her in the room and then carried her down the stairs to the kitchen closet. He couldn't have carried a bottle of wine, too.

"Maybe not," Giorgio said to himself. "Do we have the lab results back from the bottle in her room?"

"Not yet."

"Hmmm," he contemplated. "If he drugged her first, that would account for the lack of a struggle. The question is, how did he administer the drug?"

"Hey, Joe, glad you're here," Maxwell said, coming into the room with a fax in hand. "The coroner vacuumed Olsen's body and clothing this morning and found coarse, gray fibers on her dress and in her hair. Hey," he interrupted himself, "where'd the dog come from?"

"Joe has a new partner." Swan smiled broadly, enjoying the joke.

"My aunt used to have a Basset." Maxwell handed the fax to Giorgio and walked over to stoop down to pet Grosvenor, his protruding stomach stretching the limits of his shirt. "You don't have a pool do you, Joe?"

Giorgio was busy reading the report. "Hunh? No. Why?"

"They don't swim too good. Too heavy in the front end or something. I mean, look at that schnoz. It's a dog built around a nose," he chortled. "My aunt used to put a life jacket on her dog whenever they went boating. Looked pretty stupid, but I guess he fell in once and almost drowned."

Giorgio looked at him with a blank expression wondering why everyone suddenly seemed to have a story about Basset Hounds. He returned to the report.

"Looks like the killer wrapped Olsen in something. Maybe a blanket or a rug," he said.

"You mean the fibers?"

Swan was sitting at his desk kneading the palm of his hand and wincing as he spoke. As Swan dug the knuckle of one hand into the other, his expression seemed to vacillate between pain and pleasure.

Giorgio dropped the report to watch his partner. "Why do you do that?"

He had watched Swan manipulate his hands like that almost daily for four years, never knowing why. For some reason, now he wanted to know.

"Ever heard of reflexology?" Swan asked, shaking his hand out. "The muscles in your hands and feet are related to the muscles in your back." He got up and went around to Giorgio's desk. "Here, give me your hand."

Giorgio backed away, but Swan grabbed his right hand and pressed the knuckle of his index finger deep into the thick muscles that made up the heel of Giorgio's palm. Giorgio almost came out of his chair.

"Ow!" He cried, yanking his hand away. Swan and Maxwell just laughed.

"See? It works," Swan smiled.

"What works? That hurt like hell!" he snapped, rubbing his hand.

"Yeah, but if you kept it up, your back would feel great," Swan smiled.

"There's nothing wrong with my back! It's my head that hurts."

"Well, I don't think it will help that," Swan shook his head.

"Keep your hands to yourself."

Giorgio gave Swan a wary look as if he thought Swan might grab his hand and try it again, but Swan merely wandered nonchalantly back to his desk, chuckling.

"We have a murder investigation to conduct." Giorgio eyed Maxwell who quickly suppressed a smile. Giorgio glanced back at the report hoping to change the subject. "A blanket was probably used to carry our victim down to the supply closet. Get forensics on it." He said this to Maxwell, slapping the paper onto the desk a little more loudly than necessary. "And what about fingerprints?"

The young officer was rubbing Grosvenor's neck. "We found ten or twelve different prints in the closet."

"Have you identified any of them yet?"

"McCready put them through AFIS this morning." The cop stood and opened a folder he was carrying. "From our current cast of characters, we have Father Damian, Father Daniels, Father Rosario, Father Julio, Mary Fields, and the janitor. The other prints were either unidentified or came from people who no longer live on the premises."

"Check them out anyway. I wonder why Mary Fields' prints were in there."

"I think the bigger question is," interrupted Swan, "why *wouldn't* they be in there? Remember, she caters there. She could have gone back at any time looking for extra napkins or something."

Giorgio sat back. "That's probably true for almost anyone at the monastery. It would only get interesting if we found a print from one of the conference guests. We need to fingerprint everyone and then get to work on those fibers."

"I'm on it."

Maxwell gave a mock salute and patted Grosvenor once more before leaving. Giorgio looked at Swan.

"Now all we have to do is find something up there made from coarse, gray fibers."

Swan clasped the fingers of his two hands together and turned them inside out, cracking his knuckles. The sound gave Giorgio the shivers, but this time he said nothing.

† Chapter Twenty †

It was almost ten o'clock that morning when Giorgio passed through the monastery gates, guarded now by a police cruiser. They'd already turned away the construction crew that had returned to work on the bell tower, and the news vans were all lined up outside the gate attempting to interview anyone who ventured within striking distance.

Giorgio parked up near the building, letting Grosvenor out before slamming the door. The sky was a blank, gray canvas and visibility extended to only the first quarter mile of homes in the valley. The iron monk, so eerily real the night of the murder, stood calmly in the drab morning light. In fact, the entire building appeared docile now that the storm had passed. Even Giorgio's attack from the night before seemed in the distant past, though he was conscious of the dull ache in his head.

Two monks trimmed nearby bushes, while a third raked leaves just outside the cemetery. Giorgio had decided to walk a full circuit of the property this time, convinced either the grounds or the building itself held the key he was looking for. When a light breeze billowed through the trees carrying the promise of another rainstorm, he zipped up his jacket and stuffed his hands into his pockets, thinking he'd better hurry.

He skirted the corner of the building and glanced over to where a flagstone path curved down a grassy slope to a small pond encircled by a short brick wall. A rose garden was set off to the side, the last blooms having already been clipped in preparation for the oncoming winter months.

The lawn was edged carefully around the perimeter of the pond and walkways were swept clean, leaving no sign of the previous storm.

Giorgio knew the Benedictine monks lived on a timetable divided into three distinct time periods: liturgical prayer, spiritual reading, and manual labor. It was obvious from the pristine nature of the grounds that a good portion of their time was spent doing yard work.

A western-style pole fence separated the formal monastery grounds from the untilled fields below; the fence ran from Sunnyside Drive to a bank of aspen trees that marked the east property line a football field away. There were a couple of dilapidated barns just in front of the aspens. Giorgio decided he would have one of the other officers do a thorough search of those, just in case. Instead, he set out to explore the backside of the property, hoping to discover how the murderer had invisibly deposited Mallery Olsen in the kitchen supply closet.

He crossed to the east side of the monastery. In between the refectory and the bakery was a storm cellar with heavy plywood doors. He pulled one door open and descended halfway down a set of steps. The cellar was similar to the one he'd grown up with back in New York, just a square box with a hard packed dirt floor. This one held large canisters of lard, grain, and spices, with steel bins on the floor marked for flour and sugar.

Giorgio remembered the storm cellar he'd grown up with had been dark and dank, filled with spiders and other creepy crawly things. In one particularly wicked moment, he had locked a scrawny neighbor boy inside while he and Rocky sat outside and laughed. The boy grew up to be a judge, and Giorgio always silently wondered if becoming a judge was his way of turning the tables on the bullies in his life. Fortunately, Giorgio had never had to testify in his court to find out.

Since there was no door linking the cellar to the main building, Giorgio backed out and turned toward the cemetery, where a young monk raked leaves from around a large oak tree. Several plastic bags filled with debris sat next to him.

The monk introduced himself as Father Francis, and Giorgio remembered he was one of the new recruits. Dressed in a long brown robe and black rubber boots, the young monk appeared to be in his mid-twenties. He had blonde hair, dark eyes, and an easy manner. Giorgio paused to talk with him while Grosvenor took the opportunity to lift his leg on one of the leaf bags. Giorgio grimaced.

"It was a terrible thing, Detective," the monk said, stopping to lean on the rake. "I hope you'll have more luck today with your investigation. Father Joseph said we've already lost some bookings, so I hope you'll be able to finish up soon."

"We can't be finished until we've found the murderer."

"Of course," the young monk said with an apologetic nod. "Is that why you're back here today, Detective? Are you hoping the murderer will return to the scene of the crime, just like in the novels?"

"My guess is the murderer never left."

The dark eyes flashed in mild surprise. "You think it's one of us, then?"

"Not necessarily. But it was someone here that night and most likely they were here the next day as well."

"I see."

Father Francis had a swarthy complexion and strong hands with thick fingers and calluses. The fingernails showed dirt in the crevices, a result of working outside for long periods of time. Giorgio thought about the difficult life the monks led as he watched the young man lean over to pull a twig from the pile of leaves.

"I was never very good at puzzles," he continued amiably. "I admire your ability to sort all this out. Even in Jesuit school I had trouble with, what did they call it, cognitive thinking." He used the rake to shape the loose pile into a neat dome as he spoke. "I'm better at supplication I suppose."

"You enjoy being a monk, then?"

He turned to look at Giorgio, his whole face aglow. "I do. It's given me a purpose, a reason to get up each day, to serve God."

"Where did you grow up?" Giorgio asked, feeling the need to change the subject.

"San Francisco. I love it there. There's nothing quite as beautiful as the San Francisco Bay on a clear day. Then there's the culture and, of course, the diversity. You can be whoever you want to be there, no questions asked."

Giorgio wasn't sure what he meant and remained silent. Father Francis must have misinterpreted his silence, because he was quick to clarify his comment.

"I know what you're probably thinking," he said, his face flushing slightly. "People think all priests must be gay, or that we hate women. That's not me. That's not even true."

The misunderstanding had opened a floodgate, and Father Francis was now a bundle of nervous energy.

"I like women a lot and I've dated more than my share," he said, trying to strike a masculine pose.

Giorgio chuckled inside, thinking he'd either just exposed a latent homosexual or a kid with an ego problem.

"Did your parents encourage you to go into the church?" he asked, thinking of his mother and trying to change the subject again.

The young man's face grew dark and he leaned on the rake again, all bravado gone. "Both my parents are gone."

Grosvenor sauntered up, sniffing the ground as he came and stepping on his ears every few feet. Father Francis finally acknowledged the dog.

"I see you have a friend today."

He leaned over and invited Grosvenor to approach. Grosvenor responded with his head lowered almost to the ground. Francis knelt down and drew his hand across the dog's broad head in a friendly gesture, alleviating Grosvenor's shyness.

"A friend of mine in college had a Basset. She had to leave him on her small patio when she went to classes. That dog howled from the moment she left until the moment she got home. She was kicked out of two different apartments and finally had to get rid of him." He chuckled. "She swore that dog was smarter than most people though."

Giorgio was beginning to wonder if just about everybody had owned a Basset at one time or another.

"He's a new addition to the family," he replied. "We're just getting to know each other."

The monk patted Grosvenor on the back and lifted the rake again. "Well, I must get back to work."

"Before you do, maybe you could answer a few more questions. Does Father Damian always lead the nine o'clock prayer?"

"Yes, unless he's sick or otherwise detained."

"Does he usually arrive on time?"

"He's very punctual. Is there a problem with Father Damian, Detective?"

"I'm just trying to establish some timelines. Do you know what time he arrived the night of the murder?"

"Actually, as I told the officer who interviewed me, I was a little late that night myself. I got caught up writing some letters. I arrived just before Father Damian."

"When was that?"

"A few minutes after nine, I guess. He came in and told us about the body being found. He called for Brother Joseph and asked all of us to stay there. I believe the police had already been called. Brother Joseph led a short service to offer a prayer for the young woman."

It was the first time he'd heard any of the monks express concern for Mallery Olsen. Giorgio stroked his chin. "Was anyone else late or absent?"

"Only Father O'Leary. He was taken ill right after the evening meal. I'm afraid he's still not feeling well."

A damp breeze brushed against Giorgio's cheek. He'd have to hurry if he was going to finish his inspection before it rained.

"Well, thank you, Father Francis. I'll let you get back to your leaves."

"We're all here to help in any way we can."

Giorgio called Grosvenor and the dog followed, ears swaying back and forth. They passed the cemetery, moving slowly so that Grosvenor could stop every few feet to mark his territory. Giorgio had trained with a few police dogs and knew that the canine's sense of smell was some five hundred times stronger than humans. Dogs gather all sorts of information by sniffing what other dogs leave behind. Giorgio estimated that Grosvenor was gathering enough information to write a short novel on the grounds of the monastery.

Giorgio glanced over the fence to the graveyard, reading some of the inscriptions on the gravestones. At the far end was an imposing marble statue of an angel with her wings pulled back and her head lowered, as if gazing at the ground. She appeared to stand guard over the gravestones. Directly in front of him, near the fence, was a grave marker carved out of a heavy block of granite with a perfectly polished round ball on top. The inscription read, "Father Anton Wingate – Lost, But Not Forgotten." It was a curious sentiment, especially for a priest.

Giorgio left the cemetery and passed the corner of the building looking up at the windows and taking note of their proximity to each other, all the while thinking about stairways and back doors.

He strolled through the circular courtyard and climbed the hill past the abbot's cottage, then crossed over to the tool shed and the vegetable garden.

The shed's windows were almost opaque with dirt. He pulled the creaking door open and stepped inside, leaving Grosvenor to sniff his way around the garden. Inside, Giorgio found nothing more than an old push lawn mower, some weathered rakes, hoes, garden tools, and bags of fertilizer. He sifted through some shelves against the wall, lifting a layer of dust that made him sneeze. He decided there was nothing here related to the murder and emerged from the shed into a light drizzle, cursing at being caught without an umbrella.

Wiping the moisture from his face, he called for Grosvenor, but the dog was nowhere to be found. Giorgio whistled just as the skies opened up and it began to pour. He strode into the vegetable garden, angry now that the dog had strayed. He found Grosvenor at the end of a cornrow, nose to the ground, digging a hole in the quickly forming mud.

Giorgio shouted a command, but the dog's short, stubby legs worked like earthmovers, pulling up mounds of dirt while his ears hung into the ever-deepening hole. He looked up once and was hardly recognizable as the same dog. Although he looked more comical than ever, Giorgio was not amused and moved over to take hold of his collar.

"Grosvenor!" he yelled, "let's go!"

Giorgio yanked on Grosvenor's collar just as the dog's paw snagged on something, bringing it out of the dirt. Giorgio froze, holding the dog mid-air, his eyes locked on a single muddy finger casually curled up in the dreary morning light like the last shrimp on the barbee. The appendage was adorned with a blue class ring.

Giorgio pushed Grosvenor aside and squatted down, scooping out handfuls of mud, releasing several more fingers, a man's wristwatch, and shirt cuff. Grosvenor whined at having lost his prize, while Giorgio pulled out his cell phone to report what was probably a second murder on the grounds of the Catholic monastery. Then he sat back on his heels and glanced over at the dog. For the second time in two days, he said, "Good boy, Grosvenor."

† Chapter Twenty-One †

By the time a tent was erected, the ground had disintegrated into a sloppy mess, eliminating any possibility of footprints. Rain-filled pockets glistened in the mid-day light, creating small, muddy swimming pools. The police worked quickly in their slickers and rubber boots to section off the entire area with yellow tape, while Mulhaney moved around the site in a cellophane-covered hat, snapping pictures from every angle. Giorgio directed the operation, sans rain gear, looking very much like he'd just climbed out of a swimming pool fully clothed. Off duty officers had been called in to intercept anyone, especially reporters, who wished to get a closer look by sneaking through neighboring homes. Giorgio had no illusions this time that he would be able to avoid the media.

Father Damian stood by protected by a golf-sized umbrella Father Rosario held above his head, his face a bland mask of self-defeat. Several other monks, including all three young recruits, huddled a few feet away under a bank of trees. Grosvenor had retreated quietly to the tool shed.

While several officers combed the area for evidence, two more used shovels to carefully remove dirt from around the body. A shirt cuff and sweater sleeve emerged first, then an arm resting on the hip of the corpse.

Eventually, a dark-haired young man dressed in black slacks and a black sweater was revealed lying on his side only inches beneath the surface, his head twisted to one side as if he had been tossed carelessly into the makeshift grave.

Although rigor mortis wasn't evident, Giorgio knew from long experience that about thirty-six hours after death, rigor mortis reverses itself relaxing the muscles. That and the reddish-green color of the skin gave him the eerie feeling he was looking at a man who had died the same night as Mallery Olsen.

It was the dirt-stained blood caked to the side of the man's head however, that confirmed he was looking at a second murder.

Before the body could be removed, the coroner stepped in to examine the position and condition of the body. He recorded the air temperature and time of day and then extracted samples of dirt from around the corpse, checking for any insects already living on the body that might help determine the time of death. More pictures were taken, and thirty minutes later the body was loaded into the coroner's van.

Several officers continued to search the surrounding area, dividing it into grids. They pushed their way through bushes and looked under benches and in between the rows of corn. They even worked their way out a hundred feet into the underbrush. Anything found was photographed and bagged and the spot marked with a small colored flag. Giorgio had worked crime scenes with so many evidence markers they'd created a maze, difficult to negotiate without squashing one into the ground.

It was clear this body hadn't been in the grave long, and hope remained that clues could be found when the weather cleared. However, after almost four hours, the only evidence collected was an old shoe from behind the shed, a torn cover from a girlie magazine, and a half-smoked cigarette found near the burial site. The paper casing from the cigarette bore half of a capital "M." Finally, an officer was assigned to stand guard while the rest of the police entourage returned to the station. Giorgio was left to wander the crime scene alone. It was three o'clock.

Giorgio sent Grosvenor back to the station with McCready. After a cursory turn around the perimeter of the gravesite, he walked the length of the upper hillside, studying the characteristics of what he could see of the main building. Something about this building bothered him.

It was a typical Spanish design with a red-tiled roof that overhung the walls by at least two feet and a tower that extended upwards in three ornate tiers heavily supported by large masonry buttresses. The middle tier of the tower had an arched window on each wall that revealed a small hanging bell. The top level had no openings along the north side, but Giorgio had seen three arched windows along the front of the building. The roof was domed and accented with a cupola crowned with a cross and decorated with broad bands of etched stone. Cornices rimmed all three sections.

Giorgio moved off the hillside down to the path that extended along the backside of the building, mentally counting windows and imagining what lay behind them. He passed the monks' quarters and stopped at the window he believed stood at the top of the main staircase in the conference center.

Something didn't add up. Unless Mallery Olsen left her room at some point and was killed outside, she had to have been killed in her room. That complicated everything because no one could have gotten her down the staircase without being seen. And while someone from the conference could have slipped upstairs to her room unnoticed, a monk going upstairs would have stood out to the bartenders unless he was dressed in street clothes.

And what about this second murder? Whoever the young man was buried in the garden, anyone could have arranged to meet him outside during the dinner, including a monk. And did his murder have anything to do with Olsen's?

Giorgio stood contemplating all of this when a creepy-crawly feeling began to inch its way across his shoulders. He came to attention and looked around thinking someone must have come outside again. But there was no one around. Giorgio looked up the hill, but the officer guarding the muddy hole stood with his back to Giorgio. Giorgio looked toward the kitchen, but there was no one visible there, either. Was he being watched? He'd had the same feeling once at the scene of a shooting when the shooter had been standing only a few feet behind him in a crowd of onlookers.

On a hunch, he turned back to the second floor window at the head of the stairs.

An overhanging tree threw a shadow across the window, yet a faint image was barely visible behind the glass. He squinted, straining to make it out. Suddenly, a chill jolted its way down his spine. It was the boy staring at him, his white shirt and black suspenders dimly outlined in the window. The youth raised his hand to point a finger in Giorgio's direction, turning the creepy-crawly feeling into a full-blown shiver.

Giorgio turned and broke into a run, bursting through the kitchen door and sprinting down the hallway into the main lobby. Adrenalin surged through his veins as he took the stairs two at a time, sliding to a halt at the top of the landing for the second time in only a few days. But the boy was gone, leaving only a cold hallway behind.

Giorgio threw open doors on either side of the landing this time to make quick searches of the rooms, but he was left standing disoriented in the hallway feeling a chill pass to the core of his spine. What was going on? Was he seeing a ghost or just letting his imagination get the best of him? Not one person had mentioned the presence of a young boy on the premises, and yet he'd seen the same boy twice. Returning to the landing, he turned to the window where the boy had appeared. Why had the boy pointed at him?

His eyes scanned the path below and then moved out into the flowerbeds and the area around the statues. Maybe the boy wasn't pointing at him, but at something else. Giorgio surveyed the area inch by inch, quadrant by quadrant. When he found something that didn't look as if it belonged there, something that looked manmade, he paused, focusing on that spot. Slowly, an image began to emerge. Lying in between the raised roots of a large tree was a dark object about fifteen inches long.

He hurried down the stairs and returned to the area just below the window. The rain had stopped and he stepped off the path, climbing through low-growing shrubs to a small rise where a tree arched over a bank of prickly bushes. With his hands stuffed into his pockets to protect them, he pushed his way through the snagging foliage to a bare spot only visible from above. Tucked into a crevice made by two gnarly tree roots lay the object he sought. Pulling out his handkerchief, he reached out and lifted up a wine bottle labeled, "Crystal Moon Chardonnay."

Giorgio studied the bottle wondering if this was a clue or just a piece of trash. A quick glance to the window gave him the answer he was looking for. The boy was back. Giorgio held up the bottle and a moment later the boy nodded and vanished.

† Chapter Twenty-Two †

By four o'clock that afternoon the second body had been identified as Jeff Dorman, a young man who had attended the conference but left before the banquet. None of the conference organizers knew anything about him. The preliminary report showed he was killed by a forceful blow to the side of the head. Time of death had not yet been established. Officer Maxwell had volunteered to stand in on the autopsy so Giorgio could go home and change into dry clothes.

He came back wearing a Yankee baseball jacket and cap and was greeted by a small crowd of press people milling about the rear entrance. He was forced to make a brief statement, saying there would be a press conference later that afternoon. While this didn't wholly satisfy anyone, it kept the throng at bay long enough for him to slip inside.

Giorgio had missed lunch, so he stopped at the vending machine for a Coke and a bag of corn nuts. Angie hadn't been home when he'd gone back to change, which was a good thing. He could stand down a killer but didn't stand a chance with Angie. Swan was at his desk when Giorgio entered, his back arched and his head thrown backwards. The big cop let out a groan as his muscles stretched.

"Want some ibuprofen, or maybe a rack?" Giorgio inquired, not even trying to hide his cynicism.

"Naw," Swan said, straightening up. "I just need to start stretching again." He gestured to Grosvenor who was watching Giorgio popcorn nuts into his mouth. "He's turning into a first-class police dog, don't you think?"

Giorgio looked down at the dog and tossed him a corn nut. "I guess," he replied without conviction. "It was probably just dumb luck."

"I wouldn't say that. Bassets have an extraordinary sense of smell." Swan lifted his arms above his head as if reaching for the ceiling. "That's what those long ears are for, you know. They were developed to stir up and hold the scent." Swan's voice squeezed out as he stretched upwards. "Same thing for all those folds in his skin. The folds trap the scent. I wouldn't count him out. He was bred to hunt small game."

"So finding a corpse is the same as finding small game?" Giorgio crunched on a nut.

Swan chortled as he lowered both arms. "No, but he knew what he was digging for."

"He could just be a digger," Giorgio replied, taking a swig of coffee. "Some dogs are, you know."

"I doubt it," Swan said leaning over to touch the floor. "He could've dug anywhere in that garden, but he went to the very spot where a body was buried." He bounced once or twice, touching the floor and then straightened up, shaking out his shoulders. "You know about cadaver dogs don't you? They can find a dead body underwater." Swan gave Giorgio an authoritative look, as if he was selling Grosvenor's attributes short. "I think you've got a bloodhound on your hands. They are part of the hound family, you know?"

Giorgio still looked unconvinced; he flipped another nut in the air. Grosvenor snapped it up. "Well, I don't think it will make much difference to Angie."

"I take it she still doesn't like him."

Giorgio took his jacket off and draped it over the back of his chair. "Let's just say the jury is still out on that one."

Swan took the hint and sat at his own desk. "So, what do we do next?"

"If the Captain is back, I think we need to talk about meeting with the press."

"How much are you willing to tell them?"

"Maybe it's time to tell them everything. I noticed a CNN truck out there. If we don't tell them what we know, they'll find out anyway, and we'll look like we're hiding something. Can you watch Grosvenor? I'll be back in a few." He stood up and threw the last few corn nuts into his mouth before heading down the hall to the Captain's office.

Forty-five minutes later, Giorgio stood on the front steps of the police department with ten or twelve microphones stuck in his face. The small brunette was front and center. Eventually, all reasonable questions were answered and he cut it off with the traditional, "That's all for now," and went back inside. Swan met him in the hallway.

"How'd it go?"

"We'll find out on the six o'clock news. I just wish I knew how they found out about the finger. That's all they kept asking about." He threw a suspicious glance at Swan, who threw up his hands.

"Don't look at me. There were a dozen officers there that night." He turned and followed Giorgio back to their office. "Pretty hard to keep something like that a secret."

"Okay, let's start putting this puzzle together. I want to find out what was in that second bottle of wine I found." He avoided saying anything about the boy. No need to get the entire department talking about ghosts. "Get McCready and let's meet in the conference room."

The lights flickered on in the conference room as Giorgio entered with another can of pop in hand. The chipped, gray walls were covered by an old chalkboard, a large map of the county, and several corkboards. Two large file cabinets sat in the corner. The linoleum floor was scuffed and dirty, and a metal wastebasket sat in the corner overflowing with coffee cups and candy wrappers. A long tabled filled the center of the room surrounded by metal chairs.

McCready had already tacked up individual profiles of every conference guest on blue 3x5 cards, along with Polaroid photos taken the night of the murder. Information on the monks had been transferred to yellow cards. They filled one whole side of the largest bulletin board. Photos of the crime scene were tacked onto the smaller board, and a general layout of the monastery grounds was sketched onto the chalkboard, highlighting the front, side, and rear entrances. Giorgio was studying the information when Swan returned with McCready. Grosvenor plopped down on the floor near the file cabinets with a heavy sigh, fluttering his lips like the bellows of an old fashioned accordion.

"Okay," Giorgio started, "let's go over what we have. According to Anya Peters, Dorman left the conference right after the last session on Saturday. That would have been around five-fifteen. No one reported seeing him at the dinner. And we know Mallery Olsen was killed between four o'clock in the afternoon and nine o'clock that evening. So let's try to establish opportunity for our list of suspects." Giorgio circled the table and began pacing back and forth on the far side, the can of soda in his hand. "Father Damian was late to the night prayer. The janitor found him outside his office when he went to report the body."

"Do we know what he was doing?" Swan sat with his feet propped on the table. He had pulled out nail clippers and was concentrating on the little finger of his left hand.

"I'm pretty sure he was with Anya Peters," Giorgio replied.

Both men raised their eyebrows but reserved comment.

"According to him," Giorgio continued, "the two parted company around seven, and we don't know where either one of them was for a while after that. That would have given either one of them the opportunity to commit the murder."

"Which one?" McCready's question stopped Giorgio mid-stride.

"Which what?"

"Which murder?"

Giorgio sighed. "That's right. We have two murders and no idea if they're related. Let's keep going. John Marsh was absent from the dinner for at least a few minutes when he went to use the restroom behind the kitchen."

"And Colin Jewett left the kitchen for a cigarette break around eight o'clock," McCready added. "The problem is that no one remembers when either of them returned."

Giorgio approached the bulletin board, studying the cards. "So at least four people had opportunity: Father Damian, Anya Peters, John Marsh, and Colin Jewett."

"The questions seem to be whether the two murders were committed at the same time, by the same people, and for the same reason?" Swan added.

"You know we're ignoring one whole group of people."

McCready stood off to one side as if giving Giorgio ample space to think out loud. "Any one of the monks could have committed these crimes, especially if the coroner places Dorman's death before nine o'clock." He approached the wall of cards. "There are at least ten or twelve of them that reported being alone at some point early in the evening."

"Is there any way to know if a monk didn't have an alibi?" Giorgio watched McCready scan the cards.

McCready pulled several off the board.

"Okay," Giorgio said counting them. "We have four with no alibi." Giorgio looked at McCready. "I understand a Father O'Leary took a walk that night."

"That's right!" McCready went back to the board. "Father O'Leary said he took a walk about seven o'clock."

"Isn't he the one who became ill later?"

"You got a hunch?" Swan asked.

Giorgio sat on the edge of the table. "I saw someone sneak out for a smoke later that night."

"O'Leary was in the infirmary by the time we got there," McCready interjected. "But the housekeeper reported she found mud on the floor in one of the guest bedrooms."

Giorgio shook his head. "No, I saw a monk outside. Which room had mud though?"

"Room 8."

"That's Cory Poindexter's room," Giorgio confirmed. "He said he took a walk. Let's add him to our list. What else can you tell us about Olsen or Dorman?"

The young officer referred to his tablet. "Olsen sold real estate and met Beth Tomlinson when she sold her a house. Olsen told Tomlinsen about her journalism background and how much she hated real estate, so Tomlinsen gave Olsen the name of an agency looking to hire. According to Tomlinson, she began to make a name for herself pretty quickly. When Tomlinson's dad died and had to fly home for the funeral, she called Olsen to stand in at the conference."

"Was she a California native?"

Giorgio sat on the corner of the table, the empty soda pop can by his side. Swan picked it up and began punching dents into it.

"No. She was a Chicago native. She graduated from the University of Illinois with a degree in journalism, served as the editor for the school newspaper, was in the drama department, and on the debate team." He looked up to see if the others were listening, then continued. "She's never been arrested, never belonged to a political party, but she is Catholic. And," he added with a twinkle in his eye, "there is one connection you may find interesting."

"What's that?" Giorgio asked.

"She lived briefly in San Marino, where Father Damian was senior pastor at St. Anselmo's. He was asked to leave five years ago for having an affair with the wife of a church elder."

"Well, that's a nice piece of information," Giorgio cooed. "Especially since he's probably guilty of it again."

"Care to share?" Swan prodded.

"The janitor saw Peters pulling out of the parking lot when he arrived," Giorgio said, "But Peters said she left around seven that evening."

"That's not much to go on," Swan said skeptically.

"No, but she had a weak excuse for lying." Giorgio told them about Peters' earring and the fact that Syd Norville had found Father Damian in the hallway rather than in the chapel when he went to report finding the body.

"How does an affair fit into the crime though?" Swan wasn't convinced.

"Damian was publicly chastised and relocated during the time Olsen was a member of the church," McCready offered.

"And you think Olsen became aware of his little tryst with Anya Peters and he killed her to keep her quiet?"

"I don't judge the information, I just dig it up," McCready stated flatly.

"It's unlikely," Giorgio admitted, "especially if the reprimand was public, but we can't ignore it. We'll drill down further to see if we strike oil. Keep going," he directed McCready.

"Our second victim, Jeff Dorman, was twenty-three," McCready said, returning to his notes. "He lived in Altadena and worked for Sanchez Produce Company. He also registered for the conference at the last minute and didn't meet with any of the agents."

"Maybe he wasn't a writer?" Giorgio speculated.

"Possibly," McCready agreed. "I called a number of the conference regulars and no one had ever seen him before. In short, he was an unknown, much like Olsen. He was arrested two years ago for possession of marijuana, though," McCready continued. "and charged a year later with selling it, although they couldn't make that one stick."

This captured Giorgio's interest. "You think maybe he came to the conference to traffic dope?"

"I don't know, but I spoke with a young woman who attempted to engage him in conversation. She said he didn't know the difference between a mainstream novel and romance."

"Any chance he and Olsen knew each other?"

"No connection there, yet."

"And nothing in her past to suggest narcotics or a brush with the law?"

"None," said McCready.

Giorgio began to pace around the table again. Grosvenor opened his eyes and watched him.

"Okay, what else do you have?"

"One of the new recruits, Father Julio, is also from Chicago. Maybe he has a past history with Olsen," McCready speculated.

"What'd you find out at the caterers, Joe?"

Swan had found a toothpick in his coat pocket and was picking his teeth as he asked this. Giorgio turned and watched him thinking he and Rocky could compete for attention-getting mannerisms.

"Not much. You know about Marsh. But Colin Jewett, one of the servers, went outside around eight o'clock for his usual cigarette. Again, no one paid any attention to when he returned."

"Speaking of Marsh," McCready interjected. "I have something on him." He thumbed through a folder and pulled out some papers. "We found this in Olsen's office."

McCready handed a piece of paper to Giorgio.

"What is it?" Giorgio asked.

"It's what they call a query letter," McCready replied. "I asked Beth Tomlinsen about it. Writers send them out to agents and editors offering up their work. If the agent is interested, they'll ask for the whole manuscript."

"But we don't know if Mallery Olsen ever read this."

"Actually, we do," McCready countered, as he found another piece of paper. "I went through her computer files this morning and she logged in Marsh's query. I found a copy of her response." He handed the second sheet of paper to Giorgio.

Giorgio skimmed both copies. "Not only was he lying about not knowing her, this might have given him a reason to want her dead." He handed it to Swan.

Swan read a snippet out loud. "*Your descriptions are mundane. Even your clichés are cliché.* Ouch!"

"There's more," McCready continued with a burst of enthusiasm. "One of the attendees saw Marsh arguing with Olsen just before the dinner. This person couldn't hear what they said, but Olsen walked away in a huff."

Giorgio pulled out one of the chairs and sat down. "Marsh swore to me he didn't know her. Perhaps he isn't the beleaguered conference chair he claims to be."

"I'll do some more checking on Marsh," McCready offered.

"Add Colin Jewett to your list," Giorgio said as McCready wrote down the name. "And give Cory Poindexter--the guy who came to the dinner late--the once-over too. I didn't like him, or his answers. And don't forget to check the social media sites for all of these guys."

The door opened and a uniformed officer entered. He stepped over the dog to hand Giorgio a note.

"The medical examiner faxed this over. Said you'd probably want it right away."

The officer left and Giorgio read the documents. Swan and McCready waited until Giorgio finally looked up.

"He hasn't pinned Dorman's time of death down but thinks it was sometime between six and ten o'clock Saturday night. Looks like we have two murders in almost the same location at almost the same time." He handed the sheets over to Swan.

"And only about sixty possible suspects." Swan sighed, glancing at the report.

"Perhaps the murders aren't connected," McCready said.

Giorgio and Swan looked up to where McCready held Olsen's folder close to his chest like a college student about to make a book report.

"Think about it," he said. "The murders were completely different. Whoever killed Olsen wasn't afraid of the body being discovered. In fact, the body was left in the closet where someone was bound to find it, making a big news splash. On the other hand, Dorman was buried."

"Hurriedly, I might add," Swan added, catching on.

"Right," McCready agreed. "So, in one case, the body was placed where it would be found. In the other, the body was hidden."

"Two different murderers," Giorgio mused. "Could be."

"But is it just a coincidence they were murdered on the same night?" Swan asked skeptically.

"Why not?" McCready defended his theory. "You said yourself there were sixty people on the premises that night. We don't have a motive yet, just opportunity."

Giorgio looked at Swan. "Do we have anything back from the lab, yet?"

"No."

"Then ride them. I need to know about that wine glass and the wine bottles. Also that cigarette butt." He looked at McCready. "And I want to know everything you can find out about Dorman. Why he would have gone to a writers' conference. Who would have even suggested it to him? Did he know Olsen or anybody else on that list? Canvass his neighborhood, his acquaintances, even people at work."

"Right," McCready gave a mock salute as he left.

"Here's something else," Swan interrupted, reading the third page of the fax. "It says Dorman's injury was consistent with being hit from behind. What if he met someone out there to buy drugs? They got in an argument; he turned to leave and was hit from behind." Swan handed the fax back to Giorgio.

"Maybe. Okay, catch McCready and get him to check up on Dorman's bank accounts and his job. Also, anything we can find out about his personal life."

Swan got up to leave, but McCready met him on the way out.

"More information," the young cop said. "They found Dorman's car on a street called Eagleton Drive."

"Where's that?"

McCready squeezed past Swan and went to the map on the wall. He pointed to the base of the San Gabriel Mountains.

"Here's the monastery. Just west of the property is a residential area, and here's Eagleton Drive. It cuts off Michillinda and tucks back into a cul de sac. The backyards along here border the Fathers' property. The car was parked up here. Dorman must have cut in between these two houses and across this hill. There's a forest service access road in there. He must have gone through this short stretch of trees, crossed this hill, and come up through the garden. No one would have seen him."

"Which is what he wanted," Giorgio added as they all stood surveying the map.

"But why would he attend the conference and then check out, only to sneak back onto the property?" Swan asked.

"To provide cover in case someone saw him," McCready suggested.

Giorgio gave McCready an appreciative look, thinking the kid was a natural at this.

"He had to have a flashlight," Giorgio said. "Otherwise he would have killed himself in the dark."

McCready shrugged. "Unless he came back onto the property before it was completely dark."

"No," Giorgio cut him off. "If he went to that much trouble to conceal himself, he wouldn't take a chance of being seen by some neighbor out for an evening stroll." Giorgio gestured to the residential area on the map. "I'm going back up there to see what I can find."

"But, Joe," Swan began, "we searched that whole area."

"If Dorman had a flashlight, where is it?" He turned to McCready. "Keep at it. I need to know whatever we can find out about Dorman."

"Will do."

Giorgio got up, signaling to Grosvenor his nap was over. "I'm going to see Marsh first," Giorgio said pinning the fax to the bulletin board. "He has some 'splaining to do."

† Chapter Twenty-Three †

John Marsh lived in a lower middle class part of Pasadena where the houses were small, box-like structures covered in a variety of pastel stucco. His pale green house sat at the end of a tree-lined street and was badly in need of paint. An old Ford sedan sat in the driveway.

Giorgio left Grosvenor in the car and knocked on the screen door. The door opened to reveal Marsh dressed in baggy blue jeans and a faded red shirt that hung outside his pants. His hair stuck out at odd angles, and he hadn't yet shaved. A far cry, Giorgio thought, from the prim and proper image he'd presented at the conference. Marsh seemed surprised to see the detective but pushed open the screen door and invited him in.

Giorgio entered a dingy living room with brown shag carpet. Stale cigarette smoke hung in the air. Lopsided stacks of books filled either side of the brick fireplace, and writing magazines were scattered across the 1970s style wood coffee table. Mismatching table lamps cast a dim glow across a large velvet painting of a scantily clad woman with big breasts leaning against a vintage car while a pack of hungry wolves circled around her. It reminded Giorgio of the small apartment where his uncle had lived after his aunt died. Although it was clean enough, the lack of personality and musty smell, worn furniture, and dirty magazines spoke volumes about his uncle's state of mind. Either Marsh lived on a meager income or had a dim view of his prospects in the world. Giorgio suspected both.

"May I offer you a beer?"

Giorgio shook his head. "No, thank you. I just need a few minutes. I'm surprised I caught you."

"I work at home," he gestured to the dining room where a computer was set up on a small dining room table. The entire table was filled with books and dirty dishes. There was only one chair. Apparently Mr. Marsh didn't entertain.

"Please, have a seat. What can I do for you?"

Marsh sat on the frayed green sofa, extending bare feet housed in open leather sandals. Giorgio sat across from him in a rickety swivel chair. He found himself staring at Marsh's feet with their long toes and toenails. It was a moment before he realized Marsh had spoken.

"Did you find the killer?" Marsh continued.

"Not yet. We have a long way to go."

Giorgio's eyes came to rest on an ashtray sitting on the coffee table. It was overflowing, and he tried to see what brand of cigarette Marsh smoked.

"Well, how can I help?"

It was clear Giorgio's unannounced visit made Marsh feel edgy. He sat forward on the sofa, his forearms resting on his knees, his right leg bouncing up and down in a nervous rhythm.

"I was told you were seen arguing with Ms. Olsen just before dinner that night."

Marsh shifted in his seat, drawing his feet close to the base of the sofa.

"I believe I had some words with her. I'm not sure I would characterize it as an argument."

"What was it was about?" The chair Giorgio had selected had a lumpy cushion that made him feel like he was sitting over the edge of a bucket. He shifted in his seat to find a more comfortable spot.

"She wanted to sit at a front table at the banquet. But the front tables were reserved for the conference committee and a few of the more well-known agents." Marsh folded his arms across his chest in an attempt to appear relaxed, but it wasn't working. "Ms. Chase asked me to settle the dispute," he said. "Ms. Olsen and I stepped aside so she wouldn't be embarrassed, but she wouldn't listen to reason. She argued that she was as important as any of the other agents and deserved to sit at the front of the room."

"How did the discussion end?"

He hesitated as he ran his tongue across his teeth. "She said something rude and walked away."

"Mr. Marsh, are you an aspiring author like the rest of your members?"

"I write science fiction. I have four novels completed."

"Any of them ever published?"

"I'm not sure where you're going with this, Detective."

He began to wriggle his toes nervously, making them look like long worms poking their heads out of a can.

"It's a simple question. I'd just like to know if any of your work has ever been published."

"No."

"Do you have a literary agent?"

He sat forward with an angry expression. "Why are you asking me these questions? I had nothing to do with Mallery Olsen's death!"

"I like to know who I'm dealing with. Do you have an agent?" Giorgio remained calm, looking directly into Marsh's eyes.

"No," he said with exasperation. "I've received some very nice comments about my work, but so far the timing has been off."

"Did you ever submit anything to Ms. Olsen?"

"I told you, I didn't know her."

"That wasn't my question."

Marsh paused, chewing his lip. "I sent her a query letter back in August." Marsh paused again, sorting out how to continue. "She asked for the first fifty pages of my novel."

"What happened?"

As the color drained from his cheeks, he began to wring his hands. "She rejected it, but I wasn't lying to you. I had never met her before she came to this conference."

"Did you confront her about the rejection?"

"Why should I? A writer gets used to rejection. It comes with the territory."

Giorgio pulled a sheet of paper from his pocket and handed it to Marsh. "Because it seems she wasn't very kind."

Marsh glanced at the document and blanched. "I see you've done your homework, Detective."

"It's what I get paid for. Are all agents so blunt?"

"She was particularly cruel. I don't know why."

"Cruel enough for retaliation?"

Marsh looked up in surprise. "Of course not. I'm not that small." His lip twitched. "I consider the source. Many agents are themselves frustrated writers."

"And you didn't let this enter into the argument you had with her Saturday night?"

"I doubt she even knew who I was."

"But she would have known your name."

"These agents read material from hundreds of writers every year. They don't remember names. Especially those they've rejected." He tossed the paper back to Giorgio. "I don't think she even suspected who I was."

"Why did you lie about knowing her?"

"I didn't want to be connected to her. Do you blame me? Besides, there were probably several other writers at the conference who had been rejected by her."

"We'll check into that." Giorgio glanced at the ashtray. "What kind of cigarettes do you smoke?"

The question caught Marsh off guard. "What?"

"Cigarettes. What kind?"

Marsh looked confused. "Lucky Strike. Why?"

"What can you tell me about Jeff Dorman?"

"Who?"

"He was a guest at the conference."

Marsh looked truly lost. "I don't think I met him. Why? Did he have something to do with Ms. Olsen?"

Giorgio stood to leave. "I wouldn't leave town, Mr. Marsh."

"I assure you, Detective, I didn't kill that woman."

"Then it's probably in your best interests to be completely honest from now on."

Giorgio moved toward the door and Marsh followed.

"Oh," Giorgio said, stopping short. "One more thing. You left during the dinner. Why is that?"

Marsh's eyes grew wide and he stuttered, "I... needed to use the restroom."

"Is that all?"

The poor man had begun to sweat, and his jaw moved as if it had just been oiled. Finally, he answered.

"I had to make a phone call."

Giorgio thought his manner unconvincing and asked, "Who did you call?"

"My brother in Los Angeles."

His eyes shifted, and Giorgio decided to call his bluff.

"Well, that's easily checked." Giorgio turned again to leave.

"No," Marsh choked out. "He wasn't home. I couldn't get through." He sounded almost relieved.

Giorgio stared back at him. The man seemed to have trouble breathing. Finally he forced out, "I took a walk. Just to get some fresh air."

Giorgio's antenna went up. "Where did you go?"

"I walked out front, out to the fountain."

"Did anyone see you?"

"No. I was upset. It hadn't been such a good day. I struck out with two agents that afternoon. After the exchange with Ms. Olsen, I just needed some fresh air. Even if she didn't remember me, I remembered that rejection letter. I was determined not to let it interfere with the conference, but I needed to talk myself down. I did not kill her, though."

"Lying during an investigation is a serious offense. I'd be more careful."

Giorgio left Marsh looking even more disheveled than when he arrived. Giorgio would be surprised if Marsh was the killer, but there was no reason to take him off the list, yet. He might be an unlikely suspect, but Giorgio knew from experience to never make assumptions.

† Chapter Twenty-Four †

After leaving Marsh, Giorgio returned to the monastery. Rocky's truck was parked out front along with one of the squad cars. Giorgio assumed they were still conducting interviews, so he went directly to the tool shed thinking perhaps Dorman's killer might have placed the flashlight there in an attempt to hide it in plain sight. The sun had finally emerged, causing steam to rise off the corn rows like something out of a Stephen King movie.

Giorgio nodded to the officer still standing guard and then moved to the dilapidated old building. The shed door creaked open, unleashing a flurry of dust mites. Giorgio stepped inside. He shoved things aside, moved buckets off shelves, and poked behind everything on the floor, but found no flashlight.

He made a cursory search of the area around the makeshift grave, the corn stalks, and the surrounding woods. Discouraged and sweating, he finally called Grosvenor back from where he'd chased a squirrel up a tree and descended the path. He turned toward the kitchen when he heard his name called. Rocky emerged from the backside of the building. Giorgio doubled back to meet him near the statue of Mary.

"I just finished interviewing Father O'Leary," Rocky informed him. "They have a small infirmary here. Just a few beds. O'Leary went to the infirmary before the nine o'clock prayer the night of the murder. I guess he didn't feel well enough to talk to anyone in depth until today. He's quite a character."

"What do you mean?"

The two brothers began to wander along the path in the direction of the kitchen.

"O'Leary has lived here since the beginning of time, I guess, and has a reputation for making up outlandish stories. I was told no one can tell the difference between his truth and fabrication. Anyway, when Father Damian arrived about four years ago he tried to put a stop to it. I guess Damian thought it was sacrilegious for a monk to talk about ghosts and secret passageways. Anyway, no one believes the old guy, but..."

"What ghosts?" Giorgio had stopped short, staring at his brother.

"What?" Rocky stopped and looked back over his shoulder at Giorgio.

"You said stories about ghosts."

"Yeah, but I didn't ask him to tell me any," Rocky shrugged.

Giorgio suddenly grabbed Rocky's arm. "Wait a minute."

"What is it with you?" Rocky said, gruffly.

"Did you say O'Leary talked about secret passages?"

"Yeah, but like I said, nobody believes him."

"Yes, but what did he say?"

Rocky shrugged again. "According to O'Leary, several secret tunnels were created as a means of escape because of the war. But remember, he also said ghosts roamed the hallways at night. If you ask me, the guy's a little nuts."

Giorgio's face betrayed an inner thought. "When I was hit on the head last night, I heard something just before I passed out. It didn't register until just now. I heard a door close." When Rocky didn't respond, he encouraged him. "Don't you see? There's no door in that stairwell."

"There's a door to the outside."

"It's made of metal. What I heard was a wooden door."

Without warning, Giorgio turned on his heels and started back to the north door. "Follow me."

Giorgio reached the door and flung it open, leaving Rocky to wait for Grosvenor. When the door closed behind them, there was the distinctive sound of metal against metal.

"You see," Giorgio said, pointing at the door. He glanced around the stairwell and then stepped forward to the underside of the staircase. There was a small door tucked into the shadows. "I thought so." He opened the door to find a narrow storage closet with a ceiling that followed the slant of the staircase overhead. He stepped inside and began running his hands over bare walls.

"What are you doing?"

"Looking for a lever."

"You've got to be kidding? You think there's a secret passage in there?"

Giorgio turned to his brother with a stern look. "I heard this door close. So if someone went in here, how did they get out?"

"They could've gone down one of the hallways."

"No one went down the hallway."

"How do you know? You were out cold!"

Giorgio pulled on coat hooks and protruding nails, but nothing moved. Rocky leaned against the doorjamb with a smug look on his face.

"Damn!" Giorgio cursed, pushing his way past his brother. "When I followed the monk into the stairwell, I looked down both those hallways and up the staircase. But he'd disappeared. I came back in here and stopped to think, right here. That's when someone stepped out of nowhere and nailed me from behind. He had to be hiding under there. But why?" he said looking around the staircase for clues to this new mystery. "I think he ducked in here to use a secret passage, but had to wait until I left because I would have heard him."

"Was this door open or closed?" Rocky pointed to the door to the closet.

"I'm not sure. It was too dark."

As he said this, the outside door opened. Father Damian entered carrying a stack of books. He looked surprised to see the two policemen and the dog.

"Detective! What are you doing here?"

"Trying to solve a puzzle. Father, can I get my hands on the original plans to the monastery?"

Father Damian glanced at Rocky and back to Giorgio. "Yes." He hesitated. "We have a copy in the safe, but what are you looking for?"

"I just need a footprint of the building," Giorgio replied, feeling the need to be deceptive. "It will help us plot where the two bodies were found and any connecting possibilities."

"I see. Well, follow me. I'll get them for you."

The abbot led them to his office where he went to the large painting of Christ and the Last Supper. He pulled the painting away from the wall, and with a few flicks of the wrist, opened a hidden wall safe.

A moment later he handed Giorgio a roll of yellowed paper. "Please be very careful. These are very old."

"We handle all potential evidence carefully," Giorgio clipped.

The brothers walked out to their cars where Giorgio rolled out the drawings on the hood of his sedan. Grosvenor relieved himself on a nearby azalea bush. The two men studied the huge sheets of paper, running their fingers along the defining lines of the building, looking for something that might indicate a hidden passageway. They found nothing.

"Damn," Giorgio exclaimed again.

"Well, what did you expect – big arrows pointing to a sign that said 'Secret Passage Here?' I think you've starred in too many mystery plays."

Giorgio ignored him and started to roll up the plans when Rocky stopped him. He pointed to the lower right corner. "Applebaum is a fairly common name in this area isn't it?"

Giorgio looked up. "What?"

"The name of the architect. Joseph Applebaum." Rocky was pointing to where the architect's name was printed in block letters at the bottom. "Maybe his relatives still live here."

Giorgio's eyebrows shot up. "You're right. Maybe I can track down a direct descendent."

"It's a long shot," Rocky warned.

"Right now, anything seems like a long shot." Giorgio rolled the oversized papers back up. "Listen, thanks for your help."

"I'll type up my notes and get them over to you tomorrow," Rocky offered. "Let me know if you find anything. I'm going home to catch a nap."

They said goodbye, and Giorgio climbed into the sedan with Grosvenor on the seat beside him. He always carried a current phone book in his car and found it under the seat. He looked up Applebaum and was dismayed to find six names, all living in Sierra Madre or Pasadena. He got out his cell phone and began making calls. After the first three, he hit pay dirt. The woman who answered was Joseph Applebaum's daughter; she said she would see him the next day.

† Chapter Twenty-Five †

Giorgio spent the rest of the afternoon flipping through 3 X 5 cards, studying the file on Mallery Olsen, and following up on leads. Olsen's boyfriend had been found and claimed he'd only heard about the murder that day. He and some friends had just returned from a long weekend on Catalina Island, giving him an airtight alibi.

Giorgio checked in with the coroner to clarify a few details and then called Angie to tell her he'd be home around six o'clock. At six-fifteen, however, he was immersed in drawing a fishbone diagram, matching individuals with facts about the case. As he rifled through papers on his desk, he found a phone message tucked between two sheets of paper. Apparently Father O'Leary had called earlier that afternoon. Giorgio reached for the phone, but felt a twinge of panic when he realized he was already late for dinner. The good Father would have to wait until morning.

He arrived home just as Angie was finishing the dishes. She was dressed in gray slacks and a lavender cashmere sweater, renewing Giorgio's hope that perhaps her mood had changed.

"You're late," she snapped, barely turning from the sink. "I already put dinner away."

He stopped as the temperature in the room plummeted.

"I'll just make a sandwich," he said.

He reached for the refrigerator door, grabbed a carton of milk and a package of ham, and went to the counter where he made a dry sandwich. Angie wiped down the sink as if he wasn't even in the room.

"Where are the kids?" he finally asked, pouring himself a glass of milk.

"Doing homework."

She placed a last cup into the dishwasher, poured in the liquid soap and shut the door. The motor roared into action while she wiped her hands on a towel. Giorgio waited, wondering what word or gesture would finally melt her cold demeanor. A honk startled him, and he got up to look out the kitchen window. A Honda Accord sat at the curb with its headlights on and motor running. Angie didn't seem surprised and turned to him, hands on her hips.

"You should probably check on the children. I'll be home by nine-thirty."

"What?" But she was already in the front entry. He followed, sandwich in hand. "Angie, I have to go back to work."

"It'll have to wait, unless you can get Rocky to come over and baby-sit. I have a class that starts at seven." With that, she settled her coat around her shoulders, grabbed her purse, and started for the door.

"What do you mean, you have a class?"

"I signed up for it today." She stepped outside, heading for the waiting car. He stood in the doorframe, staring dumbly after her.

"What class?" he repeated to her retreating back. "Angie!" he yelled. "I have to go back to work!"

"Then hire a nanny," she snarled as she got into the car.

The car pulled away from the curb leaving the head of the household trying to make sense of the last few minutes. He returned to the kitchen and dropped his sandwich onto the table before grabbing the phone to call Rocky in the hopes he really could come over and watch the kids. When no one answered, Giorgio slammed down the receiver, feeling betrayed by yet a second member of his own family. When he reached for the sandwich again, it was gone.

His mouth dropped open in surprise, until he turned in Grosvenor's direction. The dog couldn't help swiping his long tongue from one side of his muzzle to the other. That, and the few crumbs on the floor next to the web-sized feet, told the whole story.

"You ate the whole thing, didn't you?" Giorgio blurted. "No, you didn't eat it! You inhaled it! I mean, why eat a sandwich when you can inhale it whole?" He paced in front of the table, venting his frustration. "Why have a conversation with your husband when you can run off to a class and avoid confrontation?"

Grosvenor cowered, his snout nearly touching the floor. Giorgio stopped, feeling ashamed. He took a deep breath, patted the dog on the head and went to the living room where he plopped into his favorite chair. Grosvenor came and sat next to him, his droopy eyes imploring Giorgio for some attention. He leaned over and rubbed the dog around the neck.

"Why is Angie so mad at me?" he said to the dog.

Grosvenor gave the back of his hand a good lick, as if apologizing for eating the sandwich.

"She can't be mad about you. Jeez, look at that face," he said, reaching out and cupping Grosvenor's chin in his hand. "How could anybody resist that face?"

Grosvenor threw his head back and wiggled happily as if he knew how cute he could be. A noise like the infantry landing at Normandy Beach announced the arrival of Tony and Marie.

"Where did mom go?"

Tony reached the dog first and was already throwing his arms around him. Grosvenor reacted as if he'd just been released from jail.

"She had a class," Giorgio replied tight lipped.

"I think she's mad at you." Marie had come to sit in her father's lap.

He settled her against his chest, smelling something fruity as she leaned against him.

"Yeah," Tony agreed. "I heard her talking to Marianne's mom. She said you could just stay home and baby-sit tonight."

Tony had draped himself over Grosvenor's back. The dog rolled over so that his feet stuck straight up in the air, his genitals flopping out in the open. Marie turned her face away in a sneer.

"What'd you do, dad?" Marie had the same look of reproach he often saw on Angie's face.

Just then, Tony burst out laughing as he wrestled with the dog.

"Don't you kids have homework?" he said, hoping to avoid any further reference to the disintegrating relationship with his wife.

"You know you could just call Mrs. Greenspan to come over, Dad."

Giorgio looked at Marie for a moment as if she might be teasing him.

"Seriously," she said. "Mrs. Greenspan loves to snoop through Mom's cupboards. I bet she could be here in ten minutes."

"I do have work to do."

Tony scratched Grosvenor's stomach causing his leg to kick as if he was trying to kick start a motorbike. The dog whined in ecstasy.

"Dad, it'll be fine." Marie seemed so grown up. "Mrs. Greenspan has come over before. She smells like garlic and onions all the time, but we'll be okay."

"Yeah," Tony agreed in between giggles. "She makes excuses that she's going to the kitchen for a glass of water. Then we find her with her nose in the cupboards. Once, she took a piece of chicken off a plate in the icebox, ate half of it, and put it back. Mom was really mad."

Giorgio frowned as if the prospect of having Mrs. Greenspan was becoming less and less a viable option. All of a sudden, Tony rolled away from Grosvenor with his hand over his nose.

"Oh, no, he farted again!"

"That's it!" Giorgio stood up. "I'm calling Mrs. Greenspan."

✝

By eight o'clock, Giorgio was parked on Eagleton Drive where Dorman's car had been found. He hadn't meant to return to the monastery, but decided on the after-dark excursion partly to get Grosvenor out of the house, and partly because it would give him an opportunity to approach the property the same way he believed Dorman had the night he was killed.

The moon sat high in the sky, illuminating a bank of clouds in a bright halo. Grabbing a flashlight and his cell phone, Giorgio got out of the car, conscious that if anyone saw the shadow of a man passing their windows they might call the police. The neighborhood was quiet except for the sound of a TV blaring.

He set off down the path towards the dirt road he assumed Dorman had used. The road was rutted with deep tire tracks and runoff trenches, so Giorgio was forced to use the flashlight to avoid twisting an ankle. He breathed in the smell of sage brush just as Grosvenor stopped to take a dump, making him hold his nose. Giorgio waited patiently while the dog did his business and then tried to mentally mark the spot so he wouldn't step in it on the way back.

He followed the road up and over an embankment until it turned north. This was a fire road that wound its way up into the hillsides. He'd participated a year earlier with the Sierra Madre Search and Rescue Team on a drill and remembered the road started to climb pretty steeply about a hundred feet ahead. It wasn't going in the right direction.

He found a small deer path and followed it over the crest of the hill in the direction of the upper gardens of the monastery. Although he couldn't see the lights from the building yet, he judged he had less than a quarter of a mile to cover. Grosvenor kept up, making Giorgio think he could see in the dark as well as a cat. They made their way through scrub oaks and scratchy underbrush until they climbed a small hill. In the distance, he could see the flickering lights from the retreat center.

Moving at a faster pace now, he made it to the perimeter of the flower garden. Lights from yet another event blazed at the entrance. Apparently not everyone had cancelled bookings. Giorgio stayed to the north of the garden until he found the vegetable garden where Dorman had met his killer. They had released the guard earlier in the day, and so Giorgio was alone. He stopped to look at his watch. It had taken him only eleven minutes to make the trip in the dark and that included Grosvenor's bathroom break.

The flashlight cut an arc around the surrounding area. To his right was a regiment of ghostly corn stalks. Together with the bushes and nearby trees, they camouflaged the building. It would have been easy for a conference guest to leave the cocktail party, kill Dorman, and return unnoticed. It would have been more difficult for one of the catering staff since they would have been missed. Giorgio remembered however, that Colin Jewett routinely came out for a smoke after dinner. Perhaps Dorman was trafficking drugs and Jewett was the buyer. Corey Poindexter had also gone for a walk that night, as had John Marsh. Even the monks had to be considered now that he knew a few occasionally left the building after dark. Grand Central Station came to mind, with people crisscrossing the yard as they hurried to their various destinations. It was a wonder they didn't all bump into each other in the dark.

He glanced over at the tool shed. A dark image stood out in relief against the deep shadow of the shed's outline. It was a tall, New England-style bird feeder. He remembered seeing it during the daytime, but hadn't thought much about it.

A hunch made him walk over and shine his flashlight up into it. It was designed like a small octagonal building, complete with shingles and windows on all sides. It was secured to a flat piece of wood that sat atop a steel pipe anchored into the ground. At the front was a wide doorway to let in its small winged visitors. The feeder itself sat about a foot above his reach. As the beam of his flashlight cut into its interior, a glint from the inside made the hairs on the back of his neck bristle.

Quickly, he surveyed the surrounding area until he found an old bucket thrown against the side of the shed. He took it back to the birdfeeder, turned it upside down and climbed onto its rickety bottom hanging onto the metal pole to gain his balance. The bucket sank into the soft earth, but gave him enough elevation so that with only a slight waver he could reach into the opening.

His fingers scraped across old birdseed, splintered wood, and bird droppings. The bird droppings made him shudder, but when his fingers touched cold metal he smiled. With his handkerchief, he reached in and carefully removed a heavy, military style flashlight. Across one side was a dark splash of color.

A little bird, he thought, may have just led him to the weapon used to murder Jeff Dorman.

† Chapter Twenty-Six †

Giorgio returned to his car to deposit the flashlight into an evidence bag and then decided to drive to the monastery. He could return the architectural drawings to Father Damian and maybe find Father O'Leary. When he got there, Anya Peters was just disappearing into her office. Not wanting another confrontation, he proceeded to Father Damian's door, but there was no answer and the door was locked. He'd have to leave them with Peters after all.

He went to her office and knocked, but there was no answer there either. Confused, he tried the door knob and found it unlocked. The room was empty. He took a quick glance down the hallway as Grosvenor pushed past him into the office, sniffing the carpeted floor. The dog stopped briefly at the desk and then made a beeline for the closet. He pressed his nose against the baseboard, inhaling with loud sucking noises.

Curious, Giorgio placed the drawings on the desk and pushed Grosvenor aside to open the full-length closet door. The closet wasn't any bigger than a phone booth, but was empty. Peters' coat was hung outside the closet on an antique coat tree, yet the smell of her perfume was overpowering inside the closet. Giorgio stared into the blank interior for thirty seconds.

What was going on here? He'd just seen Anya Peters duck into her office. But why would her scent remain in the closet if her coat was hung on the other side of the room? As his eyes roamed around the small space, the tiniest sliver of light near the floor at the back of the closet gave him the answer. He quickly flicked off the overhead light behind him and came back to the closet. He couldn't help the smile that flickered across his face. There was a light leak from somewhere behind the back wall.

He turned the light back on and then ran his fingers around the edges of the closet. He pushed knobs and twisted hooks looking for some secret lever. Nothing happened. His fingers pressed into corners and pulled on anything that hung loose. He even yanked at the coat rod. Nothing moved. He stood back and used his flashlight to play across the knotty pine panels. The beam of light inched across the wood surface, revealing the irregular wood grain that flowed in river patterns. Everything looked normal until he noticed a swirl of dark brown wood in the far upper right corner of the side panel. It appeared to be just another imperfection, but closer inspection revealed that it didn't blend into the wood as the rest of the patterns did.

His heart skipped a beat. He used the knuckle of his index finger to press the center of the demarcation. The circle receded into the wall a good half inch as the back wall opened silently toward him, bringing with it the musty smell of earth and decayed wood.

Giorgio ordered Grosvenor to stay put, grabbed his flashlight and slipped through the opening. He found himself in a narrow hallway lit by a single wall sconce, with a low ceiling and a set of stairs descending to his right into a well of darkness. A duplicate wood panel lined the opposite wall making him pretty certain Peters' office backed up against Father Damian's. If he was right, he was standing in between the two.

Remembering the lost earring and the discrepancy in time, he was forced to assume there was another hidden doorway to Father Damian's office, allowing the two to pass back and forth undetected. He listened at Damian's wall for a moment, but heard nothing. Either they were engaged in something private, or Anya Peters had taken the stairs to places unknown.

Giorgio followed his instincts and decided to descend the short set of stairs. He stepped into an earthen tunnel carved into shale rock that formed the foundation of the building. It had a low ceiling that appeared to be the underside of the floor above. The air was dank and musty and there was hard-packed dirt beneath his feet. He used the flashlight to get his bearings.

A claustrophobic tunnel twisted and turned as it followed the outline of the building above. Wherever Peters had gone, she might return at any moment and she might not be alone. He'd have to hurry.

Old wall sconces dotted the interior wall, but offered no help now; draped in cobwebs, they looked more like props from a Halloween fright house. The hard-packed floor was uneven enough to increase the chance of mishap, so he had to be careful. In fact, he nearly tripped over a timber that framed a doorway as he hurried forward. Just beyond the heavy timber a small room opened up, with a second set of stairs. A tiny light, the size of a nightlight, gave off a soft illumination at the top of the stairs. Giorgio carefully climbed the stairs but was forced to stop at a blank wall.

He used his flashlight to search for what he knew had to be there, a mechanism to open the wall. Unfortunately, this area had not been constructed in anything as nice as knotty pine and there were no visible hooks, knobs, or levers. He pushed on the wall in several places, but it didn't budge. He used the toe of his shoe to push against a shallow step. Nothing happened. He ran his fingers around what he thought must be the edges of a doorway. Still, nothing happened.

The light switch and tiny bulb set into the ceiling were the only indications any technology existed here. Using his forefinger, he flicked the light switch. The light above him went out. He quickly flicked the light back on – but not before he heard a scraping noise that started and stopped. His heart fluttered again. He flicked the light off just as the wall began to move.

"Whoa!" he whispered.

With a rush of adrenaline, he stepped back just in time for the wall to open all the way. He stopped and listened for a moment and then stepped forward. He was in the supply closet he and Rocky had visited earlier that day. The smell of turpentine and cleaning solution was intermixed with the lingering aroma of Peters' perfume. With a soft moan, the wall swung closed behind him, leaving him in the dark. Very clever. As a safeguard, the light on the other side of the secret door was set up to go out as soon as the door opened. When the door closed, the wall inside the closet appeared normal.

Giorgio was just about to find the door to the stairwell when the scraping of metal alerted him that someone had entered the stairwell through the outside door.

The closet extended all the way under the stairs, so he ducked back until he was able to effectively hide himself from view of the entrance – the way his ambusher had probably done the night he was attacked.

And just in time.

The door to the closet opened and a robed figure slipped through. The figure closed the door and flicked on a small penlight. The figure reached for something directly above the door. A moment later, the wall opened again, allowing the monk to glide silently into the tunnel.

Giorgio allowed the secret door to close again before emerging from his hiding place. Quickly he turned and shined his flashlight above the hallway doorframe where an enameled crucifix hung on the wall. He counted to twenty before reaching up and pulling on the crossed ankles of the Christ figure. The entire symbol slid silently down as if mounted on a well-oiled runner. The wall behind him opened and Giorgio wasted no time in following the furtive robed figure.

He descended the steps as quietly as possible, conscious that the person he pursued could be waiting around any corner. He hurried through the tunnel, crouching around corners and hugging the outer wall. He made it to the small hallway outside of Peters' office just as she flew backwards out of her closet, nearly landing in his arms. Her momentum actually threw him back against the wall to Father Damian's office. A sharp bark signaled that Grosvenor was the reason for her sudden emergence. Peters disengaged herself from Giorgio and turned to stare at him in surprise. The look on her face was a mixture of shock and anger as she realized her predicament.

"That dog should be caged," she bluffed. "What's he doing in my office?"

"I think the bigger question, Ms. Peters, is what are you doing making secret trips through an underground passage dressed as a monk?"

"I don't know what you're talking about. That dog nearly attacked me. I could bring charges."

She stopped talking when she realized Giorgio had noticed a set of monk's robes hanging on a hook just inside the small enclosure.

"Ah, the costume," he said, starting towards it. When his foot kicked something lying in the dirt, he looked down to find a brown paper package lying in the dust. "Well, well, what's this?" Giorgio stooped to pick it up.

The pause Ms. Peters took before answering spoke volumes. "I have no idea," she stammered, flinging her head in the air. "I'm not even sure where we are."

She made a vain attempt at looking lost, as if she'd fallen through the wall by mistake. Giorgio prodded her forward with his flashlight.

"Let's go back inside."

They squeezed through the closet door into the office again and he ordered Grosvenor to the other side of the desk. Giorgio invited Ms. Peters to take a seat.

"Want to tell me about it?" he asked, holding out the package.

"I have nothing to tell," she replied stubbornly. "I was working late and this dog attacked me in my own office. I'll bring charges."

"You may want to revise that story, Ms. Peters. I followed you in here a little while ago, but when I got here, you were gone."

She raised an eyebrow. "I think I'd like to call a lawyer."

Her eyes flitted to the package and Giorgio smiled as he began to unwrap it. As he lifted the end flap, several plastic bags filled with white powder slid onto the desk. Anya Peters sank into her chair.

"I think you'd better make that phone call right now," he said, handing her the phone.

With a grim look, she dialed a number while he pulled out his cell phone and called for a squad car. When she'd finished, he took out a pair of plastic ties, read her the Miranda rights, and cuffed her to an old radiator at the back of the room.

"Now, don't you go anywhere," he chided, pointing at her with his flashlight.

Giorgio and Grosvenor hurried to the kitchen where the catering staff had begun to pack up. Mary Fields was at the sink rinsing out a chafing dish, while Nancy placed empty platters into a large plastic storage container. Mary Fields stopped when she saw him enter.

"Detective? Has there been another incident?"

"Where's Colin Jewett?"

Grosvenor had followed him into the kitchen and started a wide loop to where one of the assistants scraped leftovers into a large trash bin. At that moment, the back door slammed and Colin Jewett strolled in.

"What's next?" he asked Mary, freezing when he saw Giorgio.

Giorgio held up his badge. "Colin Jewett, you're under arrest. You have the right to remain silent; you have the right to...."

Jewett turned and bolted for the back door. He would have made it, too, except for Mary Fields' foot which clipped him just above the ankles throwing him head first into the wall.

Giorgio pulled his weapon and ordered the man to halt as he struggled to get up. Giorgio grabbed another set of plastic ties from his pocket and forced the man's hands behind his back.

"Nice work," he said to Fields.

Giorgio pushed Jewett against the wall and reached into his jacket pocket where he was rewarded with an envelope filled with a stack of one hundred dollar bills. Just then a siren echoed in the distance, giving Grosvenor a reason to join in for a good howl.

† Chapter Twenty-Seven †

It was after eleven o'clock and the bar was full. He sat alone in a red leather booth tucked in the far corner facing the door. Two worn pool tables commanded the center of the room. Neon signs advertising Bud Light and Draft Beer glowed in the window, and an old-fashioned juke box played Kenny G, out-of-place here, especially for the group of bikers playing pool.

The Guinness in his hand felt like an old friend and his thumb was already lifting the label, a habit he'd picked up as a child. Back then, every pop bottle or juice box had to be stripped of its label. It just did. It was an obsession. A nervous habit. His mother's harsh voice still echoed in his head, screaming at him to stop making such a mess.

What was she thinking these days, he wondered? His mother. She didn't know the truth. His uncle felt she couldn't be trusted and so led her to believe he was dead. It was the only guilt he'd felt since this all began.

He glanced down at the small pile of paper on the table in front of him. What surprised him most was how lonely he was. He was isolated from everything and everyone he knew, and he couldn't be honest about anything. Every moment, every breath was a lie. And although he was good at lying – no, make that *great* at lying – living a continuous lie was harder than he thought it would be. There were moments when he wanted to scream at the top of his lungs that he wasn't who he said he was just to see the look on everyone's faces. But of course, he couldn't. He was a ghost and had to stay that way.

His short fingers cradled the cold bottle of beer while he half listened to two young women flirt with a couple of guys at the bar.

His mind drifted back to when he'd held a cold bottle of Guinness the night he and Jacko had nicked Mangano. He'd been relaxing in his apartment, reliving the swell of pride at finally avenging his father's death when a knock temporarily short-circuited his air supply. A familiar voice had called out from the hallway.

"Open the door, Cato."

His uncle. It hadn't been a spontaneous visit. Oh, no. There were people who watched and reported what went on in the neighborhood. His uncle had come for a reason.

When his uncle entered the apartment, Cato had closed the door and leaned against it in an attempt to appear casual.

"Uncle Nick, what brings you here at this hour?" The dryness in his throat had cried out for the cool ale in his hand, but he held the bottle at his side.

His uncle stood looking out the window, most likely at his black Mercedes waiting at the curb. The pure elegance of this man had always held Cato in awe. His rich black suit and blue silk tie seemed to define the very air around him.

"You been busy tonight, Cato. Am I right? I hear things, and some things I hear ain't so good.

Cato had flicked the beer bottle with his forefinger just as he was doing now, filling the small apartment with a dull echo.

"I don't know what you mean, Uncle Nick.

"You went to Alfonso's tonight. You think I wouldn't find out?

He'd tried to respond, but a papal gesture from his uncle had stopped him, the sparkle of gold glinting off the ring finger of his right hand.

"Mangano had to be eliminated. You had a right, Cato, but not like this. You're inexperienced. You should have waited. You made mistakes. Mistakes that will raise questions. Questions I can't afford.

Cato's thumb nail raked across the bottle label at the memory, shredding the last of it and forming a small pile on the bar room table.

"I'll lay low for a while. I can do that. You always said I'm like a mole that goes underground."

"Moles leave little piles of dirt around for others to find," his uncle had said. *That's how they catch moles. No, I'm afraid something more permanent must be arranged."*

The front door to the bar banged open extinguishing the chilling voice in his head. Three young businessmen entered the bar, their arrogant disregard for others preceding them. He ignored them, turning his gaze to the flat screen TV that hung behind the bar. It was tuned to the local news.

A brunette woman reported that a young man named Jeff Dorman had been found buried in the vegetable garden on the grounds of the monastery. She went on to say the victim had attended the same writers' conference as Mallery Olsen and may have been killed on the same night. The picture switched to tape of a news conference apparently held earlier in the day where the lead detective on the case, Giorgio Salvatori, was making a statement.

Cato leaned forward to listen more closely. This was the man he had seen in the gift shop. This Salvatori reported that the police didn't know if the two deaths were related, or if the two victims had even known each other. Cato smiled. He had no idea who the dead guy was, nor did he care. He only hoped the second murder would lead the authorities away from him. The detective went on to say they were still running down leads on the Olsen murder and had no idea why the killer had removed her little finger. This sparked a flurry of interruptions as reporters clamored for questions, but Detective Salvatori abruptly ended the press conference and went back inside.

Cato leaned back. His little package would have gone out in the mail today and he practically salivated at the thought of what it would do to the next press conference. Although there wouldn't be any congratulatory phone calls, his uncle would recognize the message because he'd also removed Mangano's little finger. His reward for having waited fifteen years.

Glancing at the TV again, he caught the fleeting picture of Jeff Dorman as the reporter signed off. Thinking about Dorman gave rise to a concern. He still had one loose end, a big loose end that demanded attention. It would require taking another risk, but the risk was greater if he did nothing. Jeff Dorman's murder might actually help deflect attention, even confuse the matter to the point of obfuscation. Since it was probably an amateur who had killed Dorman, the police were more likely to solve that murder. So, what if there was a third murder and they were all pinned on the same person?

He smiled.

Bodies piling up all over the place at the Catholic monastery. What a hoot. His uncle wouldn't see the poetic justice, but he would appreciate the clarity with which it was accomplished.

Cato's lips played with the rim of the bottle as he contemplated his next move. He would take no trophy this time. In fact, it was time for something bold. Something different. Something that would eliminate any patterns the police might follow. He contemplated a few possibilities and then nodded to himself.

Ah, yes. He knew just what to do.

With a quick chug, he finished the beer and slid out of the booth, leaving a small pile of shredded paper behind.

† Chapter Twenty-Eight †

Father O'Leary lifted his huge bulk out of the wooden chair in the library, stretching his arms over his head to alleviate the ache in his back. He really should lose a few pounds. Always overweight as a child, he'd grown to be an overweight adult. It had never posed a problem until the monks had begun baking bread for additional income. A freshly baked loaf of sourdough bread was something he couldn't resist. Add the real butter Mrs. Tilkens snuck to him on Sundays, and a warm slab of bread took on the mouth-watering appeal of a piece of double chocolate cake. Soon enough, his affliction had taken on new proportions, literally.

He stretched his back feeling a slight lightheadedness. These had been the first few hours out of bed and perhaps he wasn't yet fully recovered from the intestinal tract infection he'd come down with on Saturday night; the night the young woman was found hanging in the closet. He placed his hand across his mid-drift, feeling his intestines grinding slowly inside.

What was it that had made him so sick he would still be feeling the effects? Dinner that night had been a rather plain beef stew and no one else was taken ill. It might have been the sardines he'd feasted on in his room earlier that day. But most assuredly, if they had been tainted, he would have felt the effects sooner than evening time. The only other possibility was the chocolate bar one of the brothers had slipped him right after dinner in appreciation for a helping hand. But he couldn't imagine a chocolate bar giving him so much trouble. It was a mystery to be sure.

He moved into the glow of a small lamp sitting on the table next to the window and gazed out across the east parking lot, flexing and relaxing the fingers on both hands.

A cigarette right now would taste heavenly and might even serve to quiet his stomach. He was behind in cataloguing the new books delivered from the regional office, and he looked at the stack of tomes on the floor with a small pang of guilt.

This was the first time he'd felt well enough to tackle the job, which had to be finished by the bishop's arrival on Friday. Of course, he wondered if the bishop would even come. The monastery was abuzz with news of the second murder victim and the arrest of Anya Peters, the Event Coordinator. About fifteen abbots would be attending the regional forum. A multiple murder site could hardly be a place of peace and solitude, what with yellow police tape hanging everywhere, news vans blocking the entrance, and people being arrested. The more he thought about it, the more he felt certain the bishop would change plans and his deadline would be a thing of the past.

A fifteen-minute break was looking more and more like a good idea. It would refresh his spirits and allow him to work with more clarity. After all, it wouldn't do to make a mistake. And if the bishop didn't come this weekend, it wouldn't matter if he finished by Friday. He glanced back out at the night sky which displayed an inviting splash of stars and a crisp moon. Yes, a walk in the garden would surely do him good.

Father O'Leary turned on his heel and left the library, disappearing down the hallway to his room where he pulled a single Marlboro from the pack hidden behind his shaving kit, along with a small pack of matches. A moment later, he was descending the stairs, his robes billowing behind him. A furtive glance down both hallways told him he was alone. Because the night offered a clear view of the valley, he decided to take his walk at the front of the building. It was after midnight, and the monks were expected to be in bed, ready to rise at four in the morning. The grounds would be free to roam in what Father O'Leary considered his personal time for quiet contemplation.

When he reached the front door, the soft thud of a door closing upstairs warned him that someone else was feeling restless tonight. He hurried out the door and down the path leading to the large wooden cross.

He stayed to the flagstone path, crossed the drive, and then lumbered down the embankment to the small duck pond. There he lowered himself onto the wall that rimmed the shallow water and sighed.

This was his favorite spot, and the bushes gave him ample cover from prying eyes. A few seconds later, he was holding a lit cigarette and drawing the acrid smoke into his lungs with a feeling of reverence. His whole body relaxed as the nicotine flushed his veins. When he exhaled, he crossed one leg over the other and gazed with satisfaction out on the valley below.

It was a beautiful evening, though chilly, and the rich pine bouquet of the trees close by was intoxicating. Crickets kept up a healthy racket in the grasses that surrounded the pond and the soft breeze gently rustled the palm trees along the drive, making it sound as if a bubbling brook angled its way down the hill. The sound of music drifted across the open fields from one of the neighborhood houses, making him think of the conference and the murder.

He'd missed much of the excitement surrounding the investigation because he'd been confined to the infirmary. But that hadn't stopped him from thinking about it. The image of a young girl strangled and hanging alone in the supply closet was heartbreaking.

He took another draw on the cigarette, allowing it to warm his insides. His muscles tingled as the nicotine brought them back to life.

His mind drifted back to the girl in the closet and the question of how and why someone would commit such a heinous act on the monastery grounds. The monks had gossiped about it quietly all week and their speculation had reached him even in the infirmary. There was a running theory that the murder was the result of a lovers' spat gone bad, but that didn't resonate with Father O'Leary. And it didn't answer the question of how the murderer had killed her and placed her in the closet without detection. Unless she'd been killed outside, getting her down the staircase and into the closet without being seen was almost impossible. Yet, according to the police, she hadn't been outside. She'd been seen going back to her room. The only way from her room to the kitchen was either down the main staircase or down the fire escape, and carrying a body down that fire escape seemed impractical to say the least.

Thoughtfully, Father O'Leary took another draw on the cigarette, watching the ember flare.

Of course, there was one other way. A route that only he and a few living persons knew about. The thought had bothered him all week and reminded him of the Snickers Bar he'd snacked on that night and the bitter aftertaste from what he'd thought was a bad peanut.

He pulled another mouthful of smoke into his lungs, allowing it to escape slowly, curling up into the night air.

A twig snapped in the thicket of bushes behind him and the crickets' symphony abruptly ceased.

"Who's there?" he called out, his breath catching.

He let the cigarette drop to the ground and snuffed it out. It wouldn't be good to be caught smoking, even though he wasn't the only one on the premises who did. He waved his hand in front of his face to dispel the lingering evidence and then stood up and turned around.

"Anyone there?"

His eyes strained to see in the darkness. Although it was still nearly a full moon, shadows filled every gap and crevice, making it difficult to distinguish shapes and forms beyond a few feet away.

"It's Father O'Leary here, enjoying a few moments alone. Come and join me."

A rustle to his right made him jerk in that direction. Was someone circling him? Was someone there at all? Perhaps it was just a rabbit. There were plenty of the little critters at this time of year.

"Who's there? Please. This isn't funny."

His voice cracked, and he swallowed a wad of sour-tasting saliva. There was another sound behind him, and he whirled around to face the open field that stretched away towards the south. Nothing. And still no crickets. He waited, listening until all he could hear was the beating of his own heart. Finally, he backed up a few steps. This was silly. He was letting his imagination run away with him. It was time to go inside. There was work to do. Those books needed cataloguing whether the bishop arrived this weekend or not.

The trees rustled again, and the tips of the rose bushes swayed back and forth in the breeze. A chill snaked down his spine making him turn again. Someone was here with him. He knew it. He could feel it. He spun a full 360 degrees until he found a figure standing a few feet away, draped in shadows, yet fully recognizable.

"Oh, it's you!" Father O'Leary clapped his hand to his chest as he tried to catch his breath. "You frightened me. You shouldn't sneak up on people. Shame on you. You don't want a cigarette, do you? I'm flat out, and I was just thinking of going back inside."

"Good idea," the figure replied, "it's chilly out here. And you're not well."

"Yes, yes," O'Leary acquiesced, "I agree. I just couldn't resist. You know me. It's so lovely out tonight."

The figure gestured. "I'll follow you up. I want to make sure you get back safely."

Father O'Leary smiled, feeling a nervous twitch in his gut. "That's very kind of you."

He hesitated before stepping past the other figure, never seeing the arm that swung around to land a crushing blow to the side of his head. One knee buckled, and he reached out for help, grabbing only a handful of cloth as the figure pulled away.

"Please," Father O'Leary begged.

His plea was rewarded with a second blow to the crown. He collapsed sideways onto the rim of the pond, his breath coming in short rasps as he felt something warm begin to run down the side of his face and into his mouth. Incapacitated, he couldn't resist when two strong hands grabbed his legs and pulled them onto the ledge.

"Why?" he muttered through blood and spittle. "Why are you doing this?"

But he knew the answer, and before he could resist, the hands gripped the edges of his robes and rolled him into the water, face down. He struggled to get his knees underneath him, but the hand found the back of his head and pressed his face to the bottom. His nose glanced off the mossy stones and panic seized him.

He struggled to pull his head away, but the hand pressed harder, breaking his lips and cracking his teeth against the stones. Algae and blood flowed into his mouth, and he coughed and sputtered before taking a final, large gulp. The foul-tasting water filled his lungs, expanding his chest like a water balloon.

For a brief moment, he was flying above the wheat fields in Illinois where he'd grown up. Below him he saw his little sister running with her kite through the tall grasses, the family dog chasing after her. The sky was a brilliant blue, the clouds a starchy white, and then there was only darkness.

† Chapter Twenty-Nine †

Giorgio woke to a persistent ringing and turned toward the noise, his pupils bringing the room slowly into focus. Angie moved underneath the blanket, motivating him to reach for the phone before it woke her completely.

"Hello," he croaked.

"Joe," someone said sharply. "You'd better get up to the monastery. There's been another murder."

Giorgio sat up. He recognized Jack Barnes, one of the officers who worked the graveyard shift. "You're kidding?" he whispered, rubbing the stubble on his face.

"They just called it in. One of the monks was found floating in the pond."

"Jesus. Which one?" he sighed.

His eyes were fully open now. It was barely light outside and the elm tree that bordered the house danced gently to a soft breeze.

"Someone named O'Leary."

Giorgio groaned. "Okay," he exhaled, "I'm on my way."

†

He approached the duck pond by the flagstone path. There were no ducks, probably never had been, but still it was a peaceful spot, a grassy spot, a place for quiet contemplation – or a murder.

The morning sun was just rising above the sycamores, casting a warm glaze over the sky. The small body of water sat about two hundred feet down the slope from the southeast corner of the building. A bank of large rhododendron and camellia bushes rimmed the pond along the east side. Roses along the west. A stone bench offered the only seating.

The pond wasn't much larger than a backyard pool, but quite shallow. Giorgio gazed down on the dark lily pads that floated on top of the murky green water, along with the billowy shape of a brown robe. He suddenly felt very old.

A group of officers were already processing the crime scene. Mulhaney stood on the two-foot retaining wall that encircled the pond, legs spread for balance, his camera poised to take aerial shots of the dead priest. The medical examiner was close by, taking note of the air and water temperature. An officer contained a gaggle of reporters down by the entrance. Three murders at a Catholic monastery had put both the town and the retreat at the center of the media map.

Officer Barnes stood off to one side talking with Father Damian who stared blankly in the direction of the water-logged priest as if this new murder had suddenly turned him to stone. Giorgio glanced at his watch. It was only seven o'clock and he hadn't even had his morning coffee. He ignored the rumbling in his stomach and approached Barnes.

"What do we know so far?"

"Not much. Father Daniel found him. He was out for an early morning jog."

Giorgio looked over to where the good-looking Father Daniel stood with the group of monks openly gawking at the floating body of their fellow Jesuit. Daniel wore a loose-fitting black nylon running suit, with a sweatband around his thick, dark hair. His expression was placid, the brown eyes calm, in stark contrast to the tense anxiety of those around him.

"Disperse the crowd," Giorgio said tersely. "But tell Daniel to hang around. I haven't had the pleasure, yet." Barnes nodded and moved away while Giorgio stepped in to speak with the abbot. "Any reason, Father Damian, why anyone would want to see Father O'Leary dead?"

Father Damian's eyes had trouble focusing, but when they did, his expression became guarded. "Of course not. I don't know what's going on here. This is a horrible nightmare. You have no idea."

"I have far too many ideas, Father," Giorgio snapped, glancing over to the pond and the liquid figure of Father O'Leary. "Do you know of any reason why Father O'Leary would have called me yesterday?"

He watched the priest struggle to concentrate before saying, "No. I can't think of any reason."

"We'll need to talk with every monk, again." The abbot's eyes seemed to glaze over at this. "Please tell each monk to go to his room, and this time they need to stay there. I don't want anyone to leave the premises, and I don't want them talking to each other. Understand?"

Damian stared at Giorgio for a long moment without moving. Then he turned rigidly to leave, his shoulders squared and his eyes focused straight ahead. Giorgio's gaze came to rest on Father Daniel who watched Giorgio cautiously. Giorgio found Barnes again.

"Call the station and get some help. I want every monk interviewed before lunch."

Barnes rolled his eyes but left for the squad car. Giorgio pulled out his cell phone and got his brother out of bed. Rocky swore softly but agreed to come as soon as he could. Giorgio signed off as Mulhaney approached.

"The victim has a big gash in the side of his head and a hole in the top of it, so I'm guessing he didn't drown," he said, trying to smile. Mulhaney held his camera in front of him like a child he was protecting from the cold. He hadn't had time to comb his hair, and it stuck out at odd angles, accenting the apprehensive look on his face. "What's going on here, Joe? How many more murders are we going to have?"

Giorgio felt a strange sense of calm he knew others didn't share. He'd worked a serial murder case in New York where seven prostitutes had shown up dead, one by one, over a six-month period. He'd been here before. The anxiety almost bristled in the air around him, and he could see fear reflected in the eyes of the people whose job it was to document the facts. Sierra Madre averaged less than one murder a year. Now, there had been three in a matter of a few days. He would have to find answers and find them soon.

"I don't know," he replied. "But do me a favor and shoot the path and sight lines up to the monastery."

"Sure. No problem."

Getting back to business and avoiding speculation seemed to help, and Mulhaney went back to work. Giorgio turned to find Father Daniel sitting on the cement bench, his hands in his lap.

Daniel was probably only five-foot ten or eleven, but had the compact build of someone who worked out with weights. His dark hair was a shade lighter than his eyes, and he had the smooth, burnished skin of an Italian. Actually, he looked like every male Giorgio had ever wanted to look like. Before Father Daniel said a word, Giorgio knew his voice would sound like an idling car engine. Giorgio walked over silently hoping Daniel would turn out to be the murderer.

"Father Daniel?"

"That's right. I was told you wanted to speak to me."

Giorgio was wrong. His voice sounded like a cello in perfect tune.

"What were you doing out here this morning?" Giorgio immediately regretted the question because the answer was obvious.

"I came out to jog," Daniel replied politely, apparently unaware that Giorgio had stumbled. "I run two or three times a week, usually around the lower fields. I'm afraid I've almost beaten down a track out there." He smiled casually.

"Why did you come down by the pond?"

"That's how I get to the lower fields." He gestured to the sloping path above them. "I stop to stretch here. It was still dark, and I couldn't see anything clearly. I use the lip of the pond to stretch out my calves. That's when I noticed Father O'Leary."

His manner didn't change even though he'd just described finding a dead body. In fact, he displayed no emotion of any kind. Giorgio eyed him, wondering if he was just the kind of person who didn't relate to the misfortune of others, or if he was unconsciously expressing the fact he didn't care about Father O'Leary's fate. Perhaps he *was* the killer.

"It's not every day one finds a dead body," Giorgio offered.

The monk smiled briefly as if Giorgio had made an endearing remark.

"No, it's certainly not," he replied.

"What did you do when you realized it was Father O'Leary?"

The perfect features rearranged themselves into a curious expression. "Actually, it was still dark. All I saw was the outline of the robe. I wasn't even sure it was a body – that is until I reached out to grab the material and grabbed a hand instead."

He shuddered, but his revulsion seemed manufactured and passed almost as quickly as it appeared.

"I went immediately to find Father Damian. By then, it was starting to get light, and Father Damian identified him."

"I received a message that Father O'Leary wanted to see me. You don't know what that was about, do you?"

Daniel's brown eyes popped open like a child caught pulling his sister's hair. "No. I can't imagine why he'd call the police. He was a gentle soul. I can't even imagine why anyone would kill him."

"Do you have a theory about any of this, Father? Why so many people have been murdered here at the monastery?"

"Me? No." For the first time, Daniel showed signs of anxiety by flicking his thumb against the back of his index finger. "I'm fairly new here. Perhaps this all has to do with something that happened before I arrived. I really couldn't say."

"Why did you become a monk, Father?"

The question caught him off guard, and he looked up. Giorgio noticed he continued the nervous mannerism with his thumb.

"I suppose I… uh… felt the need to serve God."

"There are many ways to serve God. Why become a monk?"

Giorgio had a feeling this guy didn't belong here and was merely playing a charade of some kind. Father Damian said the young initiates came for one or two-year periods to train. Giorgio had to assume that by the time they got this far they had already passed many theological and personal tests of strength. Although clearly well-educated, Giorgio couldn't believe Father Daniel had ever passed any real personal test of value in his life. He was as shallow as the pond in which Father O'Leary now floated, but Giorgio would never hear the answer to his question because Barnes interrupted him.

"Detective? We found this tossed behind the roses."

Barnes held out a gloved hand. In it was a heavy jagged rock streaked with blood.

†

Giorgio spent the rest of the morning taking statements. None of the monks had seen or heard anything unusual. Father O'Leary had worked late in the library trying to catch up after his illness. He hadn't seemed agitated lately or spoken of anything that might indicate he was having a problem with anyone.

Rocky showed up within the first hour. He hadn't bothered to shave and looked red-eyed and disheveled. Giorgio avoided comment, choosing instead to drive down to the gated entrance to make a brief statement to the press. At noon, they met back by the pond.

"Why do I feel old before my time?" Giorgio lamented as he slumped onto the bench. "This isn't a puzzle anymore, it's a test: Figure out the answers before someone else drops dead."

Rocky stood a few feet away with his hands stuffed into his jean pockets.

"You're taking it too personally," he countered. "It has nothing to do with you, but everything to do with the people who were killed. I mean, think about it--if the first two murders were committed on the same night, then why would a monk be killed several days later?"

"Because he knew something," Giorgio said.

"Bingo! O'Leary knew something in advance or saw something he shouldn't have. The question is, what did he know?"

"He called me, you know. Yesterday afternoon. He wanted me to call him."

"Maybe he wanted to tell you something."

"Something else is bothering me," Giorgio said as Rocky lit a cigarette and took a draw. "McCready made an observation about the first two murders. He said they seemed like they'd been committed by different people because of the way the bodies were left. Mallery Olsen was left where she would be found. Jeff Dorman was buried. Whoever killed him didn't want him to be found."

"So?" Rocky egged him on.

Giorgio squinted up at his brother. Rocky's six-foot two-inch frame blocked the little sunlight there was.

"Father O'Leary was left in the same bold way that Mallery Olsen was. Almost like a statement. It reminds me of New York."

"Mafia?" Rocky asked alarmed. "C'mon," he waved it away.

"Don't you think there's a certain arrogance to both murders? It's as if the killer was bragging. Yet, Jeff Dorman was buried so that no one would find him."

"So, you think two of the murders have something to do with the mob? What? The Sierra Madre mob?"

"No. Of course not. It just seems all too familiar."

Rocky rolled his eyes. "But what about the finger? O'Leary had all ten of his."

"Yes, but something just tells me O'Leary's death is linked to Olsen's."

"If the mob is involved--and I think it's a really big if--where do you go with something like that?"

Giorgio sighed and stretched his legs out in the grass. "I don't know, but Father Daniel is the only one from New York. And he's a new recruit. I think we'll do some background checking on him."

"He's a cocky bastard anyway," Rocky said.

"And he was the one who found Father O'Leary." Giorgio looked up at Rocky again. "Besides, when was the last time you saw a Catholic monk out jogging?"

They both laughed as Giorgio stood up and Rocky threw his cigarette to the ground. Giorgio eyed the butt and then looked at his brother.

"You want to be brought in for questioning when they pick that cigarette up as evidence?"

The younger Salvatori winced and bent to pick up the trash before the two brothers started back up the slope.

"So one of us has to get to know Father O'Leary... posthumously," Rocky said. "Sounds like a job for me. I'll start asking around."

Giorgio cocked his head. "Why you?"

"Because I can get more out of people than you. Face it, you offend people. People will tell me things they don't even know they're saying."

"And why is that?" Giorgio asked cynically.

"Because they trust me."

Giorgio scoffed. "Really?"

"Don't you remember when I had to take that big history test in twelfth grade in order to graduate? And Little Joey Feldman next door had taken the test *before* everyone else because he was going out of town. Every kid in the class tried to get him to give up the questions. Jack Zelder even tried to bribe him with his BB gun. But Little Joey wouldn't budge."

"And you got him to tell you?" Giorgio said with a lift to his eyebrow.

"Yep." Rocky smiled as if he'd just had the best sex of his life. "Everything. Down to the bonus question on who won the battle between the *Monitor* and the *Merrimack*."

"The what?"

"Never mind. The point is I didn't pay him anything. I merely charmed him into telling me everything I wanted to know." Rocky puffed out his chest like a strutting penguin.

Giorgio grimaced. "I didn't realize you had such a useful talent. How *do* you manage it?"

"It's all in the body language. See, you're sort of tense all the time."

"I am not!"

"Yes, you are. Look at how you hunch your shoulders. And you raise your voice a lot."

"That's a crock!"

"Just like now. On the other hand, I keep my voice low and lean in to the person. Like this." Rocky demonstrated by leaning over Giorgio who waved him away. "I make eye contact, nod my head a lot, and listen. That's the key."

"Listening is the key?" Giorgio asked, walking ahead of his brother. Rocky followed him undaunted.

"Haven't you ever taken a communications class? Listening is everything. I merely got Little Joey Feldman talking about *why* he was going out of town, which by the way was for very personal reasons."

Giorgio stopped, his eyes opened wide. "What personal reasons? You never told me that."

"I made a promise to Little Joey Feldman." Rocky struck an insincere pose.

Giorgio started for their cars. "Well, tell me about it now. You have no right to keep a secret for that long."

"Well, it seems that little Joey was going to live with his aunt in Philadelphia."

"Why?" Giorgio's patience was wearing thin.

"Apparently his stepfather was becoming a little too friendly… if you know what I mean."

Giorgio stopped in his tracks again. "You're kidding? His step-dad was such a pious bastard."

"Yeah, well, it seems he didn't have eyes only for Joey's mom. Anyway, you're missing the point." They continued walking until they reached the parking lot. "I sympathized completely with his plight and admitted to some of my own personal difficulties."

Giorgio stopped abruptly again. "What personal difficulties? You didn't have any difficulties."

"Well, dad's death and living under the watchful eye of my big brother and all." He winked at Giorgio. "Then, I may have said something like that's why I had such a hard time concentrating in school."

"You lying bastard. You duped that poor kid."

Rocky smiled mischievously. "He thought he was helping me. And he did. I aced the test, much to Mrs. Pringle's surprise. And I think I may have helped a poor young troubled kid in the process."

Giorgio tilted his head. "Well, then, by all means, with such a rare gift, you *should* be the one to work your way into the monks' trust and find out what Father O'Leary may have known."

Giorgio opened the car door while Rocky smiled in the background. He'd left Grosvenor in the car, and the dog wiggled all over the place at Giorgio's return.

"Where are you going?" Rocky inquired.

"To meet Elvira Applebaum. You'd better get started with the monks. Meanwhile, I'll do what I can with my limited talents by interviewing people on the periphery." Rocky merely laughed good-naturedly making Giorgio add, "But before you get too close to some of those poor monks, grab some toothpaste. Your morning breath could kill a palm tree."

Rocky's smile faded as Giorgio slipped inside the car. A moment later, he started the car and left Rocky at the curb holding his hand up to his mouth.

† Chapter Thirty †

Elvira Applebaum lived in a cozy Craftsman bungalow just off Orange Grove Boulevard in Pasadena. A tall, slender woman with short gray hair and bright blue eyes greeted Giorgio and then ushered him into a comfortable living room with a wood fireplace mantel faced with cerulean blue tiles.

"May I offer you something to drink, Detective?"

She was a handsome woman in her mid-sixties, standing tall and erect, her hands clasped in front of her.

"No, thank you. I just have a few questions."

"Well, then, please sit down." She indicated a chintz-covered chair and took a wooden rocker herself. "You said on the phone you were investigating the murders up at the monastery. I read about them in the paper. I don't think anything like that has ever happened around here. Two murders," she shook her head. "The priests must be devastated."

"I'm afraid you'll be reading about a third murder tomorrow morning. I'm sure it's already on the news."

Her hand went to her chest in shock. "That's awful. What's happening up there?"

"That's what we'd like to know."

"How can I help?"

She was obviously a woman with a business temperament, a demeanor Giorgio liked.

"I've been studying the building plans for the monastery. I understand your father was the chief architect."

"Yes. The chapel was constructed in the thirties from the old church. They built the monastery around it and asked my father to do the work. He was just out of school then and eager for the opportunity. The monks didn't pay much and were difficult to work with, but my father was glad to have a paycheck in those days."

"Did he tell you anything about the building itself?"

"I remember him talking with my mother. The abbot came to see him when he finished the drawings and ordered him to redo them. They wanted something changed and my father was quite angry about it."

"He wasn't paid for the changes?"

"No. He had offered a bid on the entire project and the abbot argued that the changes were minor. It was all quite secretive, and he wasn't allowed to tell any of the other monks who were on the building committee."

"You said on the phone that your father had passed away. When was that?"

"About twenty years ago."

"And there are no other living relatives that might know more about his work at the monastery?"

Her eyes lit up. "My mother would, but I'm afraid she's quite ill."

"Is she in a nursing home?"

"She lives right here with me." She stood up. "She was napping a while ago. Let me see if she's awake. She loves having visitors, but you won't be able to stay long."

"I understand," Giorgio said, thinking he may have just hit the jackpot.

Elvira Applebaum went down the hallway to the back of the house. Giorgio roamed the living room, stopping to look at a cluster of framed pictures on a wall above a sideboard. In one, he saw a tall man with brown hair cut short, an unruly lock of hair hanging over one eye. The family resemblance was unmistakable. He was looking at Joseph Applebaum holding a croquet mallet and smiling at the camera with the same broad smile as his daughter. A moment later, Elvira Applebaum reentered the room.

"She would be delighted to see you. I must warn you though, she's very weak. She's ninety-one and has been bedridden for some time."

"I'll just take a minute."

She had him follow her to a back bedroom. The curtains were open, allowing filtered sunlight to enter the room. A frail woman lay propped up by pillows in a single bed with a high, carved headboard. The room was neat and clean, yet the smell of urine hung in the air making him think of his grandmother who had lived with his family for two years before she died. Mrs. Applebaum's hair was an iridescent white and lay in soft curls on her pillow. Milky blue eyes met him with a weak smile as she lifted a thin hand towards him.

"Mrs. Applebaum, thank you for seeing me." Her skin was cold to the touch and so fragile he felt if he squeezed too tightly he might break all the bones in her hand.

"It's a pleasure," she whispered. "Elvira said someone's been killed up at the monastery. You're the detective, is that right?"

She seemed spry, despite her infirmity.

"Yes, I'm looking into the murders. Could you answer a few questions about the building?"

"I can try," she said letting her hand fall back to the bed. "What do you want to know?"

"Your husband was the architect."

"That's right. It was Joseph's first real job."

"Your daughter said that some major changes were made to the building plans at the last minute. Could you tell me about that?"

"Joseph was very angry," she said, coughing. "He'd spent nearly a month doing the original plans. Father Simon, I think it was, ordered him to make some changes that caused Joseph to stay up for two nights in a row to finish on time."

"Do you know what those changes were?"

"He wasn't allowed to talk about them, but I remember he was asked to make some kind of internal adjustments that threw everything off. He had to practically start over, and yet the deadline for the drawings wasn't changed. Neither was the fee. We needed the money and so he completed the work."

"But you don't know what those adjustments were?"

"I'm afraid not. He was as good as his word; he didn't share anything with us." She punctuated the reply with a deep, throaty cough, which triggered a series of smaller coughs. Her daughter stepped in to pull up an afghan.

"I'm afraid you'll have to go," she said.

"No!" the old woman almost choked out the word. "Please, don't leave. I want to help." She had trouble getting the words out, but her face was set with determination.

"Would you know who did the construction work during the time your husband was the architect?" He asked the questions now with a growing sense of guilt.

"Not the name of the company," she almost whispered, her head dangling to the side weakly. "But I do know they were from out of town. Joseph commented on it a number of times. He joked once that even the Catholic Church knew how to be deceptive." She started to cough again, but put up a hand telling him to wait a moment. When her lungs relaxed, she whispered, "Please, go on."

Giorgio admired her. She reminded him of his grandmother who had fought right up to the very end, finally succumbing to the cancer that destroyed her liver.

"You wouldn't happen to have copies of the original drawings would you?" He asked this as much to the elder woman as to the daughter.

"No," the daughter replied. "We got rid of everything when my father passed away. I'm sorry."

Giorgio was disappointed. "Well, thank you, Mrs. Applebaum. I appreciate your time."

She smiled warmly. "Not at all, detective. I'm happy to help." She was wheezing now and her voice faltered. "Joseph was very proud of the work he did up there. But I was surprised he ever worked for them again."

Giorgio stopped at the door. "Again? You mean he did additional work at the monastery?"

"Yes, it was around the time of the war," she paused trying to remember. Her eyes fluttered briefly before she continued. "A Father Wingate asked him to do the work."

"Do you know what he was asked to do?"

"He was asked to separate the monk's quarters from the boy's quarters, but something about it made him very angry again. He said they're all alike. He was disgusted enough to say he'd never work there again. In fact, he said he'd never work for the Catholic Church, period."

Giorgio turned an inquisitive eye to the daughter.

"He said the monks were no better than the sinners who confessed to them, and that he was no engineer," the old woman finished.

"Interesting," Giorgio mused. "Thank you both very much"

He left the room and Elvira Applebaum walked him to the door. "I'm sorry we couldn't be of more help."

"You've helped quite a bit." He pulled out his card and handed it to her. "Please, call me if you think of anything else."

She put up a hand to make him pause and faded back into the house, returning with her own business card. It read, "Elvira Applebaum, Executive Director, The Childcare Consortium."

"I have a healthcare worker who stays with my mom during the day, but I can be reached at work."

"Thanks. I appreciate that," he said.

He left her at the door and strolled down the cement walkway thinking about what might have been contained in those original plans. He knew there were secret tunnels. If there was a secret passage between the two halves of the building, it could have provided a means for murder. But only a thorough search of the premises would answer the question, and it might take days. And he had a feeling he didn't have that much time.

†

It was almost seven o'clock by the time Giorgio arrived home. The children bombarded him at the doorway, herding Grosvenor off to the living room. He poked his head into the kitchen and spied a plate set off to one side covered with aluminum foil. The tangy aroma of fried chicken was too great, and he pulled the plate off the counter and sat at the table before seeking out his wife. The mashed potatoes were cold, so he shoved them into the microwave and was standing at the counter ripping the flesh off the chicken bone when Angie appeared at the arched doorway.

"You find food like most hunting dogs find game," she sneered.

He turned to her with a greasy smile. She passed behind him and went to the refrigerator to pour him a glass of milk. He retrieved his potatoes, quickly smothering them in rich butter. She placed the glass on the table and started to leave without another word.

"Angie, we should talk," he said, swallowing quickly.

She turned with a look of restrained patience. "We don't talk, Joe. I talk. You whine. You complain. You lecture. But you don't talk."

He stood motionless, plate in one hand, drumstick in the other. Slowly he set them both on the table, wiped his hands and sat down.

192

"C'mon, Angie. I can't stand being mad at each other. I'm sorry."

She continued to stand in the doorway, arms folded across her chest. He lowered his eyes knowing it made him look pathetic.

"Did you really think the dog would make things okay?" she asked with only slightly more warmth. "He's just one more slob for me to clean up after."

He looked up at her while a sly smile crept across his face. "Yeah, but if you put dish towels on those ears of his, he could sweep the floor."

In spite of her anger, she smiled and he felt the ice begin to break. She came to the table and sat across from him. There was a long pause before she spoke.

"I didn't mean to keep it from you, Joe. Really, I didn't."

He reached out a hand and clasped her fingers. "And I didn't mean to yell. It just scares me, Angie. We don't save enough now. How are we going to feed another mouth, save for college, and plan for our own retirement?"

She lifted those soft brown eyes and placed her other hand over his, turning his heart to mush. "We'll manage, Joe. We always do. God wants us to have this child."

Her faith was so complete, so unwavering. He'd never been able to match her in that department. As a young boy, he'd wondered if somehow God had passed him over – sprinkled the fairy dust on everyone but him.

Looking at Angie now, he knew there was no argument to win here. They would have this child, and it would warm his heart as it had twice before. A cold nose pushed up against his elbow, and Grosvenor laid his long snout across Giorgio's lap.

"Do you want me to take him back?" he asked without much conviction.

She stood and walked around to his side of the table. Grosvenor looked up with his droopy, pathetic eyes. She smiled.

"I think God meant for us to have this dog, too. I'm not sure why," she said, reaching out a hand to pull at one ear, "but there's a reason."

She bent down to kiss her husband, when suddenly they both wrinkled their noses and pulled away, looking at the dog.

Giorgio exclaimed. "Christ, what did you feed him?"

"Phew, he's worse than you!" Angie backed away, waving her hand in front of her face. "Maybe he has to go outside."

She called the kids and ordered them to take him outside. They did so willingly, and Angie left the room laughing, while Giorgio moved to the counter to finish his dinner.

That night, the couple sat together watching TV, and later, in bed, Giorgio played his favorite role – that of ardent lover. Although there would be no curtain call or applause, there was at least one repeat performance, making him feel perfectly cast for the part.

† Chapter Thirty-One †

When Giorgio arrived at the station the next day, he couldn't hide the smile. Even Grosvenor seemed to walk with an extra spring to his step. Giorgio stopped to get coffee at the vending machine and then sauntered the rest of the way down the hallway humming. Swan looked up and seemed to assess the situation immediately.

"Angie change her mind about the dog?"

The sly smile told Giorgio to be careful. He shrugged his shoulders. "It just took some time."

"And a little nookie? Glad to see you've still got it in you, Joe."

"So, what do we know about Father O'Leary?" Giorgio asked.

Swan's smile hung loosely on his face another few seconds and then he let it fade.

"The coroner's report came in early this morning. O'Leary suffered a blow to the left frontal lobe and one to the crown, but that's not what killed him. He was drowned. There was quite a bit of pond water found in his lungs. One tooth was cracked and his lip was split. It appears someone held his head under water until he stopped breathing sometime between eleven o'clock last night and four a.m."

"Another late night rendezvous," Giorgio said distantly. "Was the blood on the rock his?"

"It matches his blood type, but we don't have DNA back, yet. He might have died eventually from the blow to his head, but the pond was convenient and provided the exclamation point at the end of the sentence."

Giorgio looked up. "That's a rather poetic statement for a cop."

Swan shrugged. "Well, the good news is that we have the rock, but we'll never get any fingerprints off of it so it doesn't really help much. Anyway, chances are O'Leary was killed because he saw who killed Olsen. Maybe even Dorman."

"If O'Leary saw Olsen's killer," Giorgio speculated, "then whoever killed her must have been a monk."

"How so?"

"Because otherwise O'Leary would have told Rocky when he interviewed him. On the other hand, he might have wanted to protect a fellow monk. By the way, O'Leary left me a message to call him yesterday."

"Too bad."

The sound of rustling papers made them look up. McCready stood in the doorway.

"When you think about it," the young cop began, "if O'Leary had seen the murderer outside, what are the chances he could identify him? Father Francis said he saw someone from an upstairs window, but couldn't tell who it was."

"It was cloudy that night," Giorgio said. "I've been up there several times now in the dark. Sightlines are blocked from almost any angle, and there's no light out there. It's likely he wouldn't have been able to tell *who* it was. But I bet you twenty dollars he could tell if it was a monk."

"Only if the monk was wearing robes."

"Right again." Giorgio shrugged and glanced at his desk. "But it could have been something else. O'Leary could have known something only the killer knew, maybe something that gave the killer motive or means."

Swan leaned back and threw his legs onto the desk. "The forensics report came back on the bottle you found in Olsen's room. It was clean."

Giorgio looked disappointed. "What about the second bottle I found outside?"

Swan and McCready exchanged a glance. "No fingerprints, but it showed traces of chloral hydrate," Swan replied. "So I guess you were right. Whoever killed Olsen carried both her and the bottle outside."

"Unless he disposed of the bottle later," Giorgio offered. "He could have hidden it until the next day and then thrown it into the trees when no one was around."

"Why would he do that? Why not get rid of it?"

"Maybe we were supposed to find it. Maybe it was a red herring."

"A what?" McCready's face screwed up into a question.

"A false clue. Crystal Chardonnay was the same wine served that night by the caterers. He could have been trying to lead us to a conference attendee or a caterer."

"How'd you find that bottle anyway? We combed that entire area," Swan wanted to know.

Giorgio dared not look at either man or risk exposing his own doubts about how he found it. And he wasn't about to tell them a little ghost had told him.

"That's what makes me think it was placed there later," he said, avoiding Swan's question. "Otherwise you would've found it."

He turned to Olsen's file, which lay on top of his desk. The distraction worked, and there were no follow-up questions. Clipped inside Olsen's folder were photos of the crime scene taken from every angle. The supply closet appeared dark and crowded. Along the left wall was a peg-board covered with hammers, pliers, and other small tools used in general repairs. Two brooms and a mop hung on the far wall. Just beyond the mop was a ladder leaning up against the circuit breaker box. Built-in shelving along the right wall held bottles of cleaners, rags, light bulbs, blankets, and other supplies. In the corner sat a mop bucket, an electric floor buffer, and vacuum. Across the back was a wall-mounted coat rack. A green utility jacket hung on the first hook. Mallery Olsen hung on the third hook, partially blocked by the ladder. The shadows were deepest at that part of the small room and explained why the janitor hadn't seen her right away.

Giorgio stared at the pictures. As he recalled, several monks had either been late to compline that night or absent all together. And because of the time window, the murder could have been committed earlier, perhaps even during the five o'clock Mass. So there was opportunity. But it didn't answer the questions of why a monk would kill a young woman attending a conference in the first place, or how he could pull it off.

"We did check on those gray fibers," he heard Swan saying in the background.

"Yeah?" Giorgio replied absently, still staring at the photos.

"All of the guest rooms have blue or green chenille blankets. But the monks use heavy gray, wool blankets."

"Blankets?" Giorgio looked up as if waking from a dream. "What did you say about blankets?"

"Remember the gray fibers?" Swan said. "You thought they must have come from something the body was wrapped in. Well, we haven't found a gray carpet anywhere, but the blankets are a possibility."

Giorgio wasn't listening. He'd quickly returned to the pile of photos grabbing one from the bottom. The photo he pulled out showed the right wall of the supply closet with the built-in shelving. He picked it up and peered closely at it.

"You know when I'm reciting, I expect you to listen," Swan said in the background. "I've been forced to listen to enough of your play rehearsals."

Giorgio looked over at him with a smile. "Did you ever read 'The Purloined Letter' in high school?"

"The what?"

"The story about the guy who left the letter in plain sight. No one found it because they assumed it was hidden?"

Swan looked confused. "What are you talking about?"

Giorgio got up and moved around his desk so that he could drop the picture squarely in front of Swan. "Our murderer has a sense of humor, don't you think?"

Swan dropped his feet to the floor and looked at where Giorgio pointed a finger – the dimly lit shelves in the closet. One shelf was filled with cleaning supplies and a single gray blanket.

"Let's go get that blanket. Then, we need to figure out how a monk got into Olsen's room without being noticed." Giorgio stepped to the window to look out onto the street, talking as he moved. "We know there are secret tunnels up there; perhaps there are secret connecting doors, too."

He watched the street outside feeling the warmth of having achieved a small victory. The police station sat across from the town's mortuary, a two-story Edwardian-style building with steep front steps. Giorgio stood with his hands in his pockets thinking about a high school friend whose father was a mortician. Brady Mandero looked like one of his father's stiffs: thin and pale, with dark circles under his eyes.

He'd fascinated Giorgio with stories about how his dad fixed up dead people to look like they were still alive. He even gave Giorgio a small tin of mortician's wax once to play with.

Giorgio remembered the smell of the creamy wax made to look like the translucent color of skin. Giorgio had experimented with adding several warts to his cheek one summer, and once nearly scared his mother to death making her think he had small pox.

But all memories of the mortuary weren't fun and games. Giorgio had gotten lost at night once in the basement of Mandero's Mortuary, a cavernous three-story building on the lower east side of New York. He'd searched frantically through empty hallways in the dark looking for the elevator, but found the casket room instead. The memory still gave him a chill. Staring at the building across the street now, he pictured the string of bodies brought there recently and envisioned corpses lying behind closed doors along the same sort of narrow hallways that had frightened him as a child.

"You listening?" he heard Swan say.

Giorgio turned. "Hunh?"

"How do we find the secret doors?"

Giorgio turned back to the window. Brady Mandero and the ghosts from the mortuary had disappeared.

"We go look for them."

† Chapter Thirty-Two †

An hour later, Rocky joined them at the monastery. He and Swan waited by the car while Giorgio went to find Father Damian. The day was overcast, but there was no real threat of rain.

Giorgio found Damian clipping dead buds from a group of rose bushes clustered in the corner of the gated garden. An older monk worked nearby pulling leaves from a birdbath, while Father Francis sprayed weed killer along the fence line. Father Damian's body sagged as he worked, as if all energy had been drained away. He glanced up when Giorgio and Grosvenor appeared through the arbor. Even at this distance, Giorgio could see the dark beard stubble that rimmed his jaw line.

"Good morning, Detective." Whatever command he once had over his voice had been replaced by an empty, hollow sound that was hardly recognizable.

"Good morning, Father. I was wondering if we could talk."

The brown eyes searched Giorgio's, perhaps looking for more bad news. He dropped his hands and walked stiffly to a cement bench that sat in front of some arborvitae. He slumped down and turned to Giorgio with vacant eyes.

"What's going on, Detective? This is madness."

"What's going on, Father, are a lot of lies and deception. Starting with you."

The caterpillar eyebrows arched in disbelief. "Surely you don't think I had anything to do with those murders."

"What about the drug deals going on out here in the garden?"

His face froze. "Drugs?"

"And the affair with Ms. Peters?"

He glanced towards the nearest monk and then dropped his head as he realized there was no point in denying the charge. "Yes, we were having an affair, but I had nothing to do with the drugs. Or the murders. You must believe me!"

"I need to know more about the secret passage you and Ms. Peters used. How did you find it?"

He gazed across the garden as if talking to himself. "I found it quite by accident. I spun the wrong combination on the wall safe in my office one day, and the whole wall opened up in front of my eyes."

"And you told Ms. Peters?"

"Not right away. She was hired about six months later. When we… when it appeared we had an attraction for each other and had no place to go, I came up with the idea to use the secret door."

"Does anyone else know about the door and the tunnel?"

"I don't know," he shrugged. "Perhaps Father O'Leary did. He used to tell a story about a local man who pressured the Catholic Church decades ago to sell the property so he could sub-divide it into residential lots. Of course, the monks refused. According to Father O'Leary, the battle went on for months until local residents started reported sightings of a ghost in the bell tower. You can imagine it would have frightened the entire neighborhood. According to Father O'Leary, the ruse was eventually discovered, and the man confessed to using a secret passage to pull off his stunts. I'm afraid none of us put much stock in the story. There is nothing in the church records and none of the locals seemed to know about it. Then I found it, the secret door. I never told anyone until Anya… I mean, Ms. Peters."

"Did she tell anyone?"

"I don't think so. We were very careful. Of course I didn't know she was using the tunnel for other purposes. Perhaps you should ask her."

"I'll do that. And we'd like your permission to search the building again."

The priest dropped his head in submission. "By all means, search all you want. I just want this thing to end."

✝

The three officers concentrated their efforts on the rooms adjacent to Olsen's. Giorgio entered the supply closet on the monks' side. The room was smaller than the one in which Mallery Olsen had been left on display. There was a single wall sconce on the inside wall next to the door, but it didn't work. Shelves lined only the left and rear wall. The wool blankets were folded on two wide shelves along the left wall, while the shelves along the back wall held rolls of toilet paper, folded sheets, and towels. Giorgio pulled out his flashlight and began a thorough search, pulling items off the shelves in an attempt to get a clear view of the wall behind.

The interior walls were made out of pine, and he pressed his fingers on any piece of wood that appeared to have a knot. But nothing happened. He pushed his foot against the floor moldings and into corners and ran his fingers along all the edges of the shelving. He pulled and twisted the light fixture, but it didn't move. He worked the light switch as he had before, but not only did the wall not move, the light never turned on. Unlike the closet downstairs, there was no hanging crucifix or embellishment of any kind. Using the butt of his hand, he pounded on the inside wall hoping to hear a hollow sound indicating a passage on the other side. His reward was Rocky's voice calling back to him from the closet outside of Mallery Olsen's room. Frustrated, he descended the stairs and joined Swan and Rocky. Their search had been equally fruitless.

"If there is a secret way into or out of Mallery Olsen's room, we can't find it," Rocky almost pouted.

"I couldn't find anything on the other side either."

Giorgio did a quick search of the inside of the second closet, but it was almost identical to the one on the other side except for the color of the blankets.

"Damn!" Giorgio almost slammed the closet door closed and stood with his hands on his hips. "We have to get our hands on the original plans of this building. Rocky, why don't you take a trip down to City Hall and see if the original plans are still on file there?"

"Okay. What are you going to do?"

"I'm going to talk to Anya Peters."

† Chapter Thirty-Three †

Giorgio left Grosvenor with McCready and headed for the county jail to interview Anya Peters. He was forced to wait for Peters' attorney, a young woman dressed to intimidate men – probably not all men, just men like Giorgio, whose mere presence seemed to piss her off. Peters was as tight-lipped as ever. She continued to deny any involvement in the trafficking of drugs and blamed Giorgio for planting evidence in the passageway. She also denied knowing anything more about secret passageways.

He decided to interview Colin Jewett, who was housed in a separate building. Jewett was much more cooperative once Giorgio implied that Anya Peters had laid all the blame at his feet. Jewett's attorney was a quiet, pudgy man who sat in a corner and listened as Jewett explained how he met Peters at a party about six months earlier. Once she'd learned of his past incarceration, she presented him with an offer he couldn't refuse. She knew someone who worked for a produce company in Los Angeles. Drugs smuggled across the border were hidden in boxes of lettuce and shipped north. Her contact routed the boxes to appropriate locations where the drugs were removed.

When Peters secured the job at the monastery, she decided it would be the perfect cover. With her recommendation, Jewett got a job with the catering company, and Peters got Mary Fields to contract with the produce company. Peters' affair with Father Damian gave her an alibi and a reason to be at the monastery late at night. Colin Jewett confessed that Peters always dressed as a monk, but denied having ever seen the tunnel. By the end of the interview, Jewett's attorney was asking for a plea bargain.

Giorgio returned to the station to talk with Swan, who reported they had gotten a statement from the cleaning lady who confirmed she had found mud scattered across the floor in Poindexter's room. She had also removed an empty wine bottle and two used glasses from John Marsh's room.

"McCready already told me about the mud in Poindexter's room," Giorgio confirmed. "But why don't you find out who Marsh was entertaining? By the way, where's McCready? I need to get Grosvenor, and I want Poindexter's address. I think it's time I paid him a visit."

Giorgio found McCready in the break room feeding corn nuts to Grosvenor. He got Poindexter's address and then loaded Grosvenor into the car. A few minutes later, he was handing off the dog to the kids, grabbing a piece of cold chicken from the refrigerator, giving Angie a kiss on the cheek, and heading for South Pasadena.

It was a little after five o'clock when he arrived at Cory Poindexter's Spanish-style apartment building. Poindexter lived in a ground floor unit off an octagonal-shaped courtyard planted with broad-leafed greenery and the occasional hibiscus added for color.

Giorgio rang the bell and waited for several seconds before a young blonde dressed in a beige slinky dress and heels answered the door. She was of medium height, with large green eyes and a healthy tan.

"I'm Detective Salvatori with the Sierra Madre Police Department. I'd like to speak to Mr. Poindexter."

"He's not home from work yet," she drawled in an exaggerated Southern twang. "It's about that murder, isn't it?"

"I have some questions for him."

"Would you like to come in?" She stepped aside, her green eyes mapping his face in a way that made Giorgio uncomfortable.

"Thank you, Ms.... uh?"

"Chambers. My name is Sydney Chambers. Cory should be home in a few minutes. We're going to the theater tonight."

"Thank you, Ms. Chambers. It shouldn't take long."

The suffocating smell of cigarette smoke permeated the room, and a new carton of Pall Malls sat on the kitchen counter. While the room was filled with high-end steel-framed leather sectionals and several expensive pieces of artwork, it was clear Cory Poindexter wasn't much of a housekeeper.

A trash container filled with empty beer bottles sat next to the refrigerator, while the sink overflowed with dirty dishes. Clothes were tossed carelessly on the floor, and a pair of dirty Nike tennis shoes sat underneath the couch. A pair of women's bikini underwear hung from one of the bar stools. The girl allowed Giorgio to notice the panties and then coyly lifted them off the stool and folded them in her hands.

"Did Cory mention anything about the murder that night?" he asked, conscious that she was staring at him. He didn't figure she could give him anything of note, but occasionally he'd had luck with offhand remarks made by secondary players.

"No," she answered in her slow, Southern drawl. "Just that some poor woman had gotten herself strangled." She played with the lace panties in her hands, slipping her fingers through the leg holes.

Giorgio's eyes focused on the Nike shoes. "Mr. Poindexter has boats for feet," he joked, commenting on the size.

"Size twelve-something. You know what they say?" She smiled seductively, letting the question hang in the air. When he only smiled, she finally asked, "You're that actor, aren't you?"

She drew the last word out as if she were talking about a baby lamb. The question took Giorgio by surprise.

"Excuse me?"

"You were in that play the other night. You played a judge or something." She leaned over and grabbed a piece of paper off the glass coffee table, thrusting it in his face. It was the program from *Witness for the Prosecution.*

"Oh, yes," he faltered. "I was the prosecutor."

"You were good," she said, finally bunching the panties up in her hands. "I didn't think I'd like that play, but Cory's boss took us for opening night. He loves the theater and invites Cory all the time. We kind of have to go. How'd that guy get stabbed in the end, anyway? It looked real."

This was not the murder Giorgio wished to discuss, but he didn't know how to get off the subject without being rude.

"Oh, it's just a bunch of stage business. If I told you, you'd be disappointed at how simple it was."

Just then the door opened and Cory Poindexter walked in dressed in a crisp tan suit and blue silk tie. He carried a slim briefcase and his car keys. His mouth nearly dropped open at seeing Giorgio comfortably situated in his living room talking to his girlfriend.

"What are you doing here?" He said this more gruffly than he probably intended.

"I had some more questions," Giorgio replied.

The young man eyed him before handing his keys to the girl. "Go get the mail."

She stuffed the panties between the seat cushions of the sofa and moved obediently toward the door. "He was in that play, Cory. He's the guy with the wig." She giggled as she left the room.

"We're going out soon. What do you need to know?" He went to the refrigerator and grabbed a beer. "I'd offer you one, but as I said, we're leaving." The look on his face implied he enjoyed the opportunity to be rude.

Giorgio decided to be blunt. "You said you took a walk the night of the murder. Where did you go?"

"I told you," he said in between swigs. "Just around the building."

"But you stayed close to the building?"

Giorgio watched him. The man seemed to be calculating his answer but his nervousness showed as he tapped the side of the beer can with his index finger.

"I stayed on the path. I wasn't walking around in the flower beds if that's what you're getting at. I went for a walk, not a hike."

Giorgio wondered if Poindexter had ever competed in sports since he clearly didn't like losing. He appeared casual, leaning against the counter, but the tightness in his jaw indicated he was anything but relaxed. The two men locked eyes as if in combat until Giorgio broke the silence.

"You probably weren't aware that we found a footprint."

Giorgio was lying about the footprint, but he thought he might score a point here if his luck held.

"I hadn't heard."

"Yes," Giorgio began to wander around the apartment, casually looking at the artwork. "It was approximately a size eleven and a half. Maybe twelve."

He stopped at the end of the sofa where the tennis shoes sat and turned to catch Poindexter staring down at the shoes. Poindexter looked up with the expression of an angry cur. He pushed himself away from the counter.

"I didn't kill that girl, Detective."

The tone of his voice warned Giorgio to back off. Giorgio ignored it.

"Oh, I'm sorry. I wasn't referring to the murder of that young woman. The footprint was taken out in the vegetable garden...where we found another body. A young man named Jeff Dorman."

Poindexter's facial muscles seemed to freeze in place. He'd been caught off guard and didn't like the angle.

"Who's Jeff Dorman?" he asked, tight-lipped.

Giorgio began to circle the living room, making Poindexter rotate to follow him. "Another conference attendee. But you already knew that, didn't you?"

"I don't know who you're talking about," Poindexter replied.

"You were seen talking to him."

"I talked to a lot of people. That's what you do at a conference. It doesn't mean I knew them all."

Giorgio moved to where the ashtray sat on the counter. "Where did you go that night when the man you were walking with went inside?"

"I stayed outside and had a cigarette. There's no crime in that."

Giorgio lifted one of the cigarette butts out of the ashtray. "I picked up a half smoked Pall Mall near where Mr. Dorman was buried."

Poindexter stepped in and grabbed the ashtray, throwing the whole thing into the nearby trashcan. "It's a common brand."

Giorgio looked directly at Poindexter. "I suppose." He let his hand drop and deftly dropped the butt into his pocket.

Poindexter moved in close. "Detective, if you want to arrest somebody you should talk with the people who were outside that night."

Giorgio brightened up. "Who would that be?"

"There was a monk hidden up in the trees having a cigarette."

"How do you know it was a monk?"

"Because he was wearing robes. It was just before I went back inside." He paused as if figuring out the details. "I came down... I mean, around the northeast corner of the building and saw a flash of light. I looked up and could just barely see a monk standing under that large oak tree."

"Did he see you?"

"I don't think so," he faltered, moving away from Giorgio.

"What about the person you said you saw from the window upstairs?"

He paused. "It was just a shadow moving in the direction of the west parking lot," he said.

"Was it another monk?"

"I don't know," he snapped. "I just saw a figure in the dark. Now, if you don't mind, Detective...."

Poindexter started toward the door, but Giorgio felt like driving the needle in more deeply to see if he might yet hit a nerve.

"You know, we found mud all over the floor in your room."

Poindexter stopped and turned, his face revealing a low level of fear.

"We shouldn't have any trouble matching it to the gardens because of the high clay content." Giorgio began to move towards the door as if ready to leave. "Vegetable gardens also use insecticides and fertilizers. Shouldn't be hard to see if that's where the mud in your room came from."

"I told you I took a walk," Poindexter scowled. "Perhaps I stepped off the path into a flower bed." He pulled a pack of cigarettes out of his pants pocket. When he noticed the Pall Mall brand name he quickly put them back.

"But you just said that you didn't step into any flower beds."

"I said I couldn't remember!" he nearly shouted. He pointed a finger at Giorgio's chest. "Listen, Detective, you ought to be out running down real clues and not over here harassing me about dirty shoes."

The game had gained momentum, but Giorgio didn't budge.

"I suppose the fact you changed out of your tuxedo into casual clothes that night would be a fact more to your liking." Giorgio held Poindexter's gaze even though he had no testimony about a change in clothes. The look on Poindexter's face told him he'd hit pay dirt.

"You know, Detective, I'd be careful. You're fishing and you know it. You're just a small town cop who thinks he's finally got some big case to show off your stuff. Well, you don't have the *stuff*, not here, not with me. Now, I really have to get ready to go." He reached past Giorgio and opened the door.

Giorgio stepped into the late afternoon shadows and paused, turning back to Poindexter. "Perhaps a polygraph will change that."

"You really shouldn't carry the roles you play on stage into real life, Detective. You're not that good of an actor." With that, Poindexter slammed the door.

Giorgio turned and headed for his car, smiling to himself. Halfway there, he met the Southern Belle returning with a few letters in her hands. Giorgio stopped her, hoping to draw her into a casual conversation.

"Well, a night on the town," he smiled. "Sounds like fun. Where did you say you were going?"

"Some fundraiser for a kids' camp. After dinner we all go to the Pasadena Playhouse for the opening of some contemporary play. Cory says he has to be seen at these things." She shrugged as if she wasn't interested. "He's trying to move up into the executive office, I guess."

"Well, that's how it's done. Go out, wear your tuxedo, and attract the right kind of attention."

"Not tonight," she drawled. "His tux is still at the cleaners. He must have rolled in the dirt at that conference the other night," she said with a smirk. "He won't get it back until this weekend."

Giorgio grinned. "Too bad. Well, enjoy yourselves."

She smiled vacuously in return and continued in the direction of the apartment. He returned to his car feeling satisfied and more than a little smug.

† Chapter Thirty-Four †

Giorgio worked late that night, piecing together information that could eliminate suspects and help determine how the three murders might be related. Young Father Daniel, though a long shot with no apparent motive, certainly couldn't be eliminated. Nor could John Marsh. Then there was Corey Poindexter and Colin Jewett. Poindexter had been outside alone at the right time, but was it to kill Mallery Olsen or Jeff Dorman? Even Anya Peters couldn't be ruled out as a suspect. Mallery Olsen was quite small and Peters had both the resolve and the knowledge about the tunnels to have pulled it off. Lastly, there was Father Damian. He had opportunity, although Giorgio found it implausible that he had the constitution for murder. But he might know more than he was confessing.

It was after eleven when Giorgio finally dragged himself through his front door. He had one thing on his mind – a late supper and a hot bath. He'd only made it to the kitchen when Angie emerged from the den with a message from the theater.

"Marvin called a half hour ago," she said quietly. "Apparently there's a major problem at the theater. He wants you to come down as soon as you can."

Giorgio groaned. "Damn! I'm beat." He shuffled into the kitchen and grabbed a frozen cheese enchilada from the freezer and threw it into the microwave.

"He sounded pretty desperate," Angie added, finding a plate and silverware. She set a place for him at the table and then turned and slipped her arms around his waist as he waited at the microwave. He grabbed her hands and pulled her arms tight around him.

"How's our baby?"

She smiled and kissed him on the neck.

"He, or she, is doing just fine. I was just looking through our old baby name books. What do you think of Carter or Emily?"

He laughed and turned around, pulling her close. "Well, they're not Italian names, but I think you've earned the right to name this baby anything you want."

Just then, the microwave beeped. Reluctantly, Giorgio released his wife and turned to remove his dinner. He grabbed a can of pop and sat down to eat.

"I'll see you when you get home," she said seductively, giving him a parting kiss on the top of the head. "Fix whatever it is and come back soon."

He watched her disappear and quickly stuffed the enchilada down his throat. With any luck, Marvin would have the problem fixed by the time he got there.

He and Marvin constituted the entire theater building committee, and together they took care of a wide variety of maintenance problems. Over time they had fixed everything from a leaky roof to a squeaky stage floor. Giorgio's uncle had been an apartment super in Brooklyn, and he'd picked up a fair amount of do-it-yourself tips. Marvin worked with his father as an electrical contractor and was a whiz with anything that required wiring.

It was almost midnight when Giorgio arrived to find the two-story building completely in the dark. The nearby streetlights outlined the bloodless fingers of ivy that crawled up the brick exterior. Giorgio suspected that an electrical cable had blown and silently hoped it hadn't interrupted a rehearsal. Since Marvin was an electrician by trade, he assumed his job would be to hold a flashlight while Marvin fixed the problem.

The side parking lot was empty except for Marvin's old gray sedan. Giorgio grabbed the flashlight from his glove compartment and stepped out next to Marvin's car. A crisp breeze rustled the trees overhead, making Giorgio think of the night the button had bounced to within an inch of his foot. His fingers sought out the small piece of metal in his pocket before he climbed the short set of stairs to the side entrance.

The door was propped open with a block of wood, as they often did during a performance. He found the light switch just inside the door, but as he suspected, flicking it up and down produced nothing. He called out Marvin's name.

Only a penetrating silence called back. Giorgio passed the door to the dressing rooms and moved to the end of the hallway where a door led to the south side of the two hundred-seat auditorium. He paused in the curtained doorway, playing the beam of light over the empty seats.

There was something intoxicating about a theater, even when it was empty. Every night was different. Mistakes were made. Lines were read with passion, or not, and the audience, though sometimes feared and hated by the actors, was always the wild card. Each one of those seats held the promise of another laugh, a gasp, a tear, or the threat of awkward silence. Giorgio loved it.

He glanced around. The exit lights were dark, leaving the entire room as black as the bottom of a dry well. Giorgio called Marvin's name a second time. A noise drew his attention to the back of the stage where a door led to the basement and the fuse box. He moved down the side aisle and up the steps when an inner voice told him to stop.

Giorgio allowed the flashlight to inch across the stage where the theater company had begun building the set for their annual production of *A Christmas Carol*. The skeleton of a London street scene rose out of the murky depths of the stage floor at irregular angles. Here a pawnshop. There a bakery. Giorgio stepped onto the stage and drifted to his right, moving behind the stage-left curtains and toward the back wall.

The basement door stood ajar. He peeked around the doorframe into the basement. Marvin's red toolbox sat on the floor next to a battery operated work light. A can of gasoline sat next to the theater generator, along with the small CD player Marvin always carried. The breaker box was open on the wall above. Although Marvin wasn't visible, Giorgio relaxed.

"Marvin," Giorgio called out. "It's me. Where the hell are you?"

He moved down the steps, peering into the shadows filled with boxes of stage props. A piece of paper lying next to the toolbox caught his eye. He picked it up, using his flashlight to read a short, hand-written message.

I told you, you weren't that good!

Giorgio immediately reached for his gun, but too late.

A hammer slammed his forearm, almost cracking the bone as he drew the gun; the blow sent the gun skidding across the floor.

Giorgio spun away, tripping over the stool and landing on his back. A man in a hooded sweatshirt and ski mask lunged at him from the shadows. Giorgio fish-tailed sideways and clamped his feet around the man's lower leg, yanking him off balance and bringing him down right on top of him. His attacker rolled sideways, jumping back onto his feet and lifting the hammer again. Giorgio jack-knifed backwards, getting himself clumsily to his feet.

The man lunged a third time, but Giorgio grabbed the hammer with his left hand. The two struggled back and forth, bumping first against the generator and then slamming into the hot water heater. The other man was taller by several inches and felt younger and more agile. Was it Poindexter? At one point, Giorgio yanked one of the man's hands behind his back and then smashed his face into the fuse box. The cry of pain was a voice Giorgio recognized.

Poindexter twisted away, pulling Giorgio with him. The two fell, rolling sideways until a knee caught Giorgio sharply in the abdomen. He let go and groaned halfway to a standing position just as Poindexter headed for the gun lying on the floor a few feet away. Giorgio stumbled after him, tackling him from behind and sending the two of them head first into a stack of boxes. Giorgio grasped the arm holding the gun and yanked it behind him. First rule of the police force – never surrender your weapon.

Poindexter struggled to rise, but Giorgio pinned him with one knee while trying to release the gun. But the injury to his right arm prevented him from closing his hand around the gun, and the hesitation allowed Poindexter to jerk around. Giorgio toppled into the stack of boxes. Poindexter got nimbly to his feet just as Giorgio's good hand found something on the floor. He threw whatever it was, forcing Poindexter to jerk to his left. The skull from Hamlet smashed against the wall.

Giorgio followed it, coming in low but the younger man spun and clipped him with the barrel of the gun exactly where Anya Peters had hit him. It didn't take much. Giorgio went face down in the decades-old dirt, blinded with pain. He lay motionless, his head swimming. Within seconds, he was being dragged backwards and dumped a few feet from the water heater. A moment later, the suffocating odor of gasoline filled his nostrils, and his mind began to scream.

A soft chuckle accompanied the strike of a match, and in less than a heartbeat, the room was ablaze. As flames leapt toward him, Giorgio forced himself to his knees. The room came into focus revealing the foot of the stairs already engulfed in flames. Poindexter was gone. The room was filling quickly with a mind-bending heat. He had to move fast.

Giorgio had visited the basement only a few times before. It was situated below ground level so there were no windows. Too bad for that. Small and cluttered with cardboard boxes, furniture, and a couple of bookcases, it also provided an abundance of fuel. Really too bad. He made one attempt to break through the flames now halfway up the stairs, but was stopped by the roaring heat. He turned and searched for another means of escape as a fleeting thought entered his mind.

It was a play he'd done in college, in which a twentieth-century protagonist was trapped in a twelfth-century dungeon. The fiendish bad guy had pumped gas into the closed room leaving the hero to die. But, voila! At the last moment, the hero remembered a secret doorway and escaped. The memory reminded Giorgio there was a second door to the prop room.

When the theater was built, the basement had been used by the actors to travel unencumbered from one side of the stage to the other. Today, a catwalk at the back of the building provided easier access, but the door was still there. He'd only seen it once and was pretty sure it was on the opposite side of the room. If only he could find it through the smoke.

He staggered forward. The air was so hot his skin felt raw, and he was having difficulty breathing. Reaching inside his coat, he grabbed his handkerchief and placed it over his mouth. He stumbled past shelves of old dishes until he reached a tall stack of boxes. Somewhere in there was a door.

He threw aside containers filled with old tea sets, wigs, and artificial food, spilling their contents across the floor. A wax apple rolled into the flames and melted instantly, its red dye staining the floor like draining blood. Giorgio was coughing now and gasping for air. He was getting dizzy and tripped over an old baby buggy, falling onto one knee. One hand hit the floor and he used it to steady himself. As he lifted himself up, the same hand brushed against something metal. It was his gun.

Without thinking, he stuffed the gun into his pocket, then lunged forward again, pushing furniture and boxes away from the wall in a frenzy. He could hardly see more than a foot in front of him now and tears ran down his face as the smoke stripped his eyes like acid. A heavy beam toppled from a shelf blocking him and he let out a cry of frustration. He squatted to lift the heavy beam, but it came up so easily he was thrown backwards onto the floor. Like everything else, it was only a prop.

He looked up from the floor, his head spinning, his arm throbbing, his lungs burning. This could be his last moment alive. Just then, the hazy outline of a door tucked behind a flimsy set of movable shelves flickered through the smoke. Though his lungs felt as if they might collapse at any moment, he threw off the false beam and mustered the energy to pull the shelving unit forward, throwing its contents onto the floor. He squeezed behind it and reached for the doorknob. The door was stuck. Using both hands, he yanked and pulled, but the door wouldn't budge. In one desperate move he slammed his whole body against the door, hoping to loosen it like the stubborn lid to a pickle jar. When he pulled again, the door scraped open.

He pushed his way through to the other side, stumbling over a stack of paint cans and up a small staircase. He had to hurry. The fire would follow him now that it had a new source of oxygen. With a frantic shove, he pushed through into the scene shop, closing the door tightly behind him. Groping blindly in the dark past work tables and sinks, half painted flats and stacks of lumber, he found his way to the exit door. With a last heavy shove, he burst outside wheezing and drawing fresh air into his lungs. When he could finally fill his lungs without pain, he leaned back against the brick wall listening to the blare of a siren in the distance. At least he wouldn't have to call this one in.

† Chapter Thirty-Five †

Giorgio sat on the edge of a gurney while a young black doctor bandaged his arm. A nurse had helped him clean his face and hands so that he appeared less charred and more human, but his clothes smelled like the inside of an ashtray. This was a small community hospital where the emergency room functioned like an urgent care center. The doctor had determined Giorgio's arm wasn't broken, but the hammer had lacerated the skin and badly bruised the bone. He'd also received first degree burns to his face, much like a bad sun burn. Giorgio was warned the arm would be swollen, and an ugly bruise would probably surround his forearm for the better part of a month. The burns would heal by themselves, but they'd had to use antiseptic on his scalp where the gun butt had split the skin. All in all, he felt like hell.

The doctor wrapped his arm with gauze and Giorgio flexed his fingers just to make sure he could. When the muscles rippled across the injured bone, they created a sharp pain that made him cringe. Just then, the curtain rattled and Swan stepped into the cubicle.

"Barnes called Angie. She's on her way."

"What about the theater?" Giorgio envisioned a pile of blackened rubble.

"The fire was contained to the basement, but there was a lot of smoke damage. At least no one else was in the building."

"What about Marvin Palomar? His car was in the parking lot." Giorgio felt queasy thinking about what might have happened to his friend.

"As I said, no one else was found in the theater."

"Send someone to his apartment. I need to know he's okay."

"I'll call Samson. You think it was Poindexter?"

"I'm sure of it. I recognized his voice. And he left me a note."

Swan arched his eyebrows. "Do you still have it?"

Giorgio sneered. "Are you kidding? I barely got myself out, but Poindexter should have a large bruise on his left cheek where I smashed his face into the fuse box."

Swan grinned. "That should help."

The doctor finished taping the gauze into place and left the two men alone, but not before telling Giorgio he could pick up a prescription for pain medication from the nurse. Giorgio slipped off the rolling gurney. The gauze made it difficult to roll down his sleeve, so he left it rolled up and grabbed his coat off the back of a metal chair. One whiff of the jacket made him turn up his nose.

"Guess I'll be getting some new clothes."

He threw the coat over his good arm as Swan pushed the curtain aside. They stepped into the nursing area, where a circular nursing station filled the center of the room. Behind the nursing station were automatic double doors leading to the ambulance bay.

"I wonder what role Poindexter plays in all of this."

"What do you mean?"

"There have been three murders up there," Giorgio said, talking as he circled the nurse's station and headed for the waiting room. "And I don't think they were all committed by the same person."

"Which one was Poindexter responsible for?" Swan stepped to one side to let a nurse pass, nearly knocking over an IV pole. He caught it just in time.

"The mud and the cigarettes tell me he probably killed Jeff Dorman," Giorgio said, stopping at the end of the counter. He leaned over to speak to a young nurse.

"Dr. Bateman told me he'd leave a prescription for me."

"Yes, sir, here it is," she smiled, handing him a small slip of paper. "Take one every four hours. Preferably with food."

"Thanks." He pocketed the slip of paper and led Swan towards the door to the waiting room. "Look," he said over his shoulder, "Poindexter told me today he saw two people outside that night. He said he saw a monk tucked into the bushes having a cigarette. If he's telling the truth, then that might have been O'Leary."

"You think he killed O'Leary?"

"Maybe, if O'Leary saw him kill Dorman. But Poindexter said the monk didn't see him. However, it sounded as if he started to say he saw the monk as he was coming down from somewhere."

"From upstairs?" Swan asked.

"Or from up the hill," Giorgio said. "He quickly corrected himself and said he was coming from the east side of the building."

"Which one is it?"

"That's what I'd like to know. I've walked the property several times. Coming from the east side, as Poindexter says he was, nothing blocks your view of the back doorway. But if you're coming down from the hill...well, that's another story. Trees and bushes block you at almost every turn. He said earlier that he saw someone from the upstairs window moving along the pathway towards the kitchen. I think he saw someone, but he didn't see them clearly because he was coming down from the vegetable garden – after killing Dorman."

Swan shrugged his massive shoulders. "But why make up the story about seeing someone from the upstairs window?"

"Because he had a piece of information that could lead suspicion away from him in the case of Mallery Olsen, but he had to use it in a way that wouldn't place him on the hill, just in case Dorman was found."

"And, if he was coming down from the hill..." the big cop mused.

"He killed Dorman," Giorgio finished. "He slipped up by giving both answers. The question is - did he also see Olsen's killer or just Anya Peters going out for her drug deal?"

Swan let out a hefty sigh. "Man, that monastery was a busy place that night."

"No kidding," Giorgio agreed.

They were standing just inside the small emergency room lobby. A woman dressed in sweat pants and a sloppy t-shirt stood beside the counter holding a crying baby. The mother talked earnestly to the nurse who motioned her into the back. Giorgio and Swan stepped aside to allow her through. Giorgio watched the woman disappear, thinking about the late night feedings, dirty diapers, and trips to the emergency room that would become a part of his life again all too soon. With a sigh, he turned his attention back to Swan who was still focused on the case.

"So, did Poindexter kill Olsen?" Swan asked.

"I don't think so. Why would he bury Dorman and not the others?"

"Time?" Swan replied, playing devil's advocate.

"Meaning he had more time to bury Dorman than he did the others?"

"Could be."

"But they were killed around the same time, and there's no evidence that Mallery Olsen was killed in the storeroom," Giorgio argued. "That means her killer took great risk in carrying her body down there. Why would he do that when he could have just left her in her room? It's the same thing with Father O'Leary. The killer could have easily dragged the monk into the trees and at least *delayed* discovery, or even just left him to die on the ground. Instead, O'Leary was purposely pushed into the pond. I think it was some kind of statement. Just like hanging Mallery Olsen in the supply closet and taking her little finger."

Swan was nodding in agreement when Officer Barnes entered through the automatic doors. "Detective," he addressed Giorgio, "there's a man here who wants to see you."

Giorgio followed him outside where Oliver, the homeless man, was standing next to the ambulance bay, nervously shifting his weight from one foot to the other. The light tucked under the overhang illuminated his droopy skin, patchy with dirt. His long, stringy hair was beginning to roll itself into ringlets, and the quilted jacket was torn in several places. The ripe odor of unwashed human flesh had already permeated the air around him. He looked around with a furtive glance as Giorgio approached.

"Oliver," Giorgio started, "what are you doing here?"

"You okay, Detective?" Oliver clicked his teeth as if he wore dentures.

"I'm fine. Is there something wrong?"

"No." The little man watched the other officers anxiously as if they might produce handcuffs at any moment. "I jest wanted to make sure you was all right."

"How did you know I was here?"

"I saw the fire," he slurred through rotting teeth. "I was working the cans around the park and I saw that young guy leave in a hurry. Then I smelled the smoke."

Giorgio grabbed for Oliver's arm making him jerk away. "Wait. It's okay. You saw someone leave the theater?"

Oliver relaxed when he realized Giorgio meant no harm. "Some tall guy with blonde hair. He practically skidded out of the parking lot. Couple minutes later, I smelled the smoke and hurried to the shelter to call in the fire."

"What car?" Giorgio pushed him.

"Well, there was only one other car in the lot besides yours. That gray sedan."

His answer hit Giorgio like a body blow. There could be only one reason why Poindexter would be driving Marvin Palomar's car.

"Any chance you could identify that man again?" Giorgio asked somberly.

The old man appeared to chew on the inside of his cheek. "I saw him pull in earlier. I asked him for change, but he told me to fuck off! Yeah, I could probably identify the cheap bastard!" He grinned a nearly toothless grin.

"Oliver," Giorgio said, putting his hand on the thin shoulder. "I owe you. Will you give an official statement? Will you do that for me?"

Oliver clicked his teeth anxiously. "Maybe. Okay, Detective." Oliver looked unsure.

"Barnes!" Giorgio addressed the other officer. "Give Oliver a ride to the station and take his statement. Then, buy him a big dinner – a good dinner on me."

Barnes looked less than enthused about traveling in an enclosed car with the homeless man, but turned around and led him across the parking lot to a waiting squad car.

"Well, well, well," Swan chided, turning towards his own car. "You have more than a Guardian Angel by your side tonight. You've been visited by Lady Luck herself."

"Chuck, I've told you a thousand times, good detective work is fifteen percent brains, fifteen percent timing, and seventy-five percent luck."

The two men laughed as an ambulance entered the ambulance bay, cutting off its siren. They glanced over as two emergency medical technicians quickly pulled a gurney from the back of the vehicle. Swan turned back to Giorgio and offered him a ride home, but Giorgio declined, saying he'd wait for Angie. As Swan pulled out of the parking lot, a male nurse came running across the parking lot.

"Detective," the young man said breathlessly. "You need to come back. It's your wife."

Giorgio bolted for the entrance.

The blonde nurse behind the counter looked up in alarm when he burst through the ambulance bay doors. The mother and sick baby occupied the first treatment area. The second cubicle was empty. Across the central core of the room, medical personnel crowded around a third bed. He rushed in that direction. A stout woman intercepted him.

"Detective," she said, grabbing his good arm. "Let them do their work."

"What happened?" he asked, straining to see around her.

His muscles had bunched up, and the throbbing in his arm was almost unbearable. He put his hand over the wound as a way to calm the trauma. The nurse was a good three inches shorter, but her hand remained on his elbow as a caution. A stethoscope hung lifeless around her neck.

"Your wife fell down some stairs," she replied in a soft voice. "They're checking for broken bones, internal injuries, maybe a concussion."

He stared unblinking at her, thinking she had probably spent the last twenty years explaining the obvious to anxious family members. He was about ready to step inside the enclosure when the doctor moved, giving Giorgio a glimpse of Angie. Her lustrous eyes were closed, and she appeared like a small child in the bed. The brown hair he loved to stroke lay in soft curls on the pillow. She looked so peaceful – too peaceful – and he wanted to die.

"They'll probably send her up for X rays and maybe even a cat scan," the nurse spoke gently beside him. "She'll be okay."

"Tell them to check her abdomen," he whispered breathlessly to her.

"What?" the nurse looked confused.

"Her abdomen," he choked, tears blurring his eyes. "Tell them to take a picture of her abdomen. She's pregnant."

†

Giorgio sat drumming the fingers of his good hand on the armrest of a vinyl chair in the hospital waiting room as if drumming would make things happen faster. He'd tried to get information from the nurse, but hospitals were a little like the FBI; information was dribbled out little by little until they thought you were qualified to have it all.

The nurse had said the doctor would be there in a few minutes, but how many was a few? Tony had asked him that question a dozen times growing up, usually when he'd been told he could only have a "few" of something. Giorgio's answer had always been the same: *A few is more than a couple but less than you probably want.* Now Giorgio wanted to know, how many was a few?

It was almost an hour before the doctor finally came out to join him. The news he had wasn't good, making the walk to Angie's room the longest few minutes of Giorgio's life. The lights in her room were off, leaving the small room in shadow. A narrow window looked out on the street. He sat by the bed with Angie's slender fingers laced through his. It was some time before her eyelids fluttered open, and a brown eye peeked out from under a long lash. Then both eyes opened dreamily, and she smiled.

"Joe," she whispered.

He hushed her like a small child and patted her hand. "Just rest."

She looked around, allowing her eyes to focus. "Where am I?" Her voice was weak and her words came out a little garbled.

"You fell. Do you remember?"

Her brows knitted as she tried to recall. Then she nodded slowly, turning her brown eyes to search his face.

"You might have a concussion," he said.

He tried to maintain eye contact, but dropped his head to stare at the crisp white bed sheet. Slowly, she regained wakefulness and understood without being told. The rich sienna eyes went dull as if looking into a deep well. She turned her head toward the windows, and he squeezed her hand as a tear trailed down his cheek.

"Where are the children?" she asked after a long moment.

Her voice was like a breeze on a summer afternoon, no force behind it, just a gentle movement of air in an otherwise still environment.

"They're with Mrs. Greenspan." He wiped his eyes with the back of his hand.

She nodded and when he reached for her hand again, she drew it away and curled into a fetal position turned to the wall.

"I'm sorry, Angie," he practically swallowed the words. "I'm so sorry."

The tears began to flow, and he buried his head and wept. The doctor had said that she'd fallen hard, landing on her back across the bottom step, detaching the small embryo from the uterine wall. The news had swelled his heart so that he found it hard to breathe. How could this happen to his Angie? He'd promised her only the other day that she'd never lose a child.

His tears soaked the sheet until a feather-light hand reached out and stroked the top of his head. He lifted his chin to see her soft gaze and reached up to brush her cheek with the back of his hand. He knew the rough texture of his skin had to feel like sandpaper against hers.

"I love you, Angie."

She gave him a half smile. "I know. When God is ready, Joe, he'll bless us with another child. Perhaps this little one was just a wake-up call."

"What do you mean?"

"Telling us to be more careful, Joe. To cherish each day. That life is precious."

"Oh, Angie," he choked, climbing onto the bed next to her.

They curled into each other's arms and cried together until he rocked her back to sleep, smoothing her hair with his hand.

✝

Later, as Giorgio lay in bed at home, he reached out to the spot where Angie usually lay beside him. The sheets were cold, and the room felt empty. He stared at her pillow wondering how he could heal this hurt. No dog would fix this. This was a life-changing event. He didn't pretend to understand a woman's need to have more children. Giorgio only knew that Angie had desperately wanted this baby. And now he wanted it, too.

His mind began to ponder a variety of solutions, including taking a cruise, buying new furniture, or a car. But it wasn't about all of that. It never had been. With Angie, it was all about children.

Giorgio continued to concentrate, sifting through potential options until his head began to throb. He rolled onto his back and stared at the ceiling, letting his mind play across the last few days. The murders. The monastery. The theater. By the time his eyes began to close, he thought he had an answer.

† Chapter Thirty-Six †

The next morning, Giorgio moved about the house on autopilot, doing what had to be done without registering pain or pleasure. The doorbell rang around seven-thirty. It was Mrs. Greenspan returning the children. She asked about Angie and said she'd stop by later in the afternoon. Breakfast with the children was a quiet affair. No yelling or fighting. No running after Grosvenor. Only cereal and bananas, and then Giorgio bundled them off to the school bus.

He returned to clean the kitchen and put clean sheets on the bed. He even threw a load of laundry into the washer before going to Angie's garden to find a mixture of red and pink camellias. These he arranged in a shallow bowl and placed on her nightstand. Grosvenor followed him wherever he went as if he somehow understood Giorgio's despair.

Swan called to say they had arrested Poindexter earlier that morning. He did, in fact, have an open cut on his left cheek. He was scheduled for a line-up as soon as they could bring Oliver in for identification. There was no sign of Marvin Palomar or his car, but they were still looking. With a silent prayer, Giorgio hung up and left to pick up Angie at the hospital.

He brought her home around noon, carefully helping her up the stairs and into bed. Her face was as pale as the clean sheets he'd just laid out. They hadn't spoken at all in the car, letting a suffocating pressure build around them. Now Giorgio wasn't sure what to say, so he just tucked her into bed and kissed her gently on the forehead. Her eyes found his for a brief moment, but there was no message in them, only a deep pain. His fingers stroked her cheek before he turned to leave the room.

"Joe," her voice stopped him. "You knew why, didn't you? About the baby? The kids are growing up. They don't need me anymore. That's why." She turned to the window, ending the short-lived conversation.

He left the room and made it to the head of the stairs before stopping and grasping the banister in a vice-like grip. All his life, he had taken the good with the bad. *Take it one day at a time,* his dad had always said. *Things will always look better the next day.* It was a motto he'd lived by. From the time he was rejected by the most popular girl in the ninth grade, to when he was cut from first string football, to when his father died. But this was different. This was Angie. As far as he was concerned, his father's motto didn't apply to Angie. For Angie, he expected life to be good all the time.

Giorgio took a deep breath and descended the stairs, thinking about fixing Angie some lunch when the doorbell rang. He hurried to open the door and found Mrs. Greenspan standing there. She was a short, spry woman, about thirty pounds overweight, with quick movements and bright, gray eyes. She stood straight as a pin, with her knitting bag in one hand and a recipe book in the other.

"I saw you bring the missus home."

"We'll be okay, Mrs. Greenspan. The children are in school."

"I'm here to take care of Angie, not the kids. You go on to work." She brushed past him, heading for the kitchen.

"No, really, Mrs. Greenspan," he said, closing the door and following her. "I can stay home. I'm *going* to stay home."

She ignored him and entered the kitchen, laid the cookbook on the counter, and began putting on one of Angie's aprons.

"I don't think Angie is hungry right now," he said, thinking he wanted to be the one to make her lunch. "She's resting."

Mrs. Greenspan turned to him, her gray hair curled into tight little knots about her head. "I don't care if anybody eats it," she snapped. "It's the smell I'm after." She turned and opened the cookbook and then went to the spice cupboard. "It's cinnamon and vanilla I want. Cookies and maybe a cake. Maybe even some bread."

"But Mrs. Greenspan…"

"The smell will make it all the way upstairs. You'll see," she said over her shoulder as she rummaged through the spice shelf. "She'll feel better for it."

Giorgio stood in the kitchen doorway feeling helpless for the second time that morning. When the phone rang, he returned to the hallway. It was Rocky, responding to the message he'd left the night before. He passed along the information about Angie and told Rocky he'd see him at the station. Giorgio hung up and went upstairs.

The hospital had given Angie a sedative, and she was already asleep. So he left her a note telling her to call him if she wanted him for any reason, and warning her about Mrs. Greenspan. By the time he returned to the kitchen, the neighbor already had a large ceramic bowl on the counter and was opening the sugar canister. Grosvenor sat behind her. Giorgio snapped his fingers and the dog reluctantly obeyed.

"I can be reached on my cell phone, Mrs. Greenspan. For *anything*. Please don't hesitate to call."

"Yes, yes. I have the number in my bag," she waved him away without ever turning around. Instead, she deftly cracked an egg with one hand and dumped it into the bowl.

†

Swan looked up in surprise when Giorgio appeared in the office doorway.

"You okay?"

Giorgio didn't answer. He merely slumped into his desk chair. Swan got up and lifted the glass coffee pot off the burner, poured out a cup and set it in front of his partner.

"Thanks." Giorgio started to pick it up with his right hand, but the muscles flared into action. He picked up the coffee with his left hand and took a sip. "Angie is asleep," he said finally. "The neighbor lady, Mrs. Greenspan, is conducting a one-woman aromatherapy experiment, and I feel like someone rolled over me with a truck." He flexed his fingers again. "Any news on Marvin Palomar?"

Swan replaced the coffee pot and returned to his chair where he picked up his pencil before answering. Giorgio looked up and mentally braced himself for the truth.

"They just found his car in a ditch. He was in the trunk. Samson is on his way over to his parents' house."

The cup of coffee slipped in Giorgio's hand, spilling hot liquid onto the desk blotter. He put the cup down and just stared at it, remembering how the janitor felt the night of Olsen's murder. Swan kept quiet in the background. Giorgio got up and grabbed a paper towel to wipe up the spilled liquid. Then he retrieved the cup and went to refill it.

"OK, tell me the rest," he commanded, before returning rigidly to his desk.

"The car was wiped clean. Palomar was killed by a blow to the head. No weapon was found, but he was lured down to the theater the same way you were. We've been to his apartment and there was a message on his answering machine asking him to come to the theater. The voice is disguised, but the call was made from a pay phone only two blocks from where Poindexter lives."

"You've been busy."

"Yeah, well, the problem is he was found on Kramer Ave. in Pasadena, so we had to bring in the Pasadena department."

"Shit!"

"It's okay. We'll have joint jurisdiction since Poindexter probably killed him down at the theater, but I had one of their detectives here for the lineup. By the way, Oliver picked him out about twenty minutes ago. That and your testimony about the note you found in the basement should put him away."

Giorgio stared out the window. All he could think about was young Marvin Palomar stuffed into the trunk of a car and Angie lying upstairs at home, her dream of a baby gone. His insides roiled to the point he was actually jittery, as if he'd already drunk the entire pot of coffee. He would have to find a way to deal with this. Find a way, or fall apart.

"I want more," Giorgio snapped. "There were three murders up there, dammit! We don't have any proof that Poindexter killed anyone at the monastery, only that he killed Marvin and tried to kill me."

Swan tapped the pencil on his desk, eyeing Giorgio as if measuring the extent of his stress. "There were two sets of fingerprints on that flashlight you found in the birdhouse. One was Dorman's. The other was Poindexter's."

"I want more than that," Giorgio snapped before getting up and going to the window. "I want this guy put away for life." He was wound as tight as the underpinnings of a tennis ball.

"There's dried blood on the ridge of the flashlight. It's being checked, but Poindexter must have killed Dorman. Why else would he have come after you?"

Giorgio slammed his fist into the side of a file cabinet. "I want this guy to fry!"

The air between them bristled and Swan let his eyes drop. Grosvenor slunk away to the cover of a nearby desk. Giorgio turned away from the file cabinet, rubbing his forearm.

"You don't need to be here, Joe," Swan reassured him. "We'd all understand. Go home and take care of Angie."

Giorgio stared across the street at the funeral home for a full minute, thinking how close he'd come to being another one of the mortuary's guests. At this very moment Marvin Palomar was probably laid out in a cold storage unit there. He took a deep breath and leaned into the wall.

"I moved here to get away from all of this. I wanted Angie to have a better life. Now, because of me…"

"You didn't do this to her, Joe. Cory Poindexter might have, but you didn't."

"Poindexter was after *me,*" he said, turning to Swan. "I got injured and went to the hospital and because of that, Angie fell."

"Right, and don't forget, because you were born, went to high school and married Angie, none of this would have happened. I mean, if you're going to blame yourself, get it right."

Giorgio had heard that same tone in his father's voice many times when he'd blamed himself for some failure he felt could have been avoided if only he'd tried harder. He thought Swan was just acting like the big brother he didn't have. Giorgio felt some of the weight lift from his shoulders as he sat back down, putting his hands flat on the desk in front of him.

"It's not that easy, you know. This is my Angie we're talking about."

"I know that, Joe, but this didn't happen just because you're a cop. You could have been hurt in a baseball game, or in a car accident, or on stage for God's sake. Christ, some of those plays you're in have nearly killed *me.*"

He smiled and Giorgio felt the wall begin to crack.

"Thing is, Joe… life is what it is. Don't try to second-guess it."

"You get what you get and don't throw a fit," Giorgio said under his breath.

"What?"

Giorgio looked up, "Nothing."

McCready entered the room holding one of the blue note cards. "I found something."

Giorgio perked up with the first hint of interest. "What is it?"

"I was re-reading the cards and noticed something we missed. Remember the woman who said she spoke with Mallery Olsen as she left the cocktail party? And Olsen said that she would be late for the dinner because she was having a drink with a friend?"

"Yeah?" Giorgio prodded.

McCready's eyes were alight as if he'd just found a ten-dollar bill. "Actually, that's not what this woman said. She quoted Olsen as having said she was going to have a drink with an *old* friend."

Giorgio took the card from his hand and read the notation. "You're right. An *old* friend." He got up and wandered around his desk with the card in his hand. "Someone from the past."

"That leaves out the boyfriend," Swan offered.

"I would assume it leaves out Father Damian, too." McCready said this almost sadly since the connection with Damian was his idea.

"It would leave out Marsh as well," Giorgio added. "She wouldn't have referred to him as a friend at all."

"I think it means she met someone at the conference she hadn't seen in some time," Swan speculated. "How long did we say she'd lived here?"

"Four years," McCready answered readily. "She came from Chicago."

Giorgio turned to him, his face re-animated. "Didn't she go to school there?"

"She studied journalism," McCready said.

"We need to know who else may have known her in Chicago," he said, slapping the card on the desk. "And we need to know now."

"Okay," McCready agreed. "By the way, this came in the mail this morning. It's addressed to the Homicide Unit." McCready chuckled. "Wonder who thinks we have a Homicide Unit."

Giorgio spied the padded brown envelope with suspicion. He reached into his drawer and pulled out a pair of rubber gloves.

The handwriting was a ragged, irregular block style as if someone had tried to disguise it, and the envelope felt as if it was filled with padding. Giorgio turned it over and saw that it had been taped shut. Taking a letter opener from his desk, he carefully lifted the tape without touching it. McCready watched with interest. Swan even got up from his desk to come over and look over Giorgio's shoulder.

"What do you think it is?"

Giorgio could only look at him with the kind of deadpan expression that meant he thought this wouldn't be good. He used the letter opener to pull the ends of the envelope apart and then slid out a thick wad of toilet paper. When he turned it over, they all stared at a pale red stain that spread across one corner, as if something inside had leaked through. The tension in the room quickly rose.

"Jesus, Joe, what *do* you think it is?"

Giorgio slowly unrolled the toilet paper to reveal the blood soaked baggie with the tip of Mallery Olsen's little finger peeking through.

"Christ," McCready whispered.

"I think it's a message," Giorgio whispered.

† Chapter Thirty-Seven †

The baggie and envelope were sent to the crime lab in Pasadena. The envelope had been postmarked in Sierra Madre. A phone call to the post office confirmed that mail was picked up at the monastery every day around noon, except Sunday. Since Mallery Olsen had been murdered Saturday night, the envelope wouldn't have gone out until Monday. Why then had it taken two days to arrive at the police station? The answer would take a second call to the Monastery. It seemed Father Damian had sent the gift shop volunteers home the morning Jeff Dorman's body was found in the vegetable garden, so the gift shop was closed when the mail man arrived. Mail hadn't been picked up until Tuesday. Today was Wednesday.

"Cap'n wants to know what you're going to do about the envelope," Swan said in the background.

Giorgio looked up from his desk. "I'm not sure, yet."

Swan leaned against the doorframe, a toothpick stuck between his teeth. Opening the envelope had cast a pall over the entire station. These officers weren't used to multiple murders, let alone having body parts mailed to them as casually as a greeting card.

"The mayor is hounding him for answers. There's talk of a major press conference."

"No," Giorgio suddenly came to attention. "That's what this guy wants. This is all for attention. Just like hanging her by her bra strap in the closet. He's showing off. Better to keep him off balance. I'll talk to the Captain."

†

When Giorgio returned he found Swan guzzling a soft drink while he contemplated a chess move by the window. "What did Captain Ramos say?"

"He's getting phone calls and letters demanding answers and the mayor is breathing down his neck. Even the Governor has weighed in. They want these murders wrapped up. If we don't get some answers soon, he'll be forced to bring in help." Giorgio sighed and dropped into his chair. "We have twenty-four to forty-eight hours."

"Well, then, I guess it's back to work," Swan said, returning to his desk.

Giorgio filled out paperwork on the fire and then put in a call to Marvin's father. That afternoon, Giorgio visited with the District Attorney who would prosecute Poindexter. Poindexter wasn't talking, and they had yet to pin down a motive for Dorman's murder, but a partial fingerprint had been lifted off Marvin's sedan. That and Oliver's testimony should make Poindexter spend the rest of his life in jail. Giorgio's job now was to find out how, or if, Poindexter was connected to any of the deaths at the monastery while Swan and McCready mapped Mallery Olsen's life in Chicago.

He checked in twice with Mrs. Greenspan during the day. His first call was all but drowned out by the whirring of the electric mixer. He only hoped Angie didn't feel well enough to come downstairs. The sight of Mrs. Greenspan firmly planted in her kitchen would be enough to send her into a tailspin. The second time he called, Mrs. Greenspan was on her way upstairs with a tray of tea and freshly baked cookies, and, no, now was not a good time to talk with Angie. She would pass along his well wishes and tell his wife he'd be home before eight. Feeling a little put out and more than a little unnecessary, he returned to his paperwork.

By seven-thirty, he came through the door with a bouquet of flowers and a box of Mallery Olsen's college papers. Grosvenor headed straight for the kitchen with his nose in the air, sucking in the odors of roast beef and onions. Saliva filled Giorgio's mouth like a tub filling with water, and he dropped the box on a chair when Tony appeared at the doorway to the den. His son's normally jovial manner had disappeared, and he seemed on the verge of tears.

"What's the matter, buddy?"

The boy faded back into the room without a word. Giorgio followed and found Marie on the sofa with her hands in her lap, her features pinched, a sullen Tony beside her. It was obvious they'd both been crying. The heart wrenching tableau made Giorgio turn and go directly to the kitchen where he found Mrs. Greenspan cleaning up the dishes.

"Mrs. Greenspan..."

She turned in surprise, a dish between her hands. "Oh, Mr. Salvatori, I didn't hear you come in."

"What's wrong? How is Angie?"

The stern little woman set the bowl on the counter and grabbed a towel to wipe her hands. "As good as can be expected," she mumbled.

"What do you mean, as good as can be expected?"

She paused, using the towel to distract her attention. Then she sighed and sat at the table while Giorgio's heart raced.

"The doctor stopped by. He spoke to Mrs. Salvatori." She stopped again, avoiding his gaze. When a tear appeared in the corner of her eye, Giorgio ran for the stairs.

He burst through the bedroom door only to find the bed empty. Angie sat at her dressing table in a long blue robe, staring at her image in the glass before her. He went to stand behind her.

"Angie, what is it?"

She looked up, her eyes floating in pools of tears. "No more, Joe. No more." Her voice was so soft he could barely hear her.

"What do you mean, Angie? No more what?"

She began shaking her head slowly and then dropped her head and wept, her narrow shoulders convulsing in spasms. The flowers fell to the floor in a heap of petals and stems, and Giorgio swept forward and lifted her out of the chair, carrying her to the bed where he laid her gently down. She continued to sob, her hands covering her face. Distraught, he stretched out on the bed next to her, encouraging her to curl into his arms. He stayed with her, holding her, rocking her, until her sobs subsided and she finally fell asleep.

Later, he slipped downstairs to get the children to bed. Mrs. Greenspan had left a note to call if she was needed. A plate of food sat in the refrigerator in plastic wrap, but he had no appetite now. Instead, he settled down in his big chair in the den and stared at the television's blank screen. Grosvenor moved in to sit by his side. The two of them remained like that for more than an hour.

Angie would have no more children. That was a fact. It had only been a short time ago when she had announced they would have a third child, trapping him into a lifetime of limitations. Now, he felt trapped in despair. God had taken the choice away, leaving a hole where his chest used to be. How odd life was. Now, more than anything else, he wanted that child. He wanted to go through the late night feedings. The thought of tiny feet and baby powder made his heart ache now that there wouldn't be any. They wouldn't go shopping for a new baby crib or stroller, nor would Angie's eyes light up at the thought of buying a whole new set of baby clothes. When the tears threatened to explode, he quickly rubbed his eyes and jumped up to grab Mallery Olsen's box in the hall, feeling the need to stay busy.

He placed the box at his feet and spent the next hour sifting through old college papers, photos, and yearbooks – only really seeing half of what he handled. He pored over articles she'd written for the school newspaper, book reports, and notes from boyfriends. There had been several men in her life. It seemed she was desirable in ways only a twenty-year old male can adequately express. None of the letters were current, and Giorgio found himself wondering if the old friend she had referred to lay hidden in any of the paperwork before him. He decided he would give them over to McCready in the morning.

When the clock in the entryway struck ten, Giorgio heard a soft rustle behind him. Tony stood in the doorway in his pajamas, one pants leg tucked up above his socks. His hair was tangled, and he carried the raggedy teddy bear he hadn't played with since he was a toddler. Giorgio gestured and the boy came forward and crawled into his father's lap.

"Is mom going to be okay?"

Giorgio held him tightly. "Yes, she'll be okay. We'll all be okay." He could smell the bubblegum toothpaste Tony insisted upon using and the artist's clay that was stuck underneath his fingernails from school.

"Is it a bad thing?"

"What?"

"That she can't have any more kids. She isn't going to die, is she?"

His voice quivered, and Giorgio noticed he clutched the teddy bear as if he might squeeze the life out of it.

"No, she isn't going to die, buddy." He wrapped his arms around his son's shoulders. "She'll be fine. She had an accident. That's all. And now she won't be able to have any more children."

He said it simply, but knew it wasn't such a simple thing.

"But mama loves us, doesn't she? She doesn't need another baby, does she?"

Giorgio nearly cried out in pain. How complicated life was. Angie had just wanted another baby. In the process, she'd been verbally abused by her husband, lost the baby, lost the chance to have another one, and somehow made her own children feel unwanted.

"Mama loves you both very much," he said, feeling his own voice catch. "We both do. I can't explain why your mama wanted another baby. She just wanted to hold another baby in her arms." He stopped to control his own emotions. When he continued, he lowered his voice. "Your mama will be very sad for a while. It will take some time for her to heal. But then she'll be fine. She'll love you like crazy, just like she always does."

He tousled Tony's hair and attempted a smile. Tony smiled weakly in return.

"You'll have to help mom around the house, though, clean your room, you know, things like that. Can you do that?"

Tony's eyes lit up at being given something concrete to do. "Sure I can. I'll tell Marie too. We can help."

"Good boy. Let's just take it one day at a time. Let's give your mom some time. Okay?"

"Okay."

Giorgio hugged him and he slipped onto the floor. "Okay, I've got some work to do. You take off to bed."

"Okay, Dad." Tony glanced into the box before leaving. "What's all that? Are those our old pictures?"

"No, just stuff from work. Get to bed."

But Tony reached for a picture stuck inside one of the box flaps. "Look, dad. Just like Grosvenor!"

He handed the picture to his dad and leaned over to pat the dog before leaving the room. Giorgio stared at the photo for the first time feeling a chill extend the length of his spine.

A much younger version of Mallery Olsen sat on a lawn in front of what appeared to be an apartment building. Sprawled in front of her was a Basset Hound. A familiar looking blonde-haired young man sat on the grass next to her, his head thrown back in laughter. A second man stood in the foreground, his back to the camera, his light brown hair obscuring the top corner of the picture.

Giorgio concentrated on the blonde next to Olsen, trying to figure out why he looked familiar. He had a narrow jaw line, a straight nose, and looked to be about five-foot ten. His face was in profile, making it difficult to identify more than that. The second man stood close to the camera and off to one side, facing Olsen. Only his right forearm and hand were visible. In his hand was a cigarette. Across the back of his hand was the tattoo of an eagle. Something about the photo tugged at Giorgio's memories, but the harder he tried to release the connection, the more stubborn it became.

It was nearly eleven o'clock when Giorgio finished going through the box. He kept the picture with the Basset Hound on top, thinking he'd talk to McCready about it the next day. He went upstairs to check on Angie, but she slept peacefully. Her mere presence filled the room with the same mellow warmth he felt when he swallowed a good brandy. It was good to have her home.

Downstairs, he was just finishing some roast beef and potatoes when the phone rang.

"Hello, Detective, this is Elvira Applebaum. I'm not disturbing you, I hope. I know it's late."

She sounded very tired herself, and Giorgio rubbed his face, feeling the fatigue of the last few days catch up with him.

"No, it's fine. What can I do for you?"

"Mother remembered something. I just got home and thought I should call you right away."

All the fatigue washed away in an instant, and he was alert and listening. "Yes, what is it?"

"There was a time capsule. You know those things they bury and then dig up years later. I guess the monks buried one back in the Fifties. Dad was asked to put copies of the building plans inside, and so he included both sets of the original plans. Mom said he wasn't supposed to put in both sets, but he did. He told mom that someday, somebody would find out the truth. I hope it helps." Her voice caught and he heard a deep sigh on the other end of the phone.

"I'm sure it will, Ms. Applebaum. Did she say where the capsule might be buried?"

"Only that it was near the statue of a large angel. That's all mother knew. She wanted to help." Her voice faltered this time and Giorgio caught her.

"Ms. Applebaum…how is your mother?"

"She died this afternoon, Detective." There was a pause. "She was a good woman, Detective. I'm going to miss her terribly."

"She's been a big help, Ms. Applebaum. I'm sorry for your loss, but thank you for calling."

A glance up the stairs reminded him there was nothing he could do for Angie. Yet finishing his task in the den seemed too passive. He needed to take action, so he picked up the phone and talked briefly with Father Damian before calling his brother. The last call was to Mrs. Greenspan.

✝

He and Rocky approached the cemetery carrying a shovel and two high-beamed flashlights. A soft breeze crept through the trees and the lonesome hoot of an owl punctuated the fact they were about to dig up a graveyard. The clouds covering the moon made a sojourn into a cemetery at night all the more spooky.

Father Damian had given them permission. The headstones were arranged into quadrants around a tall, stone cross rising like a maypole from the middle of the graveyard. The life-sized statue of the angel sat directly behind the cross, positioned on a six-foot square block of granite. It was the one Giorgio had seen the day he'd found Dorman. The angel didn't have a name, but held a book or tablet in her hand. At the base of the statue an inscription read, "For He shall give his angels charge over thee, to keep thee in all thy ways. ~ Psalm 91:11."

"Okay," Giorgio began, "Ms. Applebaum didn't know where this time capsule was buried – just that it was somewhere near the statue."

"Then I'd better go back and get the pick. This ground is as hard as rock." Rocky sent a spray of dust up with the heel of his boot to emphasize his point.

"You might want to keep your voice down a bit," Giorgio warned. "It's almost midnight. The monks are asleep."

Rocky silently handed the shovel to Giorgio before disappearing down the path. Giorgio felt adrift in a sea of darkness and directed the flashlight around him in order to identify his surroundings. The beam revealed grave markers one row at a time while the leaves continued to murmur in the background like an audience waiting for the curtain to rise. At one point, the flashlight flickered and went out.

He shook it hard, slapping the batteries back and forth inside the metal casing. A cold breeze swirled around his neck, making him wish Rocky would hurry up. He shook the flashlight again, and the beam burst into action making an erratic arc across a line of gravestones. When it caught something in its path, Giorgio froze, sucking in a blast of cold air.

Slowly he brought the light back until it came to rest on the large granite ball mounted atop the grave with the weird inscription. Giorgio paused, feeling his chest tighten. Framed by the depthless shadows on either side, a shimmering image of the young boy appeared next to the grave.

He was dressed in the same dark knickers and starched white shirt, and although it was a fogless night, a mist hovered about his narrow shoulders. The boy stared at Giorgio, his arms dangling by his sides, something clutched in his left hand. Giorgio felt rooted to the spot, cement flowing in his veins. He wasn't even sure he was breathing. Seconds passed. Finally, the boy extended his hand. In it was a long, serrated knife.

The cement slipped through Giorgio's veins like cool gel, and he felt his bowels shift uncomfortably. He stared at the boy wondering what he was supposed to do. The police manual didn't cover anything like this. Where the hell was Rocky?

"What do you want?" he whispered.

Giorgio's hand trembled. He had been in many dangerous situations before, even facing down a maniac strapped to a bomb. Yet, he'd never felt cold fear like this.

"Please, what do you want?"

The boy pointed the knife directly at the grave by his side. Giorgio strained to remember who was buried there. The sound of crunching gravel made him glance over his shoulder. Rocky was returning.

When Giorgio turned back, the boy's image dissipated into a misty trail and swirled past his right shoulder. Giorgio flinched back from the blast of cold air only to find the boy right in front of him, floating a few inches above the square of bricks at the angel's feet. With a quick snap of his wrist, the boy flung the knife to the ground where it stuck in between two bricks.

"Hey, Jo Jo, what are you looking at?"

Giorgio's head snapped around.

"You're supposed to be looking for the time capsule, not staring at the statue," Rocky snarled. "Point that light at the...whoa!"

Rocky stopped ten feet from the statue. He carried a pick over his shoulder, and his own flashlight now crisscrossed with Giorgio's. The knife was caught in between the two beams, wavering slightly in the night air. There was no sign of the boy.

"Where did that come from?"

Giorgio's tongue had swollen to fill the inside of his mouth. It was clear Rocky hadn't seen the apparition, and yet it didn't seem reasonable to say a ghost had thrown the knife. Fortunately, Rocky didn't leave much room for idle chatter.

"That's one of those bread knives, isn't it?" Rocky stepped forward and retrieved the knife. "You'd think the monks wouldn't leave these things lying around. Wonder why it's out here? Oh, well," he dismissed the thought and tossed the knife aside. "Let's get busy. Where should we dig?"

Giorgio watched the knife disappear into thin air. A glance at his brother told him Rocky had missed the special effects and was already wandering around looking for the time capsule.

"Don't bother looking," Giorgio said, swallowing hard. "I think we'll find what we're looking for right there." He pointed to where the knife had been.

Giorgio squatted down and began brushing dirt off several bricks, looking over his shoulder once or twice to see if the boy was nearby. Rocky grabbed the shovel, slipping the tip of it under the corner of the first brick until it gave way. He did the same to five or six more.

Giorgio used the pick to lift bricks, throwing them carelessly aside. While they worked, the bank of clouds above them separated into long strands, finally revealing a full moon.

"What if we don't find it?" Rocky asked, out of breath.

"Then we come back tomorrow with a backhoe."

They continued to work silently until all the bricks lay in a large pile. Then Rocky put his boot against the back end of the shovel and starting digging, relying on Giorgio to loosen stubborn chunks of soil with the pick. After only a few minutes, they were rewarded with the sound of metal hitting metal.

"Hot damn!" Rocky exclaimed.

Rocky used the shovel to pull away the dirt around a metal tube the size of a child's coffin. The size and shape stopped him, and he looked at Giorgio with trepidation.

"Go ahead," Giorgio encouraged. "If it's not the time capsule, at most, it's probably a dog or something." He said this with only mild conviction as Rocky lifted the container out.

Once it was above ground, they both leaned in to get a better look. It appeared to be made from corrugated aluminum or light steel. A metal band encircled it. Giorgio took out his Swiss blade to break the seal. The lid popped up, and Giorgio flashed the light into the interior, revealing a roll of papers set atop several smaller items.

"Let's take it inside," Giorgio said, feeling the need to leave the graveyard behind.

They carried the container through the large kitchen and stepped through a back door into the dining room. Giorgio flipped on a light, and Rocky laid the capsule on the first long wooden table. Giorgio grabbed a thick roll of aged, stained paper, while Rocky sifted through the rest of the contents. Giorgio had the original architectural drawings of the monastery.

He rolled them out onto the table. The first was dated March 1925. Edward Applebaum's name was carefully printed in the lower right hand corner. Giorgio grabbed his flashlight and used his finger to locate the main entrance and what was now Father Damian's office. Following the corridor around to the right, he came to Anya Peters' office. Then he traced his finger along the area in between the two offices where the tunnel existed, but it wasn't indicated in any way.

He set aside this first set of drawings and pulled forward the second set, which was dated October 1938. Applebaum was again listed as the architect, but, again, Giorgio couldn't find a tunnel.

"I don't get it," he said to Rocky. "The secret tunnel doesn't exist according to these plans. Yet, I'd swear this set includes the renovations for the boy's school."

Rocky stopped reading an article he held and looked over at his brother. "Did you look at the second sheet?"

Giorgio looked at him stupidly and then lifted the top sheet to reveal identical plans underneath. The year was the same, but it was dated two months later. In the area between Father Damian's and Peters' offices were two dotted lines. The dotted lines extended north to a set of steps, then turned east and wound along the north side of the building, ending under the east staircase. Giorgio grinned.

"Bingo!"

Rocky looked to where Giorgio pointed at the tunnel and nodded. "Okay, but we already know about that one."

"Yes, but look here." Giorgio pointed to the bottom of the sheet where a duplicate outline of the exterior of the building had been drawn and labeled "Second Floor." A large water stain smudged the northern side of the monks' quarters, but Giorgio located the two staircases leading to the second floor.

"All along here are the monks' rooms." His finger trailed along a solid line with doorways clearly indicated and stopped at a small square at the end of the hallway. "I'll bet anything this is the upstairs supply closet." His finger traced a dotted line ran across the interior wall of the closet. No such line appeared across any other doorway. "Look at this dotted line. This wall was built to separate the boys' bedrooms from the monks' quarters when the school was in operation."

"Okay, but what's the significance?"

Giorgio looked at Rocky. "I think this is what insulted Applebaum's sense of morality. It appears the monks didn't *want* to be cut off from the boys' quarters after all."

Rocky's eyebrows lifted as he understood the implication. "So, you were right. There is a secret door?"

"Now all we have to do is find it."

"Take a look at this." Rocky held up an old newspaper clipping in which the headline read, *Monk Murdered!* "It was tucked inside this little pouch. There are several more."

Rocky held up a leather pouch and laid out the other articles, all having to do with the murder. He found one dated December 27, 1943.

"This was five years after the monastery was turned into a boy's school."

He picked up a second article and began to read. *"St. Michael's Catholic Boys School will be temporarily closed due to a series of incidents involving suicide and murder. On the day before Christmas, while most of the boys were away for the holidays, Father Anton Wingate was found stabbed to death in his bed. A day later, Christian Maynard, a fifth-year student, was found hanging from his window. Maynard confessed to the murder in a note found in his room. While priests refused comment, fellow students reported gross misconduct by several priests."* Rocky stopped. "I wonder if this murder has anything to do with ours." When Giorgio didn't respond, Rocky looked up but Giorgio was staring off into space. "What's the matter?"

Giorgio turned slowly in his direction. "What did you say about a boy hanging from his window?"

Rocky picked up one of the clippings and skimmed the copy until he found the spot he was looking for. *"A day later, Christian Maynard, a student, was found hanging by a rope from his window. Police believe he murdered the monk out of rage, committing suicide afterwards. According to his roommate, a Robert O'Leary, Maynard was a quiet boy who was deeply ashamed."*

"So, he hung himself." Giorgio's face had lost all its elasticity. "Is there a picture?"

"Yeah, but they're not too great."

Rocky placed the paper on the table and pulled out his flashlight. Two small pictures accompanied the article. One was of a man with a long pious face and gray hair cut so close he looked nearly bald. He was dressed in a black robe and collar, with a large metal cross hanging around his neck. The caption read, "Father Anton Wingate." The second picture looked like one of the school pictures taken for parents' day. The boy in the picture was dressed in a crisp white shirt and black jacket, with a black ribbon tied at the neck. His curly dark hair was cut above his ears, and he offered only a half-smile to the camera. Giorgio stared at the picture so long, Rocky finally spoke.

"What are you thinking? You don't think this murder is connected to ours?"

"I'm not sure, but I am beginning to think this monastery is an unholy place."

A cold frost had settled into his bones as a decades-old murder collided with his present-day investigation.

The young boy staring back at him from the newspaper article was Christian Maynard. And it was Christian Maynard who had just led them to the time capsule in the graveyard. It was also Father Wingate's grave that Christian Maynard had pointed to with the knife. Giorgio forced himself to shift his gaze back to the building plans as the only way to quiet the raging thoughts in his head.

"The monks used the closet to gain access to the boys," he said. "And young Maynard must have used the same secret door to get to Father Wingate's room in order to kill him."

"Just like our murderer?"

Giorgio looked at his brother. "Just like our murderer."

Rocky went back to reading one of the articles when Giorgio grabbed his arm and stopped him again. "Rocky, what did you say Maynard's roommate's name was again?"

Rocky looked back at the clipping. "Robert O'Leary. Oh, hell...you don't think...could this be Father O'Leary? After all these years?"

"O'Leary had to be in his seventies. I don't know how old these boys were, but they were probably pretty young."

"So O'Leary was a student here. That means he probably knew about the secret door."

"And I'll bet he shared that information with someone living here now who used it for the wrong reasons."

"And that person killed O'Leary to make sure the secret died with him."

Giorgio rolled up the papers and stashed everything back in the box. "I think we have more digging to do, but not in the graveyard. It's too late to do anything more tonight. But tomorrow we find that secret door."

† Chapter Thirty-Eight †

Giorgio slept little that night. His mind raced over the details coming together to form the narrative of a first-class ghost story, complete with child sexual predators, murder, and suicide. And that wasn't even the case he was working on.

The next morning he asked Mrs. Greenspan to stay with Angie while he went to the station. He left Angie dozing peacefully by the fire, with Mrs. Greenspan making homemade chicken soup in the kitchen. He pulled into the back parking lot of the small police station, ignoring the swarm of press that clamored for a statement. His deadline for the press conference was looming, and he still had no idea what he would say. Swan wasn't in yet, but McCready was at his computer.

"Anything new?" Giorgio looked over the young cop's shoulder.

"We have a list of people Olsen hung out with in Chicago and we're tracking down their current addresses. We also talked to the family again, getting some background information on anyone they were familiar with."

"Any familiar names?"

"Not yet." McCready nodded towards his flat screen monitor. "I'm doing background checks on everyone at the conference, including whatever financials I can find. So far, a woman named Barbara Yanks was arrested for a DUI six years ago; a guy named Peter Wright served time for petty theft; and Marsh has filed twice for bankruptcy."

"It just gets better and better for Mr. Marsh doesn't it? Listen, I want you to find out everything you can about a murder committed at the monastery back in 1943."

McCready looked up with surprise. "You don't think we have enough murders to investigate?"

"They may be related." Giorgio needed to know what, if anything, the decades-old murder had to do with the three killings facing him now. "A monk was murdered up there by one of the students when it was still a boys' school. We found these," Giorgio gave him the articles from the time capsule. "See what else you can find out."

If McCready suspected anything, he said nothing. He took the articles to photocopy them and then log them in as evidence. Giorgio went to his desk to sort through his messages. There was a message from the District Attorney and one from Elvira Applebaum.

He glanced at his watch and decided to take a chance Ms. Applebaum would be up early. She answered on the third ring.

"I hope I didn't disturb you."

"No, Detective. I'm glad you called. I had trouble sleeping. I've been up most of the night going through mother's things. It helped me hang on to her a little longer. You understand?"

"I do. I did the same thing when my father died."

"I found a box of my father's things," Elvira Applebaum said with a sigh. "It's very old and filled with many of his original drafting tools. I think I may have something for you."

"I don't want to disturb you," he said apologetically, but knew he would go right away if she offered.

"It's all right, Detective. You can stop by any time. My mother's presence is still here. If I go to sleep, I'm afraid she won't be here when I wake up. I know that probably sounds foolish." Her voice wavered.

"It doesn't sound foolish at all. I'll be right out. Thank you."

He put in a call to the District Attorney and found that Anya Peters was holding fast. Giorgio still couldn't eliminate Peters as a suspect, but something in his gut said she was just a cold-hearted businesswoman and drug dealer.

He arrived at Ms. Applebaum's spacious home only twenty minutes later. She answered the door in a wrinkled pantsuit. Her makeup had worn off, and the skin around her mouth sagged, but she attempted a smile when she invited him inside.

"Come in, Detective. Can I get you anything?"

Giorgio remembered the granola bar he'd eaten in the car and pondered a cup of hot coffee, but the house was cold and still and somehow asking her to brew coffee seemed invasive.

"No, thank you. I just had a full breakfast. What is it you wanted to show me?"

"It's over here."

She drew him to the dining room where the bay window allowed filtered light to warm the room. A cherry wood table with four matching chairs and a china cabinet filled the small space. Laid out on the lace tablecloth were tools of another age; a thick, worn pencil, a metal triangle, and a gum eraser.

"I don't know why my mother kept all of this stuff."

"We keep memories alive through the things that were important to the people we loved," he observed.

She looked at him with a weak smile. "You're not what I thought a detective would be like."

"What did you think we'd be like?"

"Callous and shallow, I guess. Maybe I've seen too many bad movies." This made her chuckle, lifting the pall that hung over the room. To fill an awkward pause, she reached out and lifted up an iron key about two inches long. "My father loved ornate things. He made that buffet." She pointed to an elaborately carved oak buffet that sat under the window. "He was good with his hands. Even though the priests didn't want embellishments, he often added accents in subtle places, like the spindles on the staircase. Like this key. This is what I was talking about," she said, holding it out for him. "It was in the box with his tools."

Giorgio took the long, graceful key, embellished with an intricate set of curls. It was labeled with a tag inscribed with only four capital letters.

"The tag made me think of your investigation," she finished.

Giorgio stared at the tag. "It looks like 'ORI...something."

"The letters spell ORIG, meaning it's the original," she replied. "There were probably duplicates made, but he kept the original key. I'm not sure why."

"Why do you think this could be useful to me? It could be a key for anything."

"My father wouldn't have kept it unless it was important. And it was in this."

She handed him an envelope browned with age. The envelope had a single word written across the front in the same cursive handwriting – "Monastery."

†

Giorgio was back in his car contemplating the antique key when his cell phone rang. It was McCready telling him that Father Damian had called to say that one of the monks had gone missing. Since Giorgio wanted an opportunity to research the key's significance anyway, he made a beeline for Sunnyside Drive.

He entered the familiar lobby, going directly to Father Damian's office. He knocked softy and was admitted with an even softer reply. The monk stood staring at the painting of the Last Supper, one hand tucked behind his back. In the other, he held his crucifix. Giorgio was shocked by his appearance when he pivoted to receive him. The monk seemed to be deteriorating right before his eyes. The man's gray eyes seemed to have sunk into his skull, and the pallid cast to his skin was alarming. Though he was looking directly at Giorgio, he seemed to stare straight through him.

"He's gone," the monk said flatly.

"Who's gone?"

"Father Daniel. When he didn't come to breakfast, we checked his room thinking he might be ill. He was gone."

"I take it he didn't just go for a run." Giorgio couldn't help feeling smug at the thought of putting handcuffs on the handsome young monk. But again something told him he wouldn't get that pleasure.

Father Damian dropped into the chair behind the desk. "If only he *had* gone for a run. His closet and drawers were cleaned out." He dropped his head to his chest. "I can't believe it. I can't believe he did it. He had such good references."

"Did what?"

The other man lifted his chin with a pale glint to his eyes. "It's clear isn't it? He ran. He's the one. The murderer. It was one of us after all."

His hand rested on the desk, but Giorgio could tell he was nervously tapping his heel against the floor. He was on the verge of a nervous breakdown.

"Father, I'm not sure that's what Father Daniel's disappearance means. Was there a note, or did he talk to anyone? Was there any indication as to where he went?"

The monk shook his head without a word, staring at the blotter on his desk.

"All right. Please block off his room. I'll send someone up here right away to inspect it. We'll check the bus and train stations, airlines, and car rentals to see if we can track him down. You don't know if a taxi arrived here today, do you?"

Damian looked up as if he'd heard a distant bird call. It was a full ten seconds before he shook his head no.

"Okay, we'll check on that, too."

The monk seemed oblivious that anyone else was even in the room. Giorgio left him that way and went looking for help. He found Father Francis, the young monk he'd met raking leaves, and asked him to take matters in hand. As Father Francis left for the Abbot's office, Giorgio went outside to call Swan at the station.

An hour later, Swan and two other policemen finished searching Father Daniel's small room. It was clear Daniel had left in a hurry. McCready called every bus station, train station, and local taxi service within thirty miles. No one remembered a young man with Daniel's description. Giorgio wondered if Daniel was even his name. Priests were often asked to take a new name when they took their vows as a sign they were leaving their old lives behind. It would make identifying the "old" friend difficult. He went upstairs to locate the secret door he now knew had to be there.

He opened the closet door on the monks' side of the building, this time pulling down blankets and whatever else lined the shelves. Since the bulb in the closet didn't work, it was almost impossible to see any irregularities in the wood paneling. Giorgio pushed the door all the way back and threw open the heavy drapes covering the hallway window only a few feet away. He studied the small enclosure, trying to see the space as Edward Applebaum would have seen it when he designed it. His fingers played with the key in his pocket, but there was no keyhole.

He began running his fingers into every crevice, across every surface, and into every hole he could find. He pushed anything that looked remotely like it might be a lever. After five minutes he stopped and tried to think clearly.

Wherever the lever was positioned, it had to be in a place that wouldn't be found by mistake. That eliminated the wall sconce because routine maintenance might reveal its secret.

As he contemplated the situation, a cold draft filled the enclosure, forcing him to step back and check the window. It was closed. A clinking sound made him turn back to see if something had fallen to the floor. His eyes caught sight of an old button sitting on the bottom shelf. A familiar chill swept through him.

Slowly, he bent down to pick it up, wondering if the boy would make himself known. As his fingers reached out for the brass object, however, he paused. The shelf support just below the button was finished with a small finial, as all the others were. Elvira Applebaum had said her father loved to add embellishments to otherwise plain architecture. Closets didn't normally have finials.

He crouched down and shined his flashlight underneath the shelves and into the crevices where the shelf supports met the wall. All the supports had been cut flat and butted up against the inside wall except for the one on the far right. It seemed to extend into the wall and sat ever so slightly above the supporting bracket. Giorgio could hardly contain himself as he backed up and grasped the small finial that embellished the front edge of that support.

With a solid tug, the knob slid easily forward and the wooden beam came free of the wall. The wall didn't move, but he could feel it release. With a shove, it swiveled away from him about two feet, scraping softly across the floor and allowing just enough space for a person to slip through to the other side. He crossed into the adjoining closet and out the other door. Mallery Olsen's room was the first door to his left.

Giorgio pulled out his cell phone and called the station. Then he slipped back through the opening, remembering the sound that had led him to his discovery. He bent down to pick up the old brass button, just as a voice whispered past his ear. The sound sent him tripping backwards into the hallway so quickly that he actually fell onto his backside.

Giorgio sat there dumbfounded for a moment, the button still held tightly in his hand. He stared into the closet, waiting for the boy to materialize. A clicking noise made him turn towards the window instead. The old-fashioned window clasp had unlatched, letting in a draft of fresh air, the same way the window by the main staircase had the night of the murder. The boy had been trying to communicate with him from the moment he was presented the case – from the theater parking lot to now. What had the voice just whispered?

Giorgio got to his feet and glanced down into the courtyard. He could see a portion of the path below. But from where he stood, he couldn't see the statue of the Virgin Mary. Yet according to McCready's notes, Father Francis had claimed to see someone that night moving past the statue of Mary. The moment he made the connection, the window latched again with a loud snap, and he remembered what the voice had whispered.

"*Mary.*"

† Chapter Thirty-Nine †

Giorgio found Father Francis in the small kitchen helping with the noon meal.

"I called the doctor for Father Damian," Francis reported. He wiped his hands on a towel as they stepped into the hallway. "The doctor just gave him a light sedative. He's resting now. Did you find Brother Daniel?"

His voice didn't register the same accusation expressed by Father Damian. Perhaps the two men had become friends.

"No," Giorgio replied, watching him. "We're checking all the bus and train stations, though. Listen, I just found a secret doorway between the east and west wings of the building."

The young priest's eyes grew wide, causing his contact lenses to float free. "Another secret passage! This is beginning to sound like some cheap crime novel," he lamented, shaking his head. "I'm worried about Father Damian. I don't think he can stand too many more surprises."

"Father Francis, you reported that you saw someone outside the night of the murder."

The monk's eyes lit up. "Yes, I did. I couldn't see very well. I mean, I couldn't see who it was. It was very dark."

"You said you were in the upstairs hallway when you saw this person?"

"Yes, I was just coming out of my room. As I told you before, I got caught up writing some letters and was a little late getting to compline."

"Where is your room?"

"At the end of the north hallway − first one around the corner."

"And you saw this person somewhere near the statue of Mary, out on the walkway?"

"That's right."

"I was just up there, Father. You can't see the statue from up there."

There was a pause in which the monk merely stared back at Giorgio, his face a mixture of curiosity and inner thought. Finally, his eyebrows creased and he replied.

"I'm sure you're wrong. Where were you standing?"

"At the end of the hallway by the last window."

His whole body relaxed. "Well, there are three windows along that hallway, Detective. That wasn't the window I spoke of."

"Would you mind showing me?"

"Of course not."

The two men climbed the staircase and followed the hallway to the end, passing Father O'Leary's room, now barricaded by yellow police tape. Giorgio trailed the young monk who moved with an athletic sense of grace.

"This is my room right here." He indicated the first room around the corner, about twenty feet from the hall closet. "I came out of my door and turned down the hallway like this." He imitated his movements, inching closer to the outside wall as he turned the corner. "I was somewhat distracted, and when I got to this second window I stopped to look at the pond. It's lovely when it's lit up at night. Anyway, I noticed a man moving along the path toward the kitchen." He turned and gestured in that direction. "You see, from here I can just barely see the statue."

Giorgio stepped forward. The statue of Mary was tucked in an alcove along the pathway to the left. From this vantage point, only her arm was visible.

"How do you know it was a man?"

His face fell. "Well, I guess I don't know for sure. All I really saw was a shadow." He stopped and thought for a moment. "I assumed it was one of the monks. The robes, you know."

"You saw the robes?"

"Well, not clearly. I only saw an outline, but I think they were robes. Of course, it could have been a long dress. Ms. Peters was caught wearing robes, wasn't she? This is all becoming so complicated. I guess I'm not positive of anything, other than I saw *someone*."

Giorgio stood for a moment, looking back along the pathway.

"Is there anything else, Detective? I'm in charge of lunch today."
He smiled affably.

"Thank you very much, Father."

The young monk disappeared down the stairs. Giorgio continued to look out the window, wondering why the monk would have stopped to gaze out the window in the first place when he was already late for prayer that night. A thought made him cross back through the secret door to the west hallway. There, he pulled aside the curtain that framed the window across from Mallery Olsen's door. As he suspected, the statue of Mary was fully visible below him.

As Giorgio contemplated Francis' story, Swan approached from the main staircase.

"I thought I'd find you up here. McCready called. The crime lab report came in on the fibers they found on Mallery Olsen. The fibers match the blankets used by the monks. No surprise there, I guess."

Giorgio stuffed his hands in his pockets and returned his gaze out the window. "And we now know how the killer accessed her room."

Swan poked his head into the closet to see the secret door. "Well, well, well. You found it. I wonder how many more of these things are around here. Did you call for Fong?"

"He should be here soon," Giorgio confirmed.

Swan came and stood beside Giorgio at the window. "So, it *was* a monk."

"I didn't say that, but we have three unsolved murders and no connecting motive. I've never believed in coincidences, but that may be what we have here."

"Not the death of Father O'Leary."

"No. I think Poindexter killed Dorman, and O'Leary's murder had everything to do with whoever killed Mallery Olsen. That's the reason I think we're looking for a monk. However, while they all had opportunity, none of them seem to have had a motive."

The two men stood shoulder to shoulder, staring out the window for a long moment. Finally, Giorgio spoke.

"I'm going to talk to Father Damian."

"I'll wait here for Fong."

"Do me a favor. Call the janitor and ask him about this key."

Giorgio showed him the ornate key Elvira Applebaum had given him.

"Describe it and see if he has any idea what it belongs to. We think there's at least one duplicate. If so, I'd like to know who has it."

Swan turned the key over in his hand before giving it back to Giorgio. "I'll see if I can find him. We might be able to get a locksmith to take a look at it too."

"Okay, catch up with you later."

Father Damian's bungalow was tucked in a grove of trees directly up the hill from the courtyard pond. It was a small, square building with a tiled roof. Giorgio knocked on the arched door and then stood back and waited. He heard a toilet flush and then a moment later, the door opened and a haggard looking Father Damian appeared.

"Detective," his voice had weakened to just above a whisper. "I'm sorry, I was resting. What is it now?"

"I wanted to ask you a few questions about Father O'Leary. May I come in?"

He sighed but stood back to allow Giorgio inside. "Certainly."

Giorgio followed him to the small sitting room furnished in turn-of-the-century antiques. The bedroom lay at the back of the sitting room, and Giorgio could see the single bed from which Father Damian had just risen. A studio-sized kitchen was set in a small alcove to the right. The bathroom door was to the left of the entry. Giorgio waited until the monk had taken a straight-backed chair in the middle of the room and then sat on a Queen Anne-style sofa.

"I'm afraid the doctor gave me a light sedative." The once proud and erect man was slouched in the chair, his hands limp in his lap.

"We found the time capsule last night." The monk's eyebrows arched, but he didn't say anything. "Just in front of the statue of the angel."

"Yes," he nodded in understanding. "After you called last night, I got to thinking that I remembered reading something in the old records about a time capsule. Did you find anything of value?"

"We found the original drawings which indicated a secret door on the second floor."

Father Damian sat back as if he expected another blow, his face drawn with suspicions.

"I found the door this morning. It's in the upstairs closet…the one that separates the east and west wings."

Giorgio paused, letting the significance of that information settle in. Father Damian's face relaxed, and he looked out the window to a large eucalyptus tree that shaded the corner window. His skin drooped around his jawline making look a good ten years older than he probably was. When he looked back, he sighed again.

"You should know there were problems here a long time ago, back when the boys' school was here."

"Indiscretions with the boys?"

He nodded and dropped his shoulders. "It almost ruined the monastery. They had to close the school, and the church was forced to pay a lot of money to the families in order to keep things out of court."

"What about the murder?"

"You mean Father Wingate. The boy who committed the murder killed himself. Back in those days, the Rectory was up on that floor, at the end of the hall. I didn't know about the secret door, but I suppose that's how Father Wingate gained access to the boys."

"Was it only Father Wingate?"

"I don't think so. I have some letters written back then from the Bishop. Several monks were relocated and a new Abbott was brought in. It was a difficult time."

"Was Father O'Leary a student then?"

"I don't know. I suppose he was old enough to have lived here then. We have the records. You could take a look."

The look on his face made Giorgio believe he really didn't know.

"What was his job here?"

"He worked in the library and served as the building manager. He hired the janitors and oversaw all aspects of the building's maintenance." Father Damian shifted uncomfortably in his seat. "The Bishop has cancelled the forum this weekend. He doesn't want to draw any more attention to the monastery, although he will be coming here directly after the meeting early next week. He wants to lend a 'steady' hand, as he put it."

"I'm sorry. I know how difficult this has been. May I take a look at those old records?"

"I keep my keys in that little carved box on the top shelf of that bookshelf. The small silver key unlocks the file cabinet in my office. If you look in the bottom drawer, you'll find a set of old files."

Giorgio located the box and the key. As he lifted them out, he noticed the door to the bathroom stood ajar. The light was off, but the toilet was still running. Water was pooling on the tiled floor just inside the door.

"Father Damian, your toilet is running over."

Giorgio reached in and turned on the light. Water was cascading over the top of the commode, soaking the floor mat and getting ready to invade the living room. He reached behind the commode and turned off the valve that fed the toilet. Father Damian appeared at the doorway and moaned.

"Oh my. Let me get a mop."

The monk disappeared into the kitchen, while Giorgio grabbed a few hand towels. When Damian returned, he asked, "Do you have a plunger?"

"Yes, of course."

The man seemed disoriented and left the mop propped against the door while he went in search of the plunger. Giorgio used the mop to soak up some of the water, but had nowhere to dispose of it except the sink.

"Here it is," Father Damian said, appearing with a long-handled plunger. "But I can call Father Abernathy. He'll take care of it, Detective. Please, you don't have to do this." He hadn't handed over the plunger yet, making Giorgio reach for it.

"Don't worry. I'm chief handy man at home."

Giorgio took the plunger and lifted the lid to the toilet, placing the plunger over the opening. "I have two children, Father. I've found all sorts of ghoulish things in the toilet." He gave the plunger a shove. "I think we need one more," he exclaimed and pushed the plunger in again.

As he pulled it back, he reached for the handle hoping to flush the toilet and be done with it, but an inadvertent glance into the bowl stopped him. Floating in the shallow water was the tip of green fabric. He reached inside his coat and grabbed a rubber glove before pulling out the obstruction. When a long, green silk scarf emerged, Giorgio heard a loud thud behind him and turned to find Father Damian out cold on the floor.

† Chapter Forty †

Father Damian was sent to the hospital, with a cop assigned to watch him. Giorgio believed it unlikely he had it in him to commit murder; it was more likely he'd been set up. But by whom?

Giorgio was spared the news conference. The Captain had taken the lead instead, refusing to confirm any information about the missing finger or secret passages. There was enough information about Anya Peters, Corey Poindexter, Jeff Dorman, and Marvin Palomar to keep the reporters happy. He did say, though, that they were making progress.

Since the children were spending the next few days with a friend to give Angie a break, Giorgio decided to work and called his brother. Mrs. Greenspan had made only soup that night for Angie, so Giorgio and Rocky shared artery-clogging drive-thru burgers and fries at the kitchen table, while Angie rested upstairs.

"So, you think whoever killed Olsen is living a secret life," Rocky slurred through a mouth full of food. "Someone trying to hide his identity, but Olsen recognized him, and he killed her."

Grosvenor had planted himself next to Rocky, his eyes fixed on the French fry clutched between the detective's fingers. The poor dog's head turned circles as Rocky drew invisible curly cues in the air as he talked.

"She didn't plan on that drink," Giorgio replied, swallowing. "It came as a surprise. She was already dressed for the dinner. At some point in between the time she dressed for dinner and when she was seen going back upstairs, I think she ran into someone she didn't expect to see. We've cross-checked names of people she knew in high school and college, even a couple of part-time jobs she had, but nothing matches."

"So you think either a monk or one of the conference attendees was using a fake name?"

Rocky had finished his burger and got up to throw his trash into the can underneath the sink. Then he leaned against the counter and pulled out a cigarette and lighter.

"It could have just been someone who changed his name," Giorgio said.

"Which is it, though? A monk or a conference attendee?"

"I think the answer lies in why the two of them went to her room in the first place," Giorgio replied. "If the old friend was a conference attendee, they could have shared drinks at the cocktail party rather than going to her room. On the other hand, a monk couldn't be seen drinking socially with anyone."

Rocky flicked the lighter to life and was about to light the cigarette, when Grosvenor suddenly barked at him and began to growl. Rocky stopped and threw the cigarette into the sink.

"Wow," Giorgio exclaimed, leaning over to pat the dog. "It's okay, little guy."

"Sorry, Grosvenor," Rocky said.

Grosvenor scooted over next to Giorgio, watching Rocky with anxiety. Rocky remained with his back against the sink.

"I didn't mean to scare him."

Giorgio stroked Grosvenor's head. The dog began to pant.

"I think he remembers all too well how he got those burn marks. We'll have to be careful around him."

"Maybe there's a doggie therapist somewhere who can help him."

"Maybe," Giorgio mused, watching the dog. Grosvenor seemed to relax now that the item in question was gone. He turned and gave Giorgio a quick lick as if to tell him everything was okay.

Rocky returned to the table. "Well, no biggie. I should stop smoking, anyway."

Giorgio gave Grosvenor a last pat and sat back in his chair.

"Wouldn't it have seemed suspicious that a monk wanted to have a drink at all?" Rocky continued, grabbing his cup and sucking on the straw.

Giorgio shrugged. "My guess is that Olsen knew him before he was a monk. She might not have questioned the walk down memory lane."

"And the monk arrived through the secret door," Rocky said.

Giorgio nodded. "That's another reason why I think it had to be a monk. A conference attendee wouldn't have known about the door. The program chair said she heard someone knocking on Olsen's door when she went to look for her mystery props. That meant Olsen was waiting inside for him."

Giorgio got up and tossed the last of his fries to Grosvenor who snapped them up like a flytrap, all signs of his previous rage gone. Giorgio threw away his trash and reached into the refrigerator for a can of pop.

"Our killer took a big chance if Levinsky's door was open," Rocky speculated.

"Yes, but if he used the secret door, he wouldn't have had to pass Levinsky's door. And he may not have been dressed in his robes at that point. So he wouldn't have raised suspicion."

"Right, but then he must have drugged Olsen first so there wouldn't be any noise, killed her, wrapped her in a blanket, and carried her out through a secret door after Levinsky left, down the *back* staircase and around the exterior of the building to the kitchen? Pretty gutsy," Rocky said skeptically.

"But only a monk would know that much about the property and everyone's routine. Olsen was petite. Wrapped in a blanket, no one outside would have been able to tell what he was carrying."

Rocky leaned back in his chair, finishing his drink. "Still pretty gutsy. There's a light outside the kitchen door, and someone could have seen him go to the closet."

"The back door is blocked by the bend in the hallway. His only risk was if someone was going out to the parking lot."

"Which, in the case of Colin Jewett, was a pretty big risk!"

"Yes, but our monk didn't *know* that," Giorgio emphasized with a raised finger. "This monk was not only gutsy, he was extremely lucky. He could've run into Colin Jewett, Anya Peters, Corey Poindexter, or Jeff Dorman."

"Not to mention Father O'Leary smoking his lungs out."

"I don't think Tommy Tune could've choreographed it any better," Giorgio laughed. "He must have hit the perfect time window."

"Of course," Rocky said, as he twirled the straw in the bottom of the cup. "He could have been seen by *all* of those people and they just didn't report it. O'Leary was killed before he could tell us anything useful, and none of the others would have said anything because they would have incriminated themselves if they did."

"Poindexter was the only one who tried and he botched it."

"And remember, O'Leary was taken ill that night. It's just possible our man made sure O'Leary would be out of the way." Rocky took a last drink and began a loud slurping noise.

"You know, if you rip the cup apart you could lick the sides clean," Giorgio smirked.

Rocky smiled as he threw it away. "Very funny. Okay, so how do we figure out which monk we have to arrest?"

Giorgio was already heading for the living room. "I want to go back through Olsen's box one last time and see if we can find anything that would lead us to the old friend she mentioned."

†

The brothers spent the next hour re-reading old love letters and searching through photo albums. Giorgio recognized several individuals from pictures on the wall in Olsen's home, but very few were identified by name. They thumbed through college annuals, reading the notes written by friends. It seemed Olsen was popular, especially with young men who often referred to her smile lighting up a room. Giorgio suspected they really meant she had big breasts. There was nothing that would lead them to one of the monks.

By eleven o'clock they were both rubbing their eyes. Rocky got up to stretch his legs and was about to go to the kitchen when Giorgio called out, "Ah ha!"

"What is it?" Rocky asked, coming back to look over his shoulder.

"Look at this kid."

Giorgio was sitting on the ottoman and held a picture taken on the steps of a gothic looking fraternity house. Three rows of young men grinned into the camera, each wearing dark fraternity sweaters. He pointed to the middle row where an athletic-looking kid with glasses and brown hair stood next to a gothic column.

"I'll bet next month's salary that's Father Francis."

"Francis has blonde hair."

"Easily fixed. It's obviously a younger version, but he's the same, I'd swear it. And one more thing," Giorgio went to the box and took out the picture Tony had found of Mallery Olsen with the Basset Hound. "Here he is again, and in this picture he's blonde." He pointed to the kid sitting next to Olsen.

Rocky studied the two pictures. "Wait a minute, Joe. They look alike, but not exactly alike. It's hard to tell because in this picture we only see the blonde from the side. I wonder, though...." Rocky picked up a college annual from the floor and flipped to the back. "I saw a guy that might be a match to the brunette." He spent several minutes going through Mallery Olsen's senior yearbook. "I thought so. Here, take a look."

He handed the book to Giorgio who peered down at a picture of the college theater club. The picture was a scene from *Camelot* in which Lancelot sings his heart out to Guinevere. Giorgio could almost hear the words from, "If Ever I Would Leave You," as the young man playing Lancelot stood center stage, one hand on the hilt of his sword, his mouth open in song. Although his hair was tied back into a pony tail, and he wore stage make-up, he looked just like the brunette in the fraternity picture.

"This guy's name is Marino," Rocky said, reading the caption. "Danny Marino."

They looked back and forth between the blonde and brunette. "They look almost exactly alike," Giorgio muttered. "And look at this." He pointed to Guinevere. "That's Mallery Olsen. Damn! See if you can find a name for the blonde."

Rocky searched through the book again, coming across a picture of the college president with three student officers. "Hold it! Here's the blonde. This is a better picture, too." Rocky took the book to the light. "Give me your magnifying glass."

Giorgio rummaged through a drawer and pulled out an old magnifying glass. Rocky leaned in to study the photos, flipping back and forth from one picture to the other.

"It's uncanny," Rocky murmured, holding the book out for his brother. "They do look like twins, or at least brothers. They're about the same height and same build, although the blonde is slightly taller. And, they have the same general facial features."

"The brunette seems a little stockier and more muscular, with a fuller jawline and he wears glasses, although on stage he was probably wearing contacts." Giorgio said, peering through the magnifier. "And, here," Giorgio exclaimed, reading the small text beneath the picture of the blonde. "This guy was Senior Class President. His name is Jack Brye." Giorgio felt a familiar tingling sensation as his eyes shifted back to the Camelot page.

"The question is," Rocky started, "which one do we have?"

Giorgio stared at the picture of Lancelot, his eyes riveted on the tattoo on the back of the actor's hand grasping the sword.

"I think I know. Let's go find out."

† Chapter Forty-One †

He sat in the garden at the foot of Christ, where he'd seen another monk sit on the night he'd killed the girl. He wasn't looking for any kind of solace, just a quiet place to think. His room had become claustrophobic. Out here the air was crisp and cool, allowing his lungs and mind to expand. Dressed as he was, fully clothed beneath his robes, he didn't feel the cold. He felt invigorated and ready to take this little saga to the next level.

Things at the monastery were coming to a close. He could feel it. The police had found the secret door; confirming the killer had to be a monk. He'd attempted to frame Father Damian, but the evidence against him was weak, and the police would quickly eliminate Damian as a suspect. Father O'Leary was dead and couldn't tell what he knew, but he and Father O'Leary had worked closely together in the library. Eventually, they would make the connection and come looking for him. Perhaps that would be soon. Perhaps not. Either way, something was about to break.

He stroked the tattoo and contemplated his options. He needed to create a distraction, something to lead the police away from him. Mailing the package to the police station hadn't worked. None of the media outlets had run the story. That bothered him. Maybe the police had never received it. Maybe they'd received it but sent it off to a lab somewhere. Either way the things he wanted, recognition and chaos, had been withheld, and the sour taste of disappointment roiled in his belly.

He glanced up at the statue's face. The alabaster expression was benevolent, with the eyes lowered with a graceful smile.

The image moved Cato, as it always did. He couldn't help but wonder at the serendipity of his being here at the monastery. His father had been killed on the steps of a Catholic church, yet instead of shunning the church, his mother had forced Cato to attend Catholic schools and even serve as an altar boy.

It was one of the reasons he'd been able to pull off this masquerade so easily. Then, his best friend in college had moved to San Francisco after his senior year to become a priest, a fact he now used to his advantage. Finally, he and Jacko had shot Mangano on Easter Sunday. And, now, here he was not only living on the grounds of a Catholic monastery, but living as one of the monks. What were the odds? What did it mean? Would he somehow die by the cross? Was he meant to repent? Or, was it just life coming full circle?

He stared at the face of Christ thinking about the convergence of all these things. He didn't think this was the end of the road, but he would accept it if it was. He wasn't afraid. On the other hand, he wouldn't go easily if caught. He had no intention of spending the rest of his life in jail. If all else failed, he could run, but this time there would be no place to go.

He took a deep breath and stood up, thinking perhaps it was time to leave and get out from under the watchful eyes of the police. He needed time. San Francisco popped into his head and an embryo of an idea began to form. Jack, the real priest, no longer existed except in the minds of the people who had once known him. Maybe he could stretch the charade out a little further. He decided to return to his room, craft a plan, and be gone by morning.

As he stepped away from the bench, something clinked at his feet. He glanced down to find a small, round object glistening in the moonlight. He bent down and wrapped his fingers around an old brass button. Holding it up, he could see it was imbedded on one side with a Latin cross.

Suspicious, he looked around wondering who had thrown it. There was no one else in the garden, and all the windows to the monk's rooms were closed. Only two of them were even lit. The air had grown cold, and a slow chill inched its way down his spine.

Cautious now, he decided it was time to go inside. He was getting spooked and that could spell disaster.

He tossed the coin into the flower bed, turned toward the door and stopped cold. Standing in the middle of the cactus garden was a boy of about thirteen. The youth wore dark knickers and suspenders and was eerily transparent. Cato stared with horror at the flickering image, because the boy was suspended about six inches off the ground. A moment later, a second boy, dressed nearly the same, appeared next to a rose bush a few feet away, his image as transparent as a piece of gauze. Two more boys hovered near the far wall.

Cato backed away, trembling. Not from the chill, but from a fear he'd never known. Father O'Leary had talked about ghosts at the monastery, but he'd never believed him. Is that what this was – ghosts?

Slowly Cato edged to his right along the path, never taking his eyes off the apparitions. They didn't move to stop him, but merely watched him from where they shimmered in the moonlight. When something moved to his left, his head snapped in that direction. A large, dense shadow emerged from the garden wall like someone stepping through a doorway. The shadow had a vaguely human shape, but was much taller and larger than the boys. As Cato watched in a near panic, the shadow took on the distinct shape of a rotund man dressed in the traditional robes of a monk.

Father O'Leary!

Cato turned and ran for the double doors, grabbing the knob and flinging the door open so violently it slammed against the wall. He entered the hallway breathless, searching the shadows for more apparitions. In a panic now, he ran for the stairs to his left.

"Father!"

Cato whipped around to find Father Rosario in the kitchen doorway, a dish towel in his hands.

"Are you alright? You look frightened."

The small priest stepped forward as if to comfort him.

"No, Father, I'm fine," the young monk responded rapidly. He held up a hand when Father Rosario started to move towards him. "Really. I'm fine," he gulped. "I just had a bit of an anxiety attack out there, out in the garden. I was thinking about that young woman and then Father O'Leary and Father Damian. All the murders. It's just so tragic, so horrifying. All of this."

His breathing came in short gasps and he struggled to calm himself. He couldn't help stealing glances back towards the garden, but nothing had followed him through the door.

"I understand," Father Rosario commiserated. "Perhaps you should lie down. You don't look well."

"Yes. Yes. It's time I retired anyway. And then, I think, Father, I may choose to leave the monastery." The moment the words left his mouth he realized he may have hit on just the excuse he needed. "I'm just not sure I can take much more of this. I'm scared, Father. I feel any one of us might be next. You understand, don't you? Aren't you frightened?

"Of course, my boy. We all are. You didn't bargain for this when you came here. No one could blame you. Get some rest and perhaps things will look better in the morning."

"Thank you, Father. I will." Cato started backing up the staircase, nearly tripping on his robes. "Good night, Father."

Both men were surprised by a flash of headlights that swept across the front windows.

"Now, I wonder who that could be so late," Father Rosario said, moving in that direction. "I'll take care of it, Father. You go to bed." The little priest wandered down the hallway towards the front door saying to himself, "I do hope it's not that detective again."

† Chapter Forty-Two †

The huge building sat docile in the cool night air, a complacent child compared to the storm-raged teenager it had been only a few nights before. A light glowed from within as if the building were half asleep. Rocky had barely turned off the truck's sputtering engine before Giorgio jumped out, heading for the chapel. He felt the same kind of excitement he'd felt as a child on Christmas morning when he knew what presents he would get. They'd solved the crime. Now all they had to do was reel in the killer.

Father Rosario met them at the door, and Giorgio asked to see Father Francis.

"Detective, it's late and Father Francis just retired," the small monk said with restrained patience. "He helped me clean up earlier, but something has upset him and he's gone to bed. Perhaps this could wait until tomorrow."

"No, Father, it can't wait." Giorgio brushed past him. "We need to see him tonight."

"All right, but I hope there won't be any more surprises."

"I think you can count on at least one more surprise, Father," Rocky said.

"Stay here," Giorgio said to the small priest.

He ordered Grosvenor to stay put as well and turned away.

"Please, Detective," the small priest raised his voice as they moved towards the stairs. "We've lost bookings and bread orders. The Abbot is in the hospital under suspicion, and the monks are feeling the strain. Father Francis just said he plans to leave the monastery tomorrow. What more could you possibly find?"

"The killer," Giorgio replied with a level gaze. "Please, watch the dog."

The two officers left Father Rosario staring after them. They crossed the carpeted hallway and took the back stairs two at a time. The residence hallway was no more than a dimly lit tunnel at night, but they caught a retreating figure at the far end. The figure turned back as the brothers reached the landing. It was Father Francis. Giorgio called out, but Francis turned with a jerk and rounded the corner, robes flying. An instant later, a door slammed and the brothers broke into a run.

Giorgio arrived first, but the door was securely locked. He pounded on the worn wooden door calling out the monk's name. When no one answered, he pulled his weapon, stepped back and splintered the old door with a well-placed kick. Giorgio burst into the room just as a doorway across the hall opened to reveal the grizzled face of one of the older monks.

"Police. Go back inside!" Rocky barked at the surprised man.

The door slammed shut, and Rocky joined Giorgio in an empty room. They made a quick search. Francis was nowhere to be found. Both men looked around bewildered as if the rabbit had just disappeared out of the hat.

"Shit! Here we go again," Giorgio exclaimed, holstering his weapon.

At his feet was a brown robe. Giorgio spied it suspiciously.

"There must be another secret door in here," he snarled, kicking at the robe.

"Shouldn't we wait for a search warrant?"

Giorgio glared at him. "We had permission to speak with Father Francis and he ran. I'll deal with any fallout later. Check the rooms on either side. Make sure he didn't sneak through to one of those. I'll search in here."

Rocky hurried out and banged on the door around the corner. Giorgio scanned the room he was in. It was larger than the other rooms, reminding him this one had once been the room Father Wingate had been murdered in. It held a single bed, a small desk, and a built-in closet along the back wall.

The closet presented the only possible place for a secret door. He approached it and threw both doors wide.

Two dark pullover sweaters were folded neatly on an upper shelf, while two black shirts and a pair of black pants lay on the floor as if they'd fallen off their hangers.

There was nothing else in the closet except a pair of work boots and a set of faint scratches across the closet floor. There was only one reason for those scratches. He began looking for the mechanism that would release the secret door.

The closet was divided from top to bottom by stained-to-match molding that ran along the interior walls. There were no hooks, knobs, or other embellishments, and the wood had a stringy grain which meant there were no visible knots to push. Frustrated, Giorgio studied the clothes bar which extended the entire width of the closet. The closet was only about two and a half feet deep, making it impossible for the back wall to open without hitting the bar. The bar also made it impossible for either of the side walls to open since it was braced against them. Yet the scratches didn't lie.

He eyed the molding that extended like a chair railing around the interior. It gave him an idea. Why would a closet have decorative molding? Perhaps only the lower half of the wall moved. He reached in and knocked in several places on the back wall and then along the inside right wall where the scratches were. The hollow thud that greeted him along the right wall prompted him to glance at the shirts lying on the floor. He reached for the clothes bar and wrapped his hands around it, twisting it towards the back wall. Nothing happened.

"I've checked both rooms," Rocky said behind him. "A Father Emanuel lives in the one around the corner. He heard the door slam but that was all. A Father Cannon lives on the other side. He was praying, but also heard the door slam. What are you doing?"

"He went through here," Giorgio said, staring into the closet. "I'd bet my life on it."

He grabbed the clothes bar again, this time twisting it towards him. The lower half of the right interior wall popped opened.

"Whoa! You're getting good at that," Rocky whistled.

Giorgio pulled the panel open as far as it would go, allowing the two brothers to peer into what looked like an old, dark elevator shaft with the top of a wooden staircase barely visible. Around the corner was a shelf where Giorgio found a wooden box filled with some stage makeup and a grayish-brown goatee. Next to the box was a pair of brown pants, shirt, and shoes.

"Damn! I saw him."

"What d'you mean?"

"In the gift shop. In disguise. This guy has balls. Let's go," Giorgio commanded.

He took out his weapon and squatted down to climb through the small opening. The rickety wooden staircase swayed under his weight but made little noise as he began to carefully descend.

"Leave the door open to give us some light," he called back to Rocky.

Rocky followed, bumping his head as he bent his lanky frame into a pretzel to squeeze through. They emerged into a dark, musty alcove.

"Where the hell are we?" Rocky whispered, producing a small LED flashlight attached to his key ring.

Giorgio pulled out his own pen light and squinted into the inky blackness that crowded around them.

"I don't know," he replied, stepping away from the stairs.

His eyes strained to find identifying landmarks. The pervading damp, stale air gave rise to a brief catch of claustrophobia, and Giorgio had to cough to relieve the anxiety building in his chest. Rocky moved in front of his brother, his light revealing the tomblike quality of an ancient mud-caked hallway with a low-beamed ceiling that angled upwards to the right. While the walls appeared to be made from an adobe mixture of clay, straw and pebbles, everything was reinforced by a matrix of wooden supports.

"I think we're below the other tunnel," Giorgio said with the back of his hand pressed to his mouth.

"You mean we're underneath the other tunnel?"

"Not directly underneath, but further underground. The air is heavier and it's colder."

He followed Rocky into the passageway and felt along the walls with the flat of his hand, grimacing at how the clammy surface of the clay-dirt mixture clung to his skin.

"There used to be a Spanish Rancho located here in the seventeen hundreds, back when Mexico passed out land grants to its military and nobility. This one was built too close to the foothills and a massive mudslide buried the entire thing. From what I read, the monastery was built directly over the site a hundred years later. I'd guess we're standing in an interior hallway of that old Spanish Rancho. Look how the ceiling slants upwards to the right. That's a roof line. And from the look of these reinforcements, the good fathers found it and wanted to maintain it for some reason."

Rocky moved forward, bending over to avoid bumping his head on a crossbeam. "Didn't someone say the monks built tunnels during the war as a means of escape?"

"Yes, but be careful," Giorgio warned. "Francis could be anywhere, and we're sitting ducks with the flashlights down here."

They crept along broken adobe tiles covered with dirt and debris, their lungs filling quickly with the stench of rotting water, rat droppings, and foul air. Giorgio's hand occasionally sought the wall for support, recoiling from the touch of water seeping through the clay. Rocky cursed every so often when he became entangled in a cobweb, and Giorgio couldn't help wondering about the boy. After all, this seemed the idyllic environment for a ghost. Would the boy make himself known? Would they see other dead souls?

"Look here," Rocky whispered, interrupting Giorgio's thoughts.

Rocky had paused at the doorway to a small room. A broken wooden door lay splintered on the floor with its wrought iron hinges flattened and bent, probably the result of a large rock now propped up by a series of steel girders on the upper corner of the doorframe, forcing the whole corner to sag under its weight. A quick search of the room revealed nothing but rotting sack cloth, pottery shards, and broken shelving.

The brothers exited the room quickly. Giorgio felt haunted by the prospect of everything caving in around them. They passed another room where the door was still attached, but where the far wall had been obliterated by the mud slide.

The room still held a small shattered wooden table and three spindly wooden chairs, broken and lying on their sides. In one corner were several tanned animal skins, a couple of wine barrels, and a stack of empty, frayed cloth sacks that probably once held grain, long ago eaten by the rats. As the pen lights followed the edge of the intruding mudslide, Rocky paused when the light reflected off the long slender bones of a hand, reaching out from under the mud.

"I suppose not many people survived the mudslide," he lamented.

"No," Giorgio agreed. "Let's keep going."

They returned to the hallway. Rocky kept his flashlight focused down, throwing the light sideways every few feet to scare away the rats that scurried before the oncoming light.

"This place gives me the creeps," he mumbled.

The tunnel ended as quickly as it began. A short thirty feet from where they'd seen the skeleton, Rocky stopped at a wall of cement cinder blocks that emerged out of the compacted dirt and extended well beyond the ancient tunnel walls on either side. Inserted into the middle of the sturdy wall was a heavy timbered door. Giorgio stopped and looked up to where the cement wall extended past the ancient adobe roofline.

"This is the bell tower," he said breathlessly. "That's how they found the tunnel – when they drilled down to lay the foundation for the bell tower." The excitement in his voice was unmistakable. "Francis is in the bell tower!"

Giorgio reached for the door latch but it didn't budge. "Dammit!" he said, kicking the wall. "This is getting tiring."

Rocky leaned forward. "Here, let me run the light around the edges."

He revealed a heavy wooden frame that was bolted directly into the cinder blocks. The door was almost a duplicate of the main door upstairs, which meant it was at least two inches thick and couldn't be kicked in. Giorgio watched the light traverse the curvature of the doorframe deciding it couldn't be opened by some spectacular means, either. This was just a door, a locked door, and he needed a key. His gaze came to rest on the dark, angular keyhole that resembled the key hole from Alice in Wonderland. Instinctively, he reached into his pocket for Elvira Applebaum's key.

"Rocky, shine the light on the keyhole."

Giorgio inserted the long, Victorian style key into the lock and with a strong twist, the internal bolt slid back.

"Hot damn!" Rocky cooed. "Where the hell'd you get that?"

"We owe our thanks to a grand old lady," Giorgio whispered with reverence.

The wrought iron hinges sang as they pushed the door open. Giorgio cringed, thinking Francis would hear them, but it couldn't be helped. A dark stone staircase wound up away from them.

"Okay, be careful little brother," Giorgio warned. "Francis is up there, somewhere."

Rocky went first, holding his weapon close to his chest and scuttling up the stairs like a crab, his back flattened against the rough stone, the faint flashlight guiding his way.

The shaft was cold, and their passage raised a cloud of fine dust making Giorgio catch a sneeze. The staircase ended some thirty feet up at a small landing and another door. But this one was unlocked. Rocky threw it open, hanging back for protection.

When there was no response, Giorgio ducked inside, breaking to the left with his weapon drawn. Rocky broke to the right. They were in a long, narrow room. Their tiny flashlights cut through the darkness to reveal a broken, primitive-style bed frame at the far end, along with a stained and shabby mattress, and two sets of manacles driven into the wall. There was no exit. And the room was empty. Both brothers paused and holstered their weapons to take stock of their surroundings.

"What is this place?" Rocky asked quietly, his gaze resting on the tattered mattress.

"Originally, probably a safe room. More recently – I have a feeling we don't want to know." Giorgio fingered the steel manacles.

"Francis isn't here, so if there's another secret door, then I'd say this is beginning to feel like one of those haunted houses at the county fair."

"The question is – how do we get out of this room?"

Giorgio scanned what little floor area his light illumined. Several sets of prints crossed the room ending at the middle of the far wall.

"Look here," Giorgio pointed, following the trail. "The footprints stop at the wall, turn right and disappear."

"Something has scraped across the floor," Rocky said, pointing to a wide mark that began at the wall and dug through the dirt and grime back across the floor in a sweeping arc.

Giorgio turned back to the wall and placed his hands on the bricks just above where the footprints stopped, as if feeling the wall's pulse.

"He must have triggered the secret door here and then moved over to step through. Come on, help me."

Rocky stepped forward and pressed on the bricks above Giorgio's head. Their efforts were rewarded when Giorgio pushed a brick closest to the floor, forcing it to recede half an inch and releasing a section of the wall to their left. The entire wall popped open some three inches inwards. The expansive belfry lay beyond, letting in fresh air.

"Be careful," Giorgio cautioned, reaching for his gun.

Rocky stepped around his brother to pull open the door, his form caught in a shallow beam of moonlight. There was a sudden crack, and a bullet whizzed through the shadows catching Rocky in his thigh. Rocky fell to the floor with a cry, clutching his leg. Giorgio reached out and grabbed his collar, pulling his brother away from the opening.

"Shit!" Rocky rocked back and forth, hugging his leg.

"Hold on," Giorgio ordered. Keeping his eye on the doorway, he shrugged out of his jacket and sweater and handed his t-shirt to his brother. "Tie this around your leg." He quickly slipped back into his sweater and jacket.

Rocky took the t-shirt and did as he was told. The secret door stood open about three feet now, allowing the moonlight from the far window of the belfry to cut a shaft of light into the dungeon-like room.

"Where the hell is he?" Rocky winced, squinting through the opening.

Giorgio craned his neck to see as far as he could into the belfry. "I can't tell. We must have caught him by surprise, though. Otherwise he could have killed you."

"Then he's trapped," Rocky grunted, tightening the tourniquet around his leg.

"Not necessarily. Remember, there's the staircase we saw blocked off by construction tape." Giorgio put his jacket back on and turned to his younger brother. "You okay?"

"Yeah," Rocky groaned. "I'll nab him if he tries to come back this way."

"You have your cell phone?"

"Yeah."

"Call it in."

Rocky pulled out his phone. His gun lay beside him.

"Be careful, Joe," he said as he began to dial.

Giorgio patted his brother's shoulder. "I intend to."

Giorgio got up as Rocky dialed 911 and turned around to grab the old mattress, staying clear of the light spill. He dragged the tattered mattress back to where Rocky was propped against the wall.

He tucked his weapon into his belt, hefted the mattress in front of him, stepped around his brother and dashed through the opening.

A bullet ripped through the corner of the mattress, sending a puff of cotton batting into the air. But Giorgio continued his charge until he reached a short wall that encircled the open bell shaft. He threw the mattress aside and then ducked down behind the wall and removed his gun. A second shot ricocheted off the bell filling the tower with a thundering alarm. The sound diminished, and Giorgio looked around to map his environment.

The belfry was shaped in a square with four large columns holding up the domed ceiling. The iron bell hung from the center of the tower like a large spider perched in the middle of its web. The ropes were tied off to one side next to a hook the monks used to recover the rope.

The secret room ran along the entire north side of the tower. The west wall held a single arched window, while the south side overlooking the valley held two large square-cut windows. Cutting off the entire east side of the belfry was a temporary construction wall made of eight-foot sheets of plywood. Most likely, the construction wall cut off a third window along the south wall and a matching arched window along the east wall. He could only hope the main staircase was also behind the plywood wall so that Francis didn't have access to it.

Giorgio began to inch around the bell shaft to his right. The cement floor was cold and the rough exterior of the wall kept catching on his jacket. He'd only gone about ten feet when a sound made him stop. Was it Francis? Was it Rocky?

A glance back to the secret room told him it wasn't his brother. He listened, trying to locate the sound. A quick scraping noise made him focus his attention on the deep shadows in the southwestern corner where a large pillar and two saw horses blocked his view. Nothing moved. Sound was deceptive in this cavernous space, and he knew he might misperceive the source.

A series of hollow thuds echoed from the far side of the tower bringing Giorgio to attention. Francis had kicked something over, either on purpose, or by mistake. Giorgio sprinted towards the west wall, darting back and forth to avoid construction debris, finally ducking behind one of the stone columns. When he'd settled in behind the column, a glance to his left revealed the main staircase. Francis had either missed it, or had other plans.

Just then, a movement made Giorgio turn towards the construction area. A shadow darted towards the make-shift door. Giorgio pointed his gun and fired. The fleeting shadow spun around and slammed into the wood enclosure, emitting a loud curse. Giorgio ran diagonally to a stack of boxes about ten feet in front of him and then darted forward again like a quarterback looking for an opening. He threw himself behind a pile of cement bags and tucked himself into a crouched position, peering into the darkness, his gun at his waist. He was about half way across the tower. A restrained moan drifted across the cluttered space and then everything went quiet. Giorgio waited.

A minute went by. Giorgio didn't dare hope that Francis had been severely injured. And a moment later, a loud smash broke the silence. Francis was trying to escape through the construction door. Giorgio jumped up to stop him with his weapon drawn. A bullet tore through his right forearm, sending him spinning backwards. He dropped the gun and hit the floor next to a short stack of lumber. With a groan, he slid on his back to the safety of the pillar again. The bullet had found its mark – entering his forearm exactly where Poindexter had broken the skin with the hammer. What were the odds of that? First his head, now his arm.

With a grimace, he pushed up the jacket sleeve and then reached into one of his pockets for his handkerchief. He wrapped it around the wound, pulling it tight with his teeth. Then he looked around for his gun.

"Joe, you okay?" Rocky called out in a loud whisper.

"I need some cover."

"You got it."

Giorgio heard a shuffle and a moment later there was a crack of fire as a bullet hit the construction wall, pinning down Francis. Francis fired back, hitting the wall just in front of Rocky, sending out a cloud of plaster. Rocky's shadow moved and another shot rang out. It gave Giorgio time to find his gun, which had landed only a few feet away. A heavy plastic tarp lay folded on the ground next to him. He grabbed it and shook it out. Positioned safely behind the column, he threw the tarp out like a fishing net, to land over the gun. With a yank, he reeled in the tarp, dragging the gun with it. He picked up the gun with his left hand and leaned against the pillar for support. In the distance, a siren wailed.

"You won't get away, Francis! Give it up," he yelled. "We could sit here all night and wait you out." Although he tried to hide it, Giorgio knew the strain in his voice was evident. He took deep breaths trying to calm his nerves. Both he and his brother were wounded, and they'd trapped a killer who had few options. Not a great position to be in.

"I've known a hundred guys like you, Detective. You guys will come get me. I know I hit your brother. Did I hit you?"

Giorgio looked down to where the bullet had ripped apart the protective gauze. Blood was seeping through the handkerchief. The seared muscles were on fire, and he was having trouble making a fist. He knew he couldn't use this hand to fire his weapon, which put his life further at risk. Too bad he'd never taken the time to practice shooting with his left hand.

"You nicked me. How 'bout you?"

The young man gave a belabored chuckle. "You nicked me. Do you play chess, Detective?"

There was another smashing noise, as if Francis was battering the plywood door, but Giorgio didn't dare expose himself a second time. Instead, he made sure the gun was properly seated in his left hand with a tight grip. Rocky, however, rewarded Francis with a third bullet that took out a wood chip just above the construction door. There was a long pause of silence.

"A friend of mine plays chess," Giorgio yelled, silently thanking Rocky. Giorgio watched the shadows around him, trying to figure out what Francis might do next. He struggled to a crouching position, leaning sideways around the pillar with his right arm tucked into his chest for support. He couldn't see Rocky well enough to give him a signal and knew his brother couldn't see Francis without exposing himself.

"I think we just took each other's pawns," a breathless voice finally answered.

The sound of splintering wood meant Francis was almost through the security door. Giorgio moved to the left so that he could see across the opening.

"My guess is that right now you're positioning yourself to take my queen," the opposing voice called from the darkness. "Am I right?"

"I think I'll just skip to checkmate," Giorgio bluffed.

Francis emitted a low, strained chuckle. "I don't think so, Detective."

Giorgio searched for a shadow with a human shape, but the short wall around the bell shaft blocked his view. Rocky decided to take another shot just as the darkness in front of Giorgio moved. Francis had finally destroyed the makeshift door and gone through it as the bullet tore a chunk out of one of the nearby pillars. Giorgio knew he had to either get through that door or lure Francis out again.

"Rocky," Giorgio whispered. "Hang back and hold him off if he makes it past me this way."

"Sure thing," Rocky whispered back. "Be careful."

Giorgio left his cover and hugged the outer wall of the belfry, crouching to pass under an open window where the outdoor spotlights from the gardens below cast angular shadows onto the ceiling. He crept forward until he was positioned behind the pillar at the southeast corner of the room. The muffled sound of splashing water from the fountain below added a drumbeat to the forlorn wail of the approaching sirens.

"You won't get away."

"Don't count me out so soon," the muffled voice answered. "And I have a clear view of the doorway, so be careful, Detective. You wouldn't want to take a second bullet."

The only escape for Francis had to be over the east wall, away from the approaching police cars. Giorgio had no idea how Francis planned to do it, but he moved along the south wall of the tower towards the plywood construction. He tucked himself into the corner where the plywood had been secured to a cement buttress, and he then inched along the construction wall at a ninety degree angle coming to within ten feet of the makeshift door.

Giorgio glanced around to put his plan in play. Finding an open box of long, heavy nails, he reached in and quietly grabbed one. That little bit of effort sent fireworks up his arm, and he steeled himself for what he was about to do. He clutched the nail as tightly as he could with his right hand and then reached back over his head, gritted his teeth, and tossed it over to the wall. It hit the floor with a series of loud pings.

A bullet ripped through the door casing and Giorgio cried out, purposely knocking over a nearby stack of cans as if he'd been hit.

This time however, he was acting, remaining where he was without making a sound. If Francis came to check on him, he'd be ready. If not, he might still be able to get a jump on him.

He became aware of a strong acrid smell and glanced down to where several gallon cans now lay on their sides next to the plywood wall. Something oozed out of the can closest to the wall. He must have knocked over some kind of solvent or industrial glue.

"Gee, Detective, hope I didn't hurt you," Francis called out.

Giorgio's heart leapt, but he kept silent with his gun pointed directly at the door opening.

"Detective?"

Still, Giorgio made no sound. Francis also became silent. Giorgio tensed, bracing his left hand as best he could, ready to fire. But Francis didn't appear. Instead, he began moving again on the other side of the plywood wall. Either he assumed Giorgio was dead, or was wounded so badly he couldn't move. Giorgio reached down and carefully took off his shoes.

Crouched like a Sumo wrestler, he moved a couple of feet forward until he could see through the door and across the small space to the east window. The angle of the spotlights below threw more light into this side of the tower, revealing the window framed in new wood, the plaster having been stripped away for the repairs. A portable workbench was set up to the right. Lumber and bags of cement were stacked to the left. Francis was partially blocked, but Giorgio could see that he was concentrating on something in his hands. A moment later, he rocked back and threw whatever it was through the window and over the wall.

Giorgio's heart sank. He knew why Francis had avoided the belfry's main staircase. He'd thrown a rope over the wall and planned to lower himself down the east side of the tower. By hugging the wall below, he could move through the heavy foliage around the building to disappear into the surrounding hillsides completely unnoticed. Giorgio had to move fast.

He inched his way to the edge of the doorway, careful not to alert his quarry. He contemplated shooting Francis, but didn't trust using his left hand. Instead, he straightened up and stepped into the enclosure.

"Francis, stop," he commanded.

Francis jerked around, dropping the rope and reaching for his gun.

"Don't!" Giorgio warned, moving closer. He held his injured arm close to his waist, conscious of the throbbing pain. His left hand held the gun steady, but if Francis moved quickly in any direction, he wouldn't have enough control to hit him.

Francis paused, his hand held above the gun sitting on a stool. "Well, well, well. I thought you were dead, but then, that's what you wanted me to think, wasn't it?"

"Move away from the gun."

Francis took a step backwards as Giorgio moved in. His right arm was useless, so rather than retrieve Francis' gun, he merely knocked it into a bucket on the floor. Francis stood quietly next to the cement bags, a dark stain spread across one shoulder.

"So, what now?" he asked warily.

"We wait for reinforcements."

Blaring sirens announced the arrival of the police onto the monastery grounds. Francis looked around as red and blue lights flashed across the arched openings.

"Good timing," he said good-naturedly.

Giorgio glanced over his shoulder at the arriving police force. When he turned back, a puff of grainy dust hit him in his face. He stumbled backwards and Francis pounced, grabbing the gun from his hand. Giorgio's eyes burned and he slid down the wall onto his haunches. When he got the grit out of his eyes, he looked up to find Francis pointing his own gun at his chest.

"What now?" Giorgio mimicked Francis.

"Now I kill you and get out of here."

"You won't get away," Giorgio bluffed.

"I'll get out of here, or die. I'd be dead within the week anyway. My uncle would see to that," Francis said, glancing around him.

Francis was caught in the spill of moonlight and suddenly, Giorgio recognized him. "Your uncle?"

"Robert Marino."

The last piece of the puzzle fit. "Your Uncle runs with the mob."

Even in the dim light, the self-satisfied grin on the young man's face told a story. "He doesn't run *with* the mob, Detective. He *runs* the mob."

Francis' eyes kept darting around the enclosure as if looking for something. Giorgio used the moment to turn towards the shattered door where a white flash on the far side of the belfry caught his attention.

"Whoa!" Francis exclaimed.

Giorgio snapped to attention. Francis was moving. Hopefully, the white flash meant Rocky was positioning himself for a rescue. Francis circled around Giorgio until he was just inside the broken door. He stopped and glanced down to the floor next to the construction wall, sniffing. The solvent had seeped under the wall, spreading several feet into their space. He looked at Giorgio with a smile.

"It seems my luck hasn't run out, yet," he sneered.

A tapestry of voices reached the bell tower as officers emerged from their squad cars and monks hurried from the monastery to meet them. The entire grounds seemed alive with activity. Giorgio knew time was short and that Francis would have to make this quick.

"Get over here," he barked.

Francis wanted him to move into the oozing solvent.

"Now!" he ordered, waving the gun at him.

Slowly, Giorgio got up and sidestepped into position as Francis reached into his pocket and removed a match. With a flick of his thumb, the match flared to life. Giorgio felt the blood drain away as he realized he was about to face death by fire for the second time in just a few days.

"You're my diversion, Detective," he smiled wickedly.

Francis raised his hand ready to toss the match, when a large shadow lunged at him from behind, grabbing his arm with a vicious growl. Francis emitted a sharp cry as the match flew safely onto the floor behind him.

He lurched sideways, twisting and turning, dragging the heavy object with him. Giorgio ran for the bucket, while Francis swung around trying desperately to dislodge the snarling monster attached to his wrist. Giorgio retrieved Francis' weapon and turned, ready to fire, but Grosvenor kept getting in the way. As Francis swung from side to side, Grosvenor swung with him.

Francis finally stopped, bringing up the hand holding the gun, pointing it straight at Grosvenor, who continued to snarl and rip at the man's arm. Giorgio steadied his hand and took a shot. He hit the young monk in the left shoulder again, this time blowing out the rotator cuff and splattering blood and bone fragments across the wall. Francis spun around, slamming against the new window supports, cracking the top boards. Grosvenor was thrown clear, but came back to stand squarely in front of Francis now, barking at him.

"Drop your gun, very slowly," Giorgio ordered him.

Francis' face registered excruciating pain, and yet he raised the gun just enough to point it directly at the dog.

"You can shoot, but I'll get your dog first."

Loud shouts drifted up from the grounds below. The police had heard the shots and were trying to get into the tower.

"Put your gun down, Detective," Francis said. "I'll do it. I swear."

The monk was listing to one side, his left shoulder a bloody mess. But his eyes said it all. He would kill Grosvenor, even if it meant losing his own life. And he would enjoy doing it. Giorgio couldn't take the chance. And he couldn't defend killing the bastard over a dog.

Giorgio was about to lower his gun, when Francis suddenly shifted his gaze to something in the corner. His eyes grew wide and his face distorted into a look of abject horror.

"What? Get away!" he screamed.

He raised his gun and fired wildly. Giorgio ducked as the bullets whizzed past him, hitting the wall behind him. He raised his own gun and fired twice, hitting Francis in the chest.

Francis flew backwards into the window frame, smashing through the boards with a sickening crack. He teetered for a moment on the edge, and then the young monk fell away from the building into empty space.

Then all went quiet.

Giorgio took a deep breath. With the threat gone, Grosvenor lumbered over to Giorgio as if asking for forgiveness.

"Good boy, Grosvenor," he said, bending down to give the dog a hug. "Good boy."

With a deep sigh, Giorgio straightened up and went to the window to look over the edge. Things below were eerily silent. Three squad cars stood head to toe along the driveway with their lights flashing. Monks and officers had gathered into a tight knot, staring speechless at the iron priest.

Giorgio followed their gaze, and a chill fluttered across his chest. Father Francis hung as lifeless as a fish on the tip of the priest's raised sword. It was a haunting tableau and one Giorgio wouldn't soon forget.

When a sudden cold spot enveloped him, Giorgio turned to find the boy standing about five feet away.

This time, the boy showed the hint of a smile, telegraphing that it had been his ghostly image that Francis had been shooting at. Giorgio nodded in the boy's direction, but before the boy could respond, a second image materialized right next to him.

It was the misty outline of a tall monk. Giorgio took a step back, his heart rate picking up again. He'd gotten rather used to the boy, never considering there were other ghosts on the property. But this one he recognized. It was the infamous Father Wingate.

The monk appeared to place a languid arm around the boy's narrow shoulders and draw him in, as if he owned him. The boy tried to pull away, but the monk held him tight. They stood together in a second strained tableau, before the monk actually smiled. Giorgio's stomach turned over. He started forward, as if he hoped to somehow rescue the boy. But Father Wingate forcibly turned the boy away and the two images evaporated before Giorgio's eyes. A moment later, Rocky appeared in the doorway, leaning against the doorframe.

"Looks like I missed the theatrics," he said weakly.

Giorgio glanced at his brother, but once again, he wasn't referring to the ghostly images. Giorgio looked back at the gruesome scene below, where Mulhaney was already shooting pictures of the dead Father Francis.

"Yeah, well, it looks as if this time, Francis won't be taking a curtain call."

† Chapter Forty-Three †

Giorgio and the family were just arriving home from church when Swan pulled up to the curb. While Giorgio had taken the last couple of weeks off to be with Angie, Swan had put the final pieces of the investigation together. The look on Angie's face as Swan ambled up the drive though, made Swan raise his hands in surrender.

"I'm only here to make a report."

"Then why don't you come in, Chuck?" she said with a skeptical smile.

Grosvenor greeted them all at the door, bristling with enthusiasm. After a lick here and a lick there, he followed the kids upstairs. Giorgio and Swan disappeared into the living room while Angie headed for the kitchen.

"How's Angie?"

"She's doing okay," Giorgio answered. "We're all taking it slow. I've had to help out around the house a bit." He gave a shrug as if vacuuming and doing the laundry were no big deal. "The kids have been great though, and I've even become a little fond of Mrs. Greenspan."

Swan laughed as he planted himself on the sofa. Giorgio took his favorite chair.

"How's the arm?"

"Good," Giorgio replied, flexing his right hand. "Good enough that Angie ignored me last night when I tried to use it as an excuse to get out of doing the dishes." They both chuckled. "So, anything new on the case?"

"A couple of things. Apparently Dorman was part of Anya Peters' scheme. Dorman had the same job as Colin Jewett at another catering company, meaning he'd take a regular break during the event to pass off the drugs and collect the payment. *But* he was starting to cause trouble. He wanted more money and more control over the operation. Peters decided it was time for him to go and got him to enroll in the conference on the pretense he was going to pick up another drop."

"And Poindexter was hired to get rid of him?"

"Not exactly. Poindexter is her brother."

Giorgio's eyes opened wide. "Hell, I didn't see that one coming."

"Poindexter is the shipping manager for the produce company," Swan continued. "He handled all the scheduling. It's a big company and they have satellites all over the basin, including one only a few miles from the Mexican border. The drugs would be shipped north hidden in boxes of lettuce. Poindexter was in a perfect position to orchestrate the drops without raising suspicion."

"What about Father Francis? Or should I say, Danny Marino?"

"We did some checking on both him and Jack Brye, that guy you pointed out in the college yearbook. Brye actually *was* a priest…"

"And Marino killed him in order to take his identity," Giorgio interrupted him.

Swan threw up his hands in supplication. "Why do I even bother?"

"I ask myself that all the time," Angie interjected, entering with a tray of cheese and crackers.

Angie put the tray onto the ottoman just as Rocky came through the front door with a bunch of flowers. He sauntered into the living room, gave the flowers to Angie, gave her a peck on the cheek, and swiped a hunk of cheese off the tray all in one movement.

"Thank you, Rocky," Angie smiled, taking the bouquet.

"He only wants to stay for dinner," Giorgio sneered.

Angie disappeared into the hallway chuckling as Grosvenor came lumbering down the stairs. He made a beeline for Rocky who stooped down to pet him.

"So, what else did you get?" Giorgio asked.

"We contacted your old department in New York. Some guy named Frank Mangano was murdered there about seven months ago. According to the street, Mangano murdered Marino's father when he was just a kid. Looks like fifteen years later, son takes revenge. The police arrested a guy named Jacko Galiano who fingered Marino as the shooter. But Marino had already been killed in a car accident the night *before* Mangano was killed. So the case was closed."

"Wonder how they managed that sleight of hand." Giorgio leaned forward to grab a cracker. "Francis said something that night just before he went over the edge. He said if he didn't get away, or die in the process, his uncle would kill him."

"Marino's uncle announced his intention to run for Mayor just last month. I suppose if his nephew had been arrested for Mangano's murder, it would have derailed any chance he had of winning."

Grosvenor had rolled over now to let Rocky rub his stomach. "Obviously they staged the kid's death," Rocky added. "Then the uncle exiled him."

"That's what we think," Swan agreed. "We can't prove it, and of course the uncle denies any connection to Mangano's murder or his nephew's disappearance. But the kid's mother says that even though the family told her he drove his car off a cliff the night before Mangano was killed, someone came by the next day and picked up some of his belongings."

"Where did the name Francis come from?"

"His mother's name is Francis. I suppose it was a familiar name. And, as you suspected, Brye was in the same class with Mallery Olsen and Marino. In fact, the three of them hung out together. Brye was a quiet kid, good student, studied a lot, and finally went into the church. The two men looked enough alike to switch places occasionally when it was convenient. Back then, Brye just put on a dark wig and added glasses."

"Just the opposite of what Marino did this time," Giorgio added.

"I guess that's what got her killed," Rocky speculated out loud, wiping crumbs from his lower lip. "Olsen probably saw him at the monastery and thought he was Brye. Then, on closer inspection, she realized it was Marino in disguise, or something like that."

Angie appeared again with several cold beers. Swan thanked her, popped his can open and then grabbed a chunk of cheese as Angie left again.

"We also have a better idea of when Olsen was murdered," Swan said. "Father Rosario finally remembered seeing Francis slip out of the five o'clock Mass. He assumed he was going to the restroom, but admits he didn't see him return."

Rocky reached for more food. "Do we know what happened to Brye?"

"The last time we can confirm anyone seeing him was two weeks before he was scheduled to come to the monastery. He told a neighbor that a college friend was coming for a visit the next day. The San Francisco police are looking into it."

"Some friend," Giorgio mumbled.

"McCready also found out that O'Leary was actually Christian Maynard's roommate when Father Wingate was killed."

"Bingo," Rocky blurted, spitting out a spray of cheese and crackers. "He showed Francis the secret door. That's gotta be what got him killed."

"By the way, we found the suave Father Daniel," Swan said. "He's living with an old girlfriend. Apparently, he decided the monastic life wasn't for him."

Angie re-entered with a vase filled with Rocky's flowers, and the men fell silent. She placed the vase on the desk and turned to them.

"Don't stop on my account," she quipped.

Giorgio was about to say something just as the doorbell rang. Rocky grabbed Grosvenor as Angie left to get the door.

"By the way," Rocky began, "what are you going to do about Grosvenor?"

"We found an animal psychologist," Giorgio said.

Swan chortled out loud.

"I'm not kidding," Giorgio said, smiling. "Matilda has already spent two sessions with him and thinks he'll be just fine."

Voices in the hallway interrupted them, and Elvira Applebaum entered the room with Angie close behind. She was dressed in brown slacks and a tan sweater. Her face was a little pale, but she had a cheerful smile.

"Ms. Applebaum, it's nice to see you again," Giorgio said, standing up and extending his hand. "Thanks for stopping by."

"It's no trouble, Detective. I'm glad to help if I can."

Everyone remained silent while all eyes shifted to Angie. She seemed to sense the awkwardness and stepped forward.

"Won't you sit down, Ms. Applebaum? Can I get you something to drink?"

"Oh, no, I just had a late breakfast. I was hoping we could look around the house."

Angie's eyes grew wide. "Look around the house? What for?"

Elvira Applebaum turned to Giorgio. In fact, the whole room turned their focus on him. He moved over to take one of Angie's hands just as the children came bounding down the stairs. They skidded to a halt in the hallway as if knowing something big was about to happen. Angie looked at her husband, the furrow already deepening in her brow.

"What's this all about, Joe? We're not selling the house are we?"

Her lip began to quiver and Giorgio knew he had to act fast.

"No. We're not selling the house. Ms. Applebaum runs a consortium of day care centers."

The crease between Angie's eyebrows deepened. "What?"

"She wants to talk to you about running a day care."

He said it quickly and then held his breath. He hadn't dared say a word to Angie until he'd worked out some of the details, but he'd been thinking about it for weeks.

Angie just stared at him without blinking. Then she turned to look at Elvira Applebaum and then at the children. A moment later, the tears began to flow. Her hands flew to her face and her slender shoulders shook. Giorgio panicked.

"You don't have to, Angie," Giorgio put his hands on her shoulders. "It was just an idea. I thought you'd like it. I wanted to make you happy. Angie, stop. Please."

Everyone else in the room stood as still as statues. Finally, Angie let her hands drop, and she turned back to her husband, her face flushed and wet with tears.

"Oh, Joe, I think it's a wonderful idea!" Her face was alive with a light that had been missing for weeks. "Thank you, Joe. Thank you so much."

She threw her arms around his neck and hugged him fiercely. The tension broke and everyone smiled. Rocky even patted Swan on the shoulder as if they'd just delivered a baby together.

"Your husband said you were a teacher once," Ms. Applebaum said in the background.

Angie turned, wiping her eyes. "Yes. I taught second grade. I miss it terribly."

"Well, having a house full of children should fix that."

Giorgio thought for sure he saw the glint of a halo above Elvira Applebaum's head.

"Shall we take a look around? We'll need to do a formal inspection later, but let's just talk it through to see first if the house will work."

Angie threw a last, grateful look at her husband and then led Elvira Applebaum into the hallway. "I'll show you the kitchen first," she said as they disappeared.

The children followed with Grosvenor not far behind. All three men stood immobile as if holding their breath. Finally, Giorgio turned to them and let out a deep sigh.

"That was close."

"Yes, big brother. You finally pulled one off. Good job."

"Listen, I gotta go," Swan cut in. He grabbed a last piece of cheese and started towards the hallway.

"Wait." Giorgio stopped him. "How's Father Damian?"

"He's been relocated again. And, I'm told they plan to tear down the entire west wing of the monastery."

Giorgio stopped short. "What?"

Swan stood in the entryway with his hand resting on the doorknob, his mouth curved into a sly expression.

"Don't look so surprised," he said, draining the beer before handing the empty can to Giorgio. "The Bishop said you took him up to see that room with the shackles and made sure he got copies of those newspaper articles you discovered. It was all the ammunition he needed. When did you slip away to do all of that?"

Giorgio shrugged nonchalantly, but didn't say anything.

"Anyway," Swan continued, "the whole west wing and the tower will go. He wants to erase the past as quickly as possible. The other tunnels within the main building will be filled in and sealed for good."

Giorgio kept his thoughts to himself, but the vision of Father Wingate pulling Christian Maynard to him had crept into his dreams for the past several weeks. Perhaps with the building gone, Christian Maynard would be free to rest in peace.

"I'd like to be there when they send in the wrecking ball," Giorgio muttered to himself.

"By the way, Rocky, you know there's an opening in the department," Swan offered. "Samson took a job in San Diego. The Captain mentioned your name. You interested?"

Rocky stole a quick glance at Giorgio who only lifted his eyebrows. "Can they give me a couple of weeks? I have to finish something first."

"Don't see why not. I'll tell the Captain."

Angie and Elvira Applebaum came in from the backyard just as the phone rang. Giorgio picked up the extension next to the staircase.

"Hey, Wally," he greeted a friend from the theater. "Yes, thanks, we're doing fine. Yes, the investigation is over. What's that? Yes, I should have some time. When do rehearsals start? Okay, get me a script and let me take a look. Thanks again." He turned to his waiting audience with a broad grin.

"I've seen that look before," Rocky quipped.

"So have I," Angie agreed. "What is it this time? A musical?" Her brown eyes danced.

"No," he said, filling his chest like a balloon. "*Arsenic and Old Lace*. They want me to play Teddy Roosevelt."

Everyone groaned in unison, but Giorgio ignored them and grabbed the banister and swung himself around to the lower landing. Then he ran full speed up the stairs yelling, "Chaaaarge!!!"

When the bedroom door slammed closed, Prince Albert's visor shut with a bang giving Grosvenor a reason to throw back his head to indulge in a good howl.

The End

Thank you so very much for reading *Mass Murder*. If you enjoyed this book, I encourage you to go back to Amazon.com and leave an honest review. We indie authors thrive on reviews and word-of-mouth advertising. This will help position the book so that more people might also enjoy it. Thank you!

About the Author

Ms. Bohart holds a master's degree in theater, has published in Woman's World, and has a story in *Dead on Demand*, an anthology of ghost stories that remained on the Library Journals best seller list for six months. As a thirty-year nonprofit professional, she has spent a lifetime writing brochures, newsletters, business letters, website copy, and more. Recently, she did a short stint writing for Patch.com, and teaches writing for Green River Continuing Education. Mass Murder is her first novel and was endorsed by Compulsion Reads as an "excellent read." She also self-published a book of creepy short stories and mysteries called, *Your Worst Nightmare* and has a second paranormal novel, *Grave Doubts* published on Amazon.com. Her third novel, *Inn Keeping with Murder,* remained in the top 100 mystery/ghost stories on Amazon for over eight months.

Ms. Bohart also writes a blog on the various aspects of writing and the paranormal on her website at: www.bohartink.com. She lives in the Northwest with her daughter, two miniature Dachshunds, and a cat.

Follow Ms. Bohart

Website: www.bohartink.com
Twitter: @lbohart
Facebook: L.Bohart/Author

67004113R00180

Made in the USA
Charleston, SC
02 February 2017